You & Me & You &

FREE PROOF COPY – NOT FOR RESALE

This is an uncorrected book proof made available in confidence to selected persons for specific review purpose and is not for sale or other distribution. Anyone selling or distributing this proof copy will be responsible for any resultant claims relating to any alleged omissions, errors, libel, breach of copyright, privacy rights or otherwise. Any copying, reprinting, sale or other unauthorized distribution or use of this proof copy without the consent of the publisher will be a direct infringement of the publisher's exclusive rights and those involved liable in law accordingly.

ALSO BY JOSIE LLOYD AND EMLYN REES

[To Come]

JOSIE LLOYD & EMLYN REES

You & Me & You & Me & You & Me

HARVILL

1 3 5 7 9 10 8 6 4 2

Harvill Secker, an imprint of Vintage, is part of the Penguin Random House group of companies

Vintage, Penguin Random House UK, One Embassy Gardens,
8 Viaduct Gardens, London SW11 7BW

penguin.co.uk/vintage
global.penguinrandomhouse.com

Penguin Random House UK

First published by Harvill Secker in 2026

Copyright © Josie Lloyd and Emlyn Rees 2026

The moral right of the authors has been asserted

[Insert any further credit lines/information here]

Penguin Random House values and supports copyright. Copyright fuels creativity, encourages diverse voices, promotes freedom of expression and supports a vibrant culture. Thank you for purchasing an authorised edition of this book and for respecting intellectual property laws by not reproducing, scanning or distributing any part of it by any means without permission. You are supporting authors and enabling Penguin Random House to continue to publish books for everyone. No part of this book may be used or reproduced in any manner for the purpose of training artificial intelligence technologies or systems. In accordance with Article 4(3) of the DSM Directive 2019/790, Penguin Random House expressly reserves this work from the text and data mining exception.

Typeset in 11.2/15pt Minion Pro by Six Red Marbles UK, Thetford, Norfolk
Printed and bound in Great Britain by Clays Ltd, Elcograf S.p.A.

The authorised representative in the EEA is Penguin Random House Ireland,
Morrison Chambers, 32 Nassau Street, Dublin D02 YH68

A CIP catalogue record for this book is available from the British Library

HB ISBN 9781787305373
TPB ISBN 9781787305380

Penguin Random House is committed to a sustainable future
for our business, our readers and our planet. This book is made
from Forest Stewardship Council® certified paper.

MIX
Paper | Supporting responsible forestry
FSC® C018179

For our daughters, Tallulah, Roxie & Minty, who have taught us how precious time is.

'If you were on your deathbed and could relive one day of your life, perhaps a day you were falling in love, you'd see all the seemingly banal things you did and weep at how precious it all was.'

– Alexander Payne, screenwriter and director

'If time travel to the past is possible, it really should be possible to change things – but doing so will create an alternate timeline. Instead of creating a Universe-breaking paradox, you would create a second universe with a different history.'

– Barak Shoshany, theoretical physicist and composer

'A dream you dream alone is only a dream. A dream you dream together is reality.'

– Yoko Ono, artist and musician

This book is about the magic of music too. So here's a Spotify playlist to go with it: https://open.spotify.com/playlist/0rbrInGMWczHH5Zr IoRo8u

Chapter One

Jules – 'Seaside'

'Time,' I call, hitting the service bell, before wiping a tiny basil emulsion smear from the edge of one of my signature risottos and tweezering the home-grown micro herbs perfectly into place. The handsome waiter takes the dish from the pass.

'Come out. They want you, Jules,' he says, with a smile.

I turn to look at my kitchen brigade. Delicious smoke rises from the chargrills, knives flash, and the air is filled with focused commands. They can cope without me for a moment.

Following the waiter through the service doors, I see the sun is setting over the magical view of the Golden Gate Bridge, bathing the restaurant in ethereal warm light. I greet the diners around the white-clothed tables on the veranda, most of whom have been on the waiting list for a year. Their hands press mine, but I demurely bat away their congratulations. Hey, I'm just me . . . doing me.

At the private table, I sink into the comfortable batik cushions beside my business partners, both of them famous Hollywood actors, as this season's must-have Zinfandel from Paso Robles is poured into my outstretched glass. They're here to persuade me to recreate my culinary alchemy elsewhere, but, seriously, no, I can't. Didn't they read the profile piece in *Time* magazine about how I've got my work–life balance just right?

We chat briefly and, as the stars twinkle, I tell them to hang around. This place always turns into the hottest nightspot after dark. Later, when the DJ arrives, I hear the familiar tango beat of Gotan Project's 'Mi Confesión' bleeding louchely from the speakers. Then suddenly Adam's here and my heart soars at the sight of him striding confidently across the restaurant in his svelte, ivory Tom Ford suit. My Adam. He extends his hand and I take it, feeling a heady, thrilling jolt of connection as we touch. He twirls me onto the small dance floor, tipping me over his arm before flipping me up against his firm body, his hand caressing my face as he stares into my eyes with such intense passion, it takes my breath away. His lips a breath from mine, he sensuously smooths his knee between my thighs . . .

Although . . . hang on . . . no, he'd better *not* do *that* . . . because I really, really need to . . .

What the . . . ?

Huh?

Oh . . . You've got to be kidding me.

Squeezing my eyes shut against the piercing daylight splaying around the sides of our threadbare bedroom curtains, I try desperately to go back to sleep, but it's no good. My dream has vanished. And I really do need to pee.

Yawning, I remove my earplugs, the squalling seagulls outside suddenly competing with Adam – the *real* Adam, not dream tango Adam – who is snoring loudly beside me. I swing my legs out of bed and he subconsciously, yet somehow victoriously, snatches my portion of the duvet and re-cocoons himself, wrapping it tightly around his furry belly.

In the bathroom, as I notice he's left the loo seat up, as per usual, I turn on the masochistic mirror light.

Bloody hell. I look like Shrek.

This hydrating avocado and apple cider vinegar face mask was meant to 'invisibly absorb overnight'. Instead, I look more like I've face-planted in the dip section at a wedding buffet.

Washing it off hardly improves matters. Rather than having fewer wrinkles, if anything, I seem to have more. When I was clearly living my best life in my dream a minute ago, it feels like an extra slap round the face.

Great. So much for looking younger. For being party-ready.

Adam's best mate Darius is hosting a 'Pool, Fun, Barbecue and DJ Beats' get-together today to celebrate moving back from the States, having sold his video gaming company there for a whopping fifty million bucks. He's just bought a humungous mansion overlooking the whole of Brighton, which he'll no doubt pack with the kind of cool, beautiful people I'm always seeing on his Insta feed – the fairest-of-them-all kind of people that this old magic mirror tells me I am not.

Of course I'm looking forward to hanging out with Darius again, we both are. We haven't seen him since his last fleeting visit a couple of years ago. Since then, he's developed that same chiselled, mega-wealthy, multivitamin sheen as the rest of his Insta buddies. What if he finds us horribly parochial? What if that's all we are to him now? Just people from his past?

Stop it. It'll be fine. It's Darius. I'm being ridiculous.

I open the posh moisturiser Ngozi got me on her last breeze through duty-free, accidentally dropping the little plastic disc covering the product onto the floor. Cursing, because that *always* happens, I scrape the expensive gloop from the faded lino with my finger and apply it to my face. Disgusting, I know, but three-second rule and all that.

As I rub it in, I glance down at the glossy cover of last Sunday's newspaper supplement magazine, left beside the sink. IF YOU DON'T USE IT, YOU LOSE IT, the dubious headline reads. The woman on the front, a self-proclaimed 'sexpert', has enviably pert breasts underneath her tight top. I suspect she's airbrushed, though I do recognise that smug sex-glow that I used to have.

The article inside is all about the importance of regular 'relationship maintenance sex', along with some dire warnings about the consequences of women my age failing to be spontaneous and not putting out. As if worrying about my face wasn't enough, apparently I've also got to 'make an effort' to keep toned . . . you know . . . *down there*.

But Fridays and Saturdays I'm out cooking for private dinner parties in the posher parts of town, if I'm lucky. The weekdays go by in a flash and most nights after supper – invariably cooked by me – Adam and I end up vegetating on our separate sofas in the living room. Me craving a foot rub while secretly snaffling my stash of Maltesers I keep hidden down the side of the cushion, and him channel-hopping between the several subscription services the kids insist are their birthright, before switching over to some obscure retro rock biopic, or other boysy documentary, like *Secrets of the Neanderthals*, his current favourite.

The sound of the *News at Ten* music usually wakes me up, leaving

Adam muttering at all the doom and gloom in the world while I slope off to bed.

Which means that if we are going to have 'relationship maintenance sex', or any kind of sex at all, it has to be in the morning.

As in . . . I suppose . . . *now*.

I pad back into the bedroom, past Adam's dirty socks and T-shirt, lying near the wicker laundry basket, and sit on my side of the bed.

'Shall we have sex?' I ask him, matter-of-factly. I know he's only pretending to be asleep.

My husband of nearly twenty-five years looks at me, like I'm a stewardess who's just asked him if he wants to be upgraded to business class. With complimentary drinks.

'Hell, yeah,' he says, after a beat just to check that I am being serious.

We begin the once titillating and fun, but now somewhat perfunctory, task of getting up close and naked. We don't kiss. Or talk. Or giggle. Not like we used to. Back in the day, Adam and I used to jump all over each other all the time. So much so, it used to feel like being between the sheets was our real life and everything else was just a distraction.

Right now, though, there's not much 'mood setting' – something else the article recommended. We both know how to get the mechanics going on autopilot and soon I'm groping about in the bedside drawer for some lube and trying not to mind that his stomach squashes my diaphragm. Or that his beard really does sometimes make me want to scratch.

Even so, a few minutes later, the movement we're creating makes my body remember what it's supposed to be doing. All of which leaves me thinking: *Get me! I've spontaneously instigated relationship maintenance sex on a Saturday morning!* But then my mind starts wandering and I'm thinking about the catering job I've got on for the council tomorrow. How about I knock up some Key lime pies for dessert? Oh, actually, that's a great idea.

No. You're having sex, I remind myself. *Concentrate. Whip out a fantasy. Get in the zone.*

My sexual fantasies are largely informed by 1980s romcoms, and these days they're a little tatty and worn, but I mentally dust off a scene at a retro Hollywood-style pool party. It's got a sleazy vibe and there's a Tom Cruise peak *Top Gun*-era lookalike approaching me in just a skimpy white hand towel.

Oh yes, now we're talking . . . I'm on the pleasure tracks. *Oh . . . oh . . . and yes, enjoying it . . . very, very –*

'Mum!' Nelly's scream from downstairs pops my erotic bubble.

'Ignore her,' Adam says, burying his face in my neck.

Good. I'm not the only one having a good time. But just a few seconds later, as we happily get going again, Adam freezes mid-thrust as our bedroom door bursts open.

Glancing over his shoulder, I see our twenty-four-year-old daughter, horror-struck in the doorway at the sight of us humped on top of each other under the duvet.

'Oh, Jesus!' she says, shielding her eyes with the arms of her pink towelling dressing gown.

'What do you want?' I shout, pulling the duvet even tighter around us.

'It's done it again. The Bot thing.' She now has her back to us, but she hasn't left the room, like no matter what we might or might not be doing, her need is still greater than ours.

'We're coming,' Adam groans, before his eyes flash wide at me, clearly realising just how this might sound.

'To help,' I quickly add. 'We're coming to help.'

With a pained yelp of disgust, Nelly storms off downstairs, her curly ponytail swishing.

'For God's sake,' I mutter, squeezing out from underneath Adam and flinging on my cotton robe.

The Kooks' 'Seaside' is drifting out from Liam's room as I hurry past, along with the stale stink of that disgusting weed he smokes, even though Adam and I have been over all the reasons why he should quit countless times. He's usually so nocturnal, I'm surprised he's awake at this hour. Or maybe he's been up all night again?

I find Nelly in the kitchen doorway downstairs, her nose buried into the crook of her arm.

'It's a shitshow,' she winces, as I squeeze past. 'Literally.'

Liam, twenty-one, really is up. Wearing boxers and a black T-shirt, he's squatting on a kitchen chair clutching a mug of coffee, while Groucho Barx, our senile – and frequently incontinent – black-and-white collie dog peers up at me with guilty brown eyes from where he's quivering by the back door.

'We can't find the remote,' Liam says, nodding down at Mop Bot, the new robot vacuum cleaner, as it continues merrily smearing one of Groucho's more exuberant deposits over the tiles in blissful, space-aged arcs.

Striding across the kitchen, I pick the damn thing up.

'Mum! Gross,' Nelly cries.

I jab at the button on Mop Bot's top until it dies abruptly in my arms. Gagging from the smell, I dump it on the floor.

In the moment of silence that follows, Liam snorts with pent-up laughter.

'Not funny,' I snap, glaring across at him and his pale skinny legs, rife with line tattoos. I hate the fact that he's done this to himself over the past year, but it's not like I'm in much of a position to criticise him. I got a drunk tattoo myself in my misspent youth – to my everlasting shame. A cartoon rat on the back of my shoulder in honour of my boyfriend at the time, Mickey Ratty. But at least I very rarely see mine.

Climbing down from his kitchen chair, still laughing, Liam half hops, half dances across the messy tiles into the hall like he's playing Twister.

'Oi. That's mine!' Nelly exclaims, pulling at the hem of his T-shirt. 'You pig! It stinks of smoke.'

Backing off, his slopping coffee cup held aloft, Liam sidesteps her as she gives chase, like they're both still kids, just as Adam arrives in his pyjama bottoms and faded Nirvana *Nevermind* T-shirt. He flattens himself against the wall as Liam and Nelly tumble past, shrieking and swearing.

I slowly survey the wreckage Mop Bot has left in its wake. The kitchen floor looks like a Jackson Pollock if he ever had a Brown Period.

'I didn't want that bloody thing anyway.'

Adam holds up his hands, as if fending off a bear. 'Only trying to help,' he says.

It takes all my self-control not to yell that this *isn't* helping. *He's* not helping. He never helps. None of them do. Or never *enough*.

Which is why I called a family summit last month and pointed out that, since Liam had dropped out of uni and Nelly was working from home, and since they're both now technically adults, they could start helping out around the place. But it fell on deaf ears, until my 'aggressive tone' was noted by Nelly, while Liam, who never misses an opportunity to gang up with his sister, added that I was 'having a go'. Then Nelly accused me of being menopausal in such a condescending way that I honestly wanted to stab them all with a fork.

Adam decided that the best solution was to buy me a robot vacuum for my birthday.

Yeah. Right. *Lucky* me.

Negotiating his way across the clean patches of tiles, Adam lets Groucho out into the back garden from the utility room and starts wafting the door to get rid of the smell. He looks at me as I snatch the mop from the cupboard.

'Um, you wanna leave that and maybe . . . ?' He gives me a hopeful smirk, glancing back upstairs.

I can't actually believe what I'm hearing. 'No, Adam,' I tell him. 'I really think the moment has passed.'

It takes an age to wash the floor while Adam takes Groucho Barx for a loop around St Ann's Well Gardens in case he does it again.

When I'm finished, I survey the kitchen with its ancient green units that Adam refuses to get rid of because of their 'sentimental' value. It's like he's trying to keep his parents' kitchen as it was when they were still alive and lived in this house, as a kind of mausoleum to his childhood. He even had the cheek to say the other day that everything here's so old, it's come back into fashion, but I don't buy it. It looks like what it is – a dump.

Out in the utility room, I tentatively sniff my original 1970s Missoni sundress hanging on the drying rack. Phew, now that I've washed it, it doesn't smell too musty. And just as well, because there's no way I can afford anything new for the party, so when Nelly suggested going down the vintage route, I ventured into the loft and found this old friend I bought in Camden Market back in the nineties. I'm hoping it'll look cool and vibey.

As Adam gets back, Groucho skitters across the wet kitchen floor with muddy paws, and I huff.

'Don't forget you said you'd take this lot to the dump,' I remind him and point as he heads out towards the shed. There are several boxes of loft junk that I've left piled up by the back door. The first lot of many, I hope. It's stuffed to the rafters up there, but if we cleared it out, we could turn it into a home office for Nelly. That would be one way of getting her out of our dining room, where she currently works.

As he takes the lid off one, I feel an urge to slap his hand away. Why can't he ever just do what I ask?

'Is that my wedding suit?' He sounds dismayed.

'It's wrecked. The loft wildlife have had a field day,' I reply defensively.

Rummaging down, he pulls out my wedding veil which is covered in mouse droppings along with my lovely silk dress that the moths have chewed into lace.

'Oh my God. Can't any of it be salvaged?'

'It's all ruined. Just take it. I want it out. Gone.'

Pulling a pained expression, he moves like a government inspector at a customs checkpoint to the next box. Under the lid is a dog-eared backgammon set.

'But we used to love playing,' he says.

'Used to. Twenty years ago. Because that's how long it's been up in the loft. Just give it to a charity shop, OK?'

Oh God. Here we go. I see his frown as he spots what's underneath. A jumble of his broken childhood *Star Wars* figurines. I chew my lip, the ghost of our Spectacular Fucking Row from 2014 suddenly looming large.

Apart from our increased scratchiness of late – well, *scratchiness* might be an understatement – mostly over the years we've rubbed along pretty well. Neither of us is particularly volatile, preferring the kind of stealth combat offered up by silent, simmering sulks and petty digs. But occasionally there's enough umbrage taken for one of us to blow.

The violent fate of Adam's *Star Wars* collection caused a pretty major explosion.

I stare down at the survivors' dusty faces and partially melted limbs. 'Maybe someone else's kid might want them? I suggest.

'No. Dad gave them to *me*,' he says, like he's a schoolkid and I've just tried to snatch something off him at the school gates. No, he hasn't forgotten the Spectacular Fucking Row either.

He puts the box on the floor reverentially, making it clear he'll be taking it elsewhere, but certainly not to the charity shop, then starts on the next box.

He holds up a bundle of my old diaries. 'Seriously? Do you want to throw all our old stuff out?'

'The past is a foreign country. Isn't that how the saying goes?'

Anyway, what's the point of keeping that old drivel? Especially if Liam or Nelly accidentally got to read them. Or Adam. There's lots of stuff about him in there too.

I sigh, moving next to him as he digs deeper.

'No way. Not all our mixtapes.' He sounds horrified.

I stand next to him and peek at the jumble of tapes and CDs we used to make for one another, until his last laptop with a CD burner died a few years before lockdown.

He picks up one of the cassette tapes and dusts it off, examining its ancient track names written out in his sloping handwriting. Along the spine it says, *For Juliet 1989* in faded blue pen.

'But you love "Ride on Time" and "Eternal Flame".'

The accusation – *no*, the *betrayal* – in his voice makes me flare with anger. All I want to do is to clear some space, get some order. He's such a bloody hoarder. It's suffocating.

'It's old tech, Adam. Just chuck it.' Snatching the lid from him, I replace it firmly on the box. 'Or, I don't know . . . recreate them all on Spotify, if you must . . .'

But from the way he looks at me, I might as well have thrown the whole box at his head.

Chapter Two

Adam – 'Strangers'

I gaze across the posters and old vinyl covers taped to every available inch of wall in Liam's bedroom, with that phrase 'recreate them all on Spotify' still ringing in my ears, but then I force myself to focus back in on Liam again. He's glaring up at me malevolently from his bed and I feel that same sense of dread over how far we've drifted apart.

I was good at it to begin with. The whole dadding thing. Sure, I couldn't actually grow the kids inside me or give birth to them or breastfeed them like Jules. But after that, I loved doing my bit to raise my own little flesh and blood Tamagotchis and do it right. To change the Huggies during the red-eye Saturday-morning *Teletubbies* shifts. To NutriBullet the broccoli and choo-choo-train it in.

I kept on being good at it too. Right through the Hama Bead, Bop It, Heely, Minecraft, Beyblade, Micro scooting, PTA camping, Pokémon, pirate party years.

The older the kids got, the more I thought I'd just keep levelling up, like in a computer game. Acquiring new skills and avatar gear. Until I was like Superdad. And not just me, *us*. The Holes. I thought we'd be like the Incredibles. Or the Guardians of the Galaxy. That, no matter what, we'd always stick together and triumph in the end.

'Why can't you just leave me the fuck alone?' Liam growls, back in his bed in his blinds-drawn, lava-lamplit, sweat pit of a bedroom, like this is his plan for the rest of the day.

As an affronted adult, part of me wants to snap right back at him.

As his dad, to ground him, or tell him there'll be no more Xbox, ever. But he's twenty-one. Too old for me to be here pestering him to type up his CV so I can give it to my banker mate Zack who'll be at Darius's party later, and who might – just might – give Liam some work experience before he goes back to uni to resit his accountancy exams at the end of the year.

'There's no need to swear,' I tell him instead. Pathetic – and hypocritical, because God knows I swear enough myself – but going in too hard will only lead to another fight.

'Isn't there?' he demands, gripping his pillow behind his head like he's considering hurling it at me. 'Because sometimes that's the only way you ever listen to what I've got to say.'

I bite down on my lip and take a deep breath, as I stare across the mess of what I like to refer to as his 'walk-on wardrobe'. 'Which is?' I ask.

'That I just want to be left alone.'

Great. He means to do nothing. Except maybe go out and get hammered again tonight, just like he did last night, and get into even more debt. 'I don't want to play the bad guy,' I say.

'So don't.'

'But you can't just spend all day in bed, and all night out.'

'I wasn't out. I was at Max's.'

Like there's a difference. Max and him used to be such great little buddies growing up, but now Max has dropped out of college too, and the two of them just seem to be dragging each other down.

'Doing what?'

'Oh, you know, mainly heroin and crack.'

'Not funny.'

'Why? Because you're worried it might be true?'

'No,' I say through gritted teeth. Even though I *do* worry, not so much about Liam experimenting with hard drugs, more about him getting mixed up in the same full-on clubbing lifestyle he got caught up in at uni, leading the pastoral team there to flag up to us that he'd stopped going to his lectures, and then Liam himself admitted he'd burned through his entire year's money in under ten weeks.

'We were just playing,' he says.

'*Dragon Age*?' My attempt at a joke, at peace-making, because old-school dungeons and dragons-style games were what we used to play together when he was a kid, before he got into *Fortnite* and *Call of Duty* and even more hardcore shooters like the ones my best mate Darius makes now.

'No. Bass,' he says.

For a second, I think I've misheard. My eyes even flick to the corner of his bedroom, to where he used to keep his two acoustic and one electric guitar, before he smashed them into a tangle of splinters and wires when he was eleven, about a week after he got discharged from the hospital.

'I've been playing Max's old one,' he says, as though reading my mind.

'Well, I suppose it's good to have a hobby.'

'It's what I want to do again.' His eyes flash defiance.

Again? He can't be serious. As in what he was 'destined' to do? The exact word we both once used, without irony, about him playing. A dumb King Arthur word, but Liam was so goddamned gifted, it felt true.

'But I don't understand,' I say, trying not to look at his left hand.

'Me and Max, we're setting up a band,' he tells me. 'Me on bass and him on lead.'

No. The word detonates inside me. Because as well as suffering major motor nerve damage, Liam lost two fingers in his accident. Meaning whatever he's planning now, it'll only lead to more heartache, and God knows he's already had enough of that.

'But what about going back to finish college?'

Silence.

'You promised me you'd give it another go.'

Still nothing.

'And you know how good that course is,' I tell him, my voice rising, 'and how great your employment prospects will be –'

'I never wanted to study accountancy,' he says, jaw clenched, jutting. 'That was always just you.'

That whole mess of feelings I got snagged up in after his accident, it starts gnawing into me again now.

'You do know I'm only try to help?'

'Yeah . . .'

Only he doesn't finish his sentence. Doesn't need to. I can already hear it like he's screamed it into my face – *but you're not.*

I find Jules in the kitchen, listening to Ed Harcourt's 'Strangers' as she writes out menu cards for the buffet she's running for the council event tomorrow.

'That work placement Zack might get Liam, he's refusing to even apply,' I tell her. 'And he's not going back to uni. He says him and Max are starting a band.'

'I know.' Her bright blue eyes fix on mine. 'I could hear you shouting from down here. That's why I just turned the music up.'

'I was *not* shouting,' I say, before realising that she's got me – because I *am* now. 'I was just trying to get him to listen,' I hiss. 'To common sense.'

'Is it really so bad if he tries?'

I can't believe she's asking me this. That she's supporting this insane idea of his.

'Yes, yes, it bloody well is. Because it's . . . it's pointless.'

'Why?'

'Because he's never going to be as good as he was.' It's the truth. 'And he'll hate that and people will just . . .'

'What?' She crosses her arms.

'You know what. You know what people are like. Like with him playing cricket at school. They took the piss constantly.'

'He still made the second team, didn't he? He proved them wrong.'

'This is different.'

'How?'

'It's the music industry. It eats its own bloody children alive.' We both know this from the few friends we've got who've worked in it.

'But it's always been his dream,' she says.

'Yeah, well, dreams aren't reality. And anyway, *has* it? *Has* it always been his dream?' I ask. 'Because as far as I know, he's not talked about making new music in ten years.'

No, not since I heard Max screaming that day in the garden with Liam. Not since I ran out to find my little boy bloodied and unconscious with his hand trapped and mangled in that zip wire's pulley.

'People are allowed to change their mind,' Jules says.

And there it is. Her jaw's set. Just like his. Oh yeah, no question, he's inherited his mule-grade stubbornness from her.

She stares at me like this whole thing's down to me. Or maybe that *is* how she sees it, because if it wasn't for me rigging up that zip wire from the old bay tree, our son would never have got hurt in the first place.

Me.

Something I've thought about every day since.

Only now, whenever I try to make his life better, he just pushes me away.

'Fine. You deal with it. With him,' I tell her.

Quickly turning, so she won't see how pissed off I really am, I march down the garden into the supersized shed Dad built as his workshop back in the seventies, pulling on the *plink-plinking* overhead strip lights before slamming the warped wooden door behind me, sealing myself in.

Squeezing past the bulging shelves of gaming manuals and science-fiction novels, I knock P. Bill Howarth's *Game Design & the Pixelated Brain* and Kurt Vonnegut's *Slaughterhouse-Five* onto the floor. I stick on Dad's sixties wooden Bang & Olufsen player which my tech-savvy pal Doodles refurbed for me, and pump the Who's 'My Generation' up loud.

Almost instantly, I feel better. Insulated. Not just from Liam, but from Jules, because us not clicking, it's happening more and more. Even our surprise fu – half-fuck – this morning wasn't enough to stop us dive-bombing into another bickerfest.

Whatever happened to reason? To just being nice?

I shut my eyes. Breathing in, breathing out. Feeling my heartbeat slow.

Glancing across at those two boxes I dragged in here earlier instead of taking to the dump, I dig out my ruined *Star Wars* figurine collection and stand them up in a line on Dad's old lathe, leaving them looking like some crazy, futuristic bus queue. I remember every single Christmas and birthday I got each one. Like they're etched into my mind. In every memory, Dad's smiling down.

Reaching into the other box, I grab a couple of the mixtapes. That same *For Juliet* tape from '89 I pulled out before and *Flat Party* from '98. I can't believe Jules wanted to chuck these out. A part of me still swoons at the nostalgia of these tapes, because I love music, like it's something my core needs to function properly. And me and Jules, it always used to be our thing, too. It's how we raised our kids. Like the von Trapps, but with beats. Until what happened to Liam. Until our whole family singalong and playalong vibe died out into each of us retreating to our separate devices and our separate rooms.

For a second, with the bright morning sunlight filtering in through the shed's ivy-throttled windows, *For Juliet* almost looks like it's glowing in my hands. But even if I could find a way to play it, I'm still too pissed off with Jules to pay her this kind of homage. She wanted to throw it out. Which is kind of like wanting to throw *us* out, right? Everything we were. What brought us to here. The soundtrack of our lives.

I toss it back into the box instead and turn Roger Daltrey up to 9.

Stripping off to my shorts, I get going on Dad's squeaky exercise bike. It's only day six of my new routine, but I swear it's getting easier already.

I think about Darius and his party as I cycle, pushing myself harder and harder. His face is dotted all over the old photo board gathering dust on the wall. Shots of him here in Dad's 'Aladdin's cave' at weekends. Dad teaching us how to build toy guns and kites as kids. And always with that sawdust – or 'man glitter', as Mum always called it – in Dad's hair. Then Darius and me playing *Super Mario* and *Sonic* as teens and teaching ourselves how to code and design our first rudimentary games, after Dad started hanging out more in the pubs and betting shops on Western Road.

Twenty-five years later, me and Darius even turned this into an office for a while. Some of the ideas we came up with are still pinned to the board. Including the proto logo for Totally Sirius Games, the company that only he went on to run when he moved to the States nine years ago.

Christ, it seems impossible now that we were ever so nearly the same.

After ten minutes, I'm knackered. Standing on Mum and Dad's crappy old analogue bathroom scales, I weigh myself. One pound. One measly sodding pound. That's all I've lost in six punishing days. I glare down at last night's Pronto in Tavola pizza box in the bin, on top of Wednesday's Kambi's Kebab wrapper. I pull off my sweat-heavy shorts, hoping it'll make another pound's difference. Does it hell. Maybe I've at least toned up instead? I turn to the tarnished mirror on the wall.

Big mistake. The pool-ready-me I've been hoping might put in a surprise guest appearance before Darius's homecoming party is emphatically *not* staring back. Instead, it's the usual me. With my little round belly leaving me looking like I've swallowed a car headrest.

Koala. My colleague Meredith gave me that cutesy nickname. On account of my beard and the way it's starting to grey, she says. But no doubt because of my dad bod, too. I picture her for a second, smiling across at me from where she sits in between me and Doodles in our messy little basement office at Quark Studios, with its reams of mobile role-playing games scripts and character traits taped to the walls.

She'd no doubt find this moment funny, watching me half sweat myself to death, because she thinks I'm comfy with who I am. But I still can't help wondering if she'll notice the new, slimmer, fitter me, if he ever does show up.

'Knock knock,' a heavy Manchester accent calls out.

Shit. Doodles. He's early. I nearly fall flat on my bare arse trying to snatch my shorts off the workbench as the shed door creaks open and Big D stoops in under the door frame, wearing leather sandals, rolled down cobra-patterned dungarees and a faded Frankie Knuckles T-shirt.

'By all the ancient gods. What seventh level of hell and decadence is this?' He grins, peering down at me from his six-foot-three vantage point as he takes off his mirrored Wayfarer shades.

'Piss off,' I say, quickly pulling on my shorts. 'I was just –'

'What, starting a one-man nudist colony? Or don't tell me, it was a full moon last night and you've just woken up here naked after ripping through several flocks of baby lambs on the moor overnight?'

'I was just weighing myself, OK?' I mumble.

'Oh, yeah, sure. Because we all, like, do that naked in our sheds.' Striding past me smirking, with his straggly long blond hair and weed-shot eyes that have always made him look like Gandalf the Grey's stoned kid brother, he grabs a couple of cold cans of Stella from the fridge.

'Here.' He chucks me one. 'Rub it on your forehead. It might help soothe your dignity.'

Jerking the dustcover off the TV, he sits down on the butt-sculpted sofa. By the time I finish getting dressed, he's already got his headset on, has levered the back off one of the controllers and is busy adjusting its electronic guts with a screwdriver.

'To stop your aim pulling to the right,' he explains, tossing it back to me and switching on the TV.

Me and Doodles game together most Saturdays. For just a couple of hours unless Jules is working, in which case it's sometimes all day. It's something we've been doing on and off since we first became friends back in our twenties, but more so now I'm less busy with the kids.

Today, it's *Baldur's Gate 3*. We've teamed up with a gang of fellow berserker, half-elf warrior druids, clerics and thieves to kick ass across the fictional world of the Forgotten Realms. A bunch of nonsense, of course. But fun nonsense. The kind that lets you leave all your troubles behind.

'Adam,' shouts Jules from somewhere outside an hour later, breaking the spell.

'Sounds like someone's in trouble,' Doodles intones, before cutting off our online chat with a bunch of twentysomethings who've been quizzing us for cheats for a couple of old-school nineties games they're really into.

'Adam!' Jules shouts louder. 'The car. You promised.'

She means Mum's old Skoda. I promised her I'd change the spark plugs. Plugs I haven't even got round to ordering yet online.

'All right, all right,' I yell back. 'I'm coming. For God's sake,' I mutter under my breath.

'Everything OK?' Doodles asks.

'Huh?'

'Between you two?' Me and Jules have been a couple since before he met us. We're probably like furniture to him.

'What? Oh, yeah. Just, you know. Married bullshit,' I tell him, shrugging it off.

He shrugs back. Being a bachelor, he doesn't have a clue.

Even though I've been praying for rain so that the whole 'pool' bit of the 'pool party' gets called off, two hours later the sun is still blazing down hotter than a chicken vindaloo from a clear blue sky, as our Uber drops us off outside the electric gates of Darius's cod antebellum mansion on Tongdean Avenue, the most expensive road in town.

'Wah-hey, A-Hole and Jules! Now the party can officially begin,' Darius whoops, all grinning white teeth, as he answers the videocam to buzz us in.

'Come on, it's still funny. Always will be,' Jules says, giving my hand the same comforting squeeze Dad used to if I'd lost one of my toys as a kid.

A-Hole. The unavoidable nickname that's dogged me my entire life. Thanks to my parents being unaware of the otherwise universally known American phrase.

'Yeah, but at least I was born an arsehole and didn't choose to marry one,' I counter with my standard retort, noticing she's wearing an old dress of hers and looking great in it – only it's too late to tell her.

Another hand squeeze. From me this time. Married Morse code for putting our earlier rows behind us. As we walk past a sparkling red Ferrari parked on the flint-cobbled drive, Darius appears, arms outstretched in his pillared doorway, dressed in designer swim shorts, a white linen shirt and black Havaianas.

For a second my heart sinks, wondering what I must look like next to him in my shitty old T-shirt and shorts. Especially since, blessed with natural Greek good looks anyway, Darius Angelopoulos has now built himself a Greek hero body to match.

But then he hugs me. 'Damn, it's good to see you, Ads,' he grins. And, suddenly, he's just Darius, my old best friend.

I smile as I watch him hug Jules, seeing the way his fingertips still roam self-consciously over his old acne pockmarks and that other, deeper scar on his chin from when he fell off his BMX back in '85 and banged both his face and his balls on a bin.

'I still can't believe you're throwing a party just two days after you got back home,' Jules says, as Darius leads us inside and past what looks like a private cinema room, with unopened removals boxes stacked up against its back wall.

'Yeah, well, you know me. I hate wasting time.' He smiles. 'Plus, I did have help,' he admits, nodding at a super-tall, super-confident-looking young woman with bright red hair, who's directing a phalanx of waiters carrying canapés from the kitchen into the garden. 'Anastasija, my PA,' he explains. 'She flew in early to get everything ready.'

Grabbing us both a glass of champagne, Darius ushers us outside. Blimey, there's got to be nearly a hundred people here already, milling around the manicured lawns overlooking the city and the wide blue sea below.

'So are you flipping out yet,' Jules says, 'about leaving your whole life out there behind?'

'Not really. Especially not now Mum's dementia has got so much worse.'

He pats my back affectionately. These last years since she got diagnosed, I've been checking in on Eleni every couple of months and reporting back. I can see that same sad look in Darius's eyes that he got in school after his dad died; we both know it won't be long.

'Of course, the money made it a hell of a lot easier,' he jokes.

The fortune he exited with. Half of which could have been mine, if I'd only moved out there to work with him, after we both came up with the idea for Totally Sirius in my shed all those years ago. Something everyone else here knows about too. Making me what? The Darius that never was? A failure? A fool?

I feel my stomach twist.

'You OK?' he asks, his dark eyes narrowing as he looks into mine.

'Yeah, of course.' Or at least, I'd better be, right? Because it's sure as hell too late to change the past now. 'Happy for you,' I say out loud. 'And chuffed to have you home.'

As he and Jules get talking to a couple of his American colleagues who are staying for the weekend, I throw myself into the party. A knock-off Buena Vista Social Club-style band strikes up and the air fills with laughter, chatter and the waft of BBQ smoke.

A couple of hours later and people are starting to get in the pool. Bagging a sunbed as far from the aquatic action as I can, I get talking to some old pals while sinking a couple of beers. When Jules gets changed into her swimsuit and sarong, she asks me to come for a dip, but I stick to where I am like a limpet at high tide. No way my shirt's coming off.

'Well, hey, boss,' Meredith says, appearing by my side, pushing her hand back through her shoulder-length blonde hair. She's dressed in a strappy green cotton dress that's covering her damp bikini underneath, and for a second, I get this jolt of adrenaline and don't know where to look. 'Enjoying the schmooze?' she enquires.

'The schmooze?' Self-conscious, I tug my T-shirt down over my belly. 'Is that what this is?'

'Ah, but of course you're here in your guise as revered old school chum and bestie of our host,' she teases. 'But for the rest of us mere mortals, while this might not exactly be Gamescom, it's probably the most schmooztastic gathering of the Sillycon Valley bosses and other selected industry arsehats we're likely to see all year.'

Sillycon, her name for the three streets in Brighton where most of the city's tech firms are based. One of our little in-jokes. Darius, or Anastasija at least, has asked a whole bunch of them here today as well as all his old friends, as he's keen to reconnect with everyone in the sector now he's back.

'Hmm,' I say, looking across at a few of the other faces I recognise from our rival companies here in town. Maybe I should be schmoozing them too, because it's not like my career at Quark is exactly going stellar, is it? Something that's bothering me more the older I get. Or maybe it's just the work I've ended up doing. Mobile role-playing games based on reality TV shows was hardly what I was aiming at when I joined, but it's the way the company has skewed these last five years. 'Oh, and talking of arsehats . . .' I nod towards where I've just spotted our MD and the founder of Quark Studios, Todd Landerson, kneeling down, mouth to a vodka luge spout.

'Do you think that's how he got the job to begin with?' Meredith asks.

'Oh, come on,' I laugh. 'You're better than that.'

'Am I, though?' she grins.

As she sits down next to me, I squidge up to make room. 'Sauvignon Blanc?' I ask, nodding at her glass.

'A pint of Dark Star IPA?' she says, glancing down at mine.

Our favourite summer drinks. Just like I know she prefers Cabernet Sauvignon in the winter, and salt and vinegar crisps all year round. The kind of crucial pub details I've only known about two or three other women in my life.

I don't know exactly when it started happening, our whole walking back from Friday-night works drinks together, but it's something we've been doing more and more lately. Unspoken. Unnoticed by others too. Not that there's anything *to* notice, of course. It's just that since Meredith moved flats, we take pretty much the same route home, and there's usually work stuff to talk about. Though, in truth, we've been talking about work less and less these last few months.

'Hey, Meredith!' a voice calls up.

We both turn to look at four hunks playing an improvised game of volleyball on the tennis court below us. Tanned torsos. Six-packs glistening in the sun.

'Klaus,' she shouts. 'Looking good, baby.'

'Feeling good!' the fittest of the four shouts back, flipping his wraparound shades up onto the top of his head.

'You still good for Wednesday practice?' she calls down.

'Sure.' He blows her a kiss. 'You and me, we're going straight to the top of the league.'

I recognise him now. One of the new account directors at work. Ten years younger than me.

'Ah, so *he's* your Mr Perfect,' I say, as Meredith turns back to me. Another in-joke, because she's been single since she moved down from London three years ago and claims she can't find anyone decent. Even though I always tease her that this is Brighton and she's setting her standards too high.

'Hmm,' she considers. 'I suppose. But only when we're playing volleyball.'

'He's your partner then?'

'Court partner.'

'He looks nice.'

'Oh, he is, but . . . *not so smart . . .*' She does a funny little Arnold Schwarzenegger, *Terminator* impression that makes me laugh. 'I mean, yeah,' she continues, 'he's hot. My type. But guys like him are always so bloody arrogant. I prefer someone with a bit more sense of humour. Someone you can have a pint and a laugh with.' She punches me playfully on the arm.

Teasing, and safe, because I'm clearly so physically not her type.

She stares back at Todd, who's now chatting to Doodles, beaming like some guy out of a toothpaste commercial.

'So, what do *you* think it's all about?' she says.

I don't even need to ask. She means the companywide meeting Todd's called for Monday, something that's never happened once in all the years I've been there. And normally I'd hate being treated as older and therefore wiser by my colleagues. A bit unfair of me given most of them are at least half my age. But last year when Todd booked our Christmas party at Horizon club down on the beach I got asked twice in the queue if I was an Uber driver and once inside if I was the plumber they'd called out to unblock the drains – it's not something you forget.

But at least with Meredith there's only a few years' difference between us. The trouble is, I don't know shit. I turned down my one shot at director-level management years ago so I could help out more with Jules and the kids. Back after Liam's accident.

'Maybe we should ask *him* then,' she says, pointing across at Darius who's splashing around in the pool. 'You've always said he's got all the answers, right? San Fran Disco, your friendly part-time DJ, part-time tech bro hero.' She smirks.

'Right.' I grin back at her, feeling a little guilty about the silly nickname I've given my oldest pal behind his back.

'But just who, pray tell, is it that Mr Siriusly-full-of-himself is with?' Meredith asks. 'Because they sure do look like they're having fun.'

'Oh, that's Jules,' I say, only now seeing that it's her.

'*Your* Jules?'

'Uh-huh.'

There's an awkward little silence as we watch them laughing and scrabbling over a rainbow-coloured Frisbee that keeps popping up out of the water, with Jules, ever competitive, and Darius, equally so, both refusing to let the other one win.

Only then Jules spots me and waves me over, but I pretend like I haven't seen.

'They're old pals,' I explain.

I try focusing on Meredith, but I can still hear Jules laughing. In a way I haven't heard her for so long. What's he saying that's making her giggle so much?

I don't really see Jules again until later, after it's started getting dark, when the music cuts and Darius hops up onto the little stage with a mic in his hands.

'Soooooo . . . guess what, people? It's karaoke time,' he announces with a showman's smile, as a spotlight picks him out.

Through the gathering crowd, I see Jules looking around for me.

But I know Darius too well. I know exactly who he's going to call up first and I can't bring myself to do it. To get up there. Next to him. Here at his awesome new house. In front of everyone I know.

Grabbing another drink, I shrink back into the shadows, as that bright, ugly spotlight shines down.

Chapter Three

Jules – 'Islands in the Stream'

I might have known Darius would get the karaoke going. He loves a performance.

'Give it up for Adam and Jules, everyone,' he hollers down the mic, stabbing his finger towards me. 'You're on.'

'No, no, no,' I call back, knowing I must look a state – sweaty from dancing.

Only Darius insists and I reluctantly let him pull me up onto the stage, squinting in the glare of the rigged-up stage lights.

'Where are you, A-Hole?' he booms, scanning the crowd.

I squirm, knowing how much Adam will hate his stupid nickname getting bandied around publicly like this. Especially in front of colleagues.

Where the hell *is* he anyway? I've hardly seen him since he was chatting to that Meredith woman from his office earlier. Doodles briefly introduced us. Of course, Adam's mentioned her before, but she was much prettier and more athletic-looking than I was expecting. Not that it matters. Because Adam . . . well, he's Adam.

Darius jabs a button on the console next to him and the intro to that cheesy Dolly Parton and Kenny Rogers classic comes on. Adam and I always used to sing it as our ironic karaoke duet back when we first got together. I'm astonished Darius remembers.

Surely, Adam can't leave me hanging for 'Islands in the Stream'?

Only it seems he can, because now I do see him, skulking at the back of the crowd. Not budging, even when our eyes lock.

Come on, I mouth. But he shakes his head. What the hell? I know he's insecure about his singing, but is he really going to leave me alone up here?

'There you are,' Darius says, spotting him too. 'Come on, mate. Remember the old Lion & Lobster karaoke days? I'm telling you guys, these two totally ruled.'

Adam shakes his head again and, with the lyrics starting to roll on the screen by my feet, Darius pulls a 'your loss' kind of a face, unclips the mic from the stand, and starts to sing at me, loudly, and very, very badly indeed.

I desperately search for Adam to come and rescue me, but I can't see him any more and suddenly it's my turn to sing. My voice is nervy to begin with and I look down from Darius's intense green eyes to the screen. Even though I know this song about sailing away to another world and relying on each other by heart, it just feels wrong to sing the words to him.

As the crowd claps and bellows along, I remind myself that it's just a bit of fun, and glance out across all these faces gathered from our past. Oh my God. Is that Mickey Ratty over there? My complete jerk of a first boyfriend. *Still* with a ponytail, only now all grizzled and grey like . . . a dead rat. The tattoo on my shoulder feels like a burn. If Adam sees him that's hardly going to put him in a good mood. Even though he says he doesn't mind my little 'rattoo', as he calls it, I know he secretly hates it.

Then I spot Ngozi pushing through the crowd to the front, where she stops, grinning at me and giving me a big thumbs up. Relief floods through me, as I grin back, and by the final verse, I'm properly in my stride.

When the song ends, Darius grips my hand and makes me take a bow with him like we're onstage at Wembley. Jumping down, I feel my legs shaking, as I fall into Ngozi's arms, and we head away to the side of the dance floor as Darius pulls another victim up onto the stage.

'Would you like a glass of something?' one of the waiters asks, walking past us with a tray of drinks..

'I need water,' I tell him, taking a glass as Ngozi grabs a cocktail.

'And would you bring us two of your finest tequilas?' Ngozi adds, in that charming, yet authoritative tone that makes most people fall over themselves to do her bidding.

We all exchange a look, as an off-key rendition of Amy Winehouse's 'Rehab' starts up from the stage, then laugh.

'I was worried you weren't going to make it,' I say to Ngozi, as the waiter heads off and we sit together on the nearby bench.

She might be at the top of her game as a corporate lawyer and earning bazillions, but her job is relentless, and she's just flown in from Geneva. Not that you'd know it. It's three years since she divorced Geoff and being footloose and fancy free is clearly suiting her. She's wearing a sexy, slinky blue dress with studded ankle boots. Her hair is scraped back from her flawless face and going grey at the edges, but she's still as stylish and cool as when I met her in sixth form college.

'It was touch and go. Hey, I'm pleased to see this old thing is holding its own,' she says, tugging at my dress.

'I know, right? Proper vintage.'

'You looked great up there.'

I'm warmed by her compliment.

'Darius has thought of everything. He had nice showers with swanky hairdryers for after the pool.' I flick my blow-dried locks.

Ngozi looks towards Darius on the stage. 'Still full of himself, I see.'

She's never been that impressed by our host.

'So? How was the trip? Any GS?' I ask, and she laughs. This is our code for German Sausage – a reference to the one and only time she copped off with someone on a work trip.

'No. Not a whiff.'

The waiter returns with our shots and proffers them to us on a tray with a flourish. Ngozi and I clink glasses, downing the tequilas, making that disgusted, wincing joyful face we always do.

'O-*kay*. Let's get this party started,' she says, hauling me back to my feet.

We join in with the crowd and sing along to the karaoke numbers and then Doodles appears. He's bare-chested beneath a crazy fake-fur jacket, in tattered jeans with 'Aphex Twin' scrawled across one leg. He wraps his arms around our shoulders, leaning on us.

'My dudes,' he says. 'You look . . .' He surveys us both, grinning, but clearly a little too wasted to decide exactly how we *do* look. 'It's yours truly up next. Stay right where you are.'

A moment later, a blast of dry ice hisses up from the stage and Darius introduces Doodles like he's the headline act at the Ibiza season opening party. Headphones on, Doodles nods from behind the decks and starts his set. Ngozi puts her arms up, as the intro to her favourite song, Baccara's 'Yes Sir, I Can Boogie' starts, swaying her hips as the beat comes in. She's always been the coolest person in any room and quickly she's surrounded by other people, as the party really gets going. Only still no sign of Adam.

I step away from the dance floor and head towards the house, spotting him in the glass-sided atrium at the back. He changed three times before we left home, in the end plumping for his orange R.E.M. *Out of Time* tour T-shirt, so I know it's him, even from this distance. He's running around the table-tennis table with a bunch of other middle-aged blokes, throwing the bats down at each end so they can all take turns at hitting the ball. As I get closer, I can hear them laughing and panting with the exertion.

'Where are you sneaking off to?'

'Jesus, you made me jump,' I tell Darius, suddenly engulfed in his expensive cologne. 'I was trying to find Adam.' I point to the atrium.

'He looks just like a giant goldfish going round and round,' Darius observes.

As I'm trying to formulate a response to what he's just said, because that was a bit mean, one of the lads bundles into Adam and they collapse on their arses in a fit of laughs and chorus of jeers.

'And to think he was nearly my business partner,' Darius says conspiratorially. Like by not answering I've admitted that it's OK for him to take the piss behind Adam's back. 'Does he ever regret it?' he asks. 'You know. Not taking the chance?'

I'm amazed that he's jumped right in and asked something so personal, but it occurs to me that I don't have the foggiest idea how Adam actually feels. About not going to San Francisco. About turning their business partnership down. It's a subject we don't . . . *can't* discuss. Neither of us dares open that particular Pandora's box of resentment and recrimination.

But I'm not going to give Darius what he clearly wants – the affirmation that Adam screwed up. That he could have had all this too. Even though we're both thinking it. How can we not, when this whole party has been one giant willy-waggle?

'What about *you*?' he presses.

'I don't think about it,' I lie. Have I pulled off nonchalant? Please, God . . .

'Life would have been different, there's no denying it,' he says, with a sad sigh. 'The three of us out there together in that brave new world. Who knows how it would have turned out?'

What does he mean? Turned out for who? Me and Adam? Or me and *him*? Because that's here too. The possibility, no matter how crazy, that he's also talking about *us*.

And suddenly I can feel the *thing we're not discussing* approaching. The very specific conversation we had eight years ago, before he left, that neither of us has acknowledged or mentioned since. Well, it wasn't much of a conversation, but it still feels like a secret. *Is* a secret. One I've buried, telling myself it was too insignificant and yet at the same time too shocking to admit even to myself.

My mind now fills with the memory of how Darius tenderly wiped away my angry, disappointed tears and told me that I *could* still go to San Francisco. Me and the kids. Only not with Adam, but with *him*. And how I held his gaze, my tears stalling with shock at his offer. And in that split second, he moved his face towards mine . . .

Only I pulled away, flustered, shaken. So shocked that he'd betray his oldest friend, but even more shocked that my heart had soared for a brief moment in temptation, until, guiltily, I'd crashed back down to earth.

I never mentioned it to Adam. I never told him how close Darius and I came.

'It's a shame you didn't find someone out there,' I say, pushing the memory away. 'Or *did* you?' I ask, picturing his uber-cool PA Anastasija and the way she was staring up at him during the karaoke just now.

'Oh, I found plenty of people,' he says, that cheeky smile back, the spell he'd woven between us broken. 'Just not the right one. But *c'est la vie*, eh? Maybe one day.' He shrugs, looking thoughtful as he scuffs the path with his moccasin. 'You know I've always secretly envied you guys. What you have. Kids. Each other. I mean, you really lucked out, right? You got everything, Jules. All the really important stuff.'

This admission of jealousy momentarily floors me because, well, just look at this house. On the other hand, isn't this kind of like him saying that I made the right choice?

It's such a relief that, for a moment, I consider confessing everything to him – about how I *don't* feel like I've lucked out at all. About how far from having everything I really am. About feeling useless and unseen. About how Adam and I hardly connect any more, and I'm increasingly absorbed with layer upon layer of regret.

'Nothing's perfect,' I say. 'I mean, nothing ever is.'

'Like what?'

'Like my career . . . it's pretty much at a dead end. There were some opportunities, but . . .' I fizzle out.

I'm shocked I've been so honest. After all, I've been avoiding giving anyone – especially Adam – the full financial picture of Jules's Kitchen. Don't get me wrong. Adam's always been supportive enough of me being a caterer, so much so that he even put his own career ambitions on hold, going part-time when I first started freelancing and the private dining contracts were rolling in when the kids went to school. Back then, he did the lion's share of the parenting and was pretty incredible, but then the recession kicked in and somewhere along the line, it was decided that he should go back to being the main breadwinner, as if I'd had my turn.

Since I started back up again after lockdown things have gone from bad to worse. I've had to slash my prices to stop my regulars leaving for the competition, while the cost of all my ingredients has skyrocketed. Even though I've always promised Adam I'd stick to his golden rule of paying off our credit cards each month in full, the truth is that I've long since resorted to paying the minimum amount on my business card and now everything's snowballed.

'But, Jules, you're the best,' Darius says, as if it's a given. 'With all those big dreams to match.'

'No.' I bat away his flattery. 'That was always you. Look at all this.' I stretch my arms out wide.

He tips his head bashfully. 'OK, so this catering company of yours has somehow not taken off. How do we fix that?' he asks. Like it's just some puzzle to solve. His voice is warm and concerned and I'm relieved we're back on safe ground. We're friends, I remind myself. Old friends. The same as we've always been, except for that one tiny blip.

'I don't know. I'd love to try something else. I've always wanted to run a pop-up restaurant. Something classy. Quirky. You know?'

'Then you must,' he says decisively.

I feel it then. A beat of my old confidence. A bounce.

But before he can say any more, Doodles calls out for him on the mic to come back to the stage, and I notice Adam heading up the path towards us.

'I'll come over,' Darius tells me. 'We'll discuss.' He points at me, then Adam, as he arrives. 'Gotta go,' he says. 'DJing duties call.'

Then with that, he's off, walking backwards, gun-toting his index fingers at us like he's Kiefer Sutherland or Emilio Estevez in some Brat Pack flick, before spinning away.

'Discuss what?' Adam says, more than a little drunk.

'Jesus, what have you been drinking?'

'I'm fine. Hey, shall we go dance?'

Oh, so *now* he wants to party? Whatever that karaoke shyness was all about has just vanished.? As he slings his arm around my shoulder, I shrug him off, not wanting him leaning on me all buddy-buddy like we're students again. Not after he just let me down.

I'm also shaken by how frank my chat with Darius was, and by how good it felt to be listened to. I need some time to process what's just happened. To see if I should feel as guilty as I do.

'I think we should call it a night. I'm tired,' I tell Adam. I think of my early start and all the stuff I've still got to get organised for the council lunch tomorrow.

'French exit,' he says, tapping the side of his nose. 'Good idea.'

It's like leaving Narnia. Outside on the pavement, I shiver as we're spat back out into the real world. I pull out my only slightly moth-eaten cashmere throw from my handbag and wrap it around me. From the other side of the high brick wall, I can still hear the beat of the music and see the colourful lasers stretching up to the stars.

Despite the fleet of cabs that have been promised in an hour's time, there's not one on the street and Uber is fully booked, so we have no choice but to walk the two miles home.

I guess it's no bad thing, because the night air seems to sober Adam up, although I start limping. The blister from my pre-lockdown wedges is killing me. Adam offers to lend me his socks, and as we sit on the kerb, he takes them off and I put them on. An old custom of ours. I look ridiculous wearing slingbacks and socks, but who's judging?

There's no one around and the night is warm, the lamp posts spreading a yellow glow onto the road. An owl hoots and, ahead, a fox stops and looks us up and down with disdain.

'Why didn't you want to sing with me?' I ask. 'He was an even worse singer than you.'

'You didn't look like you needed me.'

I glance sideways at him. Is he jealous? No, just stating a fact.

'Yeah, well, you missed out.' I stop myself saying more. There's no point in punishing him. 'But all in all, a pretty good party, eh? And he had everyone there. God knows how.'

Then we're off, bantering about the outrageous opulence of the whole thing and how Darius managed to dig out all of the old crowd, putting some people's noses well out of joint with his absurd display of wealth. He doesn't mention Mickey Ratty even though we're soon on to the gossip from his schoolmates, some of whom we haven't seen for years. The who-ran-off-with-who roll call is like the Wikipedia page of a particularly tawdry soap opera.

'So, what's the deal with Meredith?' I ask.

'What do you mean?'

'Is she your office crush?' I tease.

'What? No! She's just a colleague. Seriously?' he adds, as if I could have been genuinely serious. Like he's the kind of guy who would get a crush on his co-workers.

We approach the Dyke Alehouse at the top of the hill by the Tesco garage and, without warning, he gently pushes me against the wall.

'I kissed you here once, remember?' he says, his breath a little sour with beer.

'Yes, when we were kids,' I point out, trying to wriggle away. There are people in the shop of the petrol garage opposite. 'Don't. They'll see.'

'Let them,' Adam says, stroking the hair away from my face.

There's a beat and then he kisses me. It's hardly up there with the tongue tangos of our courting years, but with our faces up close, it feels like a moment of connection, and somehow much more real than what we attempted in bed this morning.

Peeling ourselves apart, we head down towards Seven Dials, chatting again about the party. We automatically take the short cut down

Crocodile Walk, between the sixth form college and the playing fields, the familiar trees casting long shadows on the moonlit football pitch where Nelly used to play on the girls' team and Adam and I used to roar from the sidelines.

'Are you happy?' he suddenly says.

'What, right now?'

'Even though we don't have the fancy car, or the biggest house?'

Aha. Darius *has* got up his nose.

'Course,' I tell him, hoping he doesn't hear the tremor in my voice.

Why has he instigated this conversation? Has he guessed that I'm not, or not as happy as I could be? Or – and I'm nervous now – is he feeling the same way too? About me.

'But if you could change anything, what would you change? Be honest,' he presses.

He gives me that 'lay it on me, I can take it' look, when we both know for a fact that he can't. But fine. Screw it. He's not the only one who's had a drink.

'I've been thinking lately that it might be all downhill from here. Not just because of us, but because of our age. You know, we might end up doing the same old routine, on and on, until we die.'

He stops. Stares. I can almost hear the tumbleweed blowing past.

'But we've got what most people want,' he says a moment later. 'A family and . . .' But whatever long list he was thinking of seems to peter out.

'What happens when the kids go?' I ask.

'*If* they ever go.'

There's a pause as we both acknowledge the truth of this. 'One day they will,' I decide. 'And then what? Have you even thought about it?'

'I guess I've just been too busy. Dealing with the here and now.'

Only he doesn't, really, does he? Deal with much of any of that. It suddenly annoys me that he's so un-self-aware. I can see now that he's regretting asking me the question.

'We used to talk about building something together. Remember?' I say.

'Like what?'

I take a punt, my conversation with Darius fresh in my mind. 'Like my pop-up idea?'

'Oh *God*, this *again*,' he says, rubbing his head. 'I thought we'd put that to bed.'

'*You* had, maybe.'

'For good reason. It's crazily expensive and, anyway, you hardly have a platform to promote it from.'

I feel this like a physical slap. He knows I'm insecure about my social media skills and that I'm not exactly great at blowing my own trumpet. But worse is the feeling that we were about to talk properly, and even, dare I say it, be honest with each other and he's gone and shut me down.

This is precisely why we don't discuss this stuff, I remember too late. Because when we do, he does *this*.

I stalk ahead of him, feeling properly cross.

'I'm just being practical,' he says, catching up.

'No, you're pouring cold water on yet another one of my ideas.'

'I'm just pointing out the business problems you might come up against. It's called anticipating,' he says.

'Oh, piss off, Adam. Like you have any idea about business.'

'What's that supposed to mean?'

I grit my teeth. Sod it. Why shouldn't I say it? It's not like he's holding back. 'Well, if you really want to have this out, fine. Being good at business means taking risks. We could have done so much more with our lives if you were only prepared to take a risk. Just once.'

I hear my raised voice echoing in the dark.

'That's out of order,' he says.

'Doesn't it even bother you that Darius is up there flashing his cash, when half of that could have been yours?'

Boom bada boom. She lands. The elephant in the room.

In the light of the street lamp, I can see Adam's thunderous expression. 'It could have gone the other way,' he says, his voice catching. 'He could have lost everything. And then we'd have lost everything too.'

Like Adam's dad did. I don't say it, but that's what he's terrified of.

'But Darius *didn't* lose everything, did he?' I snap. 'He took the chance and you . . . you made us just carry on here and get stuck.'

We stomp on towards home, yards opening up between us like we're on different forks of a road.

I can feel angry tears shaking in my chest.

'And what about Australia?' I say, on a roll now, because if we're having it out, we might as well have it *all* out.

'You're accusing *me* of being stuck in the past? That was over twenty years ago!'

'We had it all worked out, Adam. Childcare. My dream job.'

'My parents died, Jules. I had that. Them. The house. The debts. *Everything* to bloody sort out.'

'We still could have gone after all that was sorted.'

'I had a new job by then. We needed the money.'

'Yes, but what about me? I ended up stuck at home. For the next God knows how many years.'

'You wanted that,' he protests. 'To bring up the kids. We agreed. *You* agreed. And I supported you, didn't I? Once they were older.'

'Oh, well, thank you so much,' I say, my voice laden with sarcasm. 'For being such a noble man. For actually putting a woman first.'

'It's not my fault your business didn't work out. And for your information, going part-time, *that's* what's cost me the chance of a proper promotion.'

'Oh, so now that's my fault too?'

We walk on locked in silence, the resentment crackling. We're now at our tatty cul-de-sac approaching our even tattier house at the end. I feel ashamed of myself because I know it's not bad. We have a decent roof over our heads and we're keeping the wolf from the door.

'We could have been in Australia, Adam. That's all I'm saying. We could have had a whole other life.'

'Yeah. One you wanted. Not me,' he says bitterly.

'You seemed pretty keen on it at the time,' I remind him.

'Not if I'd known how much it would fuck everything up.'

I stop by the gate, astonished he's actually said this out loud. 'What?'

'It's true,' he says, gritting his teeth. 'If we hadn't gone to the airport that day, Mum and Dad would still be alive.' His eyes blaze.

'Oh, so now it's *my* fault they died? Because *I'm* the one who wanted us to go more. *Wow*.' My voice chokes. 'Wow,' I repeat, winded.

'I'm . . . I'm not saying that.' He knows he's gone too far.

'You just did.'

I walk furiously up the path but somehow get caught on the long shoot of the rose bush. As I yank my dress away, the thorns snag and tear the fabric.

Tears blind me as I get to the front door. I fumble with the keys in my bag, my hands shaking. When I open the door, Groucho Barx growls, scared. I look back towards the gate, where Adam is standing in silhouette.

'You think I signed up for a life stuck here living in your parents' shitty house? Well, I didn't,' I hiss. 'And do you know what I'd really change about you, about us, about *all* of this if I could?'

Nothing. He says nothing.

'Everything,' I half say, half spit, the words tasting just as bitter and vile as I know they are.

But then before I have the chance to change my mind, I march inside and slam the door as hard as I can.

Chapter Four

Adam – 'Don't You Want Me'

I stand here for a second, gawping at the door my wife of nearly a quarter of a century has just slammed in my face.

I want to scream. At Jules. But not just Jules. At myself. I shouldn't have done it, hurled Mum and Dad at her like a bloody hand grenade. I shouldn't have told her how I feel – how I've always felt. That it was our fault that they died.

Only I can still hear it. Auntie Megan's voice on the phone, just after we'd landed at Hong Kong on that first leg of our journey to Australia. Telling me how Mum and Dad had been killed in a car crash less than twenty minutes after they'd dropped us off at Gatwick Airport. A journey they'd never have taken if it wasn't for us deciding to emigrate, to give Australia a go.

But to pass that hurt on to Jules? It's not right. Quickly, I dig into my pocket for my door keys. To say sorry. But then I stop. Because what about her? What about all that nasty shit *she* just said? All that vitriol she's clearly got no intention of apologising for. About me chickening out of the deal with Darius, and how everything we've built might add up to a big fat zero once the kids have left home.

Yeah, *stuck*. That's the word *Furiosa* just used. Like I'm some kind of barnacled human anchor that's held her back from sailing life's great glittering sea. Well, sod her. Wherever we are now, we got here *together*. We're a partnership. Or at least we *were*.

'And screw you too, Groucho Barx,' I hiss, glaring at the quisling little canine traitor, peeping out through the living-room curtains. It's too late for puppy-dog eyes now. After growling at me, backing her up.

You've made your flea-bitten bed and you can bloody well lie in it. No more Pringles. No more Skips.

Stumbling into the shed, I click on the flickering lights and slam the door. Grabbing a half-drunk bottle of whiskey left over from Christmas, I start necking it. One gulp, two gulps, three. Then I catch sight of myself in the mirror.

Jesus. I look just like my dad. Am probably around the same age he started doing this too. Drinking like a fish. First because of Mum getting ill, then because of his gambling debts. Debts he saddled me with when he died. Along with a giant mortgage we're still struggling to pay off. *That*'s why I turned down Australia and then San Francisco. To protect us. To avoid gambling away our futures myself. How the hell was I to know that Totally Sirius would turn out to be a winner? How the hell was I to know that this was a decision I'd regret for the rest of my life?

Another gulp.

Lurching towards the Totally Sirius logo on the cork board, I rip it down, then up. My ring finger starts stinging, bleeding. Shit. I must have caught it on the nail the logo was hooked on.

Furiously, impotently, I twist my wedding ring off, then . . . throw it, watch it ping off the dusty screen of an old Atari monitor before ricocheting off Luke Skywalker's half-melted plastic boot and out of sight.

Like even the Force is getting involved now.

Right away, I regret it. My finger feels wrong. Too light. The circular groove worn in my flesh over the last twenty-five years is already starting to itch.

Quickly turning on my phone's torch, I get down on my knees and start scanning the dusty floor. Nothing. I start to panic. Only then I see it. Inside that box of tapes and CDs Jules told me to throw out. Sitting perfectly balanced on top.

Thank God.

Snatching it up, I slip it quickly back onto my finger. Then I spot the *For Juliet* tape again. The one from '89. The year I met Jules.

And right here next to it I now notice my dusty old Sony boom box, complete with its double tape deck. Rummaging around, I plug in an extension lead, careful not to put my foot through the floorboards, which look riddled with wormholes.

I'm not expecting the Sony to still work, but miraculously it does, clicking on with a faint hum and a flutter of red and green equaliser bulbs. Sliding the TDK 60 tape out from inside its case, I slot it in.

Then *dum-dum-de-dum-dum-dum-dum-de-dum*.

On come the first throbbing synth chords of 'Don't You Want Me' by the Human League. An '81 hit but recorded on here as the opening track because it was having a total revival in the Brighton sixth form indie discos in '89.

Right away, I can feel the bass radiating out from the dusty old speakers, churning up this mad mix of emotions inside me, leaving me feeling anxious and happy and nostalgic all at once – and suddenly so bloody young again it makes me want to weep.

Because we had it all back then, didn't we? Jules and me. We had everything ahead of us. We hadn't screwed anything up.

It's like I can feel the music pumping right through me now, like it's somehow charging my very soul, as tears of loss and something like homesickness stream down my cheeks.

I can't stop looking at the tape's twin spindles as they keep on turning, staring back at me like a pair of hypnotic eyes, round and round . . . and round and round and round . . .

Then I'm jolted by a thunderous crash and a blinding flash of lightning obliterates the square of black night sky framed by the shed window – and I feel my whole universe shake . . .

Next thing – what the hell?! – it's *me* turning round and round and round, faster and faster, like I'm going to break. In a hideous whirlwind of coloured lights and rushing wind, and all the while with Phil bloody Oakey singing 'Don't you want me?' over and over again . . .

Until twisting, pulling back, desperately trying and failing to fight against the tide, I'm sucked down screaming into that churning, kaleidoscopic typhoon's shrinking black eye . . .

Darkness. Silence. Nothing, in fact.

I can't move, like there's a ten-tonne monster squatting on my back. Shit. Have I been struck by lightning? Am I paralysed? Have I had some kind of a stroke?

Think. Remember. The shed. I was in the shed. Drunk. Listening to that old tape with its spindles turning round and round and round until – *BOOOOM!* – thunder roared outside.

I try moving again. Still no dice.

Then noise. A high-pitched beeping. Like an alarm? Or some piece of hospital equipment? Am I in a coma ward?

Oh God, no. Please not that.

Then, suddenly, I *can* feel something. Yes, here, *my fingers* by my sides. *My toes* clenching, unclenching. Only not me doing it somehow. Not me in charge.

But that's not all I can feel, because this tingling sensation between my legs is unmistakable and going nowhere any time soon. Good grief. I have a *stiffy*? How in the name of all that's holy, with whatever's actually going on here right now, am I also somehow *erect*?

But at least this means I'm not paralysed, right? Then *what*? Under sedation? Drugged?

Only I don't feel like that either. Or even hungover. Not like I should after all that pissing whiskey I guzzled down. In fact, *clean* is more like it. Unsullied. Fresh. Almost kind of *brand spanking new*.

More movement: my mouth opening. Again, not like I'm doing it, like it's somehow opening itself. To yawn, a great big groan of a yawn. Only my voice is all wrong. Too high, too reedy. Too Justin Bieber or David Beckham-y, when, after smoking until I was thirty, I'm really more Tom Jones or Johnny Cash.

Then suddenly – in a rush – thoughts are hitting me. Only not *my* thoughts. Somebody else's, like a voice I'm hearing in my head, saying, *Come on, get up . . . it's Saturday . . . today's the day . . .*

Yet I've still got my own thoughts too. Not competing with these other thoughts. More coexisting, like I can simply hear both.

Then comes big movement. I roll onto my side – or rather my body does, because I'm not in charge of it. Then I'm squeezing and unsqueezing my eyes, before opening them, and bringing bright light rushing in.

I'm not quite sure what I'm expecting to see. The stereo? The shed ceiling? Or, after that insanely intense vision of the roaring hurricane earlier, perhaps the beatific face of God?

What I actually get is a floor full of grubby novelty Garfield and Mario Brothers boxer shorts, and striped and paisley socks, along with Smiths and Go-Betweens T-shirts, and crumpled chinos and Army

Surplus jeans . . . like, like an entire jumble sale has just exploded all over the room.

Then my body is tipping itself out of bed, before plucking up items in what looks like random order and pulling them on. Like a scarecrow dressing itself. Then quickly – *guiltily*, I somehow *feel* the guilt – grabbing up all the remaining clothes and wedging them into a wardrobe that I somehow just *know* they were all pulled out of the night before for a trying-on session, to see what looked *coolest*.

Cleanliness is next to godliness – I feel my eyes flick to these words stitched into a little framed tapestry on the wall.

Right, just like that one Mum made me as a kid. And I can see now that I am indeed in a kid's bedroom. Nelly's? Liam's? No. Neither of them would be seen dead with that Athena poster of the blonde tennis girl scratching her arse taped to the back of that wardrobe door.

What in the name of –

Oh, Christ alive. I suddenly *know* whose bedroom this is. *Mine*. But not mine *now*. Mine *then*. Back when I was a kid.

Meaning shit, shit, shit. Maybe I *am* in a coma. Or have had a nervous breakdown. Or am I hallucinating all this? But then, why does it feel so real? As in, like, I'm not only seeing this, but *experiencing* it. Like I can feel the cold gloop of the revolting hair gel whoever's steering this body is now slicking back through my/our hair. And I can feel the sudden double blast of ice-cold sickly teen deodorant under my armpits as it deluges the room with its skunky Pepé Le Pew whiff.

Even weirder, I can also tell how some alien part of me – of *this* – actually thinks this scent is sophisticated and sexy enough that it might one day help them get laid.

But it's my reflection that does it, as whatever the hell's in charge now smoothly steers us into the little en suite shower room – yep, the *same* damn little en suite shower room my dad built for me when I was a teen – and just stops dead centre in front of the mirror and stares.

At *myself*.

Only not the me I know now, the middle-aged me. No, this is the teenage me, the me I once was, now jauntily checking out not just his skinny, wrinkleless left-side profile, but his skinny, wrinkleless right-side profile too. Then adjusting his enormously bouffy hair at least twenty times, before squirting Gold Spot onto his tongue, squeezing a zit on his forehead and thinking *Nice one* to himself.

Nice one. Yep, again I hear this thought of his loud and clear. Like not only am I seemingly trapped inside his body – seeing everything he sees, sensing everything he senses – but I'm also eavesdropping on everything he thinks.

'Hi, Juliet,' he says out loud, trying a smile, and as he says it, I can feel something in his stomach. Nerves. 'Hey, Juliet,' he tries again, without the smile this time. 'How's your week been?'

'Ads,' a man's voice calls from downstairs. 'You awake?'

Ads. Bloody hell. What my dad used to call me. The only one apart from Jules and Darius who's ever called me that, in fact.

'Yeah, Dad,' I – he, this younger me, whatever – call back.

'Then come and get yourself some grub. We're leaving in twenty.'

Jerking on a pair of busted white All Stars, younger Adam reaches for his desk drawer. To grab the pack of Marlboro Lights he's hidden inside. Not only can I read his thoughts, but I can also feel his addiction too.

But as his hand darts out to grab them, a part of me, the *real* me, Twenty-First-Century Adam, thinks, *No.* Because I don't want them. I don't even want to touch them. I've read Alan Carr's bloody awful quitting book too many goddamned times to go through that shit again.

And – bloody hell! – somehow *my* resistance seems to have an effect, because I can feel it then for the first time: *me* imposing myself on *him*. On his hand. His fingers are now refusing to grab.

Teenage Adam tries to reimpose himself. Almost like he's sensing me inside him for the first time. But then that fleeting inkling is gone. He turns away, forgetting about the smokes, already thinking about breakfast. Like on some subconscious level, he's now accepted this intrusion of mine. Like he doesn't need to fight it or reject it, because we're both somehow already the same.

Then we're off, with him in charge again, and me riding as a passenger, as he reaches for a tape on the desk. No, strike that. Not just any tape. *The* tape. *For Juliet.* The exact same bloody one that I was just listening to in the shed before I woke up *here*.

Only it's not just *the* tape for me, it's *the* tape for him too. I can sense it. This is the one he's been slaving over making for *her*.

For Juliet, which – of course! – is what I used to call her before I really knew her. His Juliet is my Jules.

I – he, young Adam – barge out onto the landing and slide down the banister on my arse. It's a rush. A buzz. And I love it too. His body feels so damned zingy, like he could run a hundred miles right now if he wanted to. Like he could do it twice.

Only then, as we reach the bottom of the stairs, I freeze. Or rather my mind does. It locks.

Mum. My mum who died twenty years ago in a car crash. Mum, turning towards me from where she's been gazing, stooped, at her reflection in the gloomy hallway mirror.

She tuts, glowering at this younger me with his hands still on the banister. 'You're not ten any more, Adam,' she tells him. An opaqueness to her eyes. How she always looked when the pain got too bad and she ended up back on her pills. 'And you know what happens when people fall.'

He does. *I* do. That's what happened to Mum. She hurt her spine falling when she was out dancing with Dad, back when I was ten. The last time she ever did anything 'reckless' – her word – like that.

'Sorry.' And the quick way he – this young Adam – says this, reminds me how many times *I* had to say it. Because of Mum's rules, set after her fall. Don't run, be quiet, tidy up, be grateful, don't whine, don't cry . . .

'What?' she asks, clawing her wiry black hair up into a bun. 'You look like you've seen a ghost.'

And, wow, I only now realise I've imposed myself over young Adam again. Maybe just from the shock of seeing her. And, still in control, I march right up to her and pull her into a hug. So tight. This shouldn't be possible, yet she feels so alive. My nostrils fill with the forgotten smell of her perfume.

But already Adam's letting go. Pulling back and reasserting himself. A bit freaked out by what he's just done, but kind of OK with it too. She almost smiled, didn't she? She almost cracked. As though his old mum from before her accident, who he's still convinced is somewhere inside her, nearly broke out.

'What's that for?' she asks.

'Nothing, I –' Adam doesn't know why he just hugged her.

'I do wish you'd come to church,' she says, her dark eyes glazing over.

Another of her catchphrases. One she used every Sunday from the day I stopped accompanying her when I was sixteen, even though I knew she wanted me to go. Even though I knew church was the only thing that gave her relief.

'I can't. I'm helping Dad.'

Her lips purse. A staple thin line. Like this was a choice I made between them. Which it was. But I couldn't bear the suffocating silence of the drive to St Mark's and back any more. The way the other people in the congregation were with her. Like she needed their pity.

'I was talking to Gareth Thompson after Wednesday Bible class,' she says. 'He works for one of the big insurers up in London and he says that a boy like you who's good with figures should definitely do maths at university.'

'I'm more interested in computing.'

'But that's a hobby.'

A *hobby*. Christ, just like I said to Liam. A deflection I learned from her?

'Banks use computers too,' Adam points out. And I remember it now; I remember this whole conversation.

'Yes, but if you want to have a serious career . . .'

Computers are serious, he thinks. Just like I once thought. *Even, or even most especially, games.*

But he knows there's no point in trying to tell her this. Nor can he bring himself to confess that he's already applied to study computing at uni – something she'll repeatedly refer to in later years as 'one of your biggest mistakes', even *after* the internet is invented. The other being Jules, he'll come to suspect from the way she'll always look at her, like she's too flighty, too flippant, not quite good enough . . .

'Where is he?' Adam asks, quickly changing the subject.

He means Dad.

'Where do you think?'

The shed. Where he always is, at least whenever she's around, Adam's thinking. Because their marriage now is nothing like in the photos of them dancing together in their younger days, before she got hurt. Then, the two of them looked so close it's like they were one, and made of pure joy.

She leaves without saying goodbye and Adam walks through to the kitchen, telling himself it's not her, just the pills. But as much as I'm now remembering all this crazy shit I grew up with – I'm also marvelling at Adam as he scarfs down a bowl of Rice Krispies the size of a swimming pool, then two frosted strawberry Pop-Tarts, leaving me feeling his – *our* – enamel practically stripping itself off his teeth in protest, and wishing he'd rush back upstairs and brush them again. A thought that doesn't enter his mind.

He turns on the radio instead, switching it from *Sunday Worship* to Madonna's 'Like A Prayer' on Radio 1.

Taking in the rest of the kitchen, I see some things are the same. Like the lime-green laminated cabinets that Dad built that I've resisted Jules throwing out for the last twenty years. But there's a load of old eighties crap I've forgotten we ever had, too. Empty glass milk bottles next to a yogurt maker, and a SodaStream and Philips TV the size of a tank with a plug-in aerial on top.

'All right, kiddo,' Dad says, wandering in wearing paint-spattered jeans and a Motörhead T-shirt, gently patting Adam on the back.

For a moment I can't stop staring at him too. He's so alive. Just like her. Even though I know him and Mum died in the exact same crash.

'Come on. Best get a shift on,' he says, 'or we're going to be late.'

A flare of excitement bursts inside Adam. Inside *us*. I get a snapshot image of his Juliet – my Jules – as a teen. Bloody hell. That's who we're off to see now, isn't it? Right, because it's October 1989, just like it says right here on the cover of Dad's *Racing Post* that he's pulled down from the top of the cupboard where he keeps it hidden from Mum. Meaning we're off to continue fixing up the Peregrine Hotel today.

Adam follows him out into the drive and there it is. Dad's old minibus. An old school bus that he scrubbed the school's name off along with a couple more letters, so that it now reads 'C OOL US' on the side.

And we *were* cool, weren't we? *Are*. Me and my dad. In this memory or dream or whatever the hell it is. Or at least that's how it feels to both me and this Adam as he jerks open the minibus's rusty door and breathes in the familiar reek of Golden Virginia and varnish and paint drifting through from the timpani of pots and brushes in the back, before hitting 'Play' on the dashboard's tape player, cueing up the pair of them bellowing out Led Zep's 'Good Times Bad Times' in perfect caterwauling sync.

Driving one-handed, with no seat belt on, and with the minibus's tyres squealing in protest, Dad reverses out onto the road, expertly missing the low garden wall by mere inches, before revving off down the street, leaving a belch of black smoke in our wake. But even though him and Adam are grinning at each other as they continue their duet, another part of me feels sick. Like I should warn him that this is his bloody coffin. He's got no idea that this is the same minibus that him and Mum will die in on their way back from dropping us off at the airport.

Only this *isn't* real. None of this is, because it *can't* be, right?

The journey into town passes in a blur, with Dad calling in at Ladbrokes to stick a couple of quick bets on the Kempton horse meet – 'just a little flutter' – and with me freaking out inside of Young Adam, goggling at all the brand-new Audi Quattros and Ford Sierras on the road, along with the crazily sexist billboard ads for Polaroid cameras and Reebok Pumps and Drakkar Noir aftershave. All the while with Adam's thoughts burbling away in the background: homework he needs doing, ideas for a game he's been working on with Darius, but mostly thoughts of Juliet, her eyes, her hair, and that one time he once really, nearly actually made her laugh . . .

Then those butterflies he's feeling, I start feeling them too. Like my whole body's made up of them, like it might fly away. What *will* it be like to see Jules young again? Even if this isn't real.

Dad parks down the bottom of Regency Square, overlooking the churning sea. Only look, there, where the i360 observation tower should be stabbing up into the bright blue sky, there's nothing. Like the view's been Photoshopped. Even weirder, the West Pier, which I watched burn down in 2003, is still jutting out into the sea in all its dilapidated glory.

Grabbing their painting gear from the back of the van, Adam and Dad head into the Peregrine through the basement tradesman's entrance. Straight away, Adam offers to pop up to the kitchen to see if he can whip them up a cup of tea, but really because he knows it's where *she*'ll be working today.

The shock of seeing her hits me like a bucket of iced water. His Juliet. There through the kitchen doorway. Aged seventeen, dressed in waitress black and whites, with her long blonde hair tied up. She's clearing away dirty plates in the dining room. Still so young, so ridiculously young. Still just a kid. Like him.

Catching sight of him, she turns, looking radiant in the morning light, and smiles. And, Jesus, the feeling he gets. Like he's hearing a chorus of angels in his head. With a full cinematic orchestra. In Dolby Stereo. On speed.

So, say hello, I'm thinking. *Right, just like you practised in front of the mirror.*

The last couple of B&B guests have just finished their breakfast and are heading for the door, while the owner, Rose O'Grady, is still nowhere to be seen. This is his chance, and he knows it.

It's just the two of them. It's fate.

But all that *Hey, Juliet. How's your week been?* flops right out of his head. Instead, he just stares. Or, more accurately, ogles. At her legs. Then her bum. Then . . . well, everything. I mean, Jesus, isn't it so obvious that he's going to get caught?

'Do you need something, Adam?' she asks, her bright blue eyes suddenly fixed on his.

'Er, I was just looking for Mrs O'Grady,' he lies.

Right, *sure* that's all you were looking at, you little perv . . .

'Dad was hoping we could get a cup of tea,' he hurries on.

'Oh, I can sort that,' she says, walking over to a table with a stainless-steel tea urn on it.

Then finally courage erupts, welling up inside Adam, right alongside his near total fear that she's about to tell him to go sling his hook.

'Um, I got you something,' he says. And I can feel it. His hand in his pocket on the tape. 'You know, because you said you lost a lot of your music when you and your mum moved flats.'

'I did?'

These two little words send Adam's anxiety spiralling. In case he got it wrong. In case he misheard. In case he's making a fool of himself. *Shit*, he thinks, *what the hell am I meant to do now?* Because he's already pulled the tape out and she's seen it in his hand.

'You know, like the Human League, I think you said,' he finally splutters.

'Oh, yeah. Now I remember. And, yeah, I bloody love them,' she says.

Relief surges through him. 'Well, here. It's, er, a compilation of all that sort of thing, and some more modern stuff from this year too . . .'

All those songs he's so carefully selected and ordered while thinking of her, all the ones I remember recording myself . . .

'Oh, wow. Thanks, Adam. That's really . . . *sweet*?' she says.

But there's a question mark at the end of the sentence. Like he's being weird? *Is* he? he panics. Even that word *sweet* has got his mind doing somersaults. What kind of sweet does she mean? As in sappy or nice?

'Hey, you know what?' she says. 'Rose won't be back for a bit. So, what the hell, let's put it on.'

She takes it from him and switches off the crappy Richard Clayderman lift muzak Mrs O'Grady is always playing in here, and slots in the tape. When she turns back to Adam she starts beaming, just as the first beats of 'Don't You Want Me' start up.

Then it really is happening, they're talking, and it's everything he hoped . . . as the League segues into Neneh Cherry, into Young MC, then Transvision Vamp . . . and they natter about school, then gossip about mutual friends, then chunter on about where they want to go to college, and all the countries they'd like to visit around the world.

Only then the big red dining-room door swings open, and a guy walks in. I kind of flinch – even though I don't have a body to flinch with – when I recognise him at the same time Adam does. Mickey Ratty. He of Jules's shitty 'rattoo'. I mean, just look at the little scrote, in his poxy white puffy nylon shell suit, looking like an overgrown baby in Pampers. And to think I ever thought he was cooler than me, just because he was two years older and drove a black Subaru XT with gold 'go faster' stripes emblazoned on its side.

'Nice tune,' he says, mock-dancing to the Bangles' 'Eternal Flame', like it's something crap, which it's not, sashaying across the room between the tables to where Juliet is.

Right, like he'd know a good tune if it kicked him in the ponytail.

He stares down at the tape box.

'Adam made it for me,' she explains. 'A compilation.'

'Aw,' he says. 'Sweet.'

Right, and this time it's definitely code for sappy. Adam has no trouble decrypting that.

'Just so long as you're not sweet on her too, sonny,' Ratty warns him.

'Er, no. Of course not,' Adam says. OK, stutters. He stutters it.

'Good. Because she's already taken, aren't you, babe?' Ratty says, as he turns his broad, muscular back on Adam and kisses Jules smushily on the lips.

He then grabs a congealed rasher of bacon off a dirty plate, wedges it between two cold pieces of toast, and takes a massive bite, like a dog tearing meat off a bone.

'Don't be gross,' Jules says, but she's laughing.

'Needs HP Sauce, luv,' he tells her, heading for the kitchen door.

Catching Adam glaring after him, Jules bashfully pushes a stray strand of hair back behind her ear.

'What?' she asks. 'Don't you like him?'

'No, he's all right,' Adam lies. But then before I can stop myself, I'm imposing myself on him again. 'It's just he's got the worst name ever, that's all,' I make Adam say. 'Mickey Ratty. Like he's a dirty, ratty Mickey Mouse. And, I mean, imagine if you carried on going out with him and then got so drunk you had a cartoon rat tattooed on your shoulder for eternity.'

She laughs. 'But why would I? Why would anyone be stupid enough to do that?'

'You'd be surprised.'

They stare at each other for a beat.

'Anyway, it's not like your name's much better, is it, A-Hole?' she then says, a cheeky glint in her eyes.

Of course, because she'd already worked that one out.

'*A-Hole?*' Ratty cackles, marching back in, brown sauce dripping from his fleshy lips. 'Is that really your name? As in *arsehole*?' He spells it out, in case anyone else might not have got it.

'Yeah, well, at least my face doesn't look like one,' I get Adam to tell him.

'What did you say?' Ratty snaps, dropping what's left of his bacon sarnie down his crisp white front.

'And do you know why that's called a ponytail?' I then make Adam ask, pointing at Ratty's head. 'Because when you lift it up, all you'll find underneath is an arsehole.'

Now looking like he's about to explode, Ratty lunges at him.

But even as I try to get Adam to push him back, it's like I'm fading.

From the corner of my eye – or the corner of Adam's eye, at least – I catch sight of the clock on the wall. A few seconds to ten. Almost exactly an hour since I first woke up in his body.

The instant the little hand joins the big hand pointing north, I feel that hideous whirlwind of flashing lights enveloping me again . . . before hauling me out of Adam's body . . . leaving him and Ratty arguing and Jules trying to break them up . . . and with all of them completely unaware of this crazy tornado that's dragging me deeper and deeper inside . . .

Chapter Five

Jules – 'Groove is in the Heart'

Fucking birds.

I groan, the light penetrating my hangover, as the seagulls screech like car alarms outside our bedroom window. My head pounds as I roll over, my arm flailing towards Adam, but I hit a smooth, unslept-under duvet and my eyes spring open.

'Fuuuuuuuuuuuuuuuuuuuuuuuuuuuuuuuuuuuuuuuuck,' I say, crossing my arms over my head, as the walk home and the things we said last night come crashing back in vivid technicolour.

I sit up, noticing that I'm still wearing Adam's socks. My lovely dress lies crumpled on the floor where I stamped out of it. Even if it hadn't been ruined by the rose bush, I know I'll never wear it again. Not now it's cursed after our awful fight.

What if the kids heard? God, I couldn't bear it. They've both got enough to deal with already without seeing us acting out like that. I've always wanted our home to be a safe place, no matter what the outside world might throw at them.

Where *is* Adam, anyway? Did he go back to the party? I remember slamming the door, not caring where he went, before crying myself to sleep.

I pick up my phone to see if there are any missed calls from him, but there aren't. My screensaver says it's half ten. No. I should already be at Rose's and picking up everything for the venue.

'Shit, shit, shit,' I mutter as I hop around, pulling on my baggy linen trousers, a sports vest and my stained old Agnes B T-shirt.

Downstairs, Groucho Barx greets me effusively and I let him out of the back door. The living room is empty. Adam's not on the sofa, so where is he? Standing at the kitchen sink, I spot a light on in the shed.

Oh. Right. He's been out there all night, has he? Making some kind of righteous point rather than coming inside and apologising. I can't believe the shit he's been holding against me all these years. My nose fizzes with the onset of yet more tears.

Fine. Let him stew in his own juice. I'll deal with him later.

Except that, after ransacking the house, I realise he's got the bloody car keys.

In the garden, I take a deep breath as I approach the shed. I don't know how things stand. It feels like something seismic has happened. Maybe Adam is feeling as churned up as I am. Maybe he's ready to talk. Maybe, just maybe, we can laugh it off, have a hug, blame the cocktails. Though I doubt it.

Another breath and I open the door.

Adam is sitting on his dad's ripped leather armchair, staring at an old cassette tape in his hand, transfixed. His head jolts up when he sees me, like someone who's just fallen asleep on a train. He's still in last night's clothes and his eyes are red-rimmed, like he hasn't slept a wink.

There's a beat as we stare at one another, then he jumps up and lurches towards me. I can smell whiskey on him and spot the empty bottle.

Great. He's still drunk.

'Car keys,' I spit, realising that he hasn't got any intention of apologising.

'No, listen,' he starts, gingerly tapping me on the shoulder as if checking I'm real. 'There's something I've got to tell you.'

Oh God, here we go. Did he head off to some bar with Doodles which he's only just got back from? Lose his wallet? Lose the *keys*?

'About my dream,' he says, 'I mean, if it was a dream, or at least, it must have been, but there was also a lightning strike . . . But either way, seriously, Jules, it felt really real, like I was actually th—'

'Stop arsing around, Adam. I'm late for work.'

'But Mum and Dad were there and I was in my body – my young body. And you . . . you were waitressing in the Peregrine and –'

I sniff the air suspiciously.

'Have you been smoking Doodles' weed?' I ask, eyes narrowed.

'No, but what happened, it's –'

51

'Just give me the bloody keys.' My voice rises.

'But, but . . .'

I spot them on the arm of his gaming sofa and grab them before hurrying back to the door.

'But nothing,' I tell him, glaring. 'Get your shit together and get cleaned up before the kids or anyone else catches you in this state.'

I'm still muttering imaginary arguments as I drive our cranky old Skoda that nearly wouldn't start yet again towards the Peregrine Hotel and turn into Regency Square to park, cutting off Radiohead's 'High and Dry' on the radio.

Getting out of the car, I take in a deep breath, the salty breeze mingling with the familiar waft of fish and chips from the Regency restaurant on the corner, and watch as the tourists troop past carrying inflatable paddleboards, cool boxes and lilos to the pebbly beach, like we used to when the kids were younger. I can't actually remember the last time we went to the beach just for fun.

In the distance, the Palace pier stands out against the glittering sea like a cardboard cut-out, with its red, white and blue striped helter-skelter, waterslide and roller coaster, no doubt already packed with screaming teens. Nearer, the i360 observation tower reaches for the sky, while behind it, the older, burnt-down West Pier looms like a familiar skeleton, a ghost of Brighton's past, but none of these sights can brighten my mood today. Turning towards the flaky pillars of the Peregrine's portico, I head inside.

I've known Rose, the owner, since I was seventeen and started waitressing here on Saturdays. It's where I first met Adam, who used to help his dad with building work and handyman jobs, but whatever temporary improvements they made back then have long since faded. Nowadays, it's positively shabby, and with dwindling bookings to match, what with Brighton's more discerning visitors now choosing to spend their tourist buck in the swanky Artist Residence Hotel across the square or the Grand down on the front.

Once, though, the Peregrine had a dining room, with swagged red curtains framing its still magnificent sea view, and velvet relief wallpaper. The resident chef served kippers and full Englishes for breakfast and later fish suppers and coq au vin on gold-rimmed, monogrammed plates. But these days Rose can't afford the staff and can't be arsed with the faff of a restaurant, despite my protests that she's missing a trick.

Over the years, its little kitchen has become a kind of home from home for me, because Rose very kindly lets me use it to prep for my catering jobs. It hasn't changed in decades, with its scuffed, glitter-effect lino floor, large metal units and two marvellously capacious fridges, one of which is all mine. I open it now to retrieve the metal trays filled with the food for today's event.

I still can't believe that some pillock at the council scheduled this team-building day for a Sunday. But even that would have been fine if that same pillock hadn't then messed up the booking at the Racecourse where it was supposed to be held. So now the poor fuckers, who were promised a morning bazzing around in electric cars, have to schlep into the office to do pointless role-playing exercises all day.

Earlier in the week, I was looking forward to this job, although I'm barely making a profit on it, knowing that the egg sandwiches and salmon quiches they ordered were at least going to be the highlight of everyone's day, but now the last thing I feel like doing is being civil. Let alone friendly.

Rose walks into the kitchen in a lovely, if tired-looking, Indian-print dressing gown, with her waist-length grey plait over her shoulder, and smiles when she sees me. She's nearly seventy and, with my own mum having retired to North Wales and poor Dad having died of a heart attack when I was little, she's become like a surrogate parent to me, as well as a good mate.

She's holding a mug of tea and I realise that my empty, hungover body desperately needs caffeine.

'How was the party?' she asks.

'We left early.'

She frowns at my tone, studying my face and I sigh. I can never hide anything from her.

'Adam and I had a row.'

She says, 'Hmmm,' and twists her lips in an 'it's been coming' kind of a way.

She knows the last few months have been difficult since Nelly moved back home. I thought she should have stuck out her London marketing job in the sustainability company she'd worked for, despite the pitiful salary. Adam, though, unable to bear his little princess being unhappy, encouraged her to look for another job, and before I knew it, she was back home, complaining about the Wi-Fi speed and treating me like her personal runner.

As far as I can make out, her new job involves being a lackey to her arsehole of a boss who regularly bullies her and makes her cry. Even though he's on the other side of the Atlantic, he seems to know if she's so much as taken a loo break. But Adam thinks her work ethic is 'cool'. Something he deliberately said in front of Liam last week, needlessly adding that it was great to see someone her age being 'so ambitious'.

Rose got the brunt of that one.

'It wasn't about the kids. It was other stuff. About us. And now I really don't know where we stand.'

'Ah, get on with you,' Rose says, as if I'm being crazy. 'You two are destined for each other. It's written in the stars.'

I'm dubious of Rose's astrological predictions – particularly as her 'dead cert' horses have each come last in the Grand National three years running. She clocks my sceptical face.

'What happened?' she asks.

'It all started because Adam asked if I was happy, and I said I thought we were in a rut. Because it's true. Lately it feels like we're living in some kind of *Groundhog Day*, but without the romance.'

Rose smiles gently, walks over and holds my shoulders. 'There's always bumps in the road but look what you've achieved. You and Adam. A whole life together. No mean feat.'

I sniff, tears feeling perilously close. 'I guess.'

'You be careful what you wish for, missy,' she says, looking into my eyes. 'Happiness is learning to love what you already have.'

That's one of her favourites. She has that on a T-shirt, I swear.

'I mean it. The quest for perfection is a fool's errand.' Another T-shirt right there. 'He's a good egg, your Adam,' she continues. 'It'll all work out.' She brushes my cheek affectionately with the end of her plait. 'You'll see.'

She's usually right, but this time, I'm not so sure.

In the bland council office building, I set up the lunch table in the grey function room and Eva arrives, shrugging off her leather jacket to help me. She's got rosy cheeks, short dark hair, twinkly brown eyes, and is always so cheery, she instantly makes me feel better. She's an old friend of Nelly's from school, and they used to be close, especially when they won places on that organised trek in the sixth form to Kenya, an adventure I thought would be the first of many for Nelly but turned out to be her last.

Eva's worked on and off for me for the last four years to help pay for her studies and I hired her today to help with the lunchtime rush. Not that there's any need. Unsurprisingly, half the people haven't turned up. The ones who have pick at the food, looking miserable.

'Just think of it. Not long until I'm actually there,' Eva tells me. She's been saving up for her trip to Costa Rica, where she's going to be working with a charity to build a school. She gets out her phone and shows me pictures on the scheme's website. 'Look at that sloth. Isn't it cute?'

'Have you told Nelly you're going?' I ask, handing back the phone. 'She always said she wanted to do more travelling.'

'But she's a highfalutin executive now.'

I pull a face. 'It's not that glamorous, believe me.'

'She's always so busy. I ask her to come to things, but . . .' She shrugs.

'Do you mind doing me a favour?'

'Sure.'

'Can you try once more? Get her out. Tell her what you're doing. I know it's what she needs.'

'There's a DJ thing that Cody's doing at the Windmill on Wednesday. I could invite her to that?'

'That would be amazing. But promise not to tell her I asked you to.'

I hate doing this and asking Eva to keep a secret, but Nelly is so spiky with me these days, what choice do I have?

'You might as well go,' I tell Eva. I dig out my wallet and pay her for the full shift. It feels a little like bribery. 'I'm so jealous you're off,' I add, as she's leaving. 'If I could catch that plane with you, I would.' She laughs like I'm joking, but right now, I'm not.

After she's gone, I check my phone. I'm not sure what I'm expecting but there's nothing from Adam. Instead, there's an email about my latest missed credit card payment and I beat down a rising sense of panic that everything is sliding off a cliff.

How the hell am I going to get out of this scrape? Obviously, I was going to tell Adam. I was just waiting for the right moment. Only now it appears that I can't talk to my husband. About anything. Maybe ever again. The promise of the inevitable chat we need to have about last night hangs like a thundercloud above.

Back home, Liam's music is thumping out from his room – 'Deceptacon' by Le Tigre, a record he got into via me – and Nelly is competing with the much more mellow 'A Messenger' by Liza Lo in the dining room. I wonder if she'll be cross if I ask her to take Groucho Barx out for a walk, because Adam and I are going to need some serious privacy if we're actually going to have 'the chat'. Probably fifty feet of soundproofing as well.

'Where's Dad?' I ask.

She shrugs. 'He went to Waterstones in town. Came back with lots of books. But apart from that, he's been glued to the internet all day.'

'Books?' I say, confused.

'He was acting kind of weird.'

I remember how he was this morning. That glassy-eyed, fruitloop stare. So not just drunk or stoned then, because surely both would have worn off by now.

I head to the back door. On the way, feeling sweaty, I sniff my T-shirt, then take it off and drop it on the laundry pile. I adjust the racer-back vest I'm wearing and twist my hair up, stabbing it with a pencil from the pot. Then I take a breath and head for the shed.

If anything, Adam looks even more deranged than he did this morning. There are books open all over the sofa and papers with his handwriting scrawled across them.

'Sit,' he says, pointing to his dad's favourite wingback leather chair. No 'how was your day?'. No 'I'm sorry'. No bloody contrition at all. Like in his apparent madness he's mistaken me for Groucho Barx.

'Adam. We need to talk,' I tell him, still standing. 'Last night was horrible and . . . and I think we need to go to counselling.' Christ. This is so much harder than I thought. 'Or couples therapy.'

'Therapy?' he scoffs, like I've asked him to join clown school.

'We need help, Adam. You've clearly got issues with me that you've been festering on for years and, well, maybe . . .' I take a shuddery breath, '. . . maybe last night needed to happen. If we're both being really honest, things haven't been right for a while.'

It hurts to say this. To admit that something is broken.

But he barely looks like he's taking it in.

'Don't you remember how we used to be?' I try.

'Yes!' He points at me like he's a schoolteacher and I'm a student who's just made an excellent point. 'Oh my God. Yes, Jules. It was amazing. I was so in love with you. And you –'

'Adam, I'm being serious.'

'So am I. You see, what I was telling you about earlier – my dream that wasn't a dream – honestly, the more I've been reading about it, the more I think what actually happened was I somehow travelled back in –'

'I don't give a shit about your dream!'

He really isn't registering this conversation, is he? In fact, he looks absolutely bonkers and suddenly my desire to get him to listen pivots into something else. Is he having a psychotic episode?

'Adam.' I squeeze the top of my head, flummoxed. I turn away from him and then back, but his eyes have gone wide.

'There!' Lunging towards me, he spins me round and pulls my vest aside. Then scratches at the skin on my shoulder.

'What the hell are you doing?' I pull sharply away.

'Your tattoo,' he gasps.

'What tattoo?'

'Your bloody "rattoo". That you got to impress Mickey twatty Ratty when you were going out with him.'

'What are you talking about?'

'Mickey Ratty,' he says. 'The king of the bloody shell suits.'

'Yes, I do know who he is.' So Adam *did* see him last night at Darius's? Is that what's triggered this episode? Some kind of weird jealousy fit?

Only Adam's not done. 'You had a tattoo of a shitty cartoon rat,' he declares. 'Right. There.' He jabs my shoulder, twice.

'Ow!'

'Only now . . . Now you don't. Because of what I said when I went back. I told you how bloody stupid it would look.' His mouth hangs open, incredulous.

'Adam. I've never had a tattoo,' I point out.

'Well, no. Not now. Not in *this* future. Not in this new reality I guess I've just created. I must have stopped you getting one. Bloody hell.' He grins. Actually grins. 'Seriously. I really did. Don't you see what this means?'

That you've gone batshit crazy? I think. 'No,' I only just manage to say instead.

'It means that I really *did* somehow travel back in time. Into my teen body. To 1989. Only, thank God, I didn't change anything else,' he says. 'And I didn't,' he adds, almost as if he's checking this with himself, 'because everything else –' he looks me carefully up and down, before peering around the shed – 'it's just as it was.'

Right. Screw this. Enough's enough. I clearly need to get him medical help before this gets any worse.

'O . . . kay,' I say, in the same kind of 'time out' tone I used to deploy at kids' parties when they'd come up with some wacky idea like smearing jelly on the wall. 'I think I should come back when you're –' I begin backing away from him towards the door, already wondering if I've got the out-of-hours doctor's number on my phone.

Only before I can get there, he rushes past me and twists the key in the lock, then shoves it in his pocket.

What the hell? My heart is now pounding for an altogether different reason. I'm locked in a shed with my husband who's starting to scare me.

'Adam. Give me the key,' I say, holding out my hand, trying to sound rational.

'I will. If you give it a go.'

'Give what a go?'

'Going back.'

'Where?'

'In time.'

'Please, Adam. Just stop. Can't you hear how crazy you sound?'

'But that's just the point. It's not crazy.'

He lunges for the papers on the sofa, which I now see are a bunch of seemingly random articles he's printed off the internet. All over them are circled words and highlighted passages. Jagged exclamation marks abound.

'Because look. Time travel is one hundred per cent already theoretically possible via cosmic strings and traversable wormholes and machines, like this one here. The Alcubierre drive, which is this really cool speculative warp drive that a spacecraft could use to achieve apparently faster-than-light travel by contracting space itself.'

Oh. My. God. What am I meant to do?

Grabbing another article, he holds it towards me with both hands with a saint-like expression on his face like it's the Turin bloody Shroud, before thrusting it even closer, like I might have any interest in reading its incomprehensible small print.

'Or maybe it's not even just time travel we're looking at here,' he says, scratching at his beard, 'maybe it's the multiverse.'

'The multiverse?'

'Yeah. You know. Like in *Everything Everywhere All at Once* . . .'

'What?'

'That movie you fell asleep in front of.'

He's right. I did. Which is probably why I don't remember a thing about it. But he's not done.

'Because once you accept the possibility – well, no, the *probability*, actually – of the multiverse being real –'

'Which I don't,' I point out.

'Yeah, but if you did, *when* you do, then you'll see that the existence of an infinite number of universes, of *possibilities*, also means that an infinite number of timelines is also theoretically possible. For us, for whoever, maybe even all going on simultaneously all the time.'

'Yes, but we're not talking theoretically, are we, Adam? We're talking about my need to get out of this bloody shed in *this* reality right now.'

His eyes flick to his old stereo.

'But, of course, for time travel or travelling between multiverses to be practically possible, you'd still need a machine – a time machine – or some kind of bridging machine to open a portal to each parallel universe, and the energy to power it . . . You know, like a DeLorean and a flux capacitor,' he says, nodding towards an old *Back to the Future* DVD case that's lying open on the floor in front of the TV next to a copy of *About Time*.

Oh, Jesus. Maybe I can break out through the window? Maybe that's my best bet.

'Whereas all we've got is this,' he says, shaking his head in wonder at the old Sony.

'Whoa, whoa, whoa,' I finally interrupt him. '*We?*'

'Well, more *you*, really. Or at least you *next*,' he says brightly. 'Because I've already been back and so I *know* it's true. Even more so because of your tattoo. But also, it's got to be you, because I want to stay here this time to see what happens to your body here. Will it vanish? Or something else? You know, after you disappear into the whirlwind.'

Whirlwind? What the fuck? So now he thinks I'm Dorothy about to be whipped off to see the Wizard of Oz?

'And then there's the question of whether me being here when you put on the tape means I might even travel back with you, or whether it's only possible for one of us to go back at a time . . .'

'Adam,' I say, still eyeing the keys in his pocket. 'This is your last warning. You let me out of this shed. Right now. Or I will scream.'

But he just nods, as though he was expecting this too. He holds up his hands in surrender.

'Just humour me. That's all I'm asking,' he pleads. 'How's one more minute going to hurt? Seriously, you don't have to *do* anything. Just stand here, or even sit here on this chair, and put a tape in the machine.'

'That's it?'

'That's it.'

'Then you'll let me go?'

'Then you can leave, get me sectioned. Whatever the hell you want.'

I narrow my eyes.

'Come on,' he says, 'you're always telling me I don't try enough new things. Well, all I'm asking is for you to try one tiny little new thing for me.'

One tiny little new box of frogs crazy thing.

'Fine,' I say. Flatly. Not wanting him to think I'm in any way actually taking this bullshit seriously.

He does a little jump of excitement. Even pats me collegiately on the back. But then he's ranting again, like some barking mad tour guide, telling me all about how this thing *that isn't going to bloody happen* is going to *feel*.

Then I'm standing in front of the old boom box. Exactly where he wants me to be.

He blinks down at the tape he's holding in his hands, rubbing at its casing where it looks a little melted and warped. Then holds it out to me. With a roll of my eyes, I perch on the armchair next to the Sony and slot it into the deck and press 'Play'.

For a split second, I actually feel a sudden burst of apprehension. Like something really *is* about to happen. Like all this nonsense is somehow going to work.

But, of course, it doesn't. Instead, his old stereo makes a gargling, squeaking noise as the tape unspools.

Only Adam's *still* not deterred.

'Hmm. I did wonder . . .' he says, taking out the tape and carefully examining the squiggly black mess before grabbing another tape from the box, this one labelled *Move Your Body! 1993*. In my handwriting too. Christ. I wish I'd never given him the damned thing.

Eyes shining, he gives it to me, rubbing his beard and waggling his eyebrows at me, like he's a magician about to make a rabbit vanish from a hat.

'Good luck,' he says, before nodding at me again to put it into the machine.

'Ridiculous,' I start to say, as I press 'Play', but the first bars of Deee-Lite's 'Groove is in the Heart' are already thumping out . . .

WHAAAAATT? . . . straight away it's like there's a hurricane whipping my hair so violently round my face that it hurts. The floor drops out of the shed. Colours strobe all around. Faster and faster. I try to scream but all I can hear is this insane, almighty roar until –

BOOOOOM.

Music.

Dum dum-dum-dum-dum-dum, dum di-dum-di-dum-dum-di. Good God. It's Deee-Lite's 'Groove is in the Heart' still pounding through my brain.

What the hell?

My nostrils twitch from the acrid stink of stale sweat and dry ice. Opening my eyes, I don't see the shed like I'm expecting, but instead hands waving in front of me and I recognise a snake ring on one of the index fingers. Mine! I bloody loved that ring. Mum and I bought it on a trip to Blackpool for my eighteenth. Three years before . . . *now*. Before 1993.

1993!

But I suddenly know this with absolute certainty.

This really *is* me. Me in '93.

I'm *in* me. In my head. In my body.

Oh my God. How's this working? It's just like Adam said. It feels so utterly *real*.

I start looking round for him to tell him. Which is even more crazy, right? But there are too many dancing bodies in the way. Then I look at my hands again. My *old* hands. Or rather, young hands. No age spots, or cooking burns, just the smudge of the Zap Club stamp.

Of course. I'm in the Zap Club. Down on the beachfront. My old haunt. I recognise the low ceilings, the dripping walls, the sweaty fug. The homely pong of ciggies and farts. And right next to me is Ngozi.

Oh my God. She's so young too!

She's wearing a low-cut top with lattice string work up the front, her hair up high, and just a sliver of a leather skirt. Her eyes are thickly lined in gold and she pulls her dancing face at me, as she lifts her arms, wanting me to mirror her. The two of us are thick as thieves and have been since that trip in the first week of sixth form college to see *Starlight Express* in the West End, when we bunked off and went to the cinema to watch the far superior *Withnail & I* instead.

It's like I'm observing everything. Like I'm in *Peep Show* on the telly. Or *Being John Malkovich*. I can sense memories, ones the real me – the older me from the future – has forgotten. But even as I note this, I can tell these aren't just memories, these are her *thoughts*. Young Me's actual thoughts.

This. Is. *Insane*.

I can read her mind. All that's pulsing through it is Adam and how he'll be here any moment.

I'm doing it. Tonight's the night. But first I'll give him the tape.

This is what she's thinking. I feel a bulge in the back pocket of her jeans. The mixtape she's made.

Holy shit.

The same mixtape Adam put in the machine just now. I don't even need to look to know.

Jules is desperate to find a quiet moment to give the tape to Adam. Alone. Because this thing between them has been building ever since she came back from her catering course in London and walked into the

Basketmakers Arms three weeks ago and realised Adam had changed from a boy into a man. A hot one at that.

Suddenly, Ngozi nudges Jules. She nods to the door and my tummy – Jules's tummy – jolts.

There, over there . . .

He's here. Adam's here.

Ngozi grins. She knows all about my crush.

Adam's eyes lock with mine, and he puts up a hand in greeting. A wrist full of leather bangles.

Just look at him! Gangly yet lithe, undone baggy shirt, and look at those flary jeans. Black Doc Martens. That boy-grin and chiselled jaw. So like Liam's. Only Liam doesn't even exist yet, does he? Wow.

My Adam.

Her thoughts. Young me's. And mine. Only he's not mine, is he? He's hers.

They shoulder through the crowd towards each other. He's with someone. Bloody hell! Is that really young Darius? I'd totally forgotten that he used to be such a dork.

'Where've you been?' she shouts, as they meet. She, the younger me. She's so confident. So *loud*.

Adam glances at Darius and Jules sees the look that passes between them and she knows they've been gaming. The two of them are obsessed. Not that she cares, because at least Adam's here now. From the way he's looking at her, it's clear he doesn't want to be anywhere else.

'Let's go,' he shouts, pointing to the bar on the other side of the throng of dancing bodies, and Jules laughs, skipping after him, before nodding for Darius to follow too.

She's so springy. *I* feel so springy. So much energy. God, I feel *incredible*. So up for anything.

We get beers and mingle with the crowd and the music throbs through me. Darius is ogling Ngozi's bouncing cleavage. She's just announced she's got E's down her Wonderbra, but Jules isn't interested. As soon as Adam finishes his pint, she knows it's now or never.

'Come with me,' she yells and quickly takes Adam's slim, sweaty hand and they run up the stairs, past the cigarette machine, someone thumping the top of it.

I catch a flash of my reflection in a dark mirror and, oh my God, I look amazing. These low-slung jeans are so flattering. My stomach's taut and bare beneath my crop top.

I want to stop. To caress myself. To marvel.

But there's no time.

We burst through the metal push bar exit door into the night where there's still a queue, and next thing we're on the concrete slope leading down to the beach.

Our breath is clouding, the cold sea air immediately cooling our skin.

'Come on,' Jules tells Adam, pulling him onwards. Now that I can hear her properly, I notice how different her voice is to mine now. It's light and full of promise. Probably because she hasn't spent half her life nagging her husband and kids.

They run down the beach to where the waves are breaking against the stones in a silver line, as the moon rises over the sea leaving the derelict old West Pier – that won't even burn down for another decade – looming eerily like some vast and creepy set from *Scooby-Doo*.

My ears – *her* ears – feel fuzzy after the booming noise of the club.

But Adam's still craving more music and heads further up the beach until they're standing beside a fenced-off section in front of the Fortune of War pub where there's a band. They both laugh, immediately recognising the song. 'All the Daze', by the hot new local group everyone is talking about, Troubadours d'Amour.

'Shit,' Adam says, 'I didn't know they were playing. Or else we could have gone.'

Because she – Young Jules – loves this band too. He bought her their CD as a gift. For a minute they just dance here on the beach like they're the only people in the world, and I can't help myself, I'm almost swooning too. Because this song, it's my and Adam's song. The one we'll end up dancing to at our wedding in only six years' time.

I can still hear her thoughts – she's been wanting this moment for ages, it's now or never. But the risk – eek! What if he doesn't feel the same?

She's brave in spite of all this, though. A bravery I realise, plungingly, I've somehow lost along the way. She jumps towards him, planting her feet on the stones in a power stance. Eye to eye.

Bloody hell. This is the start of it . . . of *us*. It's happening right here, our future bursting, blooming out of this very moment.

'I've got something for you,' she says, reaching round and taking the cassette tape out of her pocket. She gives it to him, and grins, watching his face. 'I figured I owe you one,' she says, pleased by the smile he suddenly gives her. 'You might not like them all,' she warns.

'No, I will,' he says.

She knows he means it too, even though he hasn't even read through the whole list of songs. Because he trusts her.

Their eyes lock and I can't breathe as the moment stretches, then their faces – *our* faces – move together and his lips are on mine and I'm fizzing with every second of this magical first kiss.

Her heart, it's like a jack-in-the-box as he finally pulls away.

'Wow,' she says.

Because, hell yes, *wow*. It feels like we're the last two pieces of a jigsaw and now everything makes sense.

'I've wondered if you fancied me for so long,' he confesses.

'Really?'

'Only, I didn't want to make a move. Spoil our friendship.'

Oh God, he's so earnest. So adorable.

'Don't worry. We'll always be mates too,' she says, taking his face in her hands. 'Promise. No matter what.'

I want to weep because I can sense her optimism, her sheer faith in the world. In *him*.

'So what's all this?' she teases, rubbing his stubbly chin. 'You not shaving these days?'

'I was going to go the full George Michael.'

She twists her lips.

'What?' he asks, something close to panic in his eyes.

'No, no, it's nothing, honestly,' she says.

But it *is* something. And she's *not* being honest.

Because I've always disliked his beard. *Always*. Not because of how it looks. It's more the distraction of it. The tickliness. And not just on my mouth.

She doesn't want to ruin the moment, though. She's going to let it slide.

But before I know it, it's me who's rocking back, just as we're about to kiss again. And *me* who's somehow opening *her* mouth and putting my thoughts into words with her tongue.

'It's just I've never really liked beards,' I make her say.

Adam stares at her, stunned. And *she* feels stunned too, by these words that have just come out of her mouth. But she's not upset. Or annoyed. More relieved that she's had the courage to be honest to his face.

'Really?' he says.

'Yeah. Sorry. Really,' she answers. All by herself, with zero help from me. 'It's just the way it feels.'

'OK. Anything else you'd like to change about me?' he asks, smiling.

'No. Nothing.' She laughs, like it's a silly question, really. 'Or not yet, anyway,' she teases, grabbing at his hair.

Oh, that lovely, thick hair of his.

'Let's not worry about that now,' she says, and she pulls him close and it's as if they're melting together. And, as the seagulls caw, she snogs him like her life depends on it.

Then, finally breaking away, they laugh with the sheer joy of this, of *them*. They hold hands and walk back towards where the band is still playing. They push through into the crowd and, as he hugs her from behind, she wants this moment to never end.

Chapter Six

Adam – 'The Passenger'

Jules looks so beautiful perched on the armchair, with soft pink light slanting in through the shed window gently illuminating that triangle of pale russet freckles on her right cheek, while accentuating the fine detail of those sweet wrinkles at the corners of her eyes that make her look like she's perpetually on the brink of a smile.

Of course, the fact that her eyes are currently glazed over like she's a member of the undead does rather ruin the effect. Giving her much more of an *Exorcist* vibe.

I check her pulse for the umpteenth time as the final song on this Memorex 60 cassette – Soul II Soul's 'Keep On Movin'' – comes to an end.

Will it have worked? Will she have gone back?

As the tape stops with a click, her eyes start to clear and she groans, disoriented, gawping around.

'Jesus Christ, Adam,' she squeals, launching herself at me and throwing her arms around my neck and squeezing me tight. 'It's bloody true.'

I feel sick with relief. I'm not mad. It really does work.

'I actually went back in bloody time,' she laughs, staring into my eyes, her forehead pressed to mine.

'I know.' My heart is pounding, buzzing that she's experienced this too.

'I actually went back in bloody time and you're absolutely bloody right about bloody everything.'

'I know.' And the only thing I know more than this is how much I'd pay to have her last sentence printed on a T-shirt that I could brandish for the rest of my life.

Spinning away from me, she grabs for a bottle of water and starts glugging it down. Turning my back to her, I hit 'Eject' on the Sony. When I take out her tape, I see it's already got that same warped, half-melted look as the first one I used and I bet it'll unspool just the same if I try using it again.

'Looks like you can only use them once, like it's some kind of rule,' I say out loud. But a rule made by who? Made by what? Even just the thought of this sends a shiver down my spine.

Existential as fuck.

'It's just so crazy, Adam. So weird,' she says from where she's still standing behind me. 'How did I look when I was gone?'

'Like a zombie.'

'And you just stayed here? Didn't get dragged down into any screaming whirlwinds yourself?'

'Nope, like it only works for whoever plays the tape.'

Another rule.

'It really did feel just like you said it would,' she hurries on, pacing behind me now, as I examine the machine to see if there is anything obviously weird about it, 'like I was visiting my own head, or younger head, whatever. Like a ride. And this is all totally incredible, right?' She's rubbing her brow. 'Because I really *did* feel like I was actually there. In the Zap, with you and Darius and Ngozi. Then outside at the Troubs' gig – remember? When I gave you *that* exact tape, on the very first night we kissed.'

Twisting me round, she goes to kiss me right here right now. Only then her grin falters, and she's pulling back, cocking her head like she's never seen me before.

'What?' I ask.

'Your beard . . .'

'What beard?' I say. I might have camped out in the shed last night, but I shaved yesterday morning just the same as I do every morning. Quickly checking the mirror, I see a light dusting of stubble, a day's growth, nothing more.

'You used to have one,' she blurts out, incredulously pawing my face.

'Well, yeah.' I think back to the gig she was just telling me about, to when I did sport some sort of bumfluffy, lazy-arsed affair. 'But that was nearly thirty years ago,' I point out.

'No, an hour ago,' she says, not blinking. 'You had a beard an hour ago, Adam. Right here in this shed. You had a full-blown beard before I stuck that tape in and pressed "Play". Just like you've had one ever since you were a student.'

What's she talking about? 'You're joking,' I say.

'Do I bloody look like I'm joking?'

No, no she does not.

'But how does that even make sen—' I start to say.

Only suddenly I see where she's going with this. It's like her tattoo, isn't it? The way I made it vanish by going back in time and telling her she'd regret it. And her then not remembering she'd ever had one because she'd never got one. Even weirder, I also now have these odd 'new' memories of her *never* having had a tattoo as well, sitting right here alongside my old memories of her always having had one. Like somehow in my mind both histories now exist at once.

'Oh God, Jules,' I say, 'what did you do?'

'Nothing, I didn't *do* anything,' she tells me. 'But I might have *said* something,' she admits. 'Back on the beach after the Zap, I might have got her – the younger me – to just kind of hint to the younger you that . . .'

'That *what*?'

She throws her hands out. 'That I don't like stubble or beards, that I never have, that they've always given me the ick!' Turning to the corkboard, she plucks off one of the old photos of me in my mid-twenties. 'And see,' she gasps, 'it's gone from here too. You're clean-shaven. And here, and here,' she says, quickly pointing out several more snaps of me in the following decades.

'My God,' I say, a crazy possibility dawning on me, as I snatch up a page of my research that I printed out earlier. 'Listen, this is a quote from this cutting-edge dude – a theoretical physicist or something – Barak Shoshany. See, here in this BBC article, he says, "If time travel to the past is possible, it really should be possible to change things – but doing so will create an alternate timeline. Instead of creating a universe-breaking paradox, you would create a second universe with a different history."'

'Fuck,' says Jules.

'Fuck indeed.'

'And you think that's what we might have done? Created a new –'

'Maybe even twice,' I say, staring back at the Sony. 'Because what if this isn't just a time machine, Jules? What if it's a multiverse machine? What if both times we travelled back and changed something, we caused whole new parallel universes to be created, just like this Barak Shoshany says? Ones almost identical to our old ones, but not quite.'

I feel my mouth drying out. Because, seriously, this whole concept is so insane that I feel like I'm squeezing my brain with both hands.

'Like you created one where I didn't have a tattoo,' she says.

'Right. And only I remembered the previous universe where you did, because when I travelled back into the new future timeline I'd created, I somehow brought my memories of that previous universe with me, even as my consciousness blended into this new me.'

'And I then created another new universe – *this* one we're in now – where you don't have a beard?'

'Exactly. And only you remember the previous universe where I did. Because in *this* universe I've *never* had one since I shaved it off that night we went to the Zap.'

'But everything else that happened between me telling you I didn't like beards and now is the same as in the previous universes? Like us going to Darius's party and having that fight and you then discovering this machine?'

'Correct. Unless . . .' Another mind-blowing thought occurs to me.

'What?'

'Unless we *have* changed something else,' I say. 'By accident. Something that neither of us has noticed yet. Oh, Christ.' I feel sick. 'What about the kids?' I look across at the *Back to the Future* DVD I watched this morning as part of my research, and picture that iconic scene where Marty McFly and his siblings start fading out of existence on the Polaroid clipped to his guitar. 'What if we said or did something in the past that's changed or even erased who *they* are?'

'Nelly,' Jules says, panic in her voice. 'Our daughter's name is Nelly.'

'Born on 2 October 2000,' I chip in.

'And named after Nelly Furtado, who released her first single, "I'm Like a Bird", the month before.'

'And Liam,' I add. 'Our son.'

'Who was born 20 April 2003 –'

'And named after Liam Gallagher, who released "Songbird" in February that year, the first Oasis single he'd written on his own.'

Thank God, we both nod rapidly in agreement. Meaning these tally. We both have these same memories of them.

'But what if we've changed something else about them because of something else we said or did back then, something that made us then raise them in some other way?'

I quickly scrabble for the key and fumble it into the shed lock.

'I'll check Liam,' I shout, racing up the garden path.

'I'll do Nelly,' yells Jules, racing up behind.

Dashing past the open dining-room doorway inside the house, I glimpse our daughter pacing, talking on the phone. Everything about her fits with my memories of her.

I thunder up the stairs into Liam's room.

'What the hell?' he snaps, from where he's sitting on his bed in his underwear, strumming a Fender Duff, the same bass he told me Max would be lending him, with Iggy Pop's 'The Passenger' chugging out of his speaker. Meaning so far so good, yeah? Who he is feels completely right too.

'Haven't you heard of knocking?' he demands.

Resentment. Entitlement. Tick, tick. All pure, unadulterated Liam. Even the injuries on his left hand look the same. Making him definitely *my* Liam, right? Only . . . shit. *Jules* created *this* timeline, didn't she? This same new timeline on which I've never had a beard and have no memory of ever having had one, even though on my original timeline, I apparently did. So how the hell would I know if this Liam is the identical Liam from the last timeline that Jules left? I wouldn't. Only Jules would notice any changes that have taken place between her travelling back in time just now to 1993 and then coming back to here.

I dash downstairs and nearly run flat into Jules on her way up and explain all this. She then checks out Nelly in the dining room again, before running back upstairs to check on Liam too.

'I think they're *both* all right,' she finally gasps, breathless, catching up with me in the hallway again. 'Both exactly as I remember them from our last timeline.'

'Thank God.'

Hurrying through to the kitchen, shutting the door behind us, she cracks open a bottle of white. I'm still hyperventilating. Can't stop myself. Because yet another hideous thought has just occurred to me. Because it's not just the kids who could have changed, is it? Either one of us still could have too. Only in some way that the other's not yet noticed or pointed out. And not just physically, but psychologically too.

'It's OK,' Jules says, handing me a glass of wine and watching me glug it down. 'They're OK. We're OK.'

'But *are* we? *Am* I?' I say.

'Well, yes . . . apart from the beard.'

'But nothing else? *Nothing* else about me has changed?' I check. 'You're really sure?'

'Nothing,' she confirms. 'Unless it's so subtle that it doesn't even register and probably doesn't even matter. And when you got back from 1989, I definitely remember you telling me that, apart from my tattoo, everything else was the same too.'

'Meaning it is only the tattoo and the beard that have changed from our original timeline,' we say in unison.

'And everything else, right up to me discovering this damn machine and you then trying it out, that's the same too?'

'Yes.' She grins.

It's like a wave crashing over us – the relief. Or at least for a second.

'But, equally,' I point out, 'this means we're not the same *us*. Not the exact same Adam and Jules who started out on this whole weird adventure on our original timeline.'

'Shit.' She looks at me strangely. 'You're right.' She slowly turns and stares at herself in the mirror. 'And what about *them*? Jules with the tattoo and Adam with the beard. Where are *they* now?'

'I guess still back there in those previous universes?' I hazard. 'Like maybe there were versions of us where we travelled back in time but didn't change anything? So they then returned to their original timelines? Leaving them now just living out their lives.'

It sounds right. And comforting.

But hopefully also true.

'But apart from not being them, we're pretty much still us?' Jules says.

'Well, yeah. Or close enough,' I say, and seriously, is that really so much of a big deal if we're not *exactly* the same, because didn't I read somewhere that every cell in our bodies is constantly dying and replacing itself anyway? Meaning our bodies don't contain a single atom we were born with. So who we *are*, isn't it something slightly flexible, not fixed?

'OK.' She nods. 'But either way, we're going to have to rely on each other's observation and honesty from here on in, aren't we, if we're going to do it again?'

'*Again*?' I can't keep the panic from my voice. After our freakout about the kids just now, and our*selves*, how the hell can she be thinking about even going near that damned Sony again?

But she's not listening. 'Which is why we need to make a pact,' she says. 'To change nothing in the past. To create no new alternative timelines. So each time we come back, it *will* be to exactly the same universe. This one right now. Where you, me and the kids and everything else are the same. But if we do accidentally change something, and then notice something's different, no matter how little, then we've both still got to tell each other, OK?'

She holds out her hand – like it's a deal.

But before I get a chance to answer – to tell her that the risks are just too big, and that we still don't know the first thing, really, about how any of this works – we both hear Liam yelling..

'Hey, Dad. Uncle Dar has just pulled up in a shit-hot red Ferrari outside.'

Jules and I rush to the living-room window just in time to see Darius alighting from his flaming-red chariot, in a linen jacket and white panama. Like the man from bloody Del Monte. But he's also got a wistful look on his tanned face as he stares around, no doubt remembering how much time he used to spend here as a kid.

'What's he doing here?' I hiss at Jules. Not that I'm pissed off to see *him*. I'd be annoyed if the Pope himself turned up right now, because me and Jules have currently got bigger fish to fry.

'Shit. I forgot.'

'You invited him?'

'More he sort of just said he might come round,' she says.

We lock eyes, both panicking. Groundbreaking multiverse wanderings aside, we've been caught with our proverbial middle-class pants well and truly down. The house is a pigsty.

'You stall him,' she says, pushing me towards the door, as she snatches a line of drying knickers and socks off the radiator. 'Jesus! He can't see this mess.'

I hurry out to intercept Darius and he spreads his arms out wide. 'Mate,' he says. That slight American twang. 'Didn't see you leave last night.'

There's a lump in my throat. 'I . . . I . . . we . . .' I stumble, because, well, because me and Jules have just discovered a bloody multiversal time travel machine in our shed and he wants to chat about his party? 'We, er, weren't expecting you,' I say, trying to buy Jules some more time. 'Come round the back a minute. I was just, er, finishing something off in the garden . . .'

I lead him through the side gate and into the back garden, watching as he surveys our overgrown lawn with his hands wedged into his pockets like a disappointed cricket umpire, before his eyes light up.

'Ah, the old shederoonie,' he grins, acting like he hasn't noticed Groucho Barx quivering mid-shit on the patio.

As he follows me inside, he looks genuinely misty of eye, running his manicured fingers along the back of our old gaming sofa and even picking up the burnt-out *Move Your Body! 1993* mixtape I left on Dad's workbench. I have to summon every ounce of willpower I possess not to snatch it right back.

He stares at a framed photo on the wall of me, him, Jules and the kids on a picnic rug in front of a sunny stage at the Love Supreme Festival we all used to go to every year together before he left. Jules is in that mad daisy-patterned De La Soul hoodie I bought her from the merch stand after we'd all danced ourselves stupid to 'The Magic Number'.

'Nice,' he says, smiling. 'Now take me to your leader.'

Unable to put him off any longer, I lead him slowly back up the garden and in through the back door, whistling loudly to give

Jules a heads up, and then on past the heaps of washing still to be sorted in the utility room, and into the kitchen, where she slams the crammed dishwasher shut behind her with a swing of her hips in the nick of time.

'And here she is, the karaoke queen,' Darius says, advancing towards her and giving her a hug.

In comes Nelly, smoothing her hair behind her ear.

'No way,' Darius says. 'Even more grown up than before.' He embraces her too. 'So I guess you've graduated college by now? Edinburgh, wasn't it? Sociology?'

'Economics.'

'Even better. But still living at home?'

'Working from home,' she corrects him. 'And saving for a flat of my own. Back up in London, but not getting ripped off sharing with a bunch of random people like I was before.'

'Cool. And what is it you do?'

She talks him through her marketing job and the two of them start picking apart the pros and cons of today's hybrid economy. Then Nelly's asking him about his work and coming home, and he tells her he's got new offices in town and there'll be some spare space, which of course he'd be happy to let either of our kids use for free.

'Wow, that's a great idea,' Jules says, no doubt thinking about our dining room and how nice it would be to get it permanently back.

'Oh, and if you need any mentoring, I'm up for that too,' he adds.

Leaving Nelly looking at him like he's Father Christmas who's just popped out of the chimney in a flurry of soot.

'I didn't know you already had an office here,' I say.

'Oh yeah, and some news too, mate. But let's save that for later,' he tells me with a wink.

Then it's Liam's turn to behold Darius's munificence, bouncing down the stairs in trainers that he's even laced up for once, and wearing clean jeans and an actual buttoned-up shirt.

'I see you finally got your Ferrari, then, Uncle Dar,' he teases, still easy in his company from when he was a kid, even though he's not seen much of Darius these last ten years. 'Any chance of us going for a quick spin?'

'Sure. Why the hell not?'

I feel a pang of jealousy. Not just for the Ferrari, but the way Liam's looking at him. But then my mind flies back to the shed. To what's just happened. To how my whole world's just been *shook*.

'What's for dinner?' Nelly asks.

'Dinner?' Darius feigns shock. 'Oh God. I suppose it is that time. Do you want me to leave?'

'No, no,' Jules says, 'we'd love you to stay. But it'll be half an hour, or so,' she adds, looking at me awkwardly, a look that says, *Shit. Have we even got any food?!*

'OK, so let's do this,' Darius tells Liam. 'Ferrari time.'

As the two of them march outside, joshing like old mates, the rest of us wander out onto the driveway like the bloody Waltons to wave them off, to a fanfare of twitching curtains from the neighbours.

'God, he's so charismatic,' Nelly says, as the Ferrari purrs out onto the road. 'And he looks so good for his age, doesn't he, Mum? Were you really the same year group as him at school, Dad? Because you could definitely do with a bit of whatever he's taking,' she goes on, gently prodding me in the gut.

The bloody cheek.

I turn to Jules, embarrassed, but she's not even looking. She's watching the Ferrari rev off out of sight.

'It's only Darius,' she says – but whether to herself or me, I can't tell – before hurrying back inside.

Then we're back in full panic mode again. With no time to go to the shops, Jules throws open the freezer and shouts at me to tidy and vac the hallway and living room. Nelly even surrenders her business demesne, temporarily at least, clearing her paperwork off the dining-room table and laying it with our best cutlery and plates.

A frazzled half an hour later and we're sitting down with Darius for a supper of chilli lime prawns and tagliatelle that Jules has somehow miraculously cobbled together, while even more miraculously also managing to change into smart cargo trousers and a clean red T-shirt, with her hair coolly tied up, and a fresh swipe of gloss across her lips.

'God, this is so tasty,' Darius says, 'it's making me think more and more about that pop-up restaurant of yours, Jules. I take it you're already on board with this, Ads?'

'I . . . um . . .' It's not just Darius's eyes on me, but Jules's too. I'm not even sure how he knows about her idea. Something else they must have talked about last night before our fight.

'I'm really happy to help in any way I can,' he says. 'Financially, or otherwise.'

I feel it then. My hackles rising. Because it's not his place to come blithely cantering in on his charger to re-choreograph our lives, is it? Only he doesn't stop at Jules either. He's on to Liam next. Quickly winkling out of him how much he hated his degree and how much I want him to go back to uni, but how he'd much rather be in a band instead.

Obviously, I'm expecting Darius to back me up. Because he's an adult, and a businessman, who's worked ruthlessly hard his whole life. Meaning he and Liam have nothing in common.

'I imagine that sometimes it's hard for dads to let go,' is what he actually says, nodding to himself over this Hallmark gift card insight. 'But if you're not passionate about something, there's no point in doing it, because further down the line you're only going to quit.'

'But that's just it,' says Liam. '*I am* passionate about the band.' He taps his wine glass with the little finger of his left hand, something Darius notices too.

'Sometimes having obstacles in your way, like you've had, that's what gives you your edge.'

'Exactly.' Liam flashes me a glare – as if to say, *See. Uncle Dar gets it. So why can't you?*

'Then maybe you and your dad need to have yourselves a little chat,' Darius says, generously nodding at me now, inviting me into their newly formed circle of trust. 'To find some kind of common ground.'

I knock back my whole glass of wine just to keep myself from exploding. I know Darius is only trying to help, but he should know better. He was there, for God's sake. The day Liam got hurt. He sat up with us in the hospital and brought us coffees that whole first night. He knows how bloody awful it was and how long it took Liam to get his confidence back. And now he's setting him up for another fall?

'Ah,' Darius sighs, failing to pick up on my mood, and snaking his arm across my shoulders to give me a brotherly squeeze. 'God, it's good to be back here with you guys. I love how nothing ever changes here. Really, like it's frozen in time.'

Ha. If only he knew. I can't help making wide eyes at Jules.

Not that he notices. He's already moving the conversation on, telling Liam he'll get him listed as a beta tester for some hideous-sounding, violent new games title he's got in development called *Zombie pHUK* – 'as in pH, because they bleed acid, and UK, because it's set over here' – he tells us, with the same revolutionary zeal with which Einstein probably first uttered, '$E = mc^2$.'

'Probably not one for you, though, eh, Ads?' he says, before confiding in Liam with a wink, 'Always was into softer games, your old man. One of the reasons things would never have worked between us in business, what with *Fortnite* and *GTA* leading the market for the last ten years.'

The kids exchange a look that Jules somehow ducks. They both know we could have moved out to San Francisco and no doubt resent me for it too. Thanks a lot, Darius, for bringing that up.

'Oh, I don't know,' I say. 'There's still a market for retro games and gamers. Quite the community online.'

'Old people, man. Not where it's at.'

Another little pat on the back, but he's wrong. One of the crews me and Doodles play with online have even set us up a Reddit called the Dadass Dudes, where we answer old-school games queries from Millennial and Gen Z gamers craving tips. All way too small fry for Darius, though, so I don't bring it up. Plus I just want this conversation to end.

I have a time machine. A time machine, for Christ's sake. I have a time machine in my shed! Catching Jules's eye, I know she's thinking the same.

She starts making noises about having to work tomorrow. After a quickly orchestrated coffee, I walk Darius out front just the two of us, so I can get him into his car as fast as possible and get back inside to talk to Jules about how our whole world has been flipped upside down.

'So that, er, news I mentioned . . .' he prevaricates, leaning on the Ferrari's open door.

'Uh-huh.' I nod, barely even remembering the context of whatever it was that he said.

'It's Quark Studios,' he says. 'I've bought it.'

It takes a second for this to sink in. I picture Todd grinning like a Cheshire cat at the party last night.

'I would have told you sooner,' he says, 'and God knows I wanted to. But you know what lawyers are like. In fact, in a way, it was your idea, really. You remember a few months back when we were chatting on Zoom, and you were telling me about what a great company Quark was?'

When I was trying to big myself up to him, he means, me and my pathetic little life . . . I feel my arse cheeks clench and my stomach churn.

'And, er, what are you planning on doing with it?' I say, already thinking about Meredith and Doodles and the rest of my department. And, obviously, myself. Because, *shit*. In this babyface industry, I'm practically a dinosaur already. What if he's going to break Quark up and I'm suddenly surplus to requirement? How will I pay my mortgage? How will we *survive*?

'Well,' Darius says, 'I'm putting a management team in, so that'll be up to them. I don't want to be too hands on to begin with. There's a couple of other local companies I'm hoping to snap up too. We'll then see what we've got and maybe even try to do the whole Sirius unicorn thing all over again.'

Another gamble, in other words, but with me now just another one of his little plastic chips he's stacking up in front of his roulette wheel.

'But don't worry, eh?' he says. 'I've got your back.'

Right, because even if push did come to shove, he'd surely throw me a lifeline, yeah? Yeah. I still have that, at least.

Another wink, like the one he shot Liam just now when he was reminding him how I lost out on a fortune. A wink that tells me he's in charge.

Less than thirty seconds after Darius finally leaves, me and Jules are sequestered in the kitchen discussing the bombshell he's just dropped.

He'll make a much better boss than Todd, Jules reckons and might even put my career back on track. But what if it doesn't? I can't help thinking, as she drags me upstairs and into our bedroom. What the hell am I meant to do then?

'Listen, there's nothing you *can* do about it. So just forget it for now,' she tells me as we sit down at the end of our bed.

'But –'

'But nothing,' she says. 'You and me, we've just travelled back in *time*.'

She's grinning. Then I'm grinning too, because she's right. None of *that* – Quark Studios, Totally Sirius, *Zombie* fucking *pHUK*, my whole bloody industry – means diddly squat next to *this*.

Because *this* – our portal into the multiverse, temporal body-swapping, call it what you want – *this* is not just life-changing, it's world-changing.

And it's *ours*.

I stare at our reflections in the wardrobe mirror.

'So, all those other tapes, and maybe even those CDs, you think we can use them to time travel too?' Jules says.

'Maybe.' Although even just her considering this still does freak me out. 'Don't you think we'd be better off telling someone?'

'Like who?'

'I don't know. The government. Or maybe some Oxford professor. Whoever got Stephen Hawking's old job. They'd probably do for a start.'

'Right, and you're just going to call them, are you? Or maybe WhatsApp?'

'Well, why not? This has got to be the greatest scientific invention of all time. Or even *times*,' I joke.

'Seriously, how would we even get them to listen to us?' she says. 'Let alone believe us.'

'Just show them. Show them how it works.' Like I did with her.

'If it even *would* work for them . . .' she says.

'What's that supposed to mean?'

She frowns. 'Just that I've been thinking about, well, how *personal* this all feels. These tapes that we made for each other, with love, and with all those songs that mean so much to us and that bring back so many vivid memories . . . I mean, do you really think that if someone else listened, that the – I know you keep talking about science, but just humour me here, OK? – that the *magic* would work for them too?'

Magic. Meh. But what do I know? About life, the universe, or anything. I mean, kids are wearing Crocs again, for fuck's sake.

'I don't know,' I settle for instead, 'and have no way of knowing, not unless we give someone else a go.'

'Which we're not going to,' she says, her eyes flashing. 'Or not until we know more. No, for now, I think the first and second rule of Secret Multiverse Time Machine Club has to be that we do not talk about Secret Multiverse Time Machine Club. Agreed?'

I nod.

'Great.' She smiles. 'So, when are we going to do it again?'

The excitement in her voice is unmistakable. The glow in her eyes. The *relish*. Of adventure. Of travel. Oh God, it's Australia all over again . . .

'Really? Even knowing how bloody dangerous it could be?'

'Yeah, OK, I get it. We could mess up accidentally again, like with the tattoo and beard. The beard I really do prefer you without,' she teases, reaching out to stroke my smooth cheek. 'Or we could mess up even bigger, or even on purpose. Like maybe going back and assassinating some evil dictator,' she suggests, 'but thereby inadvertently unleashing God only knows what else in their place. Or cheating on the lottery numbers or something like that, because that would be like stealing from somebody else. But we're not going to, are we?'

'Well, no, of course not.'

'Right, because we're not dicks and we're going to be super careful. So there are going to be no new alternative timelines created and therefore no new universes, OK?' she says. 'We're just going to ride. Then return to our exact same unadulterated universe here.'

'Like tourists,' I say. 'Time tripping.' Only tourists taking notes too, I'm thinking. Tourists trying to fathom out what makes this thing tick.

'Precisely.'

But I've still got alarm bells ringing in my head. That we should *not* do this. I can't keep that panic we had over the kids out of my mind. But maybe Jules is right. Maybe we can explore this responsibly.

'And who knows,' I say, 'once we find out more about how it all works, maybe we'll discover it's not dangerous at all. Like the universe, or multiverse, or whatever, has some inbuilt law that won't let us screw it up,' I add, because I read about that too. How God doesn't play dice. Or whatever it was that Einstein said.

'Like this is just a gift,' Jules says.

Huh. 'But from who?' I ask.

'I don't know. God. The universe. Aliens. Does it matter?'

I think about this for a second, all the potential *X-Files* stuff. 'No, I suppose not,' I say.

'So, when *are* we going to do it again?' she asks, turning to face me and squeezing my hands. 'How about the next time the kids are out of the house?'

Chapter Seven

Jules – 'Alright'

It's Tuesday morning and I'm on my last length in the Sea Lanes, the outdoor fifty-metre heated pool down on Marine Parade.

'Whoa. Steady on,' Ngozi says, as I reach the end. 'You've been proper motoring.'

I nod, out of breath. 'I needed that,' I gasp, taking off my goggles.

'Everything OK? Still worrying about Adam?'

'Uh-huh,' I lie, even though I'm not thinking about Adam at all, or at least not in the context of what I told Ngozi in the changing room earlier about the shit week he's having with all the fallout from Todd breaking the news about Quark. Adam ended up having to hand-hold everyone in his department, who all wanted to know what he'd known, which was nothing, and wanted reassurance, which he at least could give them, promising them that Darius is a stand-up guy.

'It'll be fine,' Ngozi reassures me. 'Big news always takes a while to digest.'

No bloody kidding. Like the existential bonkers-ness of the fact that thirty-nine hours and fifteen minutes ago, I – *Jesus, I still can't wrap my head around it* – travelled back in time to 1993. I mean, this has to be the head fuck of all head fucks, right?

Everything is different.

Except that everything is *completely normal* too.

And *real*, because Adam continues to *not have a beard*. All of yesterday evening, I couldn't stop staring at him, and this morning it felt downright pervy watching him shave. Not to mention also kind of hot.

Even so, I'm getting used to it. Which is odd. Like my memories of the actual Adam – OG Adam, the Adam-with-the-grizzly-crumb-filled beard – are getting less dominant. Even though I know he *was* like that, it's now equally true that he *isn't*. Like my memories of him from that old timeline are now happily bobbing along with my new memories of him in this new universe. It's like owning the same pair of trousers in both blue and black.

'Can't wait for the sauna,' Ngozi says.

She's booked the Luna Wave just outside on the beach as a treat for us both.

'Me too,' I say with a smile, but it feels like I'm acting, keeping this huge thing from her. Even Ngozi, who can usually read me like a book, couldn't get close to guessing the biggest, most mind-bending secret of my life. And I can't tell her. None of it. It's my and Adam's secret. Ours to bear alone.

As we walk from the pool across the pebbles to the sauna hut, I start to feel a bit more grounded, though. She hasn't sussed anything is wrong and soon we're onto chatting about Darius's party.

'I was looking for you at the end,' she says.

'We left early.'

She smiles. 'Aye aye. You two love cats.'

If only. Not being able to talk about the time machine brings me and Adam back into focus. Because, yeah, I am still processing what we rowed about, too. 'Adam was drunk,' I say. 'We had a fight on the way home. Said a few horrible home truths.'

'Oh Lord. Shit-faced honesty,' she says. 'The worst. I don't miss those days one bit.'

I've often marvelled at how quickly she moved on from Geoff. They were never the most passionate of couples, granted, but the second their twins, Isa and Isaac went to uni, she just gave him the flick. Said she was done with that whole 'conventional relationship thing' and it was time to move on. I'm amazed that they've managed to remain friends.

She opens the door to the sauna and it's empty, which is a rarity. Beach saunas are all the rage in this neck of the woods. She takes the ladle and splashes water on the coals in the corner. A cloud of scorching steam rises, and she sits on the top bench, relishing the heat, looking through the picture window to the sea and the pale horizon in the distance.

'So? How are things now?' she asks, genuinely concerned.

'We're OK. We've made up ... *ish* ... but even aside from what's happening at his work, we're both still rattled,' I say, which is all true enough, because discovering our time machine hasn't wiped away the memories of that fight.

We sit for a moment in the heat.

'Do you ever ... I don't know ...'

'What?' she asks.

'Do you ever have that thing where something happens, and it blindsides you?'

She opens one eye. 'What's going on?'

'Nothing,' I bluster. 'Just that I've been doing a ... deep dive into the past to try and figure some stuff out. Do you remember the night Adam and I first got together? The Zap Club. You were there. You had E's down your Wonderbra.'

'Did I?' She hoots with laughter. 'Seriously? How on earth can you remember? I could get disbarred for that,' she adds, not altogether joking.

'It felt so amazing. I mean, if I could go back to how it was then ...'

'You want to go back to your early twenties? Are you mad, woman? It was shit. We were skint, remember? Everyone had bad teeth and BO.'

'I guess.'

'Oh dear,' she says, 'sounds like you're having a midlife moment.' She shakes her head, settles back and closes her eyes. 'Don't worry, babe. It'll pass.'

Only I'm not sure it will.

And it doesn't. All the way home I keep thinking about Adam and the Zap Club and that amazing kiss, but how different our lives are now.

In the kitchen, I'm about to put on Radio 4, but linger on Heart radio, as it plays first D:Ream's 'Things Can Only Get Better' and then 'Oh Carolina' by Shaggy. Both bangers from '93.

'Er?' Nelly asks, coming in to find me dancing. She looks appalled. 'What are you doing?'

'Dancing,' I say, not stopping. 'Why?'

'Well, firstly because the way you're ... moving ... is dangerously close to cultural appropriation, and secondly, because you're meant to be giving me a lift.'

I stop abruptly, remembering what she told me earlier. How Darius has come good on his offer of workspace. Only not just any workspace, workspace at Quark, where Adam says Darius and his people have already moved into the empty top two floors.

'Honestly, Mum, your brain is like a sieve.'

'What did Dad say?' I told her to check with him that it was OK, because he says there are quite a few people at work already viewing Darius as the enemy.

'He muttered something about it potentially looking weird for optics, but said I should do it anyway. It's my life.' She grins, like she couldn't agree more.

Hustling me into the hall, she points out the two large cardboard boxes she's already packed. As I open the front door, I interrupt the postman who's about to wedge a brown envelope through the letter box, addressed to me.

I rip it open and slide out the letter inside. It's a final demand from the credit card company. The figure in red leaps off the white page. Thank God Adam has no access to my business card, or he'd be freaking out.

'What is it?' Nelly asks.

'Nothing,' I say, folding it and stuffing it into the back pocket of my jeans, feeling my heart thud. I can't tell her, or anyone. Not now. Not with Adam's job up in the air. Even if Darius has assured him he'll be fine.

'We'll miss having you around,' I tell her, as I walk out with one of the boxes and unlock the Skoda.

'Yeah, sure you will,' she says sarcastically, as she loads the boot.

'But even you've got to admit, it'll be a bit more sociable than being at home.'

'I'm actually more going there for the internet.'

'Yes, but hopefully you'll meet some new people too. Go out at lunchtime. In the sun,' I offer, as I force the key in the ignition three times before the car finally starts with a shuddering cough. Bloody Adam, he'd better have ordered those spark plugs.

'Can you please stop telling me how to live my life?'

'I'm not –'

'Look. I don't know how many times I have to tell you this, but I'm working this hard because I want to save up. To move out into my own place. So I don't get . . . stuck here.'

Like you. Her voice is laden with these unspoken words. I feel my face flush, remembering how I levelled that word 'stuck' at Adam during our fight.

'But sometimes if you spend all your time focused on the future, you can get stuck too,' I point out.

'Mum. Just drop it, OK?'

Her spiky tone hurts. As does her lack of respect. I'm also frustrated by my inability to convey that I am proud of her for being a hard worker. She's always been diligent. I just wish she'd, I don't know, lighten up.

'That's weird,' she says, after a while. 'Eva's texted.'

'Oh?' I ask, as casually as I can. 'What did she say?'

'She's having a drinks thing tomorrow night.'

'That sounds fun.'

Nelly scrunches up her nose. 'I bet you put her up to it.'

'No, I didn't,' I say, trying hard not to blush. 'She's always saying how much she'd like to see you.'

Nelly's not buying it. 'Seriously?'

And something inside me snaps.

'Oh, for God's sake, Nelly. Go and have some bloody fun for once. I mean, do you even realise how lucky you are to be young? To not have any cares, or real responsibilities? To have exciting new relationships stacked up ahead of you. To have a body that will let you drink and do whatever the hell you want to it and stay up all night because you still get to look like a supermodel in the morning?'

Because that's how I felt when I went back. That's how bleedin' wonderful it was.

Nelly looks at me in surprise. 'All right, Nana, keep your hair on.'

Nana. For a second, I nearly snap something back at her. But then I stop. I'm not that girl in 1993. I *am* old.

Rolling her eyes, she starts texting. Hopefully saying yes to Eva.

When we arrive at Quark Studios, the receptionist picks up a sleek phone like she's in *The Apprentice*.

'Mr Angelopoulos says to go right on up to the eighth floor,' she tells Nelly.

'Can I go too?' I ask, because only ever having been in the basement of this building, I want to see what it's like upstairs.

'Sure.'

The lift opens onto a smart, open-plan space. A tall young woman with long, styled red hair, heavy eyeliner and an electric-blue trouser suit, who I recognise from Darius's party, steps towards us.

'Hey, Nelly, right?' she says with a Californian lilt, flashing us both a crisp, professional smile. 'Welcome. I'm Anastasija, Darius's day-to-day. You're right over here.'

Nelly's desk is in the far corner by the window. She has a view overlooking the gaudy chocolate-box Brighton Pavilion and down onto a row of hip clothes boutiques and coffee shops in the Lanes, and gives me a stern look like I'm fussing, as I start commenting on how cool it is.

'You're here,' Darius booms, sauntering towards us from a glass-fronted private office. He hugs Nelly and then me, kissing me on both cheeks. He's wearing dark blue designer jeans, a dazzlingly white T-shirt and a smart black jacket.

'Come and check out my office,' he says.

Nelly doesn't thank me, or even look at me, as I leave her by her desk with Anastasija to get 'on-boarded'. I follow Darius across the vast, grey-carpeted floor, feeling the same rejected pang I had when I left her on the first day of primary school and she was the only kid who didn't wave goodbye.

Unsurprisingly, the corner office is big and show-offy, the kind you see in TV shows like *Succession*, with low leather couches, a designer coffee table and pot plants that look so healthy, they must be fake. Except that a surreptitious squeeze of one of the fleshy leaves reveals that they're not.

I fiddle with the Skoda's car keys in my hand, feeling underdressed in my ancient jeans and hoodie.

Darius sits on one of the couches and points to the one opposite.

'Take the weight off,' he says. 'Go on. Just for a minute.'

I perch on the arm of the couch, remembering that bit-too-much eye contact we had back at the party. 'So, you liked it so much, you bought the company,' I Victor Kiam riff, peering round.

'Yeah, it looks like a good business. Or, you know, we'll see . . .'

Whatever the hell that means.

'I thought you were leaving all this to your management team?' Wasn't that what Adam said?

'Yeah, but still. I want to be close to the action. Plus, work's what turns me on,' he laughs. 'But you know that feeling. You've always been passionate about what you do. I mean, I'd forgotten how easily you can rustle up something completely delicious like that pasta dish on Sunday. Just like that.' Darius kisses his fingertips. 'So.' He claps his hands. 'On that note, I've got these French guys coming over next week. Investors,' he says. 'They want a dinner to discuss how we all might work together, and I suggested we do it here. There's an amazing kitchen and dining room through there.' He waves towards a door.

'Right?' I say, still confused as to what this has to do with me.

'And I figured you'd be perfect. You know, to cater the event. Chat them up with a little explanation of the menu, that sort of thing.'

'Me?'

'Yeah, I'll make it worth your while. Money's no object,' he says.

Enough for me to square away the credit card bill in my pocket? My mind can't help going there as he talks.

'They'll want high end, though. I know you can do anything, but I think it'd impress them to serve something properly French. You know, show them we're on the same page as them. You can do that, right?' he asks.

I swallow hard, already feeling out of my depth, but he looks so enthusiastic, so pleased with himself, I find myself mumbling, 'Sure. Yeah.'

'Great.' He grins, then stands up and I realise that my little meeting with him is over. He puts his hand on my shoulder, guiding me to the door. 'I know you won't let me down.'

Wednesday evening is the first 'alone time' Adam and I have without the kids. Liam took the bait – and the tickets Adam bought on a resale site – to see Brighton band Town of Cats at the Hope & Ruin tonight with Max. And Nelly is blow-drying her hair, ready to go and meet Eva for a burger at Salt Shed opposite Brighton Dome before heading up to the Windmill for a dance. I'm in the kitchen, slouching around and pretending to be preoccupied as I watch the clock, itching for her to depart so we can *do our thing* again.

The second she does, Adam appears in the kitchen, clearly raring to go too. He's showered and changed into his nice jeans and short-sleeved

Ben Sherman shirt. And, yeah, I get it, because this does have something of a date night vibe about it, even if our glamorous destination is the shed.

I grab a bottle of wine from the fridge and some glasses, because I'm betting even time travel goes better with Tesco's Finest half-price Chardonnay. I've spent all afternoon trying to fathom out which tapes correspond to which months and days from the clues in my diaries and making a list, since Adam reckons that each new tape we play sends us back to the day it was given. Or that's how the first two tapes seemed to work, anyway.

As we hurry down the garden path in the fading light, it feels illicit. Exciting. Like the old days. Me and Adam against the world. Or maybe 'worlds' would be more accurate, if what we've been theorising is right. Me and Adam against the multiverse. When he reaches the shed door and asks if I'm ready, just for a second, I glimpse him again, that bright-eyed boy from 1993 who's since got lost inside a man.

I've always rather resented the shed. Adam's made it clear that this is his man cave, full to bursting with stuff he won't throw out. But it's taken on a different perspective now it houses the *machine*. It feels somehow sacred and silly all at once. Like the Doctor's Tardis.

Groucho Barx gives us a funny look and cocks his head as I tell him to shush and to wait outside. I close the shed door and lock it.

As Adam opens the wine, I show him my list detailing the dates that the tapes and CDs might match and I want to squeak with excitement. This is already giving me an off-the-clock buzz.

'We could get back into it,' I suggest. 'You know, the mixtape thing. Or sharing playlists anyway. I kinda miss it.'

'Me too.'

He looks at me and I shrug and smile apologetically. 'OK. I know I wanted you to throw them out, but I do appreciate that I couldn't have been more wrong.'

He raises an eyebrow at my apology. 'Just as well I never throw anything away then, isn't it?' he says, and we both laugh.

'So, come on then. Who's going first?'

He waggles his eyebrows. 'Well, we both want to, obviously, so let's flip for it. That seems fair, right?'

I nod, grinning. Just the idea of it is so bloody intoxicating. He takes a fifty-pence piece from the pot on his dad's old workbench, and I call heads before he flips it. The late Queen Elizabeth's face sparkles as he catches it on the back of his hand. Good old Liz. I clap my hands, delighted.

'OK. So . . . where to?' I say, digging through the box. 'How about *May-hem 1995*? I found a mention of it in my diary from when I gave it to you.' I open the tape box and step towards the machine.

'Wait,' Adam says.

'What?'

'Just that . . . Look, it's a TDK 90.'

'So what? All the more room for more great tunes, right?'

'But maybe not just that . . .'

'What do you mean?'

'Just that when you went back to '93, you were there for exactly sixty minutes. I know, because I timed it. And that was exactly the length of that tape. And when I went back to '89, that was a sixty-minute tape too and I reckon that sent me back for exactly an hour.'

'So this one,' I deduce, 'means I might get to stay back for an hour and a half?'

'It makes sense. Well, as much as any of this does,' he admits.

'And you still reckon it'll take me back to the same day it was handed over? Which in this case was –' I open my diary and show him where I found a mention of it – 'Sunday, 21 May.'

'Yeah, but maybe these work even more accurately than that. What happened to me is young Adam handed that first tape over to young you in the Peregrine about halfway through my trip back.'

'And the same with me,' I quickly work out. 'I started my trip back half an hour before I gave you the '93 tape and then stayed on maybe another half-hour with you on the beach at the Troubs' gig, before I got hauled back into that whirlwind again . . .'

'Meaning this should take you back to around forty-five minutes before you give me the tape.'

'And spit me out forty-five minutes after.'

'OK.' He nods towards the open tape deck of the machine. 'But remember our promise. You can't change anything. Not one thing.'

'I won't.' I reach up and kiss him quickly, desperate to get going.

I bang in the tape and hit 'Play'.

Grinning at Adam, as the tinny piano chord riff of Supergrass's 'Alright' blasts out into the shed, for a second I think that nothing's happening, but then – the floor vanishes and I'm screaming down into that tornado again . . .

Darkness.
Then pale warm light.
I'm in the kitchen. Our *old* kitchen. In our first flat.
Oh my *God*. This is amazing.
It's worked and I'm back and I'm dancing.

I mean, *she's* dancing – the young me – with Supergrass still playing. My – *her* – hips are swinging to the now familiar guitar riff, although to her this song is refreshingly new. *I Should Coco*, Supergrass's debut album, is a recent purchase, bought just three days ago in Across the Tracks on Gloucester Road, a flash memory pops into her mind.

It's playing on the kitchen radio, with its dial covered in crusted flour, because she – the young me – always listens to the radio when she's baking.

The reason she's grinning is because she just yesterday recorded it onto a new mixtape she's giving to Adam today. That *same* mixtape that I just put into the old Sony.

And my heart is fit to burst too. Because whenever I hear this song, it transports me back to a memory I can't quite grasp – the way music so often does. Its chorus has always conjured up an intangible atmosphere of the past, and I realise it's *this*. This moment right here right now.

She harmonises with Gaz Coombes about feeling all right. Then jumps around to the instrumental bit and her body is still so fluid, so *un-achy*. Her slinky satin robe falls open and she's naked beneath. I look down at her – my, *our* – pert tits as she jigs in time with an unselfconsciousness that's beautiful.

I'm hearing her thoughts and how happy she is that it's a Sunday morning and she and Adam are actually living together. They've both got new jobs – with him now a games designer and her a cook at the Bandstand cafe – so they could afford to move out of their parents' homes and into this little one-bed top-floor flat up by Seven Dials, with a view down over the higgledy-piggledy roofs of the rest of Brighton.

I watch her hands reach for the metal coffee pot and unscrew its lid, then spoon in grinds from the jar. And I remember how years before that Nespresso machine Adam bought me, this one made great coffee and was one of the first things we bought together when we moved in. She loves it that they now have *their* stuff. These first bricks of their new life together.

'Ads, what have you done with the matches?' she calls.

Her voice is bright, but then she – I – feels great. She glances over at the table where the backgammon set is laid out from last night's session, alongside two empty wine glasses, an empty bottle of red, a full ashtray and, next to it, a box of matches. But even with the late night, she's totting up that they've still had nine hours' sleep.

A straight nine hours.

When was the last time *I* got nine hours' sleep? Without Adam getting up for a pee, or me getting a cramp, or having to beat off the duvet with the onset of yet another hot flush?

She lights the gas, jumping back as it flares, her attention already turning to the salad she's going to make for their picnic lunch. She reaches up and pulls down a large black notebook from the shelf, one left over from her food design course at college. She's filled it with recipes, along with sketches. You eat with your eyes, is what she thinks. She wants anyone who tastes her dishes to have all of their senses engaged. That's what it'll be like when she makes them in her own restaurant one day.

As I eavesdrop on her thoughts, I'm gobsmacked by how single-minded and ambitious she is. How she aches with wanderlust to experience food in different places. She knows the world is out there. Just waiting for them.

'Is that coffee?' Adam calls in a sleepy voice and her heart leaps. He's awake.

She runs into the bedroom – I'd forgotten the orange duvet and the purple sheet with the splodgy orange roses. Adam lies beneath it, and agile as a cat, she leaps onto the bed, straddling him.

Jeez, my knees could do *that*?

'Get up,' she says. 'We're going to the park, remember?'

He looks all sexy and mussed up. He's sporting long sideburns and a boxy, retro mod haircut that makes him look like someone's stuck a Lego wig on his head. I now remember it was her who severed his fringe, a month ago, on the first night they moved in here, that same night she gave herself her Justine Frischmann from Elastica slanted bob.

Liam, she wanted him to look like Liam from Oasis . . . when now we have a Liam of our own.

'Come back to bed,' he mock-whines, because he's lazy, but also because he's not as much a fan of fresh air as she is. Left to his own devices, he'd play video games round the clock, though slowly but surely she's breaking his bad habits. He's her work in progress.

'Nope, fresh air, fresh air, fresh air,' she laughs, squashing him, as she leans over to her side of the bed and grabs the blister pack of contraceptive pills and quickly pops one.

Adam laughs as she deliberately crushes him again.

'All right, all right. Get off,' he groans. 'I need a slash.'

I watch the languid way he moves. He's so comfortable in his skin. And I realise that the young me is assuming that his tight buttocks and buff biceps are a forever thing – like the contours of Michelangelo's David. She has no concept that his dad bod is patiently waiting for her on the horizon. Just like my saggy body is for him. But right now, her body is stirring at the sight of his.

She fights down the urge and quickly gets dressed – pulling her dark blue sundress with yellow suns and moons out of the wardrobe. A wardrobe that is filled solely with clothes that actually fit. She'll pair it, as she does with every outfit these days, with her Doc Martens and her black trilby.

She half watches as, in the adjoining bathroom, Adam pees, then turns to the sink for his toothbrush. A bubble of irritation rises up inside her. Yet again, he's left the toilet seat up.

I *know* I shouldn't – me and Adam have absolutely promised each other that we'll just be passengers – but I can't help myself. 1995 Jules really needs to nip this in the bud right now if she's to save herself years of looking at dribble marks on the rim of the porcelain bowl with the seat left up every bloody time.

'Oi. Put the loo seat down,' I say. Yes, *me*. Only the words come out of *her* mouth.

Whoops.

I register her shock and sudden flare of confidence now the words are out.

'What?' He glares back.

'You heard.' She stares him down, and any guilt I might have felt evaporates. Because it was *her* who just said that. She's back in control.

He puts the loo seat down and washes his hands. In the bedroom, he looks at the clothes he's left scattered on the floor. He lifts up his socks, sniffs them and wrinkles his nose, then throws them towards the wicker laundry basket in the corner, where they land on the floor.

Again, I can sense her watching, pretending to herself that she's not really minding, but actually minding a lot. While she's in shock from her last command, the daredevil in me makes her say, 'You can do better than that.'

Then I make her scoop up the socks and chuck them back at him. You know what, Adam? Sod it, this is for your own good.

He looks at her with surprise as I continue imposing myself, so that she opens the laundry-bin lid and waves her arm to encourage him to fire them in.

'Goal!' she cheers – or, rather, *I* cheer – as he succeeds with the first one. Then 'Goal!' as he gets another. 'Pants are double,' I tell him, cheering him on as he gets those in too.

There. See. I will it into my younger self's brain. You can get a man to do anything, so long as you tell him it's sport.

Younger Jules is feeling pleased that two big items are crossed off her 'Adam to-do' list. The loo seat and the laundry. Not bad for a morning's work.

He grabs her, pressing up against her. 'You're so bossy today. It's hot.'

But still she resists his advances, and ten minutes later, the salad is assembled in the empty Wall's ice-cream tub, and with beers in a backpack, they set off to Stanmer Park in their chipped cream Beetle.

Oh, our fabulous car!

'Ta-da!' Jules says, waggling the tape at Adam. 'I finished it yesterday.'

He smiles, delighted, and leans over and kisses her. He puts the tape in the player and they wind down the windows, not caring that people are giving them looks as they bellow out first Supergrass and then 'I'll Be There For You' from that new Channel 4 comedy about a bunch of squeaky-clean New Yorkers, which Jules has absolutely no clue that her kids will still be watching reruns of in nearly thirty years' time. Then, our favourite Dolly song, 'Islands in the Stream', and I remember Darius's party and how Adam refused to sing with me. Whereas this Jules is certain that he'll be harmonising badly like this with her forever.

Adam parks on the grass verge outside Stanmer House and they listen to a few more songs on the tape while they snog. Just snog. Like they have all the time in the world. Which they do.

'Fresh air,' Jules reminds herself, eventually coming up for some herself.

The park is in full May bloom, with the woods awash with bluebells, and they yomp up the winding path, holding hands. The green canopy is thick with birdsong. It's perfect.

She lays down the blanket she's brought, but even before it's evened out, he ambushes her, lying on top of her.

Flippin' heck. I'd forgotten what it felt like to have a libido this sky-high. But what's even more shocking is that neither of them seems to have the slightest fear of being caught. Their need is greater.

'Off, off . . .' he breathes, tugging at the side of her knickers beneath the short-flared dress and she laughs.

I can feel her straining, hurrying to get him inside her, but there's a worry too. Will she or won't she be able to come? It's not a guaranteed thing. In fact, it's frustrating that sometimes she can and sometimes she can't.

But *I* can help her with that.

'Wait, wait, wait,' she whispers between kisses – and I can feel her surprise that her mouth's just issued this order. She's not usually able to give instructions. 'Give me your hand,' I make her say and guide Adam's hand between her legs.

'Slower,' I say. 'Top left. No, *my* top left,' I make her clarify, guiding his fingers in a slow circle, as he continues to move inside her. And, OK, this might not be the most romantic way to instruct him. Maybe not what Dr Ruth would advise. But *tempus fugit*, and all that. I don't know how much time we've got left.

I can feel all her senses tingling. This is so damn good. That's what she's thinking, what *I'm* thinking too.

It took me years to work out how to ask for this, but now as she presses herself, grinding against Adam, his fingers move rhythmically – oh yes, yes, yes, he's a fast learner, my boy – turning her on and up and up and up.

Oh my God, this feels incredible.

My thought. Or just hers?

Because she's now firmly in charge of proceedings, leaving me literally back here for the ride . . .

'Now,' she breathes, 'now, yes, yes!' she cries out, as she startles the birds from the trees.

I come to back in the shed with a gasp, like someone's just poured ice down my back. My pulse is racing, my cheeks burn. I can't believe I've been spat back out into the present when I was in the middle of such a whopping orgasm.

I spring out of my chair. My knees are literally trembling.

'So?' Adam asks.

I fill up my wine glass and take a long slug. I can't get my head around the fact I was there. Just seconds ago.

'It was, um, it was a Sunday. We were on a walk. In Stanmer Park,' I mumble.

'Right,' he says. 'Just like you made a note of here in your diary. And you didn't change anything?'

'Uh-uh,' I lie, taking another gulp of wine. 'Nothing at all. Just passenger-ing along. Same as we agreed. And this . . . it all looks, the same too,' I say.

He nods, seemingly satisfied.

'So, how was the sex?'

His question takes me so much by surprise that I splutter my second gulp of wine back out into my glass.

'The *what*?'

'Only it says here . . .' He holds up my diary, like a preacher brandishing a Bible at a sinner. Like his mum used to do to him whenever she caught him out lying as a kid, he once told me. '*We had sex in the woods,*' he reads out. '*And I had a huge orgasm, for once, thanks to this great new trick I just kind of came up with . . .*'

Only that's something *I* never wrote, of course. Not in my old diary, on my old timeline. Her 'great new trick'? Sweet Jesus, that was *me*, just now, in her head.

'*For once?*' he says me accusingly. 'So had you been, well, *faking* it all before then?'

'No,' I bluster, scoffing at his indignant male pride. 'It's just that up until then it could be a bit random whether it happened, that's all.'

'*Random?*' He looks mortified.

'Difficult.'

Even more mortified.

'It's just that sometimes I *could* and sometimes I *couldn't* . . .' I try to explain.

'But then?'

'OK, fine,' I half shout, because sod it, he's going to work it out, isn't he? 'But then, on this particular day, I taught myself a little trick – well, taught *you*, actually,' I say, waggling my fingers and watching his cheeks mottle. 'A little trick that we wouldn't have otherwise picked up on for a few more years.'

'Oh my God,' Adam says. 'So that was *you*. The you from now. *You* were the one who first showed me how to do that to you up in the woods?'

Because, of course, he remembers *that*. Because for him in – oh, shit – this *new alternative universe* I've just created, I would have *always* taught him this trick on that date.

'So what? Is it really such a biggie?' I ask.

'Yes. Yes, it is. Because, shit, Jules. Well, for one thing, you just lied,' he says, tossing the diary onto the sofa in disgust. 'We had an agreement. And you promised –'

'Oh, stop being so dramatic.'

'But it's not even just the fact you lied,' he snaps. 'Or had sex with him,' he says.

'With *you*.'

'No, *him*. With a twenty-three-year-old.'

Jesus, I can't believe he's getting jealous about me having sex with himself. 'No, *she* did that,' I point out. 'My younger self. I just happened to be there as well.'

'But by deliberately imposing yourself on your younger self *yet again*, you've created yet another new timeline. *This* one. Which means *this* me, the me on *this* timeline, I'm not the same Adam you left on your last timeline when you just went back to 1995.'

I stare at him. Really stare. Like I've maybe never stared so hard at someone in my life. Quantumly speaking, he's correct, this *is* a different Adam, but only microscopically, right? Like when I got rid of his beard. Just now he got a bit better at sex a bit quicker than he would have otherwise.

'But you're still *you*,' I soothe.

'Well, yes. Maybe.' Although it's obvious just from his expression that he's having trouble wrapping his head around this too. 'At least, I hope. I mean, you swear nothing else has changed. You absolutely swear?'

'Yes. I double, triple, quadruple vow. And I mean, OK. I'm sorry for the lie. But apart from that, honestly, if anything, what I actually did was make our lives a little better.'

Well, a *lot* better, in fact. It's weird, but I'm now getting more of those 'new memories' of lots of other great sex we explored in those early years after this picnic. Sex that has stood us both in good stead ever since.

'And I promise, I double, triple, quadruple promise, I really won't do it again,' I say, because he's still sulking and I really don't want this to ruin our night.

Finally, he nods, but eyeing me warily, like this really is my last chance.

'So where to next?' I say, quickly drum-rolling my hands on my thighs to lighten the mood. 'What about our wedding tape? What a day. One of the best,' I tell him, full eye contact now, meaning every word. Because, crikey – a new memory informs me – the shag we had *that* night. *Way* better than the first time round.

'No, I've already got such good memories of it, I don't want to . . . risk changing them, spoiling them . . .'

By *imposing* himself. Like I just did. That's what he means. That he's better than that, better than me.

'This one,' he says, picking out a tape labelled *Flat Party 1998*. 'Sounds like fun. Another ninety-minute one too. Not that I remember this particular party *specifically*,' he adds.' I mean, we threw so many back then, they've all rather blurred into one.'

'Yeah, sure,' I laugh.

Because how could either of us forget that one? As in ever.

He takes the tape out of its plastic case and slides it into the Sony, then sits down in the armchair and tells me, 'I'll see you in an hour and a half.'

As he presses 'Play', 'Save Tonight' by Eagle-Eye Cherry starts up.

'Ooh, I love this one,' I say, perching on the edge of the bench.

But Adam's eyes have already glazed over.

'Wowzer,' I say, leaning in to look at him more closely. 'Far out.'

Chapter Eight

Adam – 'The Rockafeller Skank'

This time the landing is softer, less jarring. A glider easing down onto the runway from a clear blue sky, instead of a storm-tossed fighter fireballing into the concrete.

Twenty-six-year-old Adam already being awake helps too. But it's also like my brain – or my *mind*, what with my own physical brain being decades in the future – seems to have adjusted as well. Like two time trips in I've already got my frequent flyer badge. My *chrononaut* badge. Whatever.

A good thing too, because Adam here is on a *mission* to get things sorted before everyone else tips up at 8 p.m. to *party on* just like Wayne and Garth in what's still his favourite movie of the nineties so far.

First up on his to-do list is cleaning the bathroom, like he promised Jules he would. But he ducked out for a few beers beforehand with his new work friend, Doodles, so his first act of 'cleaning' is to pee with the precision and pressure of a fire hose at the back of the pan, in the way only a young man who's never heard the phrase 'prostate the size of a grapefruit' can.

Bloody hell! Now I know where Liam gets his slapdash attitude to hygiene from.

Me.

Putting the toilet seat down, young Adam then sets to swilling water around the washbasin and clawing toothpaste marks off with his fingernails. Because, sure, why use actual cleaning products when you can use your own body instead?

Adam feeling tipsy means *I* feel tipsy, but even weirder, another part of me feels stone cold sober. Like I'm Schrödinger's barfly or something.

Humming along to this year's ubiquitous Lightning Seeds' '3 Lions '98' football World Cup anthem that's started playing on the radio, Adam checks his reflection in the mirror – a strong Operation Desert Storm look, to say the least, consisting of a buzz cut, tan Timberlands, dark khaki jeans and an untucked military desert shirt. Only offset by a *South Park* T-shirt advertising Chef's Chocolate Salty Balls.

'Yeah, yeah, cos you're drop dead gorgeous,' teases Jules, looming into the reflection as she kisses him on the back of the neck.

His Jules. So young she blows my mind. But, yep, the feeling is mutual. Because, wow. Just seeing her is still enough to give Adam a start too. Like he's somehow still noticing her afresh. Even after it being – what? – a full three years now since they first moved into this little flat of theirs.

But while I don't remember the last time I looked at my Jules this way and I definitely like having my own space in the shed, Adam here still delights in feeling like they're a crew of two on a tiny boat in the middle of their own private sea. A feeling that's clearly mutual, because even though they've both got better jobs now – with her sous cheffing at the Grand and him working over at BeJewel Games as a junior narrative producer – not once have they talked about moving.

'What?' she asks, pushing her hand back through her Liv Tyler-esque, layered hair.

'Nothing. Just . . . you look perfect,' he says, running his eyes over her cornflower-blue dress, before pulling her into a smoky hot kiss.

Jules pulls back with a grin.

'Uh-uh. No time for that now.' Slapping a bottle of bleach and a toilet brush into his hands, she quickly pencils in her eyeliner. 'I swear it's getting bigger,' she says, glancing up.

She means the crack in the ceiling, which – bloody hell, now I remember – is destined to collapse this very night, showering plasterboard down onto Dave Scragg and Joy Chen, who'll be right in the middle of having a cheeky quickie.

I'm tempted to impose myself. To save them from their impending humiliation. But I stop myself just in time. Because of our rule. But also because, come on, Dave and Joy, who even *does* that anyway, right?

Bathroom done, Young Adam answers the front door to Young

Doodles – an even bigger hairball back then – who hurries in and starts setting up his decks. Adam heads through to the kitchen to help. Upending three bags of Doritos, Wotsits and Pickled Onion Monster Munch into a wok, he carefully balances it on the arm of the living-room sofa.

'Adam, what the hell?' Jules demands, spotting the wok, as well as Adam's *pièce de résistance*, a cereal bowl of Heinz tomato sauce, dead centre on the TV's glass table. 'Is that ketchup?'

'Yeah, for dipping,' he explains.

Only then he sees that she and her fellow hotel chef, Sabita, have been laying out their own offerings on the kitchen table – herb-spiced mixed nuts, beetroot hummus, pesto chicken meatballs and curried mango salad with endives.

'See?' she tells him. 'Better.'

Dumbly, he nods. Like a primitive man being presented with the wheel.

Christ. Was I really this unformed? Why *is* she with him? But then, am I really any more sophisticated now? In fact, shit, when did we even last have a party? Jules's fortieth? Over ten years ago. Blimey, has it really been that long?

Beating a hasty retreat, Adam stations himself by the front door as a steady stream of guests starts to arrive – his, mainly computer nerds; hers, art-school kids and chefs.

'I still can't believe you're actually going to do it,' Darius tells him ten minutes later, over the house beats thumping out from where Doodles is hunched over his decks.

Darius is dressed in the same wire specs, MOR jeans, white T-shirt and clumpy, blue-striped Reebok striders he invariably wore back then, looking like he's been teleported in from the eighties and would rather be in a coding meeting.

What are you talking about? I want to ask him. Only then I *know*. Because, suddenly, it's flashing neon right here inside Adam's mind. The ring in his pocket. And, of course, that's why *my* Jules was laughing back in the shed just now when she said 'Yeah, sure' about me forgetting this party. Because tonight's the night I asked her to marry me. It's *that* party. This is *it*.

Only right now, the only person Adam's confided in about his plans is his best mate.

'And you're still sure?' Darius asks, but like he's not a hundred per cent convinced that Adam should go through with this.

'Positive,' Adam says. Even though he's sick with nerves at the prospect of Jules saying no, he's planning on asking her tomorrow down on the beach where they first kissed and has only got the ring here in his pocket tonight to keep it safe.

'Yeah, well, what would I know?' Darius grins. 'I'm still living with my mum.'

Even though Adam knows his best pal is being self-deprecating, he feels bad for him, because Darius has never got close to finding his own Jules. In fact, he's never dated anyone for longer than a month.

'Anyone here you want me to, er, introduce you to?' Adam asks.

Darius rolls his eyes, glancing across at the fashionably attired Young Ngozi who's artily adjusting an old Kodak photo projector that's beaming random snaps up onto the wall, but she doesn't even register Darius or anyone else here. And me, I now know why. It's because she's already having a love affair with hotshot banker Geoff up in London. An affair that will eventually turn serious, but then Ngozi always seems to get what she wants.

'I don't think I'm quite cool enough,' he says.

'It's just clothes,' Adam says. 'Haircuts.'

'Easy for you to say. Jules has taught you all that.'

Taught you. Adam can't help picking up on his friend's choice of words. Like his life here with Jules is simply some code that Darius hasn't yet hacked. That it's only Jules who's made Adam who he now is. But then maybe that's true? I can't help wondering. Being back here, it's impossible to miss how much hipper than me she was. I mean, just look at her. Now holding a joint-rolling masterclass in the kitchen and making everyone laugh. Something else I guess I forgot.

'Just go and say hi,' Adam tells his friend, nodding back at Sabita who's now joined Ngozi. 'Go on, you're a smart, funny, good-looking guy.'

But something still holds him back.

'Do us a favour, will you?' Adam ends up asking Doodles a few minutes later instead, once Darius has retreated into the corridor to talk to James Peters and Ru Savage, two other nerdy guys they used to play *Dungeons & Dragons* with at school.

'What?' Doodles pushes his long Foo Fighters hair to one side.

'Can you teach Darius?'

'What, *this*?' Draining his lemon Hooch, Doodles stares down at his decks. 'But he's such a – and no offence, man, because I know you two go way back – dweeb. I mean, does he even know what acid techno is?'

'Um, sure,' Adam lies, not having a clue himself. 'I mean, doesn't everyone?'

He holds Doodles' stare. Confidently. Has to. For his friend.

'OK,' Doodles finally capitulates, 'but later, when people are more wasted.'

Over the next twenty minutes, the party gets fuller and fuller and louder and louder, until it's buzzing and every bit as good as I'd hoped. Soon I'm loving it every bit as much as Adam, relishing every acrid swig of strawberry Bacardi Breezer and drag of his spliff, and surfing off him feeling so young with his whole life ahead of him, and no mortgage, no responsibilities – and nothing to do tonight except take Jules's hand and dance . . .

Oh, except for what's coming, of course. For what he's going to ask her. Only maybe I won't even be here to witness that, because how much of my time here is already gone?

Then I get my answer. Exactly half.

'Look, I made you a new tape,' Jules says, pointing to where it's propped up on the mantelpiece. *Flat Party 1998*. 'Only it's a bit old school for Doodles here to use tonight.'

'Cool,' Adam says, picking it up and looking at the tracks. 'You got some corkers on here. We'll play it in a bit,' he says, smiling and kissing her, before noticing Darius is on his own again.

He goes over. 'Hey, Doodles wants you to take a turn,' he shouts into Darius's ear.

'At what?'

'The decks. And don't pretend you don't want to. I've seen you looking.'

True, because as with any bit of techie kit, Darius's eyes have been drawn to the decks like ball bearings to a magnet. No way is Adam letting him wriggle out of it either, because he knows this is his way to give Darius a shot of that cool his best friend so clearly feels he lacks.

'But I can't . . .'

'*Won't*, more like. You can do anything you want, Darius. You're a bloody genius, remember? An IQ higher than the sun. Go on. Try it. What's wrong with taking a bit of a risk?'

For a second Adam panics that he's pushed him too far. But next thing, Doodles and Darius are hunched over the decks together . . . and then, ten minutes later, Darius has got a pair of earphones clamped to his head, with his glasses half steamed up, and is already looking like – well, not like he feels he belongs, not yet, but not like he totally doesn't either, as everyone starts chanting along to Fat Boy Slim's 'The Rockafeller Skank'.

Darius . . . who'll DJ at my wedding in two years' time, where he'll also be my best man, playing 'All the Daze', by Troubadours d'Amour as our first song . . .

Adam's so happy to see him like this . . . but me, I feel this nip of bitterness rising up inside me, because *I*'m the one who launched him, aren't I? *I* launched Darius Angelopoulos out into the world – onto fortune and fame – and I got nothing back.

But then Jules and Adam are dancing like they just can't stop and I'm swept up in it too, loving every precious second as the time flies by . . . until, suddenly, Jules is dragging Adam away, up onto their flat's secluded little roof terrace for some fresh air, while down below, a mix of 'Gettin' Jiggy Wit It' by Will Smith is belting out and Adam can't help but grin, thinking it's probably Darius playing it.

But not like I'm now grinning inside. *Me*, who suddenly realises *what* is coming next.

'Good party?' she asks.

'The best. I don't want it to ever end. I don't want –' But he stops himself.

'What?'

Brave. Be brave, he's telling himself – because the ring, it's calling to him like he's Bilbo bloody Baggins. 'I don't want *us* to ever end,' he finally spits it out, 'because I . . . I . . .'

Go on, do it! I think.

'You?' Her blue eyes are staring hard into his.

'. . . I love you,' he says.

'Well, thank God for that,' she laughs. 'Because I love you too.'

'No, I don't just mean the words,' he says, because of course they've said them many times before. 'Or even the feeling that goes with them. More . . . everything else that might go with it too . . . The future that I want to spend with you.' And now he's found the words, he can't stop. 'And all this . . .' he says, grinning, throwing his arms outwards to encompass the entire starry sky, '. . . everything this whole wide world has to offer. I want us to share it all. To go travelling. And live crazy places. And live crazy bloody lives.'

'Me too,' she squeals. 'Like I did in Paris!' And it's like he's pulled a cork out of a bottle, because she can't stop grinning too.

'So let's make it happen,' he says. A drunken declaration. 'No matter what.'

And then he's laughing. Because he's high. And because she is too, on spliffs and on life.

But I'm not laughing. Because it was *me*, I put the idea of moving abroad into Jules's head.

Meaning it was because of *me* that Mum and Dad drove us to Gatwick Airport that day. It was *me* who caused them to crash . . .

But before I can think about changing what he's just said, Adam reaches into his pocket, nerves yo-yoing up and down inside him, like he's about to be sick. And, *whoa*, here it comes . . . He's getting down on one knee and fumbling with the little black box and finally popping its lid – panicking that this ring's not big enough or expensive enough to prove his commitment to her, this woman he loves with all his heart . . .

She beams the second she sees it and even as he starts to say, 'Jules, will you –' she's already answering, 'Yes, yes, yes, yes!' and kneeling down in front of him. As he slips the ring onto her engagement finger, she holds it up to the stars.

Then they're kissing, not stopping. Like they're each other's oxygen.

Until *WHOOOOOMPH!* They feel it like a bomb going off beneath them. *What the hell?* Adam thinks.

But I already know.

As he jumps up and rushes over to the ladder that leads down through the hatch into the corridor below, I hear that rising rushing sound.

And as the jeers start up below, and everyone crowds round the bathroom door to stare in at poor Dave and Joy grabbing for their discarded clothes, half buried in plaster, I catch sight of the nearby clock tower of St Nicholas's Church and see that I've already been here an hour and a half – and, before I can even look back at Jules for just one more precious time, I'm sucked back down into that crazy kaleidoscopic whirlwind again . . .

I wake in the shed, blinking into the light, to see Jules holding my hands. *My* Jules. Not the 1998 twenty-six-year-old Jules who Adam just asked to marry and said he wanted to move abroad with. Not the Jules who was just trying to kiss my face off under that twinkling, starry sky.

That kiss I can still taste . . . only it's *my* Jules I'm looking at now. Looking at the way Young Adam looked at his Jules in the bathroom – noticing her and being amazed.

And it's my Jules I want to kiss. The woman I've been married to for twenty-five years, who's taking my breath away all over again. Quickly leaning forward, I do. Softly.

But then it's not just noticing, it's wanting, and I can see it in her eyes . . . she's feeling this too. Then we're doing it. Tearing off each other's clothes and having wild, hungry, animal sex.

I don't care if she's thinking about me then, or me now. Or whether this is the me who got better at sex sooner, or some new version of me that I don't yet understand. Because it's all one. We're one. Until we collapse back onto the dusty shed floor in a shivering heap.

'Wow,' she pants, putting up her hand for a high five – because sex like that *deserves* a high five.

'Wow, indeed.' I glance across at the pocket of my discarded jeans. Thinking of – what? The ring Adam had inside his combats back in '98? No. It's his cigarettes I'm craving. Like that want has somehow followed me back here too.

That *need*.

'So what brought that on?' Jules asks.

'You,' I tell her.

'*Me*?' Her eyes narrow. 'Me now? Or then?'

'Both,' I say, because why lie? She's already guessed. But instead of calling me a hypocrite, she smiles. 'What?' I ask.

'Getting tangled up like this . . . in this freaky interdimensional horniness, it is kind of weird, isn't it? But in a really, really good way,' she quickly adds, taking my hand.

No denying that.

'It's like . . .' I press her engagement ring to my lips, '. . . being back there with you, at the start of us, it's like –' I hesitate, wanting to find the right words – 'it woke up those same feelings inside me. Feelings that must have got buried over the years.'

'Buried by all the shit.'

'The shit?'

'You know,' she says, 'the million and one things about getting older, about parenting, being married, that make you feel un-horny. That make you forget the whole reason you got together in the first place.'

'Right. Only now all that early wonder, it's like it's just been jump-started.' Although, if anything, this is an understatement. Because now I just want to hold her. To hold her and be held. To not let go.

'Then maybe *that's* what *this* is,' she says.

'What do you mean?'

'Maybe this whole multiverse time travel thing isn't just about re-experiencing the past. Maybe it's also about using those experiences to fix the present . . .'

Said like there are still more things that need fixing.

'Maybe. But so long as we're only learning from the past,' I remind her. 'Not actually going back there to change things here just because we can.'

'And you didn't, did you?' she checks.

'Nope. You still look like you.' I glance in the mirror. 'I still look like me.' But even as I say it, it occurs to me that this is not necessarily the same timeline, either, is it? Because me piggybacking on younger me kissing Jules back in '98 has led to us having sex tonight. We're only stark bollock naked right now because of that. Meaning maybe the future of this timeline *has* already been affected, because who knows how this will affect us from here on in?

Again, I notice that sparkle in her eyes, but what if it's not just for me, but for the old *us*? What if it's just more wanting to go back again? The sparkle of being hooked?

Only then someone's knocking at the shed door and rattling the handle, but thank God it's locked, because it's Liam's voice outside, asking to be let in because he's forgotten his house keys, as Jules and I frantically scrabble around to pull on our clothes.

Friday afternoon, four o'clock, I'm signing in at the muskily perfumed reception of the swanky Soho House private members' club that opened a few years ago on the seafront.

Walking upstairs past the slick artwork, my self-consciousness grows. I've come fresh from the office and am wearing a pair of dusty old Nikes, sawn-off jeans, and a coffee-stained T-shirt bearing the legend 'Off My Tits on Aperol Spritz'.

But Darius just smiles when he waves me over to where he's sitting out on the sunlit terrace overlooking the sea.

'Ads, good to see you. Grab a pew. What would you like?' He orders us a couple of beers. 'So what do you think?' he asks, flipping an iPad round to face me.

It's a new logo for Quark Studios, with the word 'Quark' aligned vertically with an 'S' printed behind it. All in the shape of what looks like a space rocket. Or maybe an ice lolly. Or even a dick.

'Oh, I don't know much about that sort of thing,' I hedge.

'No, I suppose not,' he agrees.

Ironic. Considering that it was me who first came up with the name of the sodding company that he's just made millions out of. But I keep the thought to myself. Because my team has tasked me with something much more important.

'But on the subject of work . . .' I say. 'Any thoughts about . . . future directions, regarding employee sustainability?' I fudge.

'Wow. Get you with the management speak.' Darius grins. 'And there was me hearing that you'd long since turned down the opportunity of climbing that greasy pole yourself.'

Someone must have told him about me passing on that promotion, when I stepped back to help out with the kids.

'I was thinking of the rest of my team,' I say. 'Doodles, obviously. But Kylie, Greg, Meredith, and the other guys too.'

'Ah, yes. Meredith Peterson. I hear she's got promise. In fact, she's working on a report for the board.'

The first I've heard of it.

'But enough shop talk,' he says. 'I'm sure everyone will be taken care of and, like I told you. I've got your back.' He smiles. 'Just like you had mine when we were younger.' He prods me playfully in the arm. 'Always including me in the cool shit.'

He can't possibly mean him DJing at that party, can he? No way, because how the hell would he remember, even though I've not been able to stop thinking about it all week? The same as I've not been able to stop thinking about Jules naked in the shed. We've already done it three times since. Another thing that's been jumpstarted, it seems.

'But we were best friends,' I point out. 'Who else was I going to include?'

Were. Oops. Not sure where that came from. Too late to correct it now and way too obvious a slip for someone as smart as Darius to have missed. Or maybe he thinks it too, after all these years apart?

'True,' he says. 'Sometimes old friendships are the most powerful things we've got.'

I chuckle. 'Sounds like something out of one of those crappy old self-motivation books you used to read.'

'*Still* read. In fact, I gave Nelly a new one this morning at work. Giles Wheatley's *Luck is a River, So Let's Fish*.' He smiles.

Well, consider me prompted. 'Ah, yes. Thanks. Again,' I say. 'For giving her the office space.'

'Not that she needs my encouragement.' He smiles even wider. 'A real grafter, that one. Impressive. Reminds me of myself when I got the bit between my teeth.'

'Yeah, but she's still young,' I find myself pushing back. 'It's not necessarily a good thing to be overly ambitious at that age, is it?' Bloody hell, the second the words are out of my mouth, I realise I'm pretty much quoting Jules from our argument about Liam last week. But *do* I want my daughter being as one-track-minded as Darius? Because even if he has made all the money, he's missed out on so many other things too.

'That might work for you, Adam,' he says, 'but she's different. She's got real fire.'

Meaning that I *haven't*?

'Yeah, but life's not just about ambition,' I double down. 'Or winning, or –' I find myself staring at his Rolex, which has got to be worth at least twenty grand – 'stuff . . .'

'Of course not. But you've got to admit that one of the perks of winning is that you *do* sometimes get to have more fun.'

I notice another smile tweaking at the corners of his mouth. 'What do you mean?'

'Troubadours d'Amour,' he says, laying on a phoney French accent.

'Huh?'

'You know, our favourite band.'

Our. He means mine and his, but it's actually mine and Jules's. Who we've seen ten times and I even know the drummer of well enough to have an occasional drink with him when he's in the Lion & Lobster.

'What about them?'

He reaches into his shirt pocket before waggling three sparkly, old-school tickets at me.

'They're playing in town in a few months. Opening night of their final reunion tour. As part of some festival.'

'I know.,' I say.

'I got us tickets. You, me and Jules.'

'But . . . but it's our wedding anniversary,' I say. Not something I'd normally give a monkey's about, seeing as we've never made much of a deal about it. But this one's different. Our twenty-fifth. Especially considering how flat things have been between us – well, before the shed.

'Oh, OK.' His face clouds, but for just a second. 'I did check with Jules and she OK'd it this morning,' he says.

Huh. Something she didn't bother mentioning to me. 'Right, well, it's just . . . I've already got us tickets too,' I explain. 'For me and Jules. As a surprise.'

He grimaces. 'Oh, shit, man, the last thing I wanted to do was tread on your toes.' He gives his tongue a little click. 'That said, these tickets *are* from this special VIP access site and include backstage passes, see?' He waggles them closer. 'But forget it, you're right, it's just *stuff*.' *Stuff* – said dismissively, like I said it before. 'Yeah, forget it,' he continues, even though he's clearly disappointed, 'I can always just give them to somebody else.'

Leaving me feeling bad, especially after he's gone to all this effort. Yeah, turning them down would be totally churlish, right?

'No,' I tell him. 'Let's do this. The three of us. We'll go together. Yeah. It'll be cool.'

'OK, phew.' He looks genuinely relieved. 'So some *stuff* can be good.' He smiles.

Too late, I see what he's done. How he's twisted what I said earlier so he gets a win.

Or maybe that's just in my head?

Come six o'clock, Doodles has taken the back panel off the Sony and is examining the wiring, while Spandau Ballet's 'True' is playing on Radio X on my phone. It's the first time I've been able to get him over since we discovered the machine.

I'm on tenterhooks, itching to see what he finds. Because Big D's got to find *something*, right? Something different about this machine. Something *technical* that can explain how this is happening, something beyond just 'magic', like Jules thinks.

'I'll be honest with you, Adman,' he finally says, scratching his arse crevice with his screwdriver. 'The only unusual thing about this antiquity is that it's still working at all.'

'You're positive? A hundred per cent? There's really nothing odd about it?'

'Yeah. It's like I said. Sony was just making music for the masses with models like this.. Which isn't to say you won't get any bids,' he quickly adds.

He means when I put it up for sale on eBay. The lie I told him to get him to come over and check it out for me before we head down the pub to meet up with the rest of our team for our usual end-of week-drink – only not so *usual* this week, of course, because the company we all work for has just been sold.

'OK.' I force a smile, but it's almost impossible to hide the disappointment in my voice.

'Not that I think you even should,' he says, wiping the dust off his favourite LCD Soundsystem hoodie.

'No?'

'Well, it's still in such good condition, why would you? I mean, you love all this old shit, don't you?' He nods across at the shelves of vinyls and at the box full of mixtapes and CDs.

'Yeah, I guess.'

My phone rings. Meredith's name flashes up on the screen, giving me that same *jolt* of connection I felt at Darius's party. That same jolt that used to exclusively belong to Jules.

'I'm just going to take this outside,' I say.

'Yeah, sure, whatever, bro,' Doodles says, already starting to screw the Sony's back panel on.

Stepping out into the sunshine, I quickly walk away from the shed, out of earshot, before glancing over at the living-room window, where I spot Jules and the kids laughing at something on TV.

'Hi,' I answer tentatively – because me and Meredith don't speak much on the phone.

'So, you guys still coming to the pub, or what?' she asks.

'Um, sure,' I say.

'Good, because they need you, Adam. We all do. Everyone's feeling a little lost, a bit shocked.'

I feel my chest kind of puff out a little at hearing this. That maybe I'm not just their boss, but something more. And not just to them, to her. But then I glimpse Jules inside again and feel this splinter of guilt. Even though I'm not actually doing anything wrong, am I? But then why does it feel so wrong?

Only then my heart stutters, hearing the opening bars of 'Seven Nation Army', by the White Stripes, thudding out of the shed. A 2003 classic that can only be from one of those tapes or CDs.

Doodles.

Christ. He must have just put it on.

'Shit, I gotta go.'

Heart pounding, cutting her off, I run back into the shed. Expecting what? To find Doodles frozen stiff with *Exorcist* eyes?

For a second, I *do* fear the worst as I spot him standing motionless in front of the Sony.

But then he turns to me and grins, blowing out a long plume of weed smoke.

'Why you looking at me like that?' he says.

'Um. Well. I . . . I just didn't have you down as a rock fan, that's all.'

'Hey, as digitally orientated as I am, I'm still allowed to dig Jack and Meg.'

'Yeah, sure. Of course,' I mutter, the words hardly coming out, my mind already racing again. Because it means that Jules is right about this too. Whatever this is, it really *is* personal.

This crazy machine of ours only does seem to work for *us*.

'And these are all yours and Jules's, huh?' Doodles says, scooping his hand through the tapes and CDs. 'Sweet. Only it all kind of died out with streaming, didn't it? Like these days most people wouldn't have the equipment left to make a new one even if they wanted,' he adds wistfully.

'Wuh? What did you just say?'

'How not everyone's got the equipment –'

'Yes.' Oh my God. But I do, don't I? I mean, if I wanted to, I *could* . . .

His Apple Watch tings. 'Kylie,' he says. 'She says they're moving to a table up on the roof terrace.'

'Um, you know what?. I think I might catch you up. There's something I need to do first.'

As soon as I've waved him off, I scuttle straight back to the shed. What if he's right? What if I *can* make more mixtapes? New ones that will allow us to travel back in time. That will allow us to continue all this even after we've burned through the others.

It takes me an age to find a blank tape among all the clutter. It's a weird one too, a ten-minute tape. Something Dad must have bought, for God only knows what. Jamming it into the machine, I eye the red 'Record' button.

But what songs? Obviously, something Jules would genuinely like, because that was always the point, wasn't it? But scrolling through my latest Spotify playlists, I can't find anything new she'd even know. Jesus. When did that happen? We always used to get into pretty much everything at the same time.

Then I find something. An old album. A vinyl. One we used to play together. Putting it on, I hit record on the tape.

Ten minutes later, I head inside to search for Jules. I end up following the sound of laughter to where she's still in the living room with the kids. Our old video tapes from way back when are scattered across the rug.

'Rewind. Show Dad,' says Liam, grinning up at me from where he's sitting cross-legged on the floor, wearing a Resident records black beanie

Dad. Said with real enthusiasm. Like he's not said it in quite a while.

Jules rewinds whatever they've been watching. A short clip of him and Nelly rolling around on the grass on a picnic in St Ann's Well Gardens. Christ, what I wouldn't give to go back there just for a –

Only then I see what Jules is doing. She's looking to see where she wants to travel back to next.

'We were just remembering all the happy times,' she says, smiling across at me.

Scanning the years on the tape spines, I see there's not one from any time more recent than a decade and half ago. Why? Because that's when all the happy times were?

'Argh, Mum. The dog's farted,' Liam says, quickly moving away from where Groucho's lying by his side.

'Oh, gross,' Jules says.

As Groucho slinks guiltily off out into the garden, and the kids continue to howl with laughter at the TV, I beckon Jules into the hall, where they won't be able to hear.

'Here,' I tell her, handing over the tape I've just made her. 'It's a new one.'

'What do you mean?'

'I recorded it for you. It's just a couple of songs long.'

She looks down at the words I've written on it. *Saturday Lift-Off.* As in tomorrow. When we're next planning to travel back.

'But why?' she asks.

'Because there's a finite number of mixtapes and CDs left in the box and we're getting through them fast. Don't you think it would be nice to find out if we can make more?'

'Damn right. Oh, and what about Doodles? He find anything weird about the machine?'

'Nothing.'

She nods, like she thought as much.

'He also put a tape on.'

'*What?*' She looks aghast.

'I know. I didn't mean him to. But he did.'

'And?'

'Nothing happened to him. Not like it does to us.'

'I knew it.' That grin again. 'This *is* just for us.' She focuses back on the tape I've just given her. 'But won't this just bring me back to –'

'Today,' I say. 'To now, to when it was given to you. Or just a few minutes before, I guess.'

Nelly shrieks with laughter, calling Jules back in.

'Did you notice she's home on time and isn't on her phone to her boss?' she says. 'She's even going out with Eva and some of her old school gang again tonight.'

I'm glad. Truly. Even if this might be down to Darius offering her that office space. Even if it's a problem I wish I'd been able to solve myself.

My phone *tings* again and I walk through to the kitchen to check it. A message from Meredith, and again I feel it – that *jolt*.

Aw, so you DID turn up, after all . . . it reads when I open it.

There's a photo attached. Of her and Doodles standing by the upstairs bar in the Lion & Lobster, both grinning. But I still don't get it. Only then I see the beer tap on the bar between them. A guest ale called Outback. With a plump little cuddly koala staring out from its tap.

Chapter Nine

Jules – 'Hey Ya'

'Oh, for feck's sake! Come on, you donkey!'

Rose leans on the bar, shouting at the wall-mounted TV. Eddy, who works at the solicitors' office next door, and has a soft spot for Rose, is in for his Saturday pint at the Peregrine. He takes a sip, catching my eye over the top of his glass, as I stand in the doorway, waiting to say goodbye.

The Royal Ascot races are always her favourite. After reading the runners and riders to me this morning to see which ones had astral or otherwise potentially lucky significance for either of us, Rose urged me to put money on her declared 'sure-fire winner', Danny Boy.

Like always, I declined. I'm not a gambler, especially after what happened to Adam's dad. I'm too long in the tooth to bet on something with so many variables, despite Rose's purported clairvoyant skills. Plus, I'm skint. That terrifying credit card bill seems to throb through my every waking thought.

In any case, I couldn't spare the time to leave the kitchen. This catering job that Darius has lined up has put me in a flat-spin panic and I've been practising a few classic dishes, but my confidence is at an all-time low.

Last night I made a boeuf bourguignon from scratch, but it had practically evaporated by the time I served it, and the gobbets of expensive meat left over tasted like shoe leather. Even Groucho Barx turned his nose up, which technically made it *worse* than a dog's dinner.

'Come on . . . come *on* . . .' Rose is properly bellowing now.

Her fist is up. 'You're nearly there, just do it,' she yells, as if the jockey can hear. The commentator's voice crescendoes to a fever pitch as the horses cross the line.

'And Carpe Diem clinches it by a hair,' the guy on the TV shouts.

'Carpe Diem, my arse,' Rose says, shaking her head and screwing up her betting slip.

She looks down at the *Daily Mail*'s sports section spread open on the tarnished brass bar. 'Pah. Twenty to one. Someone's made out like a bandit.'

The commentator's voice decreases in pitch and speed as the losers cross the line, but Rose petulantly points the remote at the TV and snaps it off.

'Ach, well,' Eddy says sympathetically. 'Better luck next time.'

Rose gives him a snide look, but he shoots her a twinkly smile and she softens.

'You off then?' she says, noticing me in the doorway.

'Yes. Oh, I left that stock in the fridge. I'll use it on Monday.'

'Doing anything fun?' she asks.

I can't meet her eye. Is this what it feels like to have an affair? What I'm doing with Adam does feel *so* illicit. For a second, I want to be glib. To tell her about our plan to spend the afternoon in the shed . . . *time travelling*. But, obviously, I can't.

'Oh, just, you know, sorting stuff out. With Adam.'

She nods as if this is a veiled reference to some kind of therapy and I want to tell her that it's not. Though come to think of it, I'm probably enjoying the best form of relationship therapy known to man. I mean, can it really only be a week since Darius's party? We've had more sex since then than in the last six months. And, dare I say it, we're connecting more and more on a day-to-day level too.

'Well, say hi to him for me,' she says.

'Will do.'

Back at home, with Nelly out on a walk in South Downs national park with Eva, and Liam on his way to London to pick up an amp, the house is quiet and I hurry inside to find Adam. As I pass the downstairs loo – the one only Adam and Liam use – I notice the loo seat is *down*.

Another little 'time kink' that I've noticed being played out, but one so small I can't see the point in mentioning it to Adam now.

'You're back. Great. Anything for a darks' wash?' he asks, stepping up behind me. He's holding a plastic washing tub, filled with a jumble of our dirty clothes. 'What?' he asks.

'Er . . . nothing.'

Because of course . . . this is another new memory I'm still getting used to. Adam always doing the washing on a Saturday afternoon, because of how I acquainted him with the dirty washing basket in 1995.

Laughing, I step towards him and kiss him, before leading him upstairs to bed by his jeans belt.

'Hey. Steady on,' he says, but he's grinning, as we strip off each other's clothes. And I can't help feeling how easy this is. To instigate sex now, and not just because the house is free, but because . . . well, because we're suddenly back in the habit. Like when we were young. That's the thing about habits, I realise. You break them, but you can make them again, too.

Afterwards, we lie on the bed smiling at each other. 'So?' he asks. 'You ready?'

'You bet.'

I gather crisps and dips and a bottle of red plonk for the shed. As if we're off on a jolly picnic, like we used to do at weekends.

Once we're settled inside the shed with the door locked, Adam holds up the tape he gave me yesterday, mock-trumpeting a fanfare, as he hands it over.

There's no writing on it like the others. It clearly isn't infused with any of our history and wasn't made with the hours of dedication and love that the other tapes were, which we both now agree might be a possible explanation as to why they have so much power. This one might not work at all.

'What did you put on it?' I ask, as he nods me towards the Sony to insert it.

'Stuff I thought you'd like. The Troubs' first album. Oh, and by the way, Darius told me about the tickets for their gig. Said he'd cleared it with you.'

'Yeah. He texted.'

'You know, I was going to take you anyway. For our anniversary.'

'Were you?' I can't help sounding surprised. Over the years Adam has tended to be ironic about our anniversary, usually getting me last-minute crappy flowers and an even crappier card.

'Yeah.'

From the way he says it, I'm suddenly annoyed that I let Darius muscle in, because while I don't need a fuss, I'm also too old to be ironic about our anniversaries any more. After twenty-five years, I *do* want it to mean something. Something special, just for us.

Maybe that's what this crazy time-warp travelling back through the years is, though. Maybe this has been sent to us as our own chance for a recap and a regroup. It certainly seems to be working, because I do feel closer to Adam than I have done for months . . . even years.

'OK, so this is just a mini tape. Ten minutes,' he reminds me. 'Meaning, if my theory's right, you should go back to yesterday, to five minutes before I gave it to you.'

He means when I was with Liam and Nelly looking at those old video tapes. The ones I hated seeing myself in, embarrassed by how I bossily pestered the kids to turn round for the camera. And sweet and adorable as the kids were, I wished I'd also filmed our friends, or Adam's parents and my mum who were so often there too.

'Ready?' Adam asks. 'But remember – change nothing . . .'

I roll my eyes at his schoolteacherly tone. 'Yeah, yeah.'

'See you in ten, then,' he grins, and I hit 'Play'.

The Troubs start singing.

'Oh, I love this one,' I reflexively start to say.

Next thing . . . *KRAASSSZZZZATTAK* . . . I'm bursting back out of the storm to find myself standing in front of the TV next to Nelly and Liam, a load of old video tapes strewn around us.

Yesterday.

It's spookily weird. Even weirder than going back further. Like a whopping double dose of déjà vu.

But whereas déjà vu ends after a few seconds, this just carries on . . . and on . . .

And just as happened yesterday . . . because this *is* yesterday . . . after five minutes, Adam appears in the doorway, and Liam and Nelly and I – well, Yesterday Jules, with me now riding inside her – stop laughing.

'Rewind. Show Dad,' Liam says.

Jules dutifully does, rewinding the tape and then showing him the footage he took of baby Liam and Nelly as a toddler in St Ann's Well Gardens.

'We were just remembering all the happy times,' Jules says, smiling across at him.

But he's looking down at the tapes in a strange way.

'Argh, Mum. The dog's farted,' Liam says, quickly rolling away from where Groucho's lying on his side.

'Oh, gross,' Jules says. A tad harsh, this, retrospectively, because I remember that one was actually me.

As Groucho slinks off into the garden, unjustly condemned, and the kids continue to laugh at the TV, Adam beckons Jules into the hall.

But it all just feels too recent, like he's acting. I want to tap his forehead with my finger and shout, 'Adam, you bellend. It's me.'

Too late. He's already talking, handing over the new tape he's made and telling her about Doodles finding nothing unusual about the old Sony.

'I knew it.' I feel her grin. 'This *is* just for us.' Then she's looking back down at the tape he's just given her. 'But won't this just bring me back to –'

'Today,' he says. 'To now, to when it was given to you. Or just a few minutes before, I guess.'

The whole thing is so absurd, so ridiculous, that I – *me*, Tomorrow Me, or whatever the hell I now am – can't help imposing myself on Yesterday Me and hissing right into his ear, 'But I already *am* back.'

Nelly shrieks, calling Jules back in. But I keep my grip tight on this other me. Keep in control.

Adam takes a sharp breath.

'Seriously?' He peers at me. 'Jules? I mean, er . . . Future Jules?'

'I think I prefer Tomorrow Jules, actually. More Marvel Universe, don't you think?' I make Jules say.

His phone *tings*, but he ignores it. 'Is that *really* you?' he says, still staring hard into my eyes.

'Yes.' Still in control. And grinning. Just from the sheer what-the-actual-fuckery madness of it all.

Adam is grinning too. Like we're a couple of naughty schoolkids who've just broken a rule. A big bloody rule. The biggest. Together. Which we have. And *still* are.

'So it works.' He laughs, before shushing me, us, both of us, and steering us further down the corridor away from the kids. 'We really can make new tapes, then?'

'But only to go back to whenever we handed them over,' I get Jules to remind him. 'Which means,' I work out, 'that if you make another one tomorrow, then in the future, say, like ten years from now, we can travel back to this weekend again.'

And while the thought of inventing a time machine just to transport me back to this otherwise pretty dull period in my pretty dull life might have once been a turn-off . . . that's all changed now we have the machine. Plus, I can imagine it now from their perspective – the older us we'll become. I bet, for them, coming back here will be a trip. To our middle years. With the kids still at home. And Adam and I starting to get on again. To all this stuff I've taken so much for granted until now.

Equally, I can feel Yesterday Me becoming confused. Like she's headachy, not quite sure what's going on. But I keep my grip on her, distracted by the smell of the boeuf bourguignon.

As I walk her through to the kitchen, and Adam follows with his eyes dancing, I can sense my yesterday thoughts – about the credit card bill and the cheffing gig Darius has offered – but then suddenly my nostrils twitch –

Oh my God. Of course! The boeuf bourguignon.

Without thinking, I surreptitiously back Jules up against the cooker.

Adam's looking at me strangely. 'Jules? Tomorrow Jules? Are you still here?'

It's hilarious, but he's actually whispering.

'Yeah,' I get Jules to tell him.

'OK, but we really shouldn't talk any more,' he says, a look of sudden panic on his face, 'because the more we do, the more we might risk changing something.'

'I completely agree,' I tell him, but behind me, without him noticing, I get Jules to turn the oven down.

I know it's wrong to change what happened to the incinerated supper . . . *potentially*. But this was only yesterday. It's only a tiny weeny thing and surely worth the risk?

'Seriously. You should stop imposing yourself now,' Adam says.

'Doing it,' I say, throwing in the kind of cutesy little sign-off salute I imagine Lieutenant Uhura or whatever her name was on *Star Trek* might use.

I pull back. I cede control to my still blissfully unaware yesterday self. Then she's moving – go, girl, all by herself! – turning slowly round and looking at Adam and around the kitchen as if she doesn't know why she's here.

'What?' she says. 'Why are you staring at me like that?' she asks him.

'Oh, nothing. Nothing.' He checks the clock on the wall, maybe thinking my ten minutes is up.

Jules walks over to the mirror and stares into it, examining her wrinkles, with obvious dissatisfaction registering on her tired face. I remember how I did this myself yesterday after watching my younger self on those videos, wanting to masochistically prove to myself how much I'd aged.

Wow. *I'm so mean to myself.*

It's only now that I'm re-experiencing it again that it dawns on me how self-critical my internal rhetoric is. How judgy. As if I'm somehow purposefully failing to change my appearance for the better. As if somewhere out there there's a perfect Jules with fewer wrinkles and a youthful glow.

Except here's the thing: yesterday I was the youngest I'll ever be.

This simple fact feels like a huge epiphany.

For the first time in my whole adult life, the futility of chasing youth hits me square-on. Along with the comforting realisation that while the youth I've been experiencing of late is fabulous, it's not the real me. Not the full package. Having this home and having raised my family is way more profound than having dewy skin and pert breasts – however marvellous it feels to re-experience that.

Right on the heels of this klaxon-like thought comes another revolutionary one. What if I just stopped worrying about it? Threw in the towel and just accepted that I'm not ever going to be young again. Or even *look* young again. Because judging from the look of Yesterday Me, she's fine as she is. Which means so am I.

Does this mean I can finally learn to be happy in my own skin? The way I look today? Right now?

I hear the kids' muffled laughter again. Adam is turning to walk back down the corridor and I know it's nearly time to go, but then my attention is snagged by the dangling felt-tip pen on its string next to the calendar and a wicked little thought drops into my head.

Oh – and it's wrong, *so* wrong. I know that – and Adam would kill me if he knew what I was about to do, but what is this trip if not an opportunity? After all, I've already managed to reignite our sex life thanks to our machine. What if I could sort out my money situation too? In a way that Adam need never know?

Quickly, I make Yesterday Me take the pen lid off in her teeth, then scrawl 'Carpe Diem' on the blank space of Saturday.

And just in the nick of time, as the wind rushes up and I'm sucked back down into the future again . . .

Adam's eyes are blazing.

'It worked,' he says – almost shouts as I snap to. 'Because . . . because *I* already *know* that you talked to me yesterday when you imposed yourself and told me that Tomorrow Jules was there. Only *you* didn't already know that on your previous timeline, did you? You had to go back to make it so.'

Make it so. And, yes, he's right. I did.

'But doesn't that also mean –' I start to say.

'That this is yet another alternative timeline? Another new universe?' He nods. 'But only fractionally. So marginally it can't really make any difference to anything, can it? The only difference is me having had that two-minute chat with you yesterday.'

I think of my addition to the calendar.

'So I reckon it was worth it,' he declares. 'Because now we know we *can* make new tapes if we want. And I think we should, right? Regularly. From here on in. That way when we're older, we can come back to today and tomorrow and the next day and onwards. We just need to keep making more and more tapes.'

'Sure,' I say.

'Good, because I've already ordered some.' He grins. 'But nothing else has changed?' he then checks, our usual debrief question.

'Everything else looks the same,' I tell him, because it does. 'You. The shed.' I look in the mirror. 'Me.'

'And what about what you remember?'

'What do you mean?'

'I mean about yesterday. And your new memories here in this universe. Nothing's too fuzzy or messed up, memory-wise, *after* you imposed yourself? Only I was wondering if there might be, like, a hangover effect or something. Like whether you'd still remember us all just having a quiet one last night, crashing out on the sofa after we ate so much of that awesome boeuf bourguignon of yours.'

I slowly nod.

Even though, *no*. That's *not* what I remember. Not with my old memories of my old timeline. I remember that I burnt it. Incinerated it. Except . . . except, right this second, I'm getting these new memories of how everyone *was* in raptures about how good that stew was. How it was slow-cooked to perfection.

Because I turned the oven down.

'But do you know what's really odd?' he says.

'Er, no . . .'

'After we talked yesterday, I tried prying, you know, subtly, to find out if you – if Yesterday You – remembered talking to me about Tomorrow Jules being there. But none of it registered, like you had no memory of it. 'Oh,' he then adds, 'and what you wrote on the calendar. Carpe Diem.' He smiles slyly. 'I saw you do that on my way out of the kitchen. Only you didn't remember doing that either when I asked.' He bobs his eyebrows. 'Meaning I'm guessing that that was still the work of Tomorrow Jules too?'

'Guilty as charged. But just as a little joke,' I quickly cover.

'What does it mean?'

'Just that, er . . . we should seize the day,' I bluster. 'That I realised that, as well as all these little adventures, we should live more in the moment too, you know?'

Only it really wasn't that at all, *was* it? Because this morning when the new me on this new timeline checked the calendar like every morning and read those two words written in her handwriting, they stuck with her just like I'd hoped. What the hell did they mean? she must have been thinking. And, yes, she was. I can suddenly now remember that too.

Then, later at the Peregrine, when Rose read out all the horse names, alongside Danny Boy, she read out the name 'Carpe Diem'.

And, Christ, that other me's heart started pounding as she worked it out. That the me of the future had left a glaringly clear message.

Which is why the new me on this timeline went right up to the end of her overdraft to put a thousand pounds on Carpe Diem to win at Royal Ascot.

At odds of twenty to one.

I have a vivid memory of standing with Rose in the bar at the Peregrine earlier, watching the race together, and when Carpe Diem flew over the line, we hugged each other and jumped up and down. She even hugged Eddy.

Then I made a jubilant Rose promise – absolutely promise – not to tell Adam as I was going to use the money for a surprise.

Fuck a duck! That same betting slip is in my purse right now, and when I cash it in, I'll have nearly twenty grand. Enough to clear my credit card at last.

I turn away to the tapes, before Adam can see my face. I want to squeal with excitement, but I can't let on. The fact I gambled at all would be bad enough in his eyes. Me, acting like his dad. But combine that with me breaking our cardinal rule and deliberately messing with the past – he'd seriously flip. Which is why I'm never going to tell him. Much as I hate to be dishonest, this one's going to have to stay in the vault.

'So, it's your turn,' I say, as with shaking hands, I rifle through the tapes. 'Where do you want to go?'

He stands beside me.

'I was thinking maybe when the kids were really little. Even one of them newborn, because my memory's such a blur from back then. I was so knackered.'

'*You* were knackered? Try giving birth.'

'But then I thought it's too much of a risk,' he says, pulling the tape named *Childbirth* out and handing it to me, as I look down the list of familiar songs, all of which I love. I remember Nelly being born to 'I'm Like a Bird' by Nelly Furtado. What a fabulous omen I thought *that* was and I still hope it's true. 'What with them being so young,' he says. 'You know, in case we did inadvertently mess something up.'

'Yes. Good point. So maybe a little later?'

'What about around the time of those videos you and the kids were laughing at when I walked in yesterday?' Adam suggests, and I smile, only a little bit disappointed, because I wanted to go back there myself.

'That was, what, 2003?' I say, digging through the box. 'How about this one?' I hold up a tape. It says 'Daddy Day Care '03' in my writing on the spine.

He gets prepared and puts in the tape and then – *click* – off he goes, out like a light, with that not-getting-any-less-creepy look of total zombification on his face, while I listen to 'Where Is the Love' by Black Eyed Peas and 'Sound of the Underground' by Girls Aloud – for which Nelly had a whole little dance I only now remember – all the while imagining Adam back there with the kids for real.

I do Wordle, Connections, the crossword, scroll mindlessly through Instagram, and an hour later, there's a soft click at the end of the tape and Adam is suddenly back.

Leaping up, he wraps me in a giant hug.

'That was . . .' He stares down into my face, obviously awed. 'Just incredible. I'd forgotten how sweet they were. Oh, Jules, they were so . . .'

He looks teary, like he's bursting with love. Why can't I remember him looking like this after the kids were first born? Was he really this enthusiastic as a young dad? How could I have forgotten something like that?

He starts telling me about his trip. About how I'd been out on one of my first weekend jobs since Liam had been born. Even though Adam was working full-time, he was more than happy to do solo dadding and to take one for the team. He describes how he'd done this mad, chaotic breakfast with the kids and he opened the tape I'd given him before I'd left that morning and he'd taken it in the portable tape player to the picnic in the park. How they'd been on all the rides and the kids had feasted on tiny Dairylea sandwich squares and Cheetos and he'd pushed Nelly on the swing and how she'd yelled at him to go higher and higher. And how he'd almost left Lion Brian, Liam's favourite toy, on the roundabout.

As he talks, I laugh along, but I'm also aching with a jealous longing to see my babies.

'Right, my turn,' I tell him, hurriedly flicking through the tapes.

'Here, look, *Bathtime Mix*. That should do it,' he says. 'That's 2004. Just a little bit later.'

'Perfect,' I say, putting it in the machine. 'Here goes. I'll see you soon.'

'Enjoy.'

As I press 'Play', sitting back, 'Hey Ya!' by Outkast fills the shed . . .

Bursting out of the whirlwind, I find myself on the Lloyd Loom chair next to the bath, in our tiny terraced house near the station that we moved to just before Nelly was born. Liam and Nelly are splashing in the water and it's like I've got vertigo.

Because here they are: my babies.

Right here.

All noisy and splashy.

I'm swooning with love, like Adam had looked just now.

Nelly, who must be three and a half, dumps a pile of bubbles on little nearly one-year-old Liam's head. They are impossibly gorgeous. Their little squidgy bodies . . . their goofy smiles . . . their fine hair . . . their little baby teeth and joyful laughter.

My tummy is doing somersaults of joy, except that 2004 Jules is not interested.

My urge to impose, to scoop my arms down into the bath and to pick up the old red dumper truck toy that Liam loved and to pour water over his shiny little body is unbearable.

But tempting as it is, I promised Adam, and I've already gone behind his back with Carpe Diem, so I really am just here for the ride this time. It's still almost impossible to resist. Because she – the 2004 Jules – is not even looking at our precious babies. Instead, she's absorbed in the chunky grey Nokia in her hand and is looking for messages from Adam.

Her emotion is fierce. An indignant fury that she's doing yet another bath time and Adam is late home from work.

I'm shocked to feel how exhausted and cross she is. She'd rather be working than doing this – the witching hour – at the end of a long day. She wants a glass of wine and not to have to do the bedtime stories.

The kids are giggling now, but she hardly hears. Her thoughts are obsessed with Adam being in the pub with Darius, who says his latest stab at running a tech business might finally be turning a corner and could even be edging out of the red.

By comparison, it feels like all her own plans are on hold. She's still getting catering gigs now and then, but not nearly enough, and even with Adam's salary, it's impossible to save for their planned big move to Oz – which is still supposedly happening later this year. Each day she feels it slipping further and further away. *Especially when Adam hangs out in the pub, spending their money on pints*, she thinks. Although is it the spending she resents, or the fact he's getting to have grown-up conversations and living a grown-up life?

Her thoughts are interrupted by screeches from the bath as a fight breaks out.

'Oh, for God's sake,' she scolds Nelly, seeing Liam has tipped back. 'You'll bloody drown him.'

She scoops up Liam, wincing as he wails in her ear. He's red-faced and upset.

'Shush,' she tells him, quickly wrapping him in a towel, then dumping him on the bath rug, while lifting Nelly from the bath, and wrapping her harshly in a towel too, before seeing her trembling bottom lip, and snapping at her to stop being a baby.

Inside I'm silently screaming, *But Nelly is a baby!* How can 2004 me ignore those big dark eyes? I feel like my heart is being lanced. It takes everything I have not to impose myself and intervene to calm everyone down.

'Cuddle,' Nelly begs, putting her thumb in her mouth, but the awful Younger Jules ignores her, throwing pyjamas at her from the towel rail, and telling her to get herself dressed. Grabbing a nappy, she lays Liam on the changing mat.

I watch, disgusted, as Jules now uncaringly rubs cream into Liam's nappy rash. She should be kneeling down and cuddling them both and showering their perfect bodies with kisses.

But instead she's hurrying them along to bedtime, like they're being punished.

Oh, and how I want to weep with nostalgia at the sight of their little room, the smell of baby talcum powder, the walls covered in Nelly's achingly cute crayoned drawings, the shelf full of sticky, well-thumbed books, and the framed imprint of baby Liam's foot.

Ignoring it all, huffing through the discarded toys strewn over the rug, Jules winces as she treads on a Lego brick. She *fucking hates* Lego! She roughly pulls down the blackout blind, the early-evening sun spilling brightly round the sides.

'Say night?' Nelly asks, standing on her pillow and consulting the world map above her bed. Her pride and joy.

I wonder where the hell that precious map went.

'Close your eyes and point,' Jules says, sighing resignedly at this nightly ritual. But she only has herself to blame for teaching Nelly about the world. A knowledge that has bloomed into an endless fascination.

Nelly closes her eyes and points. Then opens her eyes.

'Yep, Melbourne,' Jules says, matter-of-factly. 'It's in Australia. But it might as well be on another planet. Now squidge down.'

Nelly twists away, hurt that she's not getting more info about the far-flung place she's picked. She clearly wants a cuddle on the beanbag between her bed and Liam's cot where we always read stories, but tonight, Jules doesn't have the patience. She tuts, waiting for Nelly to finish lining up Mr Bear, the purple monkey, the little doll we got on holiday the year before in Cornwall that she loves – ready for story time. Liam is in his cot, kneeling in his sleeping bag, clutching Lion Brian, almost catatonic with fatigue.

I watch as Jules grabs a book off the shelf, choosing *That's Not My Teddy*, not because it's a wonderful storybook, which it is, but because it's short. And all the time that she reads, 'That's not my teddy, its nose is too rough,' she's snarkily thinking, *That's not my life, its days are too shit . . .*

I feel sick.

How could I have been so careless, so self-absorbed?

Nelly begs for another story, but Jules just gives her a perfunctory kiss on the forehead.

'Love you, Mummy,' she says, her voice small and insecure.

Jules doesn't say it back.

She doesn't say it back.

'Go to sleep,' she tells her instead.

How could I have ever looked down at that angel's face and not told her a million times over how loved she is?

But just as I'm about to impose myself, finally done with this hideous, callous display from my younger self, the front door slams.

'Daddy!' Nelly squeals, flinging back her duvet, while Liam sits up in his cot, suddenly manically wide awake, holding on to the bars and jumping.

'For fuck's sake,' Jules mutters under her breath, her bedtime routine now ruined by Adam's arrival at just the wrong time. *He always does this.*

She marches out of the room, ahead of Nelly, brushing past Adam on the stairs. 'They're all yours,' she says huffily.

Flabbergasted, I piggyback inside Jules as she heads to the kitchen and yanks open the fridge, pouring herself a hefty glass of wine, which she chugs down, almost in one, before pouring another, hoping Adam won't notice and comment about her increasing wine consumption, as he sometimes does.

Not that he's got a leg to stand on. She knows him well enough to guess he's already three pints down.

Above, she hears the sound of Adam singing out of tune to the kids – 'Mr Brightside', by the Killers, that new band he likes.

Jules sits at the kitchen table, cross that he's geeing them up just when she'd got them to bed. If he's going to insist on music, why not sing lullabies? She resents that they find him so much more fun than her. It's not fair that she's done all the donkey work, and he gets to swan in and claim all the glory.

Gripping the stem of her wine glass, she knows she should start tidying away the toys strewn across the kitchen floor, wash up the pan and clear up the scattered pieces of pesto-covered fusilli on the table, but she deserves to sit still for a moment.

'You said you'd be back earlier,' she says accusingly, as Adam appears in the kitchen doorway.

'Sorry. Couldn't shut Darius up.' Adam opens the fridge and takes out a beer. 'What's up, baby? Rough day?'

I marvel at the sight of him. He's so vital. So *in his prime*. He's filled out since he was in his twenties, but he's still slim and strong, his face unlined, although it won't be long before the beers start to show on his belly. I'm so used to him as he is now, I'd forgotten how attractive he was.

He comes over, hauling Jules off her chair. To her – to us both – he feels so familiar, so much like home, that the resentment she's feeling clashes with the relief of being held in his arms. While I'm positively ogling his strong pecs.

'Guess what? I made you a tape,' he says, brandishing the very same tape we just put on in the shed. She takes it, her heart melting at this most-needed peace offering.

'You haven't named it,' she says.

'OK, so let's call it *Bathtime Mix*,' he suggests, grabbing a pen from the pot.

He writes on the case and then puts it on. 'Hey Ya!' starts playing, and now, impossible to still be in a bad mood, with the wine softening her edges, he pulls her up off the chair and into his arms, and they dance in the kitchen, Adam playfully kicking the toys into the corner, as part of the dance.

But he knows her too well. She's not fully giving herself to him. He slows down, swaying gently against her and listens as she recounts her day. How it's so difficult to get anything done. How she's knackered. All. The. Bloody. Time.

'And I got an email from Rob,' she tells him, which is, after all, the reason she's in such a blue funk. 'You know, the chef that went out to Sydney? He's working in this amazing restaurant right on the beach called Bathers' Pavilion. He says there's a perfect job for me, but starting, like, right now. And we're nowhere near ready to go.'

Adam listens and nods, understanding.

'And it just feels . . . so frustrating. It's like there's a whole other life out there, just waiting, and we can't get there, you know?'

'But we will. It's just a matter of time. It won't be long. It will happen. I promise.'

As she looks at his face, she can see – and *I* can see – how much he means it. That he'll do anything to make this wish of hers come true.

I should be happy, like she's now happy. But suddenly all I'm thinking is, *Noooooooooooo*. My urge to put a stop to the Australian plan right here and right now is unbearably strong because it's doomed. If they go to Australia, Adam's parents will die and there'll be years of resentment and regrets. Whereas I could just impose myself. Call his dad. Somehow warn him. Change the past.

Make a new future for us all.

I know I shouldn't – that Adam would be furious if I did – but what if this *is* actually the right thing to do?

But it's too late already, as once more that tornado whips up around me, and heaves me back out . . .

My eyes spring open back in the shed and I sit for a second, shell-shocked. Something inside me feels like it's breaking.

'What is it?' Adam asks, holding my hand, as a torrent of tears is unleashed. I can't speak. 'What happened?' Adam kneels in front of me, but I shake my head. 'You . . . you haven't changed anything, have you?'

No. And that's the point. His mum and dad are still going to die. Already have. *Are* dead. But it's not just that, is it? It's everything. It's all those feelings following me back here. As real as they were then.

'I was a shit mother,' I sob. 'I was so selfish and mean and horrible to them.'

This hideous weight of shame and regret feels too much.

'But you didn't change anything?' he repeats, missing the point.

And for once I haven't, but suddenly I hate him, for all of this. For making me remember everything that was safer to forget. For smashing my rose-tinted spectacles. I've never felt less sure of who I am, or what we've become, than I do right now.

But perhaps Adam *can* read my despairing look, because he reaches forward and cups my cheek. 'You weren't a bad mother,' he says, pressing his forehead against mine. 'Not once.'

'I was,' I protest. 'You should have seen me. I was bad-tempered and impatient and –'

'It was just a bad day,' he soothes, as I cling on to him, like he's a buoy in the middle of the ocean, because that's how I feel. Lost. At sea.

'We don't have to go back,' he says. 'Not if it's upsetting you.'

I can't believe he means this. But he does. He really would give all this up, for me.

Only instead of feeling gratitude, I feel panicked, right to my core. To give this up. To be without *this*. Because we need it, don't we? Isn't *this* what's making us better, what's making us happy again?

I wipe my eyes on the cuff of my sleeve. 'No, it's OK,' I tell him, because however awful that just was, in equal measure it was still wonderful too, wasn't it? Seeing the kids. Those gorgeous little people who once belonged to me.

'I'm OK. Honestly. It was just . . . intense.'

Adam smiles at me gently. He puts his hands on his back and stretches, and then I laugh, spotting the crumbs all over his hoodie and noticing he's eaten all the crisps.

Calming down, letting the wine soothe me, we chat more about bath time 2004, but I don't mention our Australia chat afterwards, since I know it will rake up too many emotions and, like me, he'd only want to fix it.

'What about you?' I say eventually. 'You're not put off? Do you still want to go again?'

He doesn't even need to answer. I can already see it in his face. He's every bit as addicted as me.

Chapter Ten

Adam – 'Starstrukk'

Go again . . . Like I'm a kid, down on Brighton Pier, with Dad pointing at the roller coaster.

Even after seeing Jules so upset when she first came back, of course I still want to. Selfish, I know, but time travel kind of does that to you. Once you realise you can break the laws of physics at will, it's hard not to start thinking that maybe a whole bunch of other rules might not apply to you either. That you really are the centre of the universe for once.

Plus, she was smiling by the end, meaning surely the good of all this still outweighs the bad?

'So, where do you want to go?' she says.

'To see Mum and Dad.'

I'm expecting Jules to get fully on board with this right away. She knows how much I miss them. What if seeing them again – properly, not like in '89, when all Adam could focus on was Jules – makes me feel as happy as going back to see the kids? What if *that* could be my final formative memory of them instead of the crash?

If they even *have* to crash . . . because, Christ knows, I can't help thinking about that too. It's been gnawing at me for days.

'But what if you're tempted?' Jules says, as if reading my mind.

I play possum. 'To do what?'

'You know what.' She gives me that look I could spot across a football stadium, the one that says, *Do not fuck with me, mister. You don't fool me one bit.*

'To warn them about the accident,' she spells it out. 'To try and stop them getting killed.'

I wouldn't. But my eyes settle once more on that copy of *Back to the Future* over by the TV. How many times have I played it these last few days? Each time focusing in on the same few scenes. Marty McFly stuffing that note into Doc Brown's coat pocket to warn him that terrorists in the future will gun him down. Doc then wearing a bulletproof vest to change his fate. Marty thus saving Emmett Lathrop Brown, PhD's life.

'What if you can't stop yourself?' Jules says. 'Even I thought about calling your dad just now, back at bath time,' she admits, looking ashen. 'Knowing you *can* do it, Adam, knowing you *can* change history – or create a new history in a new universe, anyway – it makes it almost impossible to resist.'

'But you did resist,' I say.

'Yes, but they're your parents not mine and, as much as I loved them, for you that temptation's going to be so much worse.'

Of course, she's right, and this is also something I've been chewing over. Putting myself in temptation's way *is* risky, but not only that, it's potentially morally reprehensible too. Because what if I did cave? How might changing their fate and keeping them alive affect other people? Perhaps in bad ways as well as good? Just having them survive that car crash might mean other people die in their place in that same motorway pile-up. Leaving me playing God with other people's lives. Something Mum would hate and I know in my heart is plain wrong.

'Something else then?' I say. 'Sometime after 2004.' We both know what I mean. After they're dead.

'Oh, Adam. You look so sad.'

'Yeah, well, you know . . . I've just agreed to never see my parents again.'

But it's not even just about them, is it? It's about so many other temptations now we've got this power. Like Liam. His hand. If I wanted to, I could change that too. I *could* change anything, but *mustn't*, because of what the consequences might be.

'Let's pick something else to cheer you up, then,' Jules says. 'Something fun. Like before with the picnic.'

'Sure,' I say, feeling the adrenaline kick back in right away. That same buzz I got off my first trip today. Like I'm a smoker again and all I want is another cigarette. Like I can't help myself. Just chilling with the kids back then made me feel so alive, so integral to their lives, so *complete*.

'So, come on, what's your favourite memory?' She smiles encouragingly. 'Post 2004,' she reminds me. 'Your happiest memory?'

Shutting my eyes, I think back through birthdays, Christmases, until out of the blue I see it – a stunning Mediterranean blue. Even better, I know there's a CD for it, one Jules made in 2009, when the kids were nine and six. That same year Ngozi had booked an apartment in Mallorca but Isaac had broken his leg and Geoff had been called away to work, leaving her stuck at home and giving us the apartment for a week. The only proper family holiday we've ever had abroad.

'*Summer Lovin*',' I tell her, finding the CD and reading out the name she scrawled across it, along with a cute little stick drawing of our family holding hands beneath two cartoon palm trees.

'Do you think it will still work?' she asks, because we've never tried a CD.

'Only one way to find out. Oh, and I've already checked online. A standard CD like this is seventy-four minutes long,' I say.

'So you'll be giving me zombie face for fourteen more minutes than the normal tapes.'

Smiling, I pull a face. 'Well, lucky you.'

Pressing the CD eject button on the Sony, there's an excruciating moment as all its ancient motor does is *whirr*. But then the dusty panel slowly opens and we both grin. Turning away from Jules, I adjust my Ziggy Stardust hoodie, hating the way my spare tyre hangs over my belt like a roll of half-risen dough. Giving the CD a quick polish with David Bowie's turquoise blue jumpsuit, I slot it in.

I smile across at Jules as I quickly assume the position on the armchair, our eyes locking, as the first notes of 'Starstrukk' by Katy Perry start to play . . . before – *SKREEOWWWWWW* . . .

I'm torn back down into that howling hurricane again . . .

I *land* – now my preferred word for describing the feeling of arriving back inside my younger self – with a whoop, then a plummeting sensation, then an almighty splash.

Young Adam has got his arms wrapped round his knees and belly.

He's not breathing. Everything is blurry, *swooshy*. For a second, I freak. Where the hell have I landed this time?

Only now we're rising, buoyed up through liquid of the deepest blue, and I realise Adam's heart is thundering with joy, not fear. Whatever this is, he's loving it. We break through the surface into blazing sunlight and gasp for air.

'Ten out of ten,' Nelly calls out.

'Eleven,' Liam yells.

Ears crackling, Adam grins across at them – my God, so adorable – both miming holding up score cards like in their favourite show, *Strictly Come Dancing*, from where they're sitting knobbly-kneed in their swimming costumes, looking down at him from a barnacle-encrusted wooden jetty.

I feel Adam's joy flowing through me as Nelly tries a stand-up dive and nails it first time. His heart soars like it might never come down.

Only then Liam's in the water too. Without warning, jumping in. Instantly, I feel Adam's anxiety spike. Even though he tries to keep on smiling as both kids splash about around him, each time one of them bobs beneath the surface, his stress swells, then fades, then swells, then fades. Like he's got a booming tide inside him, one he simply can't control.

I realise then that he's gone. That happy-go-lucky twentysomething kid from the house party who wasn't afraid of risks. Ditto, that chilled guy from the picnic without a worry in the world. His mum and dad, *my* mum and dad, they died five years ago. Adam now knows the world bites.

'Back to the beach,' he tells them, still freaking out trying to keep track of them both.

'But, Dad . . .'

'Just do it.' That old Nike slogan from the eighties that him and Darius used to dare each other with.

Only from the disappointed looks on the kids' faces, *just don't* would be a better slogan for their dad.

They get back to where thirty-seven-years-young Jules is sunbathing on the beach in a polka-dot bikini. Adam's relieved to be back safe on dry land, but, even then, he worries about the kids wandering off too far. His dread of losing them too eats him up.

'Oh, shit. I forgot . . .' Jules says as they start packing up, with the midday sun already beating down too hard. 'I meant to give you this on the plane. Holiday tradition, and all that.'

She hands him an old silver Discman and a CD case. The *Summer Lovin'* mix. Meaning, shit, I'm halfway through my allotted time here already and not enjoying it either, what with Adam's anxiety seeping right through me too.

Only then a different piece of music catches his attention. Or rather, Liam's. My once-was little boy tugs at Adam and points across the beach towards where a man is playing an acoustic guitar. Liam's already hooked. Adam bought him an acoustic guitar for his last birthday.

By the time they reach the busker, he's playing a simple chugging riff, one Adam watches Liam mimicking with the fingers of his left hand as he tries to work out the chords.

The guy's voice is heavily accented, making the English words he's singing hard to decipher, but the melody is strong and super-catchy. So catchy that, next thing Adam knows, Liam is 'la-ing' along in perfect harmony, like he's known this tune all of his life.

A warm feeling ripples across Adam's chest. Pride. Pride in his little boy.

'What is it?' he asks the busker as the song finally ends, slipping Liam a couple of euros to pop in the guy's hat.

'"Ventura Highway".'

Adam nods. 'Who by?'

'America.'

The name is already familiar to him from that one song of theirs he knows, 'A Horse With No Name', but at this point in his life, Adam doesn't realise just how big they are globally. He taps their name into his new iPhone's 'Notes' app to remind himself to check them out and download a few of their albums. He's already planning on getting a subscription to that new music service Spotify when he gets back home. A little treat for the half-hour commute he does daily to the small start-up in Lewes where he's just been made project manager for a mobile phone game to be rolled out through Apple's new App Store.

'Your boy . . . he's good,' the busker says, looking up at Adam. '*Talentoso*. One day he should be a singer too.'

Little Liam blushes at the compliment, but somehow not dismissively. Like he thinks this too.

Halfway back to the apartment, Jules calls their little platoon to a halt outside the Codfather fish and chip shop. Adam sheds the beach bags one by one, like a Buckaroo! in slow motion, as she takes the kids inside to get them a bag of chips to stop them whinging about going home so soon.

Adam paces back and forth outside in the Saharan heat, wanting to sit down and wanting a cold shower, shattered from the exertion of carrying all this gear. He scratches at his belly, wishing he wasn't so unfit.

'Oi, watch where you're going, lard-arse,' someone says, bumping into him.

'You what?' Adam looks up.

The young man staring down at him has an athlete's heavily muscled frame and is a good foot taller than Adam. I recognise him, too. This bastard's face is one I'll never forget. Like the two thugs flanking him, both of them equally ripped.

'What, you deaf as well as fat?' the man cackles, leering in so close that Adam can smell the acrid stink of lager on his breath.

He waits for Adam to speak. *Daring* him to. But Adam doesn't. Like *I* didn't. As the three young men walk off sniggering, an impotent rage rises inside Adam and his cheeks burn with embarrassment.

Turning, he then sees that Jules, Nelly and Liam have witnessed this altercation as well. He catches his reflection in the chip shop window. *Koala*. Adam hasn't heard the nickname yet, but the shape is already there.

'Just ignore them. They're morons,' Jules says, tight-lipped, slipping her arm reassuringly around his waist.

All Adam can see is that the kids' cheeks are red with embarrassment and neither of them can hold his eye.

He turns to look for the men, but it's too late. They've vanished into the nearby square full of tourists, leaving Adam to pick up his clutter of bags and beach toys and follow Jules over the road.

'You're not worrying about what that drunk boy said, are you?' Jules asks him a minute later, as he continues to glare into the distance.

Boy. Her calling him this only makes things worse.

'No.' But he is, and not just him, me too. That photo Meredith sent glares back into my mind's eye. That chubby little koala on the beer tap. Then comes Darius, with Jules in the pool at his party. Darius, with his flexing, bronzed muscles. Darius, making her laugh.

Real rage pumps through him then and pumps through *me*. I try to fight it, but it's no good.

Instead, I *just do it*. Going full Nike, fucking the consequences, I quickly impose myself on Adam. Unlocking his phone, I get him to send himself another note. I use all the reasoning and language I know will hurt him and spur him into action. I don't give a shit if what I'm doing is wrong.

'What is it?' Jules asks, staring down at my phone.

'Nothing. Just . . . something I need to remember,' I make Adam say.

Already I can feel the words he's just typed getting etched into his mind. Leaving me *certain* he's going to act on them, because this is something I know he wants too.

Quick as it came, the rage passes. Pulling back, I let Adam take over again. Trying not to think about what I've just done, I block it out, in case I freak out.

Instead, I look at the kids. Marvelling at them. The way they eat, like chips have never tasted this good. How they lean into each other as they giggle, with Liam throwing a chip to a tiny little bird and Nelly 'aw-ing' as it snatches it up and darts away. My love for them stretches inside me. But with it comes fear. Only not just Adam's. This time, mine too.

'You're looking at them like you're never going to see them again.' Jules smiles.

She's right, because I won't. Or not like this anyway. Not ever again. Because this Nelly here, who likes *Gossip Girl* and algebra and rollerblading and Black Eyed Peas . . . and this Liam, who loves guitar and *Spirited Away* and climbing walls and space adventure stories and building secret dens around the house . . . I never will get to see them again, because there are no more CDs or tapes that can bring me back right here to this very day.

It feels like a death.

Two deaths.

Two axe blows to my heart. These two little people who are about to vanish, as I feel that hissing vortex whipping up around me, cutting me off from so much that I love . . .

This time it's me with tears in my eyes as I open them back in the shed.

'What's the matter? What happened?' Jules asks, glancing down at her diary. 'I thought you were going back to the first day of our holiday. I thought it would be fun.'

'It was. We were on that beach in Port de Pollença with the kids and I was teaching them to dive. But it's just that it's always goodbye, isn't it? With the kids. Each time we leave them there in the past.'

'You make it sound like we're abandoning them. But we're not. They're still here.'

'No, not like that, they're not,' I try to explain. 'Those little people are gone. And . . . and normally it would all happen so gradually, wouldn't it? Them growing up. All those thousands of days passing. But jumping back, just like that, like clicking our fingers . . . it's too much like fast-forwarding. Like they've been ripped right out of my hands.'

She blanches. She's felt it too?

'It's OK.' She presses her forehead against mine. 'It's just new, that's all. We'll find a way to wrap our heads around it in the end. We're still us,' she whispers, her eyes big as saucers, as she kisses my nose. 'We're still you and me?'

'Of course.'

'I mean, we *are*, aren't we?' She pulls back, looking me dead in the eyes.

'Huh?' Oh, right. Our debrief. 'Yeah, of course.'

'You didn't change anything?'

'No.' Only, yeah, now I remember that little note I sent myself. 'Nope. Nu-uh,' I repeat, avoiding her eyes.

I shift on my chair, ready to get up. Then I catch sight of my reflection in the mirror. Only it's not the crappy old shed mirror that was propped up by the bench before, it's one of those wide, floor-to-ceiling wall mirrors you see in gyms.

Then there's the reflection. Of course, I know it's me, because of the face, but from the neck down . . . bloody hell. What is this? Some kind of optical illusion?

Shit. Holy, moly, pissing shit.

I'm ripped. As in totally, utterly. Vin Diesely, Dave Bautistardly. With pectorals, obliques and deltoids. Oh, triple shit. How do I even know the names of all these different muscles? I swear I never did before.

That note I just sent myself back in 2009 – about losing weight, and getting fit, and toughing the hell up so that no one would ever speak to me like that again in front of my kids – without turning I somehow know that it's there behind me, printed and framed on the wall.

I clutch at my stomach. Or, rather, my *not stomach*. Because where the hell is it? Where's my spare tyre? I lift up my skintight white sports singlet to check. Then almost gasp out loud, because instead of my customary dad-bod ripples, I've got abs. A six-pack. Rock hard. Like a washboard. Like I could play fucking squash against it.

'All right, Mr Muscles. It's not like we've not seen it all before,' Jules says, rolling her eyes, looking bored.

But I just continue to stare. At my toned legs. My hamstrings and glutes. Not to mention my overly snug little gym shorts. Before finally turning to gawp back at her.

'What is it? Did you pull something this morning?'

On my *bike* ride, she means, as a new memory hits me – the *fifty-kilometre* hill ride I pushed myself on over the South Downs just after dawn.

'Um, yeah, maybe,' I answer, my mouth dry.

'But everything else here looks OK to you?' she asks, looking around vaguely. 'The shed? Me? Nothing weird or unusual to report?'

'Er, nope. Everything looks . . . just dandy.' *Dandy*? A word I've never used before. A fakey word. One I can barely get out, because everything *doesn't* look bloody dandy, does it? Not even just me from the neck down. Or this giant snazzy gym mirror. Or my slinky little shorts and tight singlet.

The shed is also filled with a ton of other professional-looking gym equipment. Free weights. A multigym. A rowing and running machine. Road bikes and mountain bikes. Even a frigging exercise bike. Only nothing like that crappy one I had before. This one's got an iPad clipped to it that I already *know* rolls out cool environments like the Tour de France stages and the Serengeti National Park for me to virtually meander through while I train.

'OK, well, that's good,' Jules says.

Good? Of course, because none of this is remarkable to her, is it? In this new alternative timeline and parallel universe I've created, her Adam has been fitness-obsessed like this since he came back from that Mallorca holiday in 2009 and unexpectedly joined a gym.

This is my chance to come clean to her and admit what I've done. A choice that couldn't be any clearer if there was a flashing neon sign pointing one way to 'LIES' and the other to 'TRUTH'.

But how can I tell her the truth without also admitting that I'm a hypocrite, a rule-breaker, a joke? Plus, even if I do tell her, then what? How the hell am I meant to reverse this? I can't and even if I could I'd be giving Jules carte blanche to do the same. To start changing whatever the hell she might not like about herself behind *my* back.

No. I messed up and have to own this. Quietly. Then make sure I never do it again.

'Yeah,' I tell her, glancing across at my biceps again in the mirror, and even giving the left one a firm little flex. 'Everything's great. Everything's totally cool.'

Through the window, I catch sight of movement in the garden. Someone in a cycle helmet, pushing a bike down the garden path towards the shed.

'It's Nelly,' I say.

'Hey, Dad,' she calls out, grinning at me as she unclips her helmet.

Automatically, I hold the door wide open for her as she kisses me sweatily on the cheek and wheels her bike through. Like I've done it a hundred times before. Which, on this new timeline, I have.

'I did Ditchling Beacon in under fifteen,' she announces, as she hangs her bike up and I high-five her, already working out that she must have been averaging at least eleven kilometres an hour to achieve such a time climbing our murderously steep local hill. 'Meaning I've beaten your new personal best,' she teases, like I haven't just worked this out too.

Because I'm now also 'remembering' that we've had this friendly cycling rivalry of ours seesawing between us for nearly two years on this new timeline, ever since I first bought her this Liv Avail AR 4 endurance road bike and started cycling with her weekends when she was home from uni.

'Bor-ring,' chimes Jules, squeezing past.

A not unexpected comment, because on this timeline, this dad/daughter *thang* of ours infuriates Jules. She hates that she's not part of 'Team Fit', as we secretly call ourselves behind her back. But . . . wow. Just look at the results. Look at Nelly. Lean and healthy and glowing from her latest triumph and loving the outdoor life. Who'd have thought it and who could deny her that happiness? That getting out there in the world. And who could deny me my part in this either? Because – *Boom!* I can feel it in my heart, and I don't just mean my epic resting sixty beats per minute heart rate, but my pride. To have helped her. To finally be an adult role model she respects.

'You'll be beating me at everything soon,' I tell her, grinning back, even though we both know that she's still got a long way to go before she catches up with my iron man credentials. Meaning more bike rides together. More swimming. More runs. More happiness.

More fun.

Monday morning 9 a.m. and I'm in the kitchen fixing myself a raw-liver protein shake after finishing a gruelling but deeply rewarding hour-long workout.

'What's that?' Liam asks, coming in.

A pleasant surprise to see him up so early. Not just in his dressing gown either. He's fully dressed in jeans and a clean hoodie. Like he's got somewhere to go. But it's the JBL Bluetooth speaker he's looking at now and I can't help but smile.

'"Ventura Highway",' I tell him. 'By America.' I've been playing *Homecoming*, the 1972 album it's from, ever since I got back from time travelling to 2009.

'I kind of recognise it,' he says, with that same look he wore back then creeping across his adult face, like a dog cocking its head at some distant sound. Then he does it again – he starts 'la-ing' along to it, harmonising to the tune.

'*Talentoso,*' I say, as it ends.

He turns to look at me blankly, the spell broken. 'Huh?'

'It means . . .'

'Talented?' he hazards a guess.

'Exactly.' As annoyed as I still am at him and his plans to quit college, and at him and Darius ganging up on me the other night, I still want to share this wonderful memory and this music I'd forgotten about. 'It's what a busker once called you,' I explain. 'In Mallorca when you were little, and you sang along to him playing this song just like you did now.'

Again I see younger Liam reflected in his adult face, as he pushes his brown hair back from his eyes, but then he's turning away and my heart sinks. So much for us having a chat.

Only then he rips a corner off the calendar and uses its dangling felt-tip pen to scribble something down.

'I love it,' he says, grinning. 'I think we should cover it. Even record it.'

'Record it?' I ask, a spike in my voice, because who the hell's he expecting to pay for that?

'If we get the chance . . .' he adds, rolling his eyes, but only a little. Signalling he expects resistance from me on what he's about to tell me.

'Go on . . .'

'Uncle Dar . . .' he starts.

I might have known . . .

'. . . he's got an old friend over at Brighton Electric . . .'

He means the little studio complex across town . . .

'. . . who says he can get me and Max some paid work setting up events and behind the bar, but that we can also rehearse there, and maybe later on me and Max and Kai can even use one of the mix studios and the mastering suite –'

'Kai?' I finally get a word in edgeways.

'She's our drummer.'

They have a *drummer*? Already. He really is serious about all this, then.

Of course, my instinct is still to shut it down. To stamp on it. Now. Before it goes any further. To save Liam from himself. But then I remember my mother on another morning, so long, long ago, telling me not to funnel my ambitions into what she considered a 'hobby' and instead to do something more boring with my life.

Next thing I hear myself saying, 'Well, if you do, and, you know, if it's any good, then I've got a few contacts who I could maybe share it with.'

Even though the truth is I've only got two. Rory, who runs the Great Escape, Brighton's annual music festival and the UK's answer to South by Southwest, so a pretty good one there. And KP from the Troubs, who plays darts down the Lion & Lobster. But who knows? Crazy busy as they are, maybe I *could* actually get them to take a look?

He looks at me like he must have misheard, but then I smile, and he smiles too.

I ride my favourite of my three mountain bikes into work – a Trek Top Fuel 5 Suspension, which is great for off-roading, but ideal for nipping around the city too.

I don't need to think about the route as I zigzag through the sun-dappled streets. I must have done it a thousand times before – well, actually no, more like *four* thousand I quickly work out. Or at least the me on this timeline has. The me I assimilated with so seamlessly when I came back from 2009.

I've also got new memories of all the thousands of hours of other exercise he's been doing since Mallorca. Which are my memories too now . . . sitting alongside my old memories of being . . . well, let's be kind here, being in *not* good shape on my other old timelines before.

I know I should probably feel guilty for getting fit for free, but it's not like I'm hurting anyone. In fact, if anything, surely, I'm doing Jules and the kids a favour by being a healthier husband and dad. Plus, I love it, don't I? The pumping iron. The workouts. The long runs and even longer bike rides. I feel happier, healthier, and clearer of mind.

Also, it's not like me taking exercise more seriously seems to have affected too much of the rest of my life. Or at least not the big-ticket items. I've still got the same home, same kids, same Jules, same worries and same problems as before. Money worries. Worries about me and Jules and the kids not getting on well enough – although, frankly, even a lot of that's now on the up. Concerns about Darius getting on maybe too well with them. Oh, but I've still got a multiverse time machine too. One I am seeing as more and more of a gift.

Even if, OK, strictly speaking, there might be a few more, shall we say, contentious little issues that have been thrown up on this new timeline too. Like the fact that for the past fifteen years I've gone on holidays with my cycling club, meaning sometimes Jules and the kids have had to go somewhere on their own, until I got Nelly on board with the cycling too. Something Jules and I have argued about – a *lot*.

Her being so pissy about all this does annoy me, of course, but I've learned to disregard her sarky little MAMIL snipes over the years and just do my thing, because why shouldn't I wear Lycra at the weekends, particularly when it looks this damn good?

I suppose there's also the Meredith thing too. The fact that I've spent so much time with her over the last couple of years now that she's my beach volleyball partner. It also might have put Jules's nose out of joint a bit more than it needed to when Meredith and I totally outplayed and outmuscled her and Darius at his party in the pool.

But you can't have everything, right? And Meredith and I are just friends, just teammates.

In fact, there she is now, waving up at me from the World Famous Pump Room cafe beach courts, because on this timeline we like to get a quick hour's practice in before work on a Monday. Same on Wednesday. So we're good and ready to get fired up on Friday nights to keep us on top of the league.

Only there is something else going on here too, isn't there? I can't help but feel that as I cycle down the ramp onto the beach to join her. A tingling deep down inside. How me and Meredith are much closer, emotionally speaking, on this timeline. So much so that I realise I've really missed her over the weekend. There's also so much new stuff I know about her. New memories from all the extra chats we've had. Like how awful it was for her with her dad dying young, and that the reason she left London was because her boyfriend was a cheat, and so now she's holding out for someone she can trust.

'Looking good, babe,' she says, as I park my bike and give her a quick kiss on the cheek.

'Feeling good, babe.' From the way we say it, the sheer familiarity of it, I realise this has become our standard greeting. Just the tip of the iceberg of our buddy banter too.

The hour goes by fast. What a team we are. Unbeatable, in fact. We win three practice matches back-to-back, all of them two sets to love. I adore it, being here, with her, our two honed bodies working in perfect tandem. Just being fully happy in the moment and not wanting to be anywhere else.

Afterwards, we chat over a broccoli juice. Only it's not the kind of chat I'm expecting. None of it's the kind of stuff I used to talk to Meredith about in the pub or on our walks home back on my old timelines. This friendship is so much more advanced. It's not just the new stuff I know about her. She knows stuff about me too. About Jules, and how lacklustre our relationship has become over the last few years. Or *had* become. Until we discovered our machine. But not even the me on this timeline has confided in Meredith about *that*. No, because the first and second rule of Secret Multiverse Time Machine Club remains that we do not talk about Secret Multiverse Time Machine Club to anyone else.

When it comes to say goodbye, Meredith goes to kiss me on the cheek again, but moves her face at the last split second, bringing her lips close to mine. I'm shocked. Even though I know she's just teasing. I jerk my head back like I've been stung.

'Everything OK?' she asks.

'Um. Yeah, sure.'

She cocks her head, confused, like I'm the one who's acting weird.

Then I know why. This *isn't* weird for them, the Adam and Meredith who've been hanging out on this new timeline. We've become so much more openly flirty. It's been months since we introduced this will we/won't we element to our play. Just for fun, though, right?

Then I see Darius, leaning over on the railings up on King's Road directly above us, looking down. No way he could have missed the two of us horsing around.

I step back. Acting like I haven't seen him, but I'm left worrying he might have guessed that something's going on. Which it's not.

Only this worry then brings up a bigger one – because, surely, even thinking this means that something already is.

Chapter Eleven

Jules – 'Somebody That I Used to Know'

I've been telling myself for ages that money doesn't matter. Being materialistic and rich is so *over*. So twenty tens. But *fuck that*. Being solvent is magical. Cash is king.

It's Monday morning and town is quiet. After a long overdue utensil and pan haul in the Cook shop, I nip into Tribeca, where I fall in love with – and impulse buy – an Isabel Marant frilly little blouse. Just because . . . well, why the hell not?

My good mood only starts to diminish when the bloody Skoda won't start in the car park. I have to borrow jump leads from a man in a white van who sucks air through his teeth, shakes his head, and tells me that the ignition system looks 'a bit fucked'.

I calculate how much money's left from the Carpe Diem windfall, but after paying off my credit card, there's not nearly enough for a new car. Besides, how would I explain a new car to Adam? And would he even want one? He's so attached to this piece of shit.

I quash down the feelings of guilt, and the horrible sense that I've cheated, reminding myself that it's not like what I've done has affected Adam. Or the kids.

At home, I gently wash my prized new pans, noting how terribly shabby they make the rest of the kitchen look. Then I open my laptop, hoping that Darius has sent the confirmation email about the dinner on Thursday, with an idea of the kind of food his clients are expecting.

He said French classics, but that's a pretty broad remit. Worse is him expecting me to talk to his clients, when I'm only on a pathetic five-day streak of Duolingo French. Which means I'm going to be exposed as the terrible fraud I am.

It's all my own fault, because, technically, I *should* be fluent. I did go to 'live-like-a-local' in Paris when I was eighteen, or at least that's what I told my mum. What I actually spent most of my time doing was getting smashed with my English mates and shagging a ne'er-do-well barman called Pierre.

I can see now that I was swept up in the fantasy of being in Paris with a lover, but I still should've been using my springy, young brain to actually learn French when I had the chance.

It's too hard now.

There's a miserable 'Whaa, whaa, whaaaa' noise as I fail the next Duolingo level.

'Bollocks,' I curse, momentarily distracted by a distant growling sound, but determined to conquer Duo's latest challenge of asking a ticket inspector what time the next train for Avignon arrives.

Next thing, Darius is knocking on the glass of the back door.

'Hey. Only me,' he says, pushing it open.

I stand up, guiltily shutting the laptop, and just like when he unexpectedly turned up the Sunday before last, I feel immediately flustered. We don't have 'popper-inners', except for Doodles, and he's used to finding us in our natural habitat – or 'shabbytat', as Adam likes to call it – and he's usually in a cloud of vape and hardly even notices the clothes I'm in, let alone our crumb-covered surfaces. If I'd known Darius was coming, I'd have zhuzhed the place up a bit. Is it a culture thing in California, that you can just turn up unannounced? Or did Darius get so used to coming to this house when he was a kid that he feels the same best-mate rights still apply?

'I thought it might be easier to drop this off,' he says, holding up something in his hand.

'Right,' I say, as he dips his head and kisses me on both cheeks. He smells of that same expensive cologne he had on at his party. He's so groomed. So polished.

He hands me a yellow card. On the top, there's a posh line illustration of what looks like a beautiful chateau, with an avenue of plane trees leading up to it, and an embossed gold crest below with the words 'Le Manoir' inscribed beneath several gold stars.

'I saved this from one of the places Sujane – she's the chief potential investor – took me to outside Paris when I last went over.'

'Thanks,' I manage, scanning down the *menu gastronomique* and trying, haltingly, to read the words. *Cromesquis de foie gras à la truffe et céleri* . . . bloody hell. *Galettes andouille de Guémené fumé* . . . what the actual . . . ? *Confit d'oignons, oeuf biologique miroir* . . .

Jesus. I can safely say that I have zero idea what *any* of these dishes are.

Darius presses his hands together in supplication. 'Jules, I can't thank you enough for agreeing to do this.'

'Uh,' I stall. 'Why exactly do you need investors, anyway?' I ask, because he's rich as Croesus, right?

'Why risk your own money when you can risk somebody else's instead?' He smiles, easy with that word 'risk' in a way Adam never could be in a million years. 'It's just part of my plan.'

'Plan?'

'World domination,' he jokes, sticking his little finger to the corner of his mouth like Mini-Me in *Austin Powers*. 'Ping me the menu you decide on later today and then we'll be all set for Thursday.'

Today? I'm meant to come up with a menu to rival this epicurean gobbledygook in mere hours?

'Uh-huh.'

There's a pause. I should ask him if he wants tea, but I don't. I'm too freaked out by what he's just said.

'What's with all the tapes and CDs?' he says, nodding at the two open Amazon boxes that arrived this morning.

'Oh, um.' I can't help blushing, feeling somehow caught out, because these are all the new tapes and CDs Adam has managed to source for us to make new playlist recordings with. 'Just some stuff Adam ordered for, er, some old school recording project of his he's nerding out on.'

'Huh,' Darius considers, like Adam's quirkiness needs no further explanation. 'I guess he's not around?' he then asks.

'No. He's at work. I didn't even see him this morning. He plays volleyball first thing.'

'Ah,' Darius says, with a knowing nod 'With Meredith, "the babe".'

I raise an eyebrow.

'Yeah, those two seem thick as thieves,' he says.

A horrible feeling settles in the pit of my stomach. What's he saying? Or implying? That there's something going on between Adam and Meredith?

But Adam is . . . just my Adam, right? I've always known he's mine. That he'll be faithful, even when he goes off gallivanting on his bike. Even when he's hanging out on volleyball courts with *her*. Besides for the last fifteen years, we've joked that he's much more interested in his own body than anyone else's.

Only my mind now fills with the image of Meredith sitting on Adam's shoulders at the pool party, both of them flexing their toned muscles after whuppin' our arses at chicken, and how unbearably competitive they were. In fact, that was one of the reasons Adam and I argued on the way home that night.

The night he discovered the machine.

I stand at the kitchen sink, watching Groucho Barx expertly piddling along the weeds next to the shed. Why didn't I ever do a proper French cooking course? Even after I got back from Paris? I had my chances. Like that time at the Foodies Festival when Chef Marcel was doing that demo.

And suddenly, a thought hits me like a bolt in the chest.

No, I can't . . .

I *definitely* can't . . .

Yet . . . as if propelled by a higher force, a minute later, I'm turning on the flickering light in the shed and staring at all the gym equipment Adam has bought over the years, stuff we can't really afford, even though most of it is second-hand. I start furtively rifling through the tapes and CDs, telling myself that I'm due this. All that time he's been cycling up mountains and I was stuck looking after the kids, when I could have been polishing my own skill set.

I'm also lucky enough to know *exactly* what I'm looking for.

As if by magic, here it is in my hand: a CD in a case with *See You Later xx May 2012* written on it in Adam's handwriting. The *exact* day of the food festival I was thinking about which just happened to be on Adam's birthday, a day he unfailingly always made a mixtape or CD on each year as a joke, because of the one year I forgot. Tucked inside there's further proof this should get me where I need to go – a receipt from the Brighton Foodies Festival that year.

Not giving myself a moment to back out, I slide the CD into the machine and quickly press 'Play' and 'Somebody That I Used to Know' by Gotye starts throbbing out –

... with a final tumbling, churning, twisting spin ... I'm flipped back out into 2012 ... into my forty-year-old body.

And I'm exactly where I hoped I'd be, on a blisteringly hot bank holiday Monday on the half-mile stretch of mown Hove Lawns running parallel to the beach, which has been taken over for the weekend by the Foodies Festival.

More importantly, it is exactly *when* I hoped it'd be. Mid-afternoon and just over half an hour before Chef Marcel's demo in the cookery tent starts.

We're by the entrance. Me – or rather, Young Me – and Ngozi. She's wearing a flowery green-and-orange wide-bottomed satin jumpsuit with a matching scarf tied around her large afro. Isa and Isaac, her twins, are with us. Isa is small and pretty, the spitting image of Ngozi, and I can already see the fashionista she'll become. Isaac – tall with geeky glasses, looking like he wishes the ground would swallow him up – is possibly already pondering the mathsy questions that'll earn him a first at Oxford in a few years.

Liam is off into the festival with Max, but we linger near where Nelly has set up a stand with an appeal for the famine in Somalia with a few other kids from school, although they seem to have abandoned her to man it alone.

My heart jolts at the sight of Nelly's earnest face, her curly hair held back by an Alice band, but Young Jules can only see the alarming posters of pot-bellied children covered in flies with skeleton legs and is worrying that Nelly's strategy of guilt-tripping people will backfire. She's taken the famine to heart in a way that's left Jules feeling guilty and slightly ashamed over how little she's motivated to do herself.

'Why don't you come into the festival with us and have some fun? Someone said Zoella's here,' Jules says temptingly.

'No way!' Isa says. She's a superfan of the young influencer. She grabs Isaac's arm, raring to set off. 'You coming, Nelly?'

'It's OK. I'm staying here,' Nelly responds, with a determined shake of her head.

'Darling. Just go –' I implore, but she crosses her arms, scowling. 'Mum.'

Wow. Even back then, she knew her own mind. And exactly how to put me in my place.

Jules shrugs hopelessly at Ngozi as the twins head off into the fair.

'Good for you, darling,' Ngozi says to Nelly, popping a tenner in her collection pot. Then Ngozi hooks her arm through Jules's and they walk into the festival, past the bouncy castle and the ice-cream van, and the red double-decker bus kitted out in Union Jack bunting for afternoon tea.

'I wish she'd enjoy herself more,' Jules grumbles.

'It's good to be engaged,' Ngozi says.

'And she's made her point, but let's be honest, it's a waste of time. What difference is one eleven-year-old going to make?' Jules protests.

How could I be so wrong? Because eleven-year-old Greta Thunberg *did* change things. Why did I have so little faith in my own daughter?

Ngozi stops by a young woman offering us paper cups of an orange liquid that looks suspiciously like cough syrup.

'Go on,' Ngozi encourages, taking one herself.

'What is it?' Jules asks, wincing at the unusual taste.

'Aperol Spritz,' the woman holding the tray says. 'It's new.'

Thanking her, we replace the empty cups and turn away.

'I don't think that's ever going to catch on,' Jules tells Ngozi.

'Not in a million years.'

Jules and Ngozi wander down the rows of stalls, tempted by titbits of weird cheeses, chilli sauces and chocolate brownies. So many hipster brands, most of which I now know will fizzle and die. Dishy James from Fishy Fishy, one of the restaurants Jules knows well, calls out and Jules and Ngozi accept a free cone of chips.

'Mum!'

Liam bounds up in his blue-and-white Brighton and Hove Albion football strip and my stomach does a flip. Look at his knobbly, mud-stained knees, his floppy brown hair!

But 2012 Jules is thinking how unbearably grown up he is. Even though he's only nine.

'Can I have some money for the ride?' he says, holding out his left hand and pointing at the kids' fairground waltzer in the distance. *His beautiful hand*, before he got hurt. My heart breaks at the sight of it and I can't help thinking about how tempting it would be to use the machine to go back and change things. I can't, though. I may be going against my and Adam's rule to change my own life, but I draw the line at messing with our kids, especially who they are. The one golden rule we can't break.

'No. That guy's always a rip-off merchant.'

He looks up with big, forlorn eyes. 'Max is going.'

Jules lets out a growl of frustration at being fleeced. Even more so, because – I get a flash of one of her recent memories – Adam's doing a half iron man today. On his birthday. Which means that he won't be back to celebrate with them until this evening, by which time the kids will be frazzled.

At least if she gives Liam money, it will give her time to chat about Ngozi's big decision about whether she joins a boutique fashion brand as their part-time in-house lawyer, or plumps for the much better paid option of joining an international law firm as a full-time partner.

I already know she'll choose the latter, just like Jules is about to advise her, but I'm itching to tell her to take the other path, the fashion brand, because that one won't wreck her marriage. But I'm not here to change her fate.

Only mine.

Jules starts rooting through her knock-off Burberry handbag, and I can't help noticing the contents, remembering that Touche Éclat concealer she's convinced she needs (but really doesn't), the small tube of BB cream that's just come out and is all the rage, and a Rimmel burgundy lipstick à la Kate Moss. Stuff I know, for a fact, she's only been able to buy on credit, a sneaky little habit she's developing behind Adam's back.

'What the hell?' she says, pulling out a CD in a cardboard case with a twenty-pound note attached to it. *See You Later xx May 2012* is written on it in Adam's handwriting. His peace offering, she realises, for being off doing his silly race today. She laughs, feeling immediately less cross with him. He's not so bad, after all.

Yet at the same time – for me – this discovery means thirty-seven minutes have gone already of the seventy-four-minute CD. Why does it always have to fly by so fast?

Jules digs out a handful of change and pours it into Liam's cupped palms. It's eight years since Adam's parents died, but even now most of his pay cheque goes to their debt and mortgage repayments. He and Jules are just about getting by, but they're still no closer to living abroad or truly getting her business off the ground – because it takes too many hours and one of them needs to be there for the kids.

Liam shouts a thanks and bounds off as Jules and Ngozi make a beeline for the fancy Albariño stand – the new wine flavour of the month. They join the queue, getting not one but two free compostable glasses each.

Oh, the ease with which I used to down my plonk in those heady pre-menopausal days, when I could get tanked up on the old-lady petrol and the effects didn't fell me for a week. The sheer joy of being, if not actually young, then at least being able to act like I still was.

From the stage come the rough chords of the local Maroon Five wannabes warming up and I spot Liam staring up at them, entranced.

Jules hardly registers it. It's no surprise to her that Liam has become distracted by the music. He's obsessed. She and Adam are convinced that he'll be in his own band one day. They talk about it in bed, late at night, fantasising about the future they see for him, although Jules is keen to keep Liam grounded in a normal childhood, even if Adam is sure fame and fortune is round the corner. Or at least in another ten years. After all, his guitar teacher of the last three years says he's already running out of new stuff to show him.

Jules feels the wine hit her system like an old friend. This is so marvellous; I can't wait to tell Adam. Oh, *fuck no. Christ, no*, I can't. He'd go nuts if he knew I – me, *his* Jules – had snuck into the shed and was here.

Eek. I get a sharp dart of terror. What if Adam walks in and catches me tranced out in the shed? What then?

'Boo!'

Jules turns to see Darius.

'Hey,' she says, looking him up and down and noting that he's grown an on-trend hipster beard.

They bump noses as he goes in for a kiss on both cheeks. He's not been around for a few months.

'Darius,' Ngozi says in a bored tone, surreptitiously poking Jules in the ribs, her message clear: she really doesn't want to get stuck talking to him. 'So how *are* things since the old takeaway food to home app fell apart?'

'Now that was just a financing issue,' he chides her. 'The basic idea's sound. And someone will do it, you mark my words.'

'Sure.' Ngozi doesn't look convinced.

'Other than that . . .' he says. 'I'd go as far as to say I'm winning.'

'And still as modest as ever,' Jules teases, while I surreptitiously keep one eye on the queue for the main events tent. I already know that she's going to make it inside on time, but I can't help feeling nervous, knowing the seconds are ticking away.

Meanwhile Ngozi is slumped on one hip, listening as Darius bangs on about his latest idea, which revolves around some virtual way to view properties for sale . . . online. *Right*, like people are ever going to do that.

'Meaning, basically, you're still going to end up a gazillionaire,' Ngozi says, deadpan, when he's finished his pitch.

'You've got to be in it to win it,' he says, all big Billy business balls.

Ngozi rolls her eyes.

'I think that cookery demo I wanted to see is starting,' Jules cuts in. Good. *Come on, we've got to get going.*

'Right, yeah.' Ngozi grabs her opportunity too. 'Sorry, Darius. We gotta run.'

Leaving him there with a wave and a promise to catch up soon, they walk off arm in arm towards the main marquee.

'That beard looks like it's just been attacked by a ferret,' Ngozi says.

'Thank God Adam hasn't got one,' Jules adds.

Only hang on, *my* Adam, my *original* Adam, *did*. And suddenly, it's like I'm not just married to one Adam any more, but like I'm somehow fragmented and multiplying . . . as though I'm walking through the hall of mirrors at the end of the pier.

Then – quite literally – not a moment too soon, we're in the queue over at the main marquee. The reason I've come back here.

As Chef Marcel's picture grins down at us from the poster advertising his cooking demonstration, Jules and Ngozi each buy a ticket and hurry inside.

There's a raised dais at the front where the cooking demo has already started and Jules and Ngozi quickly take their seats. Onstage beside Chef Marcel is a compère with a microphone asking questions.

'You look like you could do that in your sleep,' he says, as Chef Marcel finishes expertly piping freshly made truffle cream into baby mushrooms.

'*Le clef dont on se ser test toujours claire*,' Chef Marcel says in his deep, gravelly voice. 'It means,' he adds, in heavily accented English, 'one does not get rusty in what one does every day.'

Of course I'm fascinated, just as much as Jules is, and the next twenty minutes of the demonstration fly by.

'You can sign up for my course with my colleague on the stand,' Chef Marcel says, pointing towards a desk manned by a chic-looking woman in a sleeveless black dress who waves a hand in greeting at the crowd.

'That's Marcel's wife, Anna,' the compère adds. 'She's offering lessons in French too if anyone's interested.'

This is it. The moment I've been waiting for. Quickly, I impose myself. Jules would never do it in a million years, because things are still so tight at home financially. She feels guilty enough about the make-up in her bag.

Marching her straight up to Chef Marcel's wife, I make her sign up for both Chef Marcel's cooking course *and* Anna's French lessons, slapping her credit card down.

So long as I keep the credit card statements hidden and get some extra gigs to pay them off, then Adam need never find out, I leave her thinking. *And even if it means less money now, in the long term this has got to be a good thing, right?*

I gasp as I land back in the shed.

I'm shaking as I stand up and open the Sony CD panel, taking out the CD which looks blistered and burned. I nearly toss it in the bin, but then Adam might find it and work out what I've done. Panicked, I hide it at the back of a box of his dad's old sandpaper scraps, somewhere he'll never look.

Making sure nothing else appears out of place, I hurry back up to the house, slipping in through the back door, my mind whirring with what I've just experienced, but also with a twisting in the pit of my stomach.

I really have betrayed him this time, haven't I? Changing our past so purposefully.

If it's even worked . . .

Sacré bleu!

I stand in the doorway, eyes wide. *This* kitchen is not *my* kitchen.

The horrible green units have been replaced with quirky, open-plan wooden shelves. Ones that I now remember Adam fitted for me after finally relenting and then throwing himself into the kitchen renovation project, joining me on trips to antiques markets and car boot sales. He'd been triumphant when he sourced those shelves on eBay for a song.

'*C'est magnifique*,' I marvel – my accent perfect, as I admire the strings of Rose de Lautrec garlic, onions and cute crockery pot-planted herbs on display, as well as a stack of well-thumbed French cookery books.

Holy guacamole!

Je n'en crois pas mes yeux! I speak French. *Je parle français. Je parle vraiment bien français!*

Of course I speak French. My new memories hit me thick and fast. How I studied the language with Anna while simultaneously learning part-time how to cook with Chef Marcel at his cookery school over in nearby Alfriston. I also remember how, for the whole four-year period I studied for Marcel's diploma, I hid my credit card statements and lied to Adam that Mum had lent me the money for the course. How I scrimped on the housekeeping to pay for it and held back part of my money from the new weekend job I'd taken for a caterer at the football ground, even though I knew it annoyed Adam that he couldn't cycle as much as a result. Not that he said. He told me he was happy to support me as I tried to build up my clients. Memories of my culinary prowess wash over me like gentle waves on a Côte d'Azur beach. Like they're nothing to be frightened of. Like they're the most natural thing in the world.

The digital radio is playing FIP, a French internet station I now know I like to have on when I cook. I walk over to the spotless, rustic French wooden farmhouse table with its pretty pot of flowering peonies and grab the menu Darius dropped off earlier – clearly reading what I couldn't before – meaning, yeah, all *that* still happened on this timeline, like all I've really changed is my ability to speak French and to cook like a native.

Because *bon sang ouais*, I'm now fluent in French cooking too . . .

Foie gras with truffles and celery . . . *oui, d'accord*, all very straightforward. I've made that fifty times before. *Galettes andouille de Guémené fumé* . . . uh-huh, *un morceau de pisse* . . . pancakes with that delicious smoked chitterling sausage from Brittany, *un jeu d'enfant*, and yet another French staple I'm an expert at now.

And this is amazing. *Incroyable. La merde la plus cool qui ait jamais existé!*

Yet . . . hang on . . . What if something else *has* seismically changed and not just me and the kitchen? Something my new memories haven't yet informed me of? Panicking, I check my phone. Nelly is getting her bike fixed over at Gee Whizz and Liam is at the studio in town helping out on the recording session of some new band. While on my Find My Phone app, I quickly locate Adam at work.

Hmm. With bloody Meredith, the 'babe', no doubt. *Putain!*

Even so. It means everything else is normal, right?

Sitting down at my laptop, I let out an excited yelp, noticing the screensaver is of me with Chef Marcel receiving my diploma.

Bien sur. D'accord.

I'm a bloody *qualified* French chef.

Opening a new document, I start rattling off the menu I'm going to make on Thursday for Darius's corporate gig. Thanks to my new memories, I already know where I'll source all the ingredients. The guys down at the French emporium on Sydney Street keep all my favourite ingredients back for when I call. I've also remembered that after finishing my studies, I grew a thriving events catering business for posh dinner parties and the like, until lockdown scuppered it. My menu will not only be easy to make . . . it'll be a joy.

Singing along to Jacques Brel's magnificent 'Quand on n'a que l'amour', I put some tomato sauce on to simmer, expertly chopping my fresh herbs. This is bloody marvellous, but it *is* still cheating, really, right? Yet already the guilty me who just stepped out of that shed is fading. Am I really so different to how I was before? I'm still the same old Jules, aren't I?

Just a bit more French.

I'm still immersed in the cooking zone by the time Nelly gets back from work. But the second she walks in, I register that she looks different. She's thinner and somehow more brittle.

I go over to kiss her, but she shrugs me off – like I now realise she always does on this timeline. Watching her, fresh from her bike ride back from working at Darius's office, now guzzling a glass of cold water fresh from the tap, I realise that I really have been too reckless. Because *her* life on this timeline has been altered by my decisions too, hasn't it? Like me not being here over all those weekends when I was studying in Alfriston. And her and Adam getting closer as a result.

With a sickening sense of dread, I compute that my current relationship with Nelly is not good. Not good at all. In fact, I have to walk on eggshells around her, unable to mention her unhealthy relationship with food – which Adam thinks is my fault because I'm obsessed with food myself. While *I* think her unhealthy obsession with exercise is *his* fault. In fact, our conversations about Nelly have become so fraught and full of blame, it's caused a rift between us that I don't know how to heal.

And now, as I blend in with the new, French-speaking me, I long for my snarky, and sometimes difficult, but deep down always *present* and engaging Nelly. The real Nelly. I'd take that any time over this Cold War, where more and more I feel she's just freezing me out.

My need to confess to her feels so great, I almost blurt *everything* out, but instead I skirt as close to the truth as I can.

'You know, it's funny, but today I had a really vivid memory of that food festival. Do you remember? When they used to be on the lawns? And you were raising money for the famine in Somalia?'

She shrugs. 'That was just a stupid phase I was going through.'

'It wasn't stupid.'

'Yes, it was. You even said so at the time.'

'What?' I exclaim. 'No, I didn't.'

She gives me a look, clearly sceptical about my protest. 'Well, I don't remember *exactly* what you said, but that's how it felt.'

I stare at her for a beat. Oh shit. I *do* now remember how dismissive I was.

'Well, I was wrong.'

Nelly's eyebrows shoot up.

'It just made me remember that you always cared about other people way more than yourself. I mean, you should have seen the light in your eyes.'

'It was years ago, Mum. You can't possibly remember that. Besides, I'm not that little kid any more.'

'You are, though,' I insist. 'Good people don't change. And . . . I'm telling you, if anyone is going to save the world, it's still going to be you.'

I give her an encouraging smile, but she throws up her arms, her look suddenly thunderous.

'Oh Jesus! Give me a break! I've just got in from work and now you want me to save the world?'

'I don't mean it like –'

'Why are you always putting such high expectations on me? Just because your life didn't go according to plan. Not that we don't hear the bloody last of it. How you could have been this or could have done that. Could have lived somewhere else.'

Is this really what she thinks? And worse, is she right? My God, I can speak French, I have a snazzy kitchen, and a moderately successful career of sorts, but apparently, it's *still* not enough? For her, for our family, for *me*? But, yes, she's right. My new memories tell me this too.

'OK, so my big dreams may not have worked out, or not yet, but that doesn't mean yours can't,' I tell her. Nelly stares at me, and for a second, I see a chink in her armour. 'I mean it. I'm worried you're settling, darling. Or settling too young. I'm scared you're forgetting all that passion you used to have. You wanted to travel, remember? You were going to go *everywhere*.'

'I do go to lots of places. On my bike.'

'Yes, but I don't just mean Portslade and Dorking. You used to have a world map when you were little, remember? You used to say goodnight to people in places you couldn't even pronounce. You always wanted to travel the world and make a difference.'

She twists her lips and sighs. 'Yeah, well, that was then. I wouldn't know where to start.'

But as I look into those deep, thoughtful eyes of hers, I know that she's listening.

'Well, that's not surprising. You don't get a second to yourself to think. I know you've got a good job and things are better now you've got your own office space, but I'm still not convinced it's the right path. I don't think you are either.'

Her eyes narrow and I worry that maybe I've pushed it too far.

'I am not telling you how to live your life, I promise. I only want you to be happy.'

An arch of her eyebrow. 'I would be if you got off my case.'

It's the closest she's come to a smile.

'OK. I hear you, I do, and I'm going to try to do better. To be better. To be here for you more.'

She looks directly at me and nods.

'I know you think I don't, but I do trust you, Nelly. I always have.'

She tips her head to one side.

'I don't know what's going on with you, but it's weird,' she says. 'Why are you suddenly so . . . philosophical?'

'Because life is quicker than you think. And also . . . because I should have told you at the time how proud I was of you, that day. And I'm really, really sorry I didn't.'

She looks at me steadily for a few seconds. 'OK,' she says.

I nod and turn away to the cooker, swamped by a flurry of emotions that I can't even begin to untangle, picking up the wooden spoon to stir the sauce.

'That smells really good by the way,' she says, putting her hand on my shoulder, and I close my eyes for a second, the wooden spoon stopping, as my heart contracts.

The private dining room where the dinner is being held on Thursday is on the top floor of the Quark building and, just as Darius promised, there's a decent kitchen too.

I arrive early, just to make sure the ovens work, and that I've prepped everything in time. Moving around the space in my chef's whites, I already know the meal will be a success. In fact, I'm struggling to remember why I was ever worried about tonight in the first place. I've got lovely langoustines from Jack the fishmonger and some delicious fresh asparagus for my starter, and fresh gilt-head bream, capers and cream with a reduced bouillabaisse, plus my spectacular orange crème caramel and macaron dessert.

I plate up each course and Eva serves the guests, returning each time with scraped-clean plates. She raises her eyebrows at me.

'Looks like you're even more on fire than usual, chef.'

She's already delivered the cheese board stocked by Curds & Whey, Redroaster coffees and petits fours, and I'm just wiping down in the kitchen, when Darius texts me to come on through to the dining room.

To my absolute delight, the guests around the table give me a round of applause. My God, it's just like that weird dream I had a fortnight ago. Only, well . . . deserved.

The guy to Darius's left leans back in his chair and pats the front of his designer shirt. In French, he tells me that I balanced the flavours to perfection. I listen demurely, batting away his profuse praise with a self-deprecating comment in French about my disappointment about not being able to get the right courgette flowers.

Darius asks me to pull up a chair and pours me a glass of wine – one of the delicious bottles of Moscato I selected to pair with the dessert.

I can tell he's watching me as we all chat about France and then the discussion moves on to the mayoral system. Sujane is impressed when I offer my opinion, again in fluent French, on the latest local election results in the region where she's from and laughs when I tell her that I keep up with current affairs through French news podcasts because I find British politics so boring.

Back in the kitchen, Eva has almost finished the clear-up.

'I heard them laughing in there,' she says.

'Honestly, it couldn't have gone better,' I say, feeling a flush of pride.

She comes down in the service lift with me and walks me to the car and we slide the crates in. She's just a few weeks away from her big trip to Costa Rica and she's grateful for the cash I give her, plus a hefty tip.

'I'll miss you,' I tell her. 'You must be so excited?'

'I am. Can't wait. Although I'm nervous I'm going alone.'

'I wish . . . I wish Nelly was going with you, but I'm so glad you've seen a bit more of each other recently.' Although I wish they'd connected more.

Eva shrugs, like maybe she thinks this too.

'Well, good luck,' I say. 'Come and see me before you go.'

I've just got into the Skoda when Darius walks out of the office shooting me a big grin. I roll down the driver's window.

'They've signed. They're on board,' he gushes.

'That's great.'

'You literally charmed the pants off them.'

I laugh. I know he's being sweet attributing his success to me, but I'm flattered, nonetheless.

'Yeah, well, it was fun to practice the old French,' I add, barely even feeling like a charlatan any more.

There's an awkward pause.

'So . . . I'll ping over my invoice, shall I?' I ask.

'Oh, yeah. Sure, sure,' he says, putting his hands in the pockets of his beautifully tailored suit.

'Well . . . night. And . . . thanks for giving me this chance. It was fun.'

I turn the key in the ignition, but the car won't start.

'Bloody hell. Not now,' I mutter, trying again, then again. *Bloody Adam and this stupid bloody car.*

'What's the problem?'

Darius is back at the window.

'Just . . . uh . . . I don't suppose you've got any jump leads?' I ask, but as I nod over at his red Ferrari on the other side of the car park, I sincerely doubt he has. Or that his car and Adam's mum's old jalopy will be compatible. It would probably be like trying to get a golden eagle and a seagull to have sex.

'Come on, I'll give you a lift,' Darius says. 'Then you can get this towed back to yours in the morning.'

Gratefully, I follow him to his car, bumping my head as I get into the low passenger seat. It's hardly my coolest move, but Darius only laughs gently and tells me everyone does it first time.

'Hold on to your hat,' he jokes, as he launches us off down the car park ramp and gives it some gas.

The Troubs pop up right away on his dashboard playlist, singing that song Adam and I always liked the best from their third album, 'I'll Be Yours'. Darius sings along loudly and tunelessly and smiles at me, encouraging me to join in, just like he did when we sang karaoke at his party. And I do.

Is this how it'll be when we all go to their gig? Me and Darius singing, instead of me and Adam? But why does this make me feel so guilty? Adam doesn't *own* the Troubs, after all.

In no time, we're whipping along the seafront and I grip onto the seat at once thrilled and horrified. Then, laughing, he slows right down and turns up through the winding streets and swings into our cul-de-sac. He parks the car expertly on our drive and cuts the engine. The music dies.

'Thanks for the lift,' I say and undo my seat belt. Darius shifts in his seat so he's facing me.

'You know, tonight was a test,' he says.

I look at him, frowning. What's he talking about?

'And I'm pleased to say you passed with flying colours. Which is why I'm going to fund you,' he says. 'That pop-up you mentioned. If you can find a venue, then I'll invest whatever you need to make it happen.'

'*Really?* Oh my God, Darius. Thank you!' I fling my arms around his neck, because, bloody hell, this is amazing, right?

I pull back, our faces only inches apart. He looks into my eyes and then at my lips, and I can't breathe, because we've been this physically close only once before.

Except this time, there's no excuse. He's not drunk, and neither am I.

'Jules,' he whispers, but loud enough for me to hear the longing in his voice.

'Don't say it,' I tell him, seeing in his eyes that he still wants me. That he's remembering the offer he made for us to run away together all that time ago. Even though I told him no then, maybe he thinks there might be a chance.

I put my hand on his soft cheek. Then kiss his other cheek, and I pause, our faces so close, I can feel his breath on my lips.

For a second, just a second, I'm tempted. There's something so intoxicating about this moment, about him believing in me.

But . . . no. No, no. I can't.

I quickly fumble with the door and stumble out of his ridiculous car, my legs shaking.

'Jules, wait . . .' he says, reaching across to grab me, but I shake my head. I can't look at him, because if I do, he'll see how a part of me might still want this too.

Chapter Twelve

Adam – 'Happy'

What the hell? Did Darius just try to . . . ? Did Jules just nearly . . . ?

I watch through the living-room window as she walks ~~her walk away~~ from his Ferrari towards the front door. His eyes stay locked on her as she disappears from my line of sight. Then he smiles as I hear her key turning in the lock. Why? Because she just turned back to look at him before coming inside? To wave goodbye? Or even, Jesus Christ, to blow him that same kiss I think he nearly just planted on her lips inside his car?

Did he really just try to do that? No, I must have been mistaken, right?

I feel cold. I feel sick. For a second, I wonder if he spots me as he reverses his Ferrari back out of the drive and its 10 trillion-megawatt beams sweep across the tatty sofa I'm sitting on by the window.

Then he's gone and I grab a book off the table to pretend I've just been sitting here reading and not waiting up for Jules. Even though that's exactly what I've been doing. Because it's late and I'm a decent guy is what I tell myself. But it's not just that, is it? It's because I'm a jealous guy too and rattled by how well Jules and Darius have been getting on. Maybe with good bloody reason.

'Oh, you're still up,' she says, noticing me as she hangs up her coat in the hall.

'Yeah.'

'Is everything OK?'

'Sure. Why? *Shouldn't* it be?'

'Darius gave me a lift back,' she admits, either not registering or deliberately ignoring my tone. 'Because your mum's car wouldn't start. Again...'

I keep on glaring. I want an explanation. She must have worked out that I could see the two of them from here.

'Darius thinks it's the distributor,' she says. 'But he reckons the whole car is kaput. He says he knows a dealer who owes him a favour who might trade it in.'

'Saint fucking Darius,' I say.

She glances at my whiskey glass, but this has *nothing* to do with that.

'So that's what you were discussing out there so *intimately*, was it?' I say before I can stop myself, unable to keep the accusation from my voice. 'The state of our car?'

'Oh,' she says, 'so that's where you're going with this, is it? No, "Hi, Jules, how did the dinner go?" Or "Gee, honey, you must be tired after working so hard." Or "Why don't I fix you a nice cup of herb tea and run you a salts bath?" Instead, I get you sulking over some bullshit about me talking to one of our oldest friends in his car. Well, hey fucking ho, Adam. *Plus ça change, plus c'est la même chose.*'

'I don't even know what that means,' I snap. Because I don't. I'm about as fluent in French as Groucho Barx is in cat.

'So look it up in a dictionary. Although you would of course have to hold *that* the right way round.'

For a second, I don't know what she's talking about. But then I see that the book I'm pretending to read *is*, in fact, upside down.

'Or maybe I'll save you the effort,' she says, her eyes now flashing with anger. 'It means *the more things change, the more they stay the same*... Like with us. Even with everything that's been going on in the shed... even with all that... you and me, we're still... we're still...'

'What?'

'Stuck.'

'Stuck?' That same word she used against me in our fight after Darius's pool party. Only now, the way she says it, it sounds even worse, more like *fucked*. Leaving us no further on from that row when everything came spilling out, in spite of all the other good stuff that's happened since.

'In the same holding pattern, Adam,' she says, stabbing her finger at the dark sky outside. 'Like planes, flying round and round each other, only never going anywhere new. And never even landing together at the same time . . . Well, guess what? We can't fly around up there forever. Because one day we'll . . . we'll run out of fuel. One day we'll crash.'

'Oh, well, do allow me to be the first to congratulate you on your excruciatingly long and tortured metaphor,' I say, slow-clapping her.

'Simile.'

'Whatever. Because it still doesn't make any sense. Things *have* changed. *Are* changing. Like . . . like . . .' I nearly tell her about my body and how much better I feel because of it, but stop myself just in time, grasping for something else instead. '. . . like what's been happening in bed.'

'Sex. That's really all you can think of?'

'Well, why not? Because it *is* good, isn't it? *Better* than it was before. Because of us remembering how we used to be and bringing those memories back. Like *you* said,' I remind her. 'Like we're using those old experiences to fix the present.'

'Sex is just a part of a relationship, Adam. Not the relationship itself.'

'OK, then what about . . .' I almost tell her about how much better I'm getting on with Nelly because of us now getting into cycling together too, but of course that would be admitting I got fit behind Jules's back. '. . . what about the fact you and me are spending more time together, doing all this stuff, travelling back?'

'But we're not, are we? Not really,' she glowers. 'We go back one at a time, with the other one waiting on their own in the shed with just a zombie for company.'

'OK, fine, but we're still talking about it afterwards, aren't we? We're still *sharing* the experience.'

Arms folded, she's having none of it. 'All we're actually talking about is the past. Not our real lives now.'

I hate it when she does this. When she gets so bloody dogmatic. 'This is you all over, isn't it?' I snipe. 'No matter what you get, you always want more. Like I gave you a goddamned multiverse time machine and that's *still* not enough.'

'Because we're still arguing, aren't we?' she points out. 'And apart from fucking like rabbits, I can't see how we're any happier here in the present.' Her eyes narrow. 'Do you really want to know what I was talking to Darius about in the car?'

'Yeah, actually. I bloody well do.'

'Moving on. Making plans for the future.'

A sudden swell of panic rises inside me. She can't mean . . . she can't mean with *him*, can she? He can't have asked her to –

'Because, actually, Adam, the dinner *did* go well. Really bloody well. So well, that Darius is going to fully fund my pop-up restaurant.'

Oh. OK, so not *on*-on, not together . . . But still. 'You can't,' I say.

'Why not?'

'There'll be strings attached! There always are with him.' Like with him pretending that he's not micro-managing Quark when it's obvious to everyone at work that he is.

'Yes, but at least he believes in me,' Jules says. 'And knows I'll make a success of it.'

I'm about to snap back at her that she's making a big mistake by giving him control, because whatever comes out of this, it will never truly be hers. Then I hear what she's saying. That *I* haven't believed in her. I can suddenly see it right here in her eyes, how much she's wanted this.

'I believe in you too,' I quickly say, but it's only now that I've said it out loud that I realise I actually mean it. She *can* do this, can't she? She's an amazing chef. Someone who could even work in Paris if that's what she wanted. I mean, at least that's what her mentor Chef Marcel said. 'We don't need his charity,' I add, meaning this too. 'I can sell off some of my gym equipment, can't I? And a couple of my bikes.' Although, shit, even that won't be enough, I work out. Not seeing as how they're all second- or third-hand already. 'Or if that's not enough then we can –' But already, I'm faltering.

'We can *what*, Adam? We've got no spare money. Because we've never taken the risks to make any.' Her look of determination now switches to one of full-on guts. 'Which is why I'm doing this, no matter what you say. I'm taking him up on his offer and you're not stopping me. This isn't just for me. It's for us. For our family. One of us has to do *something* to fix our bloody finances and *find a way forward*, instead of just *doing nothing*. Instead of just going out on yet another fifty-mile flippin' bike ride and hoping it'll all go away.'

Speech over. She marches back out into the hall and stomps up the stairs. Leaving me in total silence, like it's not just this stupid book I've got upside down, but everything.

Slowly turning it over, I read the title. It's one of hers. In bloody French. *À la Recherche du Temps Perdu* by Marcel Proust. I type it into my phone to translate.

In Search of Lost Time.

I mean, you have got to be kidding me, right? It's like the universe is laughing in my face.

Throwing the book hard across the room, I watch its pages flap like wings for a second as it nose-dives into the glass-fronted wooden dresser, smashing its upper pane, before fluttering to the floor like a shot bird . . . landing right in front of the dresser's old wooden double drawers.

Which is when I remember – oh God . . . maybe I do have a way out of this.

Jumping up, I rush out into the hall, through the kitchen and out into the cold night. Because what if this really *is* the universe – or even many universes – talking to me? No, not as in Adam's-just-gone-totally-coco-loco-and-is-hearing-voices-inside-his-head. More like what Jules said about this whole series of crazy events being entirely personal to us.

What if *In Search of Lost Time* is a sign? About where I need to go next. And not just that, but the dresser's wooden drawers are a sign too?

As soon as I get inside the shed, I jerk the blinds down to make sure Jules can't see in from the house. Then I head for the box of tapes and CDs, already knowing what I'm looking for. Anything pre-October 2014. Right away, I find one. Again, it's like it's glowing in the moonlight. Just like with that first tape. Like this really is something the universe wants me to see.

Staycation 2014, it says on the CD cover. In Jules's handwriting in green biro. A gift from her to me in the year we didn't have enough money to go on holiday, with every penny we had going into the San Francisco fund. To keep the kids amused, we'd decided to turn the garden into a makeshift festival and adventure playground.

I picture the zip wire in my mind. Me climbing up the bay tree to tie it. How excited the kids were. Then I hear that screaming again, from later the same year.

No. I shouldn't go back to this year. Absolutely not. In case I do try to change Liam's future.

But do I have any alternative? Because the only thing I can think of that can fix everything else with Jules is also located in that year.

Quickly – before I can change my mind – I slot the CD into the Sony. Turning the volume down to 1, so no one outside of the shed will be able to hear, I hit 'Play'.

The last thing I see are my old *Star Wars* figurines still lined up in a row on Dad's old lathe, before 'Happy' by Pharrell Williams starts tinnily pumping out, and I find myself sucked into that whirling tornado, and spinning so fast I feel sick . . .

Ahhhhhand . . . I cruise down onto the runway. I'm so used to it, I might as well be some first-class passenger with my Xanax timed to perfection, before hitting the ground running the second I disembark.

Wide awake, the first thing I see are my hands – OK, Young Adam's hands – only not really that young any more, because of course here in 2014 he's already forty-two.

His hands still look younger than mine, though. Less wrinkly, less hairy. His wrist brachialis looks thinner too, along with his flexor carpi radialis muscles. Of course, because on this timeline I've only been working out for five years. Meaning I've still got plenty more volleyball, marathons, iron man comps and cycling trips to truly toughen me up.

'I think you should make them longer,' Darius says.

'But then they'll end up looking like dicks,' Adam responds. He's talking about the two i's he's currently finessing on a piece of A4 paper as part of his smile-shaped design for the words 'Totally Sirius'.

Of course. This is the exact same proto company logo that will end up pinned to the cork board right here in the shed that I'll then rip up on the night of Darius's party. A logo that Adam still hopes might become as iconic as Atari, Sega or Nintendo.

'What's wrong with dicks?' Darius asks.

'Well, nothing, per se,' Adam answers. 'But as part of a gaming logo, they might look a tad male . . . a smidgeon aggressive . . .'

'What's wrong with male and aggressive?'

'Are you serious?'

'Uh. Totally Sirius, bro,' Darius Bill & Teds. 'Because that way the market will have to sit up and notice us and therefore take us Totally Sirius-ly too.'

'I thought the whole point of Totally Sirius was to look to the future, to offer gamers something new, not just the same old guns and testosterone crap . . .'

'Yeah, but the biggest market is still teen boys. And dicks –

even just a hint of dicks in the logo – that'll make them laugh. It'll make the brand cool.'

The same old shit he'll still be peddling with Quark's new logo in ten years' time.

'A hint of dicks?' Adam mocks him. 'Maybe you should just launch that as a new aftershave instead?'

'Very funny,' says Darius.

Acting like it doesn't bother him, when the truth is he already likes being talked back to less and less these days. Especially in matters of business, still convinced he's on an upwards trajectory, despite several setbacks along the way. Leaving Younger Me already playing beta to Darius's alpha.

But enough already of this. Enough of *them*. I know how this plays out. How Adam will fail to win this battle with Darius for the soul of Totally Sirius. How all this excitement Adam is feeling right now – this whole *thirst* for the future – will fizzle out, doused by an increasing dread over the next two years that him and Darius are getting out of their depth, and that Darius is *too* confident, too reckless, and that Darius's American uncle won't come through with the promised finances, leaving Adam exposed to bankruptcy if they fail.

'Hey, where you going?' Darius asks.

Adam doesn't reply. Or even look back – because Adam is no longer in control.

Walking him past the old Bang & Olufsen record player, I make him turn up the volume so the Van Morrison record that's been playing drowns out Darius's grumblings, then steer him on out into the blazing sunlight. I turn him round to face the house, aiming to control him long enough to make him stride on up there so I can do what I came here to do.

Only then I see Liam and it shocks me how much he's grown since I last saw him in Port de Pollença in 2009, so much so that I relinquish control and just sit back inside Adam. The sweet little six-year-old I left eating chips on that bench has now warped into a feral, cheeky-looking eleven-year-old, sitting with his best friend Max by the remains of last night's staycation BBQ.

'Hey, guys,' Adam says, a little dazed from me having just imposed myself on him, and not really knowing why he's wandered out into the garden.

Darius follows him out.

'So, Uncle Dar, have you got your Ferrari yet?' Liam asks, nudging Max in the ribs. A running joke, I now remember, from back when we all thought it would never actually happen.

'Still waiting for you to get your record deal, so I can pick you up from Wembley Stadium after your first sellout gig,' Darius teases back, not missing a beat.

Liam grabs his new, bigger acoustic, that's never far from his side these days, all covered in Royal Blood and Arctic Monkeys stickers, from where it's lying by his feet, before firing off a dramatic, ironic three-chord *boom-tish-boom* strum.

I'm hardly even listening, though. Just staring at Liam's left hand. At *all* of it. At all four fingers and his thumb.

And you know what happens when people fall . . .

What Mum said after Young Adam slid down that banister that first time I jumped back to 1989.

I thought it was just a criticism, but now I see it for what it really was. A prophecy and one, no matter what the risks, I have to act on now.

I don't give myself a microsecond more to think about it. Imposing myself on Adam again, I march him back into the shed. Emerging seconds later with a ball hammer and hacksaw, I stride past Darius and the kids and saw through the end of the zip wire's rope where it's wrapped around the tree stump at the bottom of the garden. The second the forty-foot rope loses its tension, it jerks away from me, live as a snake, with its hated pulley and T-bar crashing down onto the lawn from where they'd been hooked around the top branch of the bay tree.

'Dad! What are you doing?' Liam yells.

'They're dangerous,' I make Adam say. 'I, er, read about it online.'

He's confused, but inside I'm punching the air.

'But, Dad . . .'

Liam can see it's too late. The rope's ruined. Him, Max and Darius are all staring at me like I've just gone mad.

Who knows? Maybe they're right. Maybe I have. But it's too late now to go changing things back.

Grabbing the wooden pulley, I carry it over to the nearest paving slab and smash it to pieces.

'There,' I make Adam say, grinning up at the others, his heart pounding with exertion.

'Dad! That was mental.' Liam's eyes are wide.

'Yeah, but he's right,' Darius says. 'I read that article too.'

He's lying, but backing me up. Because that's what friends do. Even when friends look like they're totally losing their shit.

'Thanks,' I tell him.

Liam looks at me nervously and I make Adam smile reassuringly, like it's no big deal. 'Just thinking of you, buddy. Keeping you safe.'

'So can you help us finish off our den?' Liam asks. 'Like you promised.'

He's right. Younger Me did promise and I've still got time. I've probably only been here fifteen minutes of what's due to be a seventy-four-minute trip.

I give Adam back control. He stares from the smashed pulley and T-bar to the cut rope and back, disorientated for a second, mentally trying to come to terms with what he's just done. Then he remembers what I made him say about the zip wire being dangerous. Him and Darius and the kids start to play

'Oh, good,' says a voice a while later.

Looking up, I see it's Jules – or Younger Jules – staring down at the wreckage of the zip wire. She's dressed in straight-cut jeans and a black, half-lace top – and I remember what we were like when we were still such a tightknit team, before we failed to move to San Francisco.

'I was worried someone might get hurt,' she says. 'I even told your dad not to put it up,' she tells Liam, 'but he wouldn't listen –' she smiles – '... until now.'

And it's only now that I remember that this is true. She *did* tell me this. Something else I'd forgotten. Or buried. Christ, how much strength must it have taken not to say this to my face over the years? To lay the blame firmly at my feet where it truly did belong.

'Here,' she says, handing me a CD. 'A bit late, but here's your summer holiday CD. And please do feel free to put it on. I don't think I can take any more Van.'

'But we love Van Morrison,' Adam, Darius and the boys protest.

'As do I,' she says, 'but that's the second time you've played the entirety of *Moondance* today,' she points out, waggling the CD until Adam takes it.

Smiling, he kisses her, just briefly, but enough to make the boys snigger and almost make me swoon, as I realise again just how far off this kind of casual intimacy we'd got before we discovered the machine.

But I also realise that now she's given it to me, I've only got thirty-seven minutes remaining here, no more, but luckily only one thing left to do.

Jules heads back up the garden, saying she's going to pick Nelly up from Eva's house. I start heading for the living room, but Liam grabs me, pulling me back down the garden.

There's still time, right? To play some more with my boy. So I let go and sit back and enjoy it as Adam, Darius, Liam and Max get building... with blankets, old bits of corrugated iron, wooden posts and anything else they can find. They make quite the space-crash-landing survivalist team too, don't they? We've been playing this new game of ours, Earth Twin, all summer. A game I'd not just been playing with the kids out here in the garden but had started storyboarding as a potential concept for pitching to Darius too. What I hoped might even one day be the first Totally Sirius non-violent survivalist game to hit the stores.

They end up rigging up the old tent skin over the clothesline and reinforcing its perimeter against freak dust storms, a regular occurrence here on Proxima Centauri, which is what they've decided to call the garden for now. Then they discuss what rations Liam and Max are going to need to get them through the night – and, luckily for them, Proxima Centauri has plenty of nearby natural deposits of Pot Noodles, Tangy Cheese Doritos and Diet Cokes. Right in the corner shop, aka NASA Supplies Depot, at the end of the road.

God, it's fun too. Just *playing* again. With Adam and Darius every bit as involved as the kids. No rules. No ideas too silly. Just egging Liam and Max on to keep on building from the sandpits of their minds.

All four of them end up howling with laughter and Darius doesn't even freak out too much about the grass stains on his tailored skinny jeans. But just when they're finalising their planet evacuation rules, he steps back, as his iPhone pings.

'Shit. Sorry. Time's up, lads,' he says. 'I've got to go and meet Lucy.'

Another new girlfriend. The boys wolf-whistle and pull grossed-out faces. It's all Adam can do not to roll his eyes too, because none of Darius's squeezes ever last long. Then Liam and Max start shrieking as a fluffball of a puppy – bloody hell, it can only be Groucho Barx – tears yapping down the garden towards us with a chewed-up teddy in his mouth.

Shit. I remember what I've actually come here to do. How long have we been playing? Bollocks. I need to move now, before my time's up. *To fix our bloody finances . . . and find a way forward . . . instead of just doing nothing.*

Quickly imposing myself again on Adam, I hurry for the kitchen doorway, reaching it just as his Jules is stepping out.

'God, I love watching you playing with Liam,' she says.

'Just Liam?' Nelly asks from behind her.

Nelly. Aged – what? – fourteen. Seeing my little girl knocks me back out of imposing myself on Adam and leaves me just staring again instead.

'And of course you too,' Adam says, with a slight slur of confusion, wondering why the hell he just walked up here.

Then he's wide awake and dadding, chatting, because these last two years that Jules has been doing the Chef Marcel French courses that her mum bought her, Adam and Nelly have spent more time hanging out. He's got her into both running and cycling, so that one day she might end up making the county team. They even have a special complex high-five round-the-side handshake that they perform seamlessly right now.

Younger Jules watches with, it has to be said, more than a little envy in her eyes.

'Did you get your logo sorted?' she asks, nodding towards the shed, as Nelly runs out to scoop Groucho up.

'Getting there.'

She grins, clearly just as excited by this progress with his and Darius's fledgling business as him. Tapping into Adam's more recent memories, I now see the hundreds of hours that he and Jules have spent discussing Totally Sirius too. Something else I've forgotten. How much she supported me. How much she wanted to make *my* dream come true.

But that's why I'm here, right? To do the same for her.

Only then Adam's watching Jules smile right past him at Darius, who's howling and prowling around the kids' den, like he's a one-man cosmic storm.

I want to tell her. About Liam. About how what I've just done will save him. Because as much as I never forgave myself for him getting hurt, I'm now not sure she ever forgave me either.

I want to tell her it's fixed.

But I can't. I never can.

'Do you think he'll ever settle down? Have kids himself?' she asks, looking at Darius. Said wistfully, like it's a waste – something the younger me misses entirely.

'Maybe,' Adam answers. Only when he looks down the garden towards where Darius is staring back up at us, I recognise that same look in Darius's eyes from when he watched Jules walking from his Ferrari to our front door.

Jules . . . my God . . . is it *her* he's been holding out for . . . for all this time?

'Where are you going?' she says.

I don't let Younger Me answer as I impose myself on him again. I don't let him stop this time until I get to the living room. Keeping Adam firmly under my control, I march him right up to the old glass-fronted wooden dresser Marcel Proust just smashed the shit out of in my future. Only the glass here is of course still intact, and I quickly open the bottom double wooden doors.

And look – just look! – they're all right here waiting for me, alongside Mum's old Royal Doulton china tea set. My old buddies. Bought for me by Dad during those seventies Christmases when Mum was giving me knitted jumpers, a new Cub Scout uniform and *The Good News Bible*.

Luke, Han, Leia, Chewy and C-3PO. My collectors' items. All still sealed in their boxes. All in pristine condition before Liam and Max get hold of them in just a month's time and 'sacrifice them' to the ancient spirits of Earth Twin on a pyre built on top of the Weber Interstellar Observation Station, aka the barbecue.

Even more important, the Mandalorian bounty hunter Boba Fett's here too, and I jarringly know an identical boxed figure will sell nine years from now to a New York collector for over twenty thousand bucks.

Quickly getting Adam to grab them all, I march him upstairs to our bedroom and make him hide them behind our heavy wooden wardrobe in the recess where I always used to hide as a kid, somewhere nobody ever goes.

I leave a message for him on his laptop too, in case the act of doing this is too blurry for him and he wonders where the hell they've gone. I remind him that they need to stay hidden in case the kids or the new puppy finds them and messes up their value by opening them or tearing them apart.

Fifty-two years old I may be, but finally – at last! – I'm getting my *Ferris Bueller's Day Off* moment, as I turn off the motorway and drive down Dyke Road Avenue and back into town.

Granted, this car is not a 1961 Ferrari 250 GT California Spyder, like the one Ferris convinces his best friend Cameron to boost from his father's glass garage in the 1986 John Hughes classic. Nor is it a 2021 Ferrari SF90 Stradale V8 Turbo like the one Darius currently bellends around the streets of Brighton. But it is at least red.

Even more important it's a Triumph Spitfire convertible, the same car Jules has shouted out the name of throughout the course of our twenty-five-year marriage whenever she's variously spotted it in episodes of *Murder, She Wrote*, *Doctor Who* and *Killing Eve*. It's her favourite car. One she's always coveted.

And one she now owns. Even if it is a bit shonky, and with only a three-month guarantee.

Admittedly, my motives for buying it are not entirely honourable. It's not just for her, is it? It's for me too. Partly because I also get to drive it, and feel deeply, Matthew Broderick-level cool in it, like I do right now with its top down and the sun beating on my flexed biceps and black knock-off, scuffed Ray-Bans.

But also because, in Freudian terms, what I'm doing here is hopefully eradicating a clear case of chronic penis envy. A subtext unavoidable even to me, in so far as I am literally, or metaphorically, giving Jules another dick. To put her off Darius's.

And while spending five K on anything would normally bring me out in hives, Jules is worth it.

I mean, why else would I have caught the train up to London first thing this morning to sell my unsullied *Star Wars* figures to a collector who probably stiffed me ten per cent more than I might have made at auction? Because I wanted to make Jules's dreams come true.

Here, in reality.

Even if this might now be a significantly different reality, indeed universe, to the one I left last night. One where Liam never did get the opportunity to cremate Boba Fett, FX-7, C-3PO et al. Meaning they were all still safely tucked behind my wardrobe when I snuck in last night after getting back from 2014.

Even more importantly, here in this alternative universe, Liam didn't have his accident. When I got back last night, the very first thing I did – before going and looking for the figurines – was to rush upstairs to his room to see how he was. Gone, was the answer. In Japan, my new memories quickly informed me. Where Liam, Max and Kai's band, Grass Stain, are touring.

Yep, my boy has only gone and made it, goddammit!

Not only did he not have his accident on this new timeline, he also pursued his dream. Relentlessly. Getting signed to a label just after his eighteenth birthday, then happily dropping out of uni and moving to London to buy a flat. Leaving him now on the verge of real success. If not yet quite a household name, then certainly well on his way.

I checked on my wonderful Nelly too. Fast asleep in bed but with her laptop still on and her phone flashing a waterfall of messages from her boss. So same as. But also with a map out on her desk showing the route she's got planned for us to go riding this weekend. Equally importantly, my new memories tell me that she doesn't seem to have been affected by Liam's rise to fame, like some overshadowed siblings might be.

What I'd done was a good thing then. *Right?* Something I don't regret. *Won't.* The only downside I've been able to think of so far is not being able to tell Jules everything I've achieved.

I flip my phone's Spotify over from Catatonia's 'Mulder and Scully' to Grass Stain's first album, *Earth Twin*. A reference to Liam and Max's childhood game back in that summer of 2014, of all things. I scroll down to track four, 'Zip Wire'.

'*And then you rush, rush, rush, down into the ground,*' Max and Liam sing, along with me too right here in the car, because I know this whole album backwards, of course.

Only now he never did rush, rush, rush down into the ground, did he? Not like in all the other universes that came before. Not into pain. Just for fun.

Jeez! What the hell?!

I slam on the brakes, narrowly missing running over the pristine white tennis shoes of a woman in lilac shorts and a matching top, who's just stepped off the kerb, cocking her hip and sticking out her thumb like she's in a movie and hoping for a lift.

I don't even need to see her face to know it's Meredith. I remember her doing this exact same thing at the bus stop just a few weeks ago when her bus pulled up. Cute. Like it was only stopping for her. Like the whole world was stopping to look too.

Not just me.

'I thought it was you.' She grins, taking off her shades, her grey eyes shining as she stares into mine. 'And, oh, my, God. May I?' She looks over the car, before climbing into the passenger seat without even waiting for a reply. 'Ooh, I love it. It's so retro. So . . . *you*.'

Me? Meaning what? That she thinks *I'm* retro too?

A car beeps behind me, and I raise my arm by way of an apology as I drive on, but to flex my bicep a little too. Out of wounded pride. To remind her I'm not quite as old as all that.

'So, what's with this baby?' she asks.

'Um . . .' But something stops me telling her that it's a present for Jules, because I've been telling Meredith too much, haven't I? On this new timeline and the last. Or maybe it's not that at all, because I can't stop myself glancing down at her long bare legs. Maybe it's that I still want this little Meredith bubble to be just about us. In spite of wanting everything sorted with Jules too.

'You got your kit in the back?' she asks.

'Huh?'

'For volleyball. That is why you're here, right? To give me a ride?'

Then I realise I *have* just driven past the end of her road. When it was totally off my route. And we *are* meant to be playing today.

'Um, no,' I say, confused.

'So, to what *do* I owe this honour? Are you planning on whipping me off somewhere gorgeous in the countryside for lunch? Because, honestly, in a car like this on a day like this, you're making it hard for a girl to say no.'

With that, she unclips her blonde hair, shaking it and letting it cascade down around her shoulders. The hairography equivalent of stripping off naked and running giggling into the woods. Jeez. What *is* this? Surely a level up even from the open flirting we were doing down at the volleyball court. An escalation. An offer. For real.

I can't believe how I've ended up in the exact same position as Jules and Darius in the car last night . . . But nothing happened between them, did it? I still have to believe that.

Even so, I can't deny I'm not tempted. Meredith is smart, she's fun, she's beautiful. But maybe this is all some needy part of me has ever really wanted from her. To be properly noticed. Because suddenly it's not her I'm thinking about. It's Jules and how she's going to look when she sees this car. How much she's going to smile.

'Sorry,' I tell Meredith, pulling over to the side of the road again, 'and . . . and the volleyball's off too. I don't think we should partner any more.'

She stares at me for a second like she doesn't believe me. I feel like a heel. I *am* a heel. This new me and the one on my last timeline, he has been stringing her along, hasn't he? Haven't *we*? Haven't *I*? Letting that whole volleyball flirting thing snowball into this.

Meredith leans in to kiss me on the cheek again regardless, just like Monday morning on the court. Only this time, she lightly touches her nose against mine.

'Just do it,' she whispers, and I can feel her warm breath on my face. 'Kiss me. Just do it and then it's done.'

But I don't want to be Nike Man. Not for her.

'No,' I tell her again. 'I'm sorry.'

Because this really is my fault, isn't it? Not hers.

Another flicker of disbelief, but then her expression hardens as she backs off and climbs out. 'You'll regret not taking this chance,' she tells me, purse-lipped, before slamming the door.

But as bad as I feel for what I've been doing and for how upset she is, I feel a rush of pure relief too. Because the original me on my original timeline would never have got himself in this fix, would he? He'd never have let things run this far. And no, not just because he didn't have the body or maybe even the confidence back then for it to ever have been otherwise, but because he only ever really had eyes for Jules.

I start driving. Heart pounding. Pedal to the metal.

To home.

To Jules.

To see what she thinks of this car and the man driving it. To see if I *can* use this old multiverse machine of ours to finally put things right between us.

Chapter Thirteen

Jules – 'The Way It Is'

I can't shake my filthy mood, so I'm cleaning the house, angrily vacuuming the stairs. Even though my meal last night for Darius was a triumph, Adam's reaction when I came back took all the glory out of it and, after our row, I felt so deflated that I barely slept.

He'd gone to work by the time I woke up this morning and he hasn't called or texted. I don't know what time he'll be home, but it looks like I've got all day to fester. I finish the stairs and head to the bathroom and start spritzing the mirrors, seeing my angry scowl.

It's not just Adam being a prick that's riled me. I'm jangled about what happened with Darius. The more I think about it, the more I can't help wondering, was our near kiss his fault or mine? Not that anything really happened, did it?

And if that wasn't enough to give me a guilty stress headache, Liam's weighing heavily on my mind too. Is there ever a universe where you stop worrying about your kids? Or feeling that you've failed them? I always thought it was a cliché, but it turns out that the saying is true: You're only ever as happy as your unhappiest child.

And something's off with Liam. I know it is.

Taking a break, I sit on the loo seat and scroll through his Instagram feed again. He hasn't posted for over a week, which is unlike him. Grass Stain has hundreds of thousands of followers and they're always hungry for snaps, or teaser videos of what they're recording, or candid shots behind the scenes backstage.

It's pathetic to cling on to these posts like a love-struck groupie, I know, but they're all I get these days, especially since Liam's been in Japan.

When he first went away on tour, across Europe and then Asia, we had a rule that he'd call at least twice a week, then it was once on a Sunday, but even that's dwindled, and I haven't actually heard his voice for nearly a month. I know he's busy. I know there's a million demands on his time, but it still hurts.

I bite my lip, debating whether or not to call Saori, Max's mum. I don't want to appear needy or uncool, but maybe she knows why there's been radio silence. I press her number. She's at the hair salon where she works, and I can hardly hear over the music and dryers as she answers.

'I just wondered . . . have you heard from Max?' I ask. 'They haven't posted online for a while.'

There's a pause at the other end. 'I didn't want to say anything,' she says, 'but there's been some issues.'

The hairs on the back of my neck stand up. 'Issues?'

'I think everything's fine now,' she says. 'Just . . . band stuff, you know. Playing too hard. There's nothing to worry about,' she adds, in a way that makes me think there really *is* something to worry about and makes me want to speak to Liam even more. 'Sorry, Jules, I've really got to go, but let's catch up properly soon.'

'Jules?' I hear Adam calling from downstairs. 'You up there?'

I stand and lean on the edge of the bathroom sink to give myself strength.

'Jules?' he calls again, this time more urgently.

'In here,' I call sharply. If he wants to talk to me, he can bloody well come up here and apologise first.

'Come down,' he calls.

'What is it?' I shout back.

'Just come. Please,' he insists, and I slump away from the mirror, annoyed.

As I walk out onto the landing, he grins at me from the bottom of the stairs. We've got so much to sort out, but he seems to have forgotten that we're not speaking.

'I've got something to show you.' He nods to the front door.

Annoyed that he's being so cryptic, I thump down the stairs.

'What?'

'It's a surprise.'

He sounds overly excited, especially when he knows I hate surprises. He stands behind me and tries to cover my eyes with his hands.

'Can you just not . . . ?' I say, elbowing him, irritated that his hands are now cupped around my face.

With difficulty, still covering my eyes, ineffectually, he hooks his foot around the front door, and I see him lever it open. Then he whips his hands away.

'Ta-da!'

There's a red convertible on the drive, gleaming in the sunshine, as if it's magically popped up out of nowhere, like one of those effects on a lottery advert. A Triumph Spitfire, no less.

'You can take it for a spin if you like. The dealer assured me the ignition works perfectly,' he says, tossing me the keys.

'*You bought a car?*'

'Not *a* car. *The* car. The one you always wanted.'

'But how can we afford it? You always said –'

'I found a way.' He rubs his hands together.

How? It's impossible. *Really* impossible. I know the state of our bank accounts. Unless . . .

Oh no. He can't have. He can't have been time travelling behind my back, can he? To get cash. Just like I did behind his.

He wouldn't? *Would* he?

I nearly ask him. Then it occurs to me that asking him might make him suspect that I've already done the same.

'Uh-hm.' I'm not convinced.

'Look, I know I was an arse last night.'

In all the muttering arguments I've had in my head with him since I got up this morning, this is not how I expected this was going to play.

'I'm sorry. Seriously. I should have been supporting you better. Because you've always supported me, haven't you? Like when I found out about all of Dad's debts. And when I tried to get that business going with Darius. Stuff I've never said thank you for. And I know you're a brilliant chef, Jules, and I know how bad things were after lockdown. Your whole pop-up thing, I should have got behind it, right from the start.'

I feel unexpected tears springing to my eyes. I hadn't prepared myself for an apology from him, let alone an acknowledgement of how I've helped him, or my talents – even if they're not strictly, actually, mine.

'I totally get why you'd accept Darius's help, especially if we couldn't afford it, but I happened to hear this news piece on the radio a while back, about how much old toys are worth these days.'

I shake my head, baffled. What's he on about?

'*Star Wars* figures especially. Then I remembered all those ones Dad had given me that I'd totally forgotten about . . .'

Didn't he used to keep them in the living-room dresser? I haven't seen them for years.

'I remembered how I'd hidden them, right after we got Groucho, in case he chewed them up. Then last night I couldn't sleep after we rowed so I went online. I always expected them to be worth a bit, but . . .' He grins. 'You have *no idea*.'

Clapping his hands with glee, he starts babbling on about contacting a dealer up in London first thing this morning and then sacking off work and jumping on the next train, and how the guy practically bit his hand off when he saw what he'd got.

'Enough for a car?' I ask.

'Yup and more left over. Enough to get your pop-up started too. Well, initially, at least. We'll have to get investors, but we can get going on planning it.'

'Seriously?'

'Yeah.' His eyes are shining. 'Seriously. We'll do it together.'

I can't believe Darius has annoyed him enough to make him pull his finger out. I've always wanted it to be something we do together, only he's always been too busy, or risk-averse. Until now.

He steps towards me, putting his arms around me, and I don't resist.

'I mean it,' he says. He looks at me with his kind Adam eyes that I know so well – but can't remember staring back into for too long.

'I don't know what to say.'

'Just say yes.'

'Yes,' I say, hugging him back. 'Yes, yes, yes.'

'Oh, but there is one more thing . . .' he says, as I finally pull back.

Oh no. Here it comes. The catch.

He grins again, his eyes twinkling. 'I need you to pack an overnight bag.'

I'll admit that I was shocked by Adam splashing out on this car, but bloody hell, it feels amazing to drive through the lanes to the countryside manor house hotel that he's booked us into. Nelly is all for the plan and is looking after Groucho Barx tonight.

We're alone on a winding, dappled road, under a canopy of trees when Adam's phone screen flickers into life on the dash – his ringtone, the guitar riff off Grass Stain's first single. My heart skips.

'It's him,' I squeal, hitting the brakes and hastily pulling over into a passing spot.

'Mate,' he says, answering the phone to Liam and switching it onto speaker. 'How's tricks?'

'Yeah . . . okay.' Liam sounds tinny – a long way away, but it's not just that. His voice is slurry. I pull a face at Adam.

'It's late there, right?' he asks.

'Yeah,' Liam says, but again too vaguely for my liking.

I picture him. How hard he can push himself, how exhausted he can get. My heart aches with longing.

'I'm here too, darling,' I burst in. 'How are you? We haven't heard from you for ages. We were getting worried.'

Adam shoots me a look, like why would we be worried, when his little boy's out there living his best life.

'You've been busy, right? Got any new songs?' Adam says, all pally.

I frown at him. Why's he turning the conversation round to music, when I need actual facts? About where Liam is, who he's with, how he's feeling. Why hasn't he even given it a second thought that Liam's recent lack of communication might be an indication that something might be up? Only that's Adam all over, isn't it? So proud of his son that he just wants to be best buddies with him, when he should be being a parent.

'I'm sending you a new one,' Liam says. 'It's kind of about you . . .'

Adam pulls his *eek* face.

'It's nice . . . or nice-ish. And about Mum too.'

'Amazing. Can't wait,' Adam says, beaming.

'How are you?' I butt in, trying to get the conversation back on track. 'What's it like there? Are you eating OK? Getting enough sleep?

'Jules. One question at a time,' Adam chides, like I'm being hysterical, and I punch him on the arm.

'I've been ... it's been a tough few weeks,' Liam says, after a pause, sending my mind springing back to Saori and the mysterious 'issues'.

'You can come home any time you want,' I blurt even though he's in the middle of a tour and I know it's impossible.

'I wish I could,' he says. 'Oh, hey, Max. Listen, guys, I gotta go. I'll call you back.'

'Don't go,' I beg, but it's too late. The line crackles and goes dead.

We stare at the phone for a second.

'Well, he rang,' Adam says, starting the car again. 'He's alive.' He chuckles, like we were stupid to think otherwise.

'Something's up,' I say.

'It's a tour. There are bound to be highs and lows.'

'Don't you think he sounds ... I don't know. Stoned? Or drunk? Or both?'

Adam's phone pings. Liam has WhatsApped him his new song, 'The Way It Is', and greedily, we play it. Once then twice. I search the lyrics for clues but find none. Even though it's kind of taking the piss out of us both a bit, at least it's doing it with heart. At least he sounds like *him*.

Adam touches my hand as I pull out and start driving again. 'Hey. Stop looking so worried. He'll be home by Christmas.'

On this sunny summer's day, Christmas feels like an eternity away.

'I just ... I just think about him all the time,' I admit. 'I mean, he'd seriously freak out if he knew how much I check my phone for news and calls.'

I sheepishly meet Adam's eye, glad that I've shared my neurosis.

'Comes with the turf. I bet Chris Martin's mum feels the same,' he says gently. 'I tell you what. Let's make a pact. Let's turn off both of our phones. Let the outside world go away just for tonight. Let's have this time just for us.'

*

The Retreat is super plush and we're staying in a suite overlooking the lake and the woods beyond.

'Bubbles, m'lady?' Adam asks, pulling a bottle from the silver ice bucket on the antique table by the window.

'Don't mind if I do.'

He's playing Ben Folds' *Rockin' the Suburbs* on the wall-mount TV's Spotify, and 'Still Fighting It' is on, a song he always says reminds him of Liam, because of how similar they are sometimes.

Outside on the private terrace, there's a wicker love seat beneath a pink clematis. We settle in and sip the fizz and soon we're onto everything that's happened to us recently.

'Maybe the shed has been leading us to this, to getting each other back?' I suggest.

We're supposed to be time travelling again tomorrow afternoon. That's what we've agreed. Just for fun. Just for the ride. Following our *rule*, although I'm feeling guiltier than ever now that I've already done it once this week behind his back. Plus, what did learning all that French and cooking really get me anyway? Another too-close-for-comfort encounter with Darius. Another fight with Adam. Fresh worries about having pushed Nelly further away. Maybe even somehow pushing my son further away too?

'To be honest, right now, I'm not sure I want to go back,' I continue, rubbing my toes against his foot. 'This is pretty kick-ass, right? This life right now?'

He smiles, surveying the view, before clinking glasses with me. 'To you and me,' he says.

'And you and me.'

He grins. 'But as long as we don't change anything, what's the harm in doing it more? I mean, Jules, it *is* incredible, this thing we've got.'

'Yes, but . . .'

'What?'

'I don't know.' I can't exactly tell him about all that French stuff and its potential knock-on effects. 'But there might be wider effects, things we don't even see,' I hedge. 'You know, like what we were saying about all those other yous and mes? In those other universes we've left behind.'

Because I haven't been able to stop thinking about them either. How we talked about them that first night after I'd travelled. About where they might be now. That me with the tattoo and Adam with the beard. As well as all the others we've now left behind.

'Yeah, but like I said . . . they'll probably just have gone back to the same futures they left. It's only us, the versions of them that *did* change something, who will have moved on to other universes like this.'

'But you don't *know* that, do you? Not for sure.'

'No . . .' He thinks for a minute. 'But isn't that a bit like worrying about Captain Kirk? Like on one level, you could say he's allowing himself to be destroyed each time he teleports, and it's just a copy of him that pops up somewhere else. Meaning you could question whether the next him he materialises is even the same Captain Kirk at all. But maybe that original Captain Kirk's just been left behind in another universe and, actually, does it really even matter if he's still out there kicking arse for a better intergalactic future for us all?'

I sort of get his point, but I also get the real point he's making. He wants to travel back again.

'I suppose,' I say, 'but either way, let's make another pact. That we also do *this* more, *us* more. Here in the present.'

'Deal. In fact, a pledge,' he says, formally, teasingly, shaking my hand. 'Oh, and talking of the future,' he says, grabbing the champagne bottle to refill our glasses. 'Now that Darius is in charge of Quark, I'm going to request a sabbatical. I've been there long enough to qualify for one of their paid ones, or where you can get half-pay, anyway. I was thinking I could use the time to really help you kickstart your pop-up. Fix you up a new website, torque the SEO, that kind of thing.'

'That'd be amazing,' I smile. And it would, wouldn't it? Him doing all the stuff that I hate.

'In any case, how about we think about some time off? New Year maybe? Once Liam's back. We could go somewhere all together if we can get a cheap enough deal. Somewhere hot.'

'That'd be bliss,' I tell him and, as we chat away, it feels like our lives really are opening up. Like I've got my old Adam back. It's like I've rediscovered the exciting, excited guy I first fell in love with.

The old Adam, the new Adam, like one.

*

By the time we leave the hotel on Saturday lunchtime, everything feels different. *I* feel different. Clearer. Not just with Adam, but somehow with the universe too.

We park up outside our house and I feel windswept, my face aching from laughing. Even though we've earmarked this afternoon for the shed, we both agreed that we are going to pick up Groucho Barx first and wander down through the Lanes to the beach and have a pint in the sun.

Groucho, who instantly senses a walk is afoot, starts doing little circles of joy the second he sees us and doesn't stop.

'Yes, OK, OK,' I tell him, as I dig out my old trainers from the wardrobe and find a towel, as he's bound to want to jump in the sea.

Adam's at the kitchen table on his laptop as his phone buzzes furiously beside him. I go over and put my hands on his shoulders, and he quickly shuts the screen with a groan, looking at his phone.

'Bollocks.'

'What?'

'I've got a bike ride this afternoon,' he says. 'I arranged it months ago. Before . . . well, before everything . . . and, shit, I'm sorry.'

'Can't you cancel it?'

'They're already on their way to meet me.'

He tells me 'they' are Marcus and Fin, two of his cycling buddies who I vaguely remember him mentioning before, and how he's going to have to get ready. He apologises again, looking shifty, but still adamant he has to go and that I should head out and do something else.

'I suppose it's a good day for it,' I say, trying to be supportive and hide my disappointment – because it's not like I haven't already had a great start to my weekend.

'How about we go out for dinner instead?' I suggest, but he's on his way upstairs to get changed into his kit.

I check my phone, noticing another missed call from Darius.

Adam's mum's car is still in his office car park, and I really should ring the rescue services to get it towed back today. I head into town in the Spitfire. The sooner I get this done, the sooner I can take poor Groucho Barx out for his walk.

When I get to the car park, I see that Darius's Ferrari is tucked round the corner and I swear, because I really don't want to see him. Then my phone pings with a message to say the tow guy won't be here for another ten minutes.

I look up at the building. OK, fine. I guess now is as good a time to clear up any misunderstanding from Thursday night.

It's weird being in the office building on a Saturday, with the atrium so quiet, and the lifts silent. I feel like Bruce Willis in *Die Hard* as I head across the vast marble floor to the lift and press the button.

When I get to the eighth floor, I notice that there are quite a few workers in the big open-plan office, and I already know Nelly is one of them because she messaged me earlier to tell me not to worry about getting anything for her lunch because she was on calls all day. I hope she doesn't see me. The last thing I need is to have to make up some awkward excuse for what I'm doing here.

I spot Darius on his phone outside his office.

'I thought you'd dropped off the face of the planet,' he says, stepping forward to embrace me.

I don't want any physical contact and so I shimmy past him into his office. He follows and closes the door.

'I've been desperate to talk to you,' he says, in a conspiratorially low voice, even though we're alone. 'Why didn't you take my calls?'

'Yeah, sorry about that. Listen . . .' There's no point in pussyfooting about. 'The thing is . . . about Thursday. I really appreciate your offer, but Adam's going to help me with the pop-up. He sold his *Star Wars* figurines. So, he's going to back me.'

Darius looks confused. 'He's going to back you with money . . . from *toys*?' He makes it sound like a ridiculous suggestion. 'Right. OK. Well, if you don't want my help, I can take the hint.'

'Darius, honestly, I'm grateful, but Adam and I have just had this amazing night away together and he was talking about the future and how we should –'

Darius just makes a 'huh' kind of noise.

'What?'

'So *that's* why he didn't respond to the email last night.'

'What email?'

'He didn't see it?'

'I don't know. He's out. He had a cycle ride . . .'

'Ah.' He pulls a wincing face. 'Well . . . there's been some big news.

'A restructure,' he says. 'I'm afraid Adam and his entire department are now . . .' He sighs and places his feet flat on the floor, staring up at me with a look of pity.

The penny drops.

'You've *fired* him?'

'Well, no, not me. *Obviously* not me. The board. It's just business, Jules.'

Something twists in the pit of my stomach as I compute what he's said. Adam's going to be gutted, not to mention how betrayed he'll feel. Also, it means that all the plans that he and I have just discussed are now totally out the window. All that money he's just made from those toys, it'll have to be our income now. What about our mortgage? All our bills? Christ, to think he's wasted however much on that bloody car.

And as for the pop-up? Well, that's a joke. There's not a chance in hell it can happen now.

'I'm so sorry I had to be the one to tell you,' Darius says.

I open my mouth to defend Adam, but then a horrible thought occurs to me. Perhaps Adam *did* know. Was that why he went rushing off on a bike ride? If indeed that is where he is.

'Look, Jules, you're the last person in the world I'd ever want to get hurt. You know that.'

'So why have you fired him? You know that's going to hurt me. Not to mention Adam. What about loyalty? Honesty? Don't they mean anything?'

'To me, maybe. But maybe not so much to Adam,' he mumbles.

'What do you mean?' I feel my head scrambling. This conversation feels like I'm on quicksand.

He sighs. 'I tried to warn you on Monday.'

'About what?'

'Meredith.'

'What about her?' I ask, but my voice is shaking.

'Look, you know how they're always together, always playing volleyball, but there are rumours that it's more than that . . .'

I stare at him, remembering how jealous it made me just watching the two of them together in Darius's pool. All those niggles about them hanging out down at the volleyball court start clawing at me too and, suddenly, I'm trying very hard not to cry.

Darius steps closer. 'I know it's upsetting to hear, but I saw them myself practically kissing down at the volleyball court on Monday morning.'

'Practically . . . ?'

'Whether they were or they weren't is not the point. They were . . . intimate.'

A tear falls down my cheek and I swipe it away.

'Jules . . . darling . .' Darius says.

I try to speak, but my chin wobbles and the tears fall faster. It's just too humiliating. Then my phone buzzes. The tow guy has arrived.

I drive home in a daze.

Adam is having an affair . . .

Adam's been made redundant . . .

And he's lied to me about it all?

It can't be true. It *can't*.

I want to confront Adam right now, but he's out on his bloody bike.

Inside, Groucho Barx scratches at the back door and I let him out, promising that we'll still go for a walk.

Adam's laptop is on the kitchen table and I eye it warily, then sit down and open it, my hands trembling. It doesn't take long to figure out his password – GrouchoBarx1972 – and suddenly his home screen is right there.

I click on the WhatsApp icon, but I don't even need to search for Meredith's name, because she's at the top of his messages.

Where are you? Call me, the last one reads from an hour and a half ago. *It's urgent.*

I guess that if she's been made redundant along with the rest of his team, she'd be anxious to talk to him, but the effusive kissing emojis at the end give her away.

Is that where Adam's really gone on his bike? To see her? Is that what he's been doing all the other times he's been out on it too? Do Marcus and Fin and all his other stupid cycling buddies even exist?

My breath leaves my body in a sudden exhale, as I scroll down the cascade of flirty messages between them.

Christ! Is Darius *right*?

The threat of betrayal makes me feel physically sick. I stagger to the sink, but just as I'm filling a glass of water, a movement in the shed window catches my eye and the glass freezes in my hand.

What the hell?

I open the back door and march down the garden path. I wrench open the shed door. Adam is hunched over the Sony.

Only suddenly seeing me, *he* now looks like the one about to puke.

'What the fuck are you doing?' I demand.

Even though it's glaringly obvious what he's doing. He's still wearing what he was wearing this morning. He's been nowhere near his bloody bike. And now he's about to use the machine.

Hurrying over, I snatch the CD from his hand. It's labelled *Smashing Pumpkins – Halloween 1995*.

'I'm . . . trying . . .' he stutters, 'to make everything OK because I've been made redundant. Which means . . .' he stares at me with bloodshot eyes, 'that now I can't afford to . . .'

'You think *this* is the answer?'

'Yes. Yes. If I can just get back to '95, I can nip down to that old toy shop that used to be in town and buy up more collectibles. See . . .' He brandishes some price lists he's printed out with an auctioneer's logo at the top. 'Even though they won't be worth anything like as much as my original *Star Wars* figures, I still think at today's prices, they'll be . . . Or I could go back later, to say 2010, and buy Bitcoin, right? But either way I can use the machine to get us more money to –'

'Whoa. What do you mean, *more*?'

As I see his cheeks colouring, suddenly the truth dawns. My instinct on first seeing that car was right. He *has* been time travelling behind my back.

'The *Star Wars* figures . . .?'

'Well, I always hoped they were going to be worth a fortune, but then Liam trashed them with Max. On the barbecue when he was a kid back on our original timeline.'

'He did *what*?'

'I know. Exactly,' Adam says, like I'm now somehow onside.

Which I'm bloody not.

'And Han and Boba Fett and the rest . . . they were always going to be my rainy-day money . . . *our* rainy-day money,' he wheedles on, 'and

I just wanted to make it so that Liam never did get hold of them. So that I'd still have them to sell for you now.'

He nods vigorously at me like one of those lucky money statuettes they sell in the Chinese supermarket on Preston Street.

'So, you see, I went back and hid them before Liam could open them so I could find them again on Thursday night . . .'

Find them? Another lie he'd planned that just came tripping off his bullshitting tongue. I rub my forehead. So, the car, the hotel, him suddenly having the money to back my business . . . that was all only possible because of this? I can't believe that he'd lie to me about something so huge and then whisk me off to a hotel and decide not to tell me? Even when we were talking about being honest with each other, he was lying.

I know it's a bit hypocritical to feel so betrayed when I went back to fix things without telling Adam too. But maybe that's the point. It was all so easy. So easy to justify it to myself, like Adam's trying to justify himself now.

Oh my God. What the hell is this machine doing to us? What's it turning us into?

'What else?' I demand, my tone icy. 'What else have you changed? Tell me right now.'

'Nothing. Nothing . . .' Only then he closes his eyes, and exhales. 'OK. You remember back when we had that holiday in Mallorca and that guy said that horrible thing to me in front of the kids . . . ?'

'*And?*'

He opens his eyes, wincing. 'I left myself a note – a really persuasive one – to join a gym, so that no one would ever speak to me like that in front of the kids and you again. So that I could get fit, and ripped, and stay that way.'

'So, what are you saying? On our original timeline, you weren't . . . ?'

'No, I was . . .' He coddles his six-pack in his hands, miming what I can only presume is a belly.

'Jesus, Adam! We had rules,' I shout, furious that we've both broken them. That neither of us could be trusted. That neither of us was strong enough to resist. 'I don't even know who you are any more! Who we are!'

I push him hard in the chest, but he catches my wrists in his muscly, bogus grip.

I wrench myself away and stumble back against his dad's workbench and – *No! No! No!* – accidentally knock the box of sandpaper to the floor.

Then out it rolls. *It*. *My* guilty little secret. Now trundling towards Adam, with a rainbow spectrum of light flickering off its half-burnt back.

'What the hell?' he says, pouncing on it before I can snatch it away. He stares down at it before holding it up so I can read what's left of its label . . . *See You Later xx May 2012* . . .

He narrows his eyes at me. 'Oh. I see. Care to explain?'

Shit.

'All right,' I admit, 'I popped back to the food festival, so I could sign up for a cookery course and French lessons.'

'Oh! Oh! Did you now? Right.' Adam is practically dancing from foot to foot.

'Don't you dare take that sanctimonious tone with me,' I snap. 'It was nothing that affected you.'

I feel my cheeks burn, because that's a lie. It *did* affect us. I think guiltily of Nelly's food issues and how distanced we've become, but this is not the moment to bring that up.

'So, let me get this straight,' he says, sounding even more pompous, 'on our original timeline, in our original universe, you couldn't speak French, let alone cook all that "frou-frou" stuff you're so precious about?'

'Oh, fuck off, Adam. At least I've been solving real problems that we actually had. Paying off my credit card bill.'

'What credit card?'

Too late, I see what I've done.

'It doesn't matter.'

'I think it kind of does.' I know . . . just know . . . that now he's back on his moral soapbox, there's no way he will ever come down.

'If you must know, Carpe Diem is the name of a horse. *That*'s what I wrote on the calendar. Then I put a grand on, knowing it was going to win.'

'You put a *grand* on a *horse*?' he squeaks, apoplectic.

'It was twenty to one. A done deal,' I tell him. 'It just meant I could pay everything back.'

'You used *this* machine – that you claim God or some bloody faeries gave us – to pay off debts you'd never told me about and then went behind my back to learn French and French cooking just to . . . to *what*? To impress Darius? Because it sure as hell isn't impressing me.'

'Oh, don't you bring Darius into this. You and your pathetic jealousy.'

'Jealousy?' His eyes blaze.

'When you went back to get yourself all fit and buff for free, I bet you didn't mind coming back to a new universe where you and your pretty little Meredith were suddenly volleyball partners, did you? Don't think I don't know what you've been up to, Adam. Darius told me.'

'Told you what?'

'About seeing you and *her* at the volleyball court. Kissing.'

'What?' He looks genuinely shocked. 'I've never kissed her.'

Yet there's a hesitancy . . . self-doubt. 'But you wanted to?'

The fact that he doesn't answer tells me all I need to know.

'This was supposed to make us happy,' I tell him, my voice catching with tears, 'but it's only made things worse.'

'Not everything is worse.'

I can't believe it. Is he really going to start talking about sex again? Then I see his eyes are closed, his lips tightly shut. When he finally meets my gaze, all I see is pride.

'What?' I ask him.

'When I went back to get the figurines, I took down the zip wire,' he says.

That old zip wire we used to have in the garden? The one I always hated. 'So?'

'So I fixed Liam,' he says

'What do you mean "fixed"?'

'His hand. His left hand. He had an accident on our original timeline. On the zip wire. He lost two of his fingers, and . . . and there was nerve damage too. But now, now he's living his dream.'

I stare at him, aghast, as he smiles as if I should be pleased.

'You changed Liam?' I clarify. 'You deliberately altered the past for him?'

'He couldn't play, Jules. After the accident. Now he's back on lead guitar. That's all he ever wanted. He's famous.'

My brain is on fire. All of Liam's success? That's *new*?

'But . . . but my Liam would have achieved so much anyway,' I say, I simply *know* in my heart that it's true, '*because of*, not *in spite of* any injury,' I tell him. 'I bet he did. Didn't he? On our original timeline. I bet he did incredible things.'

'He was starting to learn the bass. To start a band,' Adam admits. 'But he'd already dropped out of uni and was living at home with us, Jules, smoking weed and playing video games all hours. He was never going to make it.'

'How do you know he wouldn't have?' I demand. 'That's the whole fucking point, Adam. You don't know. Yet you still changed our little boy.'

'For the better. It was the only way,' Adam says, his voice cracking. 'I had to. Don't you see? I built that zip wire. It's my fault he had that accident.'

So he did it to assuage his own guilt?

I lurch away from him, trying to wrap my head around the enormity of what he's done, my heart twisting with this new knowledge of what I've lost. My son. In this new universe, he's simply not the same. *My* boy who once was. My boy *I* never even knew.

'You were the one who said this could be a force for good to change things for the better . . .' Adam pleads, clutching my arm, but I shake him off.

Because it's not just Liam that's changed, is it? It's Nelly too. Who *I've* changed because of what *I* did, and who Adam has probably changed too, with all that cycling he did when she was little and I wasn't around. My chest actually hurts as I think about all the other versions of our kids. The ones I'll never know. These ones who aren't who they should be.

I don't tell Adam this. I'm too ashamed. Too guilty.

This has to stop. *Now.*

I snatch up the box of tapes and march out of the shed.

'Where are you taking them?' Adam shouts, panic in his voice.

'Anywhere you can't get your hands on them.'

'Jules. Don't.' He rushes after me. 'Why the fuck should you decide?'

'This is wrong. Can't you see? I don't want this in our lives, Adam.' I drop the box on the grass and start loading the tapes and CDs onto the barbecue. 'Just burn them, OK? Right. Fucking. Now.'

Groucho Barx starts jumping up at me, clearly thinking this is some sort of game. He's got his lead in his mouth and cocks his head pleadingly at me.

'Jules,' Adam starts, as I snatch the lead and storm towards the garden gate, but I don't turn round.

I'm too furious.

At him.

At me.

At us both.

Chapter Fourteen

Adam – 'American Boy'

For a second, I just stare at the tapes and CDs. Like my brain's fractured. Split.

On one level, she's right. I shouldn't have given Liam a new future behind her back and deprived this new her of the old him, and all he achieved. Like overcoming all that teasing at school and teaching himself how to play bass again – albeit against my advice.

God knows I want to make it up to her, but here's what she's missing, dammit, and won't even listen to: he's happier now, isn't he? Off in Kyoto with a shot at becoming a star.

I've given back what I took away from him by building that zip wire in the first place. Given him back his true path. Haven't I?

Only now this new timeline's been wrecked too, because of Darius shooting his mouth off telling her I was fired before I could fix it, sending Jules storming down into the shed to catch me out.

No matter how bloody perfect I try to make things, he keeps undermining what we already have. Or offering her even more.

I snatch my phone from my pocket as another upset message pings in, from Kylie this time, who along with the rest of my team got the same Dear John email last night telling them they were fired.

Punching in Darius's name, I press call.

'Adam,' he answers.

'How could you?'

Silence.

'Jules told me what you . . . what you insinuated,' I snap.

'Ah, the volleyball court.' I'm expecting an apology, but instead he simply adds, 'I just told her what I saw.'

'Yeah, well, you got it wrong.'

Another pause. 'Did I? Because you and Meredith, you looked pretty close to me.'

'So you should have checked with me first.'

'Jules is my friend too, Adam. I thought she had a right to know.'

'Friend!' I scoff. 'Like that's all you want her to be.' I picture him again outside the house with her in his Ferrari. And her face when I accused her of cheating at learning French just to get closer to him.

'Now look who's insinuating,' Darius says.

'This is *my* bloody *wife* we're talking about.'

'And therefore someone you should have shown a bit more respect to –'

'How fucking dare you –'

'What? Tell you what you should already know? And *would* know, if you hadn't been too busy flirting with Meredith. In the pool at my party. And for God only knows how many months, or even years before that.'

'But that's –' Not *me*, I want to shout. Because it's not. Not the me from my original timeline, anyway. Only . . . only I *was* already flirting with Meredith too then, wasn't I? At work. After work. On WhatsApp. Even if only ineffectively. Even if she did think I looked like a koala. Maybe I did have eyes for her too?

'But *what*, Adam?' Darius says.

I don't know any more. What if he's right? What if I really have brought this on myself?

'I'm sorry,' he says, 'but not everyone gets to have a happy ending, you know.'

More Hallmark-level bullshit. Who the hell does he think he is? But . . . but also he is wrong – *isn't* he? Jules and I, we *are* so close to getting just that. To being happy. To making everything right again. Like me giving her that car. And Nelly with her cycling and Liam with his band. As well as last night at the hotel. Our pledge going forward. The money for her pop-up. Because, *right there*, that was me backing her to the hilt, wasn't it? It was *my* paid sabbatical that was going to help *her* set it all up.

Only not now. Sodding Darius has screwed that up too, hasn't he? I haven't even got a job to have a sabbatical from.

'Is that why you fired me? Because of Jules? To put the boot in on me even more?' I demand.

'I already told you. That's nothing to do with –'

'Right. That's just your management team. Because you're so bloody hands off.'

'It was nothing personal.' *It*. Like he's talking about some scuffed footprint he's left on my hall rug. Not my entire fucking future.

'Well, it sure as hell feels it.'

'Then maybe we should call this conversation off. Until you calm down,' he says.

'And what about the others?' I snap. 'The rest of my department. Doodles, for Christ's sake.' Not to mention Kylie, Greg, Daniella and, of course, Meredith too.

'It's just down to how the industry is changing, Adam. These new AI narrative engines mean we just don't need our own in-house story dev teams any more.'

I can't believe his tone of voice. How he's switched into industry chat, like he's not torn my life apart . . . Or maybe this is how he deals with it, how *all* business honchos deal with this kind of thing. By pulling back.

'Look, in the long run, it'll probably do you all a favour,' he says. 'And it's not like you were ever interested in senior management, is it? You're still young too . . . well, *ish*. Certainly young enough to retrain. The same with Doodles. Although, hey, who knows, he might even get to become a full-time DJ now?' he adds, trying to inject, of all things, a note of levity into his voice. 'Plus, it's not only cuts in your department. It's promotions too.'

'Promotions?'

'Yeah, Meredith,' he says. 'The new directors were really impressed with that report I got her to do. In fact, it's thanks to her that we've been able to restructure things the way we have.'

Meaning she's keeping her job. He's taking her from me too. Not that it matters. Not now. And good luck to her. But then I picture myself in the Spitfire yesterday and that look in her eyes when I told her to get out. Her cold fury. I pulled the rug out from under her when I really could have – should have – made more of an effort not to hurt her, and to let her down easier. But isn't that the problem with this whole time-machine thing? With each new universe that gets created, there's some new narrative already playing out by the time I parachute into it, and it's impossible to get the nuances right. Because these people, these Adams I keep becoming, they're simply not the original me.

'Yeah, so it's not all doom and gloom, mate,' Darius concludes.

'*Mate*?' I say. 'We're not mates. Not any more.'

'Yeah, well, that's a funny one, Adam, because that's exactly how I felt back in 2016, when you chickened out of signing our deal.'

There. Finally, he's spat it out. What he really thinks about that. About *me*.

'But then time passes and the betrayal, it stops hurting,' he says. 'You move on.'

I don't believe him, because he never did, did he? Or not from Jules, anyway. I can see that clear as crystal now.

I'm so angry, I hurl the phone at the shed, and pace, my heart racing. What now? Do I just let my former best friend Darius Wankopoulos get away with this? With wrecking my life and trying to break me and Jules up?

Staring back at the tapes and CDs, my eyes focus on one in particular. My heart stutters as it glints in the sun. Like it's maybe another sign. In fact, Jesus, I can almost hear Doodles, Greg and Kylie now cheering me on.

Picking it up, I read *Born in the USA* in Jules's handwriting.
2016.

Yep. This is it. The one that really could put everything right.

Yeah . . . *fuck you*, Darius, and the Ferrari you rode in on.

Fuck you very much.

And . . . *hhhhSSSSSSSSSSSHHhhhhhh* . . . I land smoothly back in 2016, with the whirling guitar riff of 'American Girl' by Tom Petty and the Heartbreakers still ringing in my ears . . .

Before, *snap*. I come round inside my forty-four-year-old body. Right away, I'm sweating, because I'm doing exactly what I said I wouldn't.

Playing God. Or *a* god. Because isn't this *exactly* what marks deities out from everyone else? The power to change whatever they want?

To make everything better again.

Adam's nostrils flare as he breathes in the delicious smell of freshly baked salmon blinis and those tiny little baked puffs stuffed with melted goats' cheese that probably do have a name, but Adam and I both just think of as plain *yum*.

It's Jules who's responsible for them, of course, fussing over them now as she plates them up in the kitchen. Flashing me a smile and a twinkle of those bright blue eyes as she ties her hair up with that blue-and-gold French Hermès silk scarf Ngozi gave her last Christmas.

'Don't even think about it,' Jules warns, slapping Adam's hand away.

Fresh on the back of his twenty-mile cycle ride less than an hour ago, Adam's flat, muscular stomach is growling so loudly that even she can hear it. As Adam steps back, he watches his wife of fifteen years mixing a vinaigrette in the Provençal shaker she picked up at a car boot sale down at the marina last month.

Even though he's told her otherwise, I feel his pang of regret over how she's been slowly staking her claim in here during these past four years, since she's got her French vibe fully on. Simultaneously continentalising Mum and Dad's tacky eighties English kitchen and replacing it with these trendy shabby chic – or, *retrouvé*, as Jules calls them – French units we'd been assiduously hunting down on eBay.

But he's not half as annoyed as I will be when I discover eight years down the line that this is all bullshit too. All rigged by future Jules when she snuck back to Frenchify her life.

To impress Darius.

But *was* it? Was it really just about that? I can't help asking myself as I continue to stare. Because this French-cheffing Jules fussing around so happily right now, she looks like she was always destined to be this way. Like she could have only ever truly done this for herself.

'The kids are so excited,' she says, shooting Adam a wide smile.

Hardly surprising either, because she's already got so much planned for them, hasn't she? In San Francisco. Where she's already been in touch with Darius's uncle and has got Nelly and Liam enrolled in high school for the fall. Where she's also been FaceTiming the owner of a hip French bistro in the super-cool Inner Sunset foodie district, who's a former student of Chef Marcel, and who says he might be able to give her a job.

'I'm so proud of you,' she adds, leaning forward and kissing Adam.

I remember this too now. How well we were getting along in the run-up to this, our second attempt at emigration – so well that the years that followed felt like a landslide from which I don't think we ever truly recovered.

At this precise point in our history, we were still in it together. We were the Holes, dammit, and about to make our great leap into the world.

I listen to them chatting for a while longer about all the other things they've got planned. Just enjoying it, enjoying the ride. What I always promised Jules we'd use our machine for. But only because – *heart thump* – this thing I've come here to do, it's still not time to do it yet.

Opening a kitchen drawer, Jules pushes a CD across the table at Adam, and I remember this so clearly, like I remember this whole evening. He kisses her, thrilled, as he reads the words she's written on it. Loving the way that, no matter how many years slip by, this ritual of theirs still leaves him feeling young, like he's seventeen again.

It's only now that I realise that this is the very last mix she ever made me. The last one either of us ever made.

He puts *Born in the USA* into the laptop they've got rigged up to their speakers. As 'Midnight Rider' by the Allman Brothers starts to play, Adam grins, because it's one of his favourites. Only instead of singing along, he once more becomes aware of the other voices in the dining room – Darius and his lawyer.

Then it's not just hunger I can feel in Adam's stomach. It's butterflies, it's nerves.

'Looks like we're ready,' Darius says, beaming as he steps through the kitchen doorway. His hair's cropped short and he's wearing a grey suit and open-collared black shirt with fawn moccasins, his metamorphosis from teenage nerd to Mark Zuckerberg and Elon Musk apparatchik now complete. He waggles an expensive-looking ink pen in his hand.

'So, shall we?' he says, before turning to Jules. 'You too, Mrs Hole. You don't want to miss the moment your bright new future begins.'

That sudden sparkle in his eyes . . . Is it just because of our impending deal, or because he's looking at *her*?

Either way, Jules doesn't need asking twice. Putting down the bottle of Tesco's champagne she's just taken from the fridge, next to the champagne flutes she's already laid out on the sideboard to seal the deal, she hurries over and takes Adam's hand and squeezes it hard. Just like my Jules did on the hotel roof terrace last night. That squeeze of sheer *strength*. Like she means it with all her heart.

It's all I want too. *Me*, the interloper here. To have *my* Jules do this to me again back in the future. But Adam barely even responds. Worse, he lets go. Not because he doesn't love her, but because . . . because . . .

And even though I've run this scene through my mind a thousand times over the intervening years, I'm still shocked by how genuinely frightened he is. His hands have started trembling. As he joins Darius in the dining room, he clasps them behind his back, while the lawyer talks him through the contract that's laid out on the dining-room table, and has already been signed by Darius's uncle in the States and by Darius here. Meaning only Adam now needs to countersign it to make it fully legally binding.

But all Adam can do is stare at the silver pen in Darius's hand and think about the four other failed businesses his best friend has already been involved in, and how this could be number five. He thinks about how much his dad ended up owing, and how if he loses the hundred thousand he's just borrowed against the house to stake this venture . . . he knows he can never bounce back.

This fear of his, it's so acutely overwhelming that it nearly overwhelms me too, because before I can stop him, he looks across the table at Jules – because, yes, this is where he does it, where *I* did it – and opens his mouth to tell her, *I can't. I just can't bring myself to sign. I'm sorry. But I can't.*

Only now it's *me* looking through his eyes at this contract too and remembering what Darius said on the phone just now about how I'd *chickened out*.

Yeah, well, *screw you*, Darius, because I'm sure as hell not chickening out now. I'm taking that fucking pen.

Imposing myself on Adam, I make him do just that.

Straight away, I can feel him resisting. Violently. Like a horse bucking, trying to throw me off. Only no matter how hard he tries, I refuse to let go.

It's because I see it now. How this was the moment, the fulcrum, where everything tilted and started going wrong between me and Jules. This is where I failed to be the man she wanted me to be. It's where I let her down.

Forcing Adam to lean over the contract, I feel Darius's hand on his shoulder, giving him an encouraging squeeze. Yet still Adam fights. Terrified of the consequences, horrified that some part of him that he doesn't understand is clearly planning on signing anyway.

A part of me also knows that this is wrong, that I should feel guilty, but Totally Sirius was my idea as much as Darius's, wasn't it? Aren't I *owed* this payback? And what was it Darius said over that dinner a couple of weeks back with the kids? How I always was into *softer games* . . .

Meaning maybe this doesn't just have to be about me making my own life and my family's life better. What if, by signing, I can make the world better too? What if I can steer Darius and God knows how many millions of kids away from games like *Zombie phUK* ? Even get them into something more constructive and positive like *Earth Twin* instead?

Then I feel it . . . Adam's resistance slackening. Like he's absorbed what I'm thinking.

As the CD in the kitchen starts up on another track – and Estelle and Kanye West's 'American Boy' starts to play – I just do it.

I sign.

I'm expecting somewhere glamorous, somewhere American. Like a condo in Pacific Heights. Or a Frank Lloyd Wright house in Montecito. Surely after signing that contract, that's the kind of luxury pad I should now be calling home back here in the future?

Instead, opening my eyes, I once more find myself back in my minging old shed in Brighton. Only this time sitting at a desk in front of a state-of-the-art laptop, surrounded by reams of paper, covered in character sketches and scrawled-out game story notes . . . notes I see pinned to every available surface and wall, and even hanging down from the ceiling like vines . . .

Right away I know something's gone deeply wrong. Even if this new me on this new timeline cashed in and exited from Totally Sirius and moved back to the UK at the same time as Darius, why aren't I now living in some tacksville mansion like his up on Tongdean Avenue, with an infinity pool, tennis court and private cinema of my own?

I stare across at the old Sony boom box. It's not switched on or even plugged in. Like it hasn't been played in years. But at least that makes sense, right? Since on this new alternative timeline, in this new universe, Jules and I wouldn't have ever had a fight after Darius's party about me not signing the contract – because of course I now did – meaning I'd never have stomped in here and discovered how our machine worked.

No – it's more why the fuck *I'm* still here that's the problem . . .

Only, ssshhhhiiiiiiIIIIIITTTT . . . here it comes . . . a tsunami of memories from this new timeline rushing over me, as old me and this new me start to merge . . .

To begin with it's great. After signing that contract eight years back, we all moved to San Francisco, where Groucho didn't like his new food much to begin with, but where the kids quickly settled into their high school. I see Nelly got her California driver's licence on first go and then bagged a place at Rutgers in New Jersey to major in American Studies, while Liam got into skateboarding right from the start and even gained himself a following on YouTube. Jules started working for Henri Chaptal in Inner Sunset, and soon made quite a name for herself as the new British chef at Bistro Bon Georges . . . and, *wowzer*, just to see it now, that look of sheer happiness and pride on her face . . . Then Doodles – yay, Doodles – moved out to California too in 2018, a couple of years after they legalised weed there for recreational use, setting up a small chain of marijuana shops called Pot Doodles – with Snoop Dogg as his partner, no less.

Only then my new memories of him, Jules and the kids get sparser, somehow *colder*, even, like I'm looking back at them through thickening ice. Because soon for me – the me on this timeline, that is – *everything* became about work. I started spending whole weekends, then whole weeks away at conventions and fundraisers, as over the next five years Darius and I built Totally Sirius into the storming success it became. I also began obsessing over *Earth Twin*, before compulsively, *addictively* developing it in-house as a rival to the more violent games Darius and his uncle insisted on launching with instead.

It wasn't just *me* I lost sight of. It was *her*. Jules. Then Jules *and* Darius, as the two of them started spending more and more time together . . .

Until . . . Jesus Christ . . . she left me. Jules left me.

She left me for *him*.

The memory leaves me iced. Frozen. But not *this* Adam, this new Adam I'm becoming one with. All he can *still* obsessively think about is his work, spending every waking moment in this fire hazard of a shed, continuing to develop *Earth Twin*, despite having enough money to never have to work again.

Only he can't give up because to do that would be to admit that his work is not of vital importance. To admit that would also be to admit that he should have been focusing on Jules and the kids instead. And he still *refuses* to admit he was wrong.

Well, *fuck* him, because I sure as hell don't want this. I don't want this life to be mine.

Panicking, I start looking round for the box of tapes and CDs. But, of course, it's not here or outside on the overgrown lawn. Jules never did clear out the loft on this new timeline, because she's still living with Darius and the kids in the States.

Happily.

Oh God, yeah. I get these new memories now too. Of her with Nelly and Liam, who stayed with her and Darius when I moved back to this, our old house, to try and tap back into my own childhood and make my new game the most imaginative it could be.

Leaving them in *their* Frank Lloyd Wright house in Montecito. With neither Nelly nor Liam really talking to me any more. Not only because they both see *me* as the one who left, but because I'm still here working behind a closed door. Still planning character arcs and storylines for a game that seems to have no end in sight – a game this me doesn't even *want* to end. He wants to lose himself in it for good.

This game that lets him forget what he's lost.

It takes a huge effort of will to drag him – to drag *us* – up to the house. To haul him up to the loft and back. As for the *BBQ King 2014* CD that I now make him put into the Sony after firing it up, he practically recoils from it. Wondering what the fuck is happening. Loathing this new part of his consciousness for reminding him of her. Loathing her for betraying him, but still refusing, for even just one second, to accept that *he* might have done *anything* wrong.

As the CD whirrs into motion, Paloma Faith starts singing 'Only Love Can Hurt Like This' and, desperately, I dive head first into the chaos of that kaleidoscopic whirlwind, craving its promise of another life – because in this universe I might as well already be dead . . .

I land in the body of forty-two-year-old Adam in 2014.

He's staring down at a row of halloumi slices sizzling on the barbecue at the end of the garden. Wearing a singlet to show off his muscles that he's been working on for the last five years since he joined the gym, he's basking in the warmth of the mid-afternoon sun beating down on his neck.

'They done yet, Dad? Can I have one?'

Liam, aged eleven, wearing a baggy old Lou Reed *Transformer* T-shirt and shorts, just a few months on from when I last saw him. This being the end of that same staycation summer and it's only this morning – a fresh memory hits me – that they've finally cleared up all those Earth Twin dens they built over the last two months. To make it look a bit more sophisticated to celebrate Jules's forty-second birthday here today.

Of course, that zip wire's still gone too. Liam's even forgiven me for cutting it down.

'There you go,' Adam tells him, forking one of the halloumi slices off onto a paper napkin. 'But don't tell your mother. She wants us to sit down and do it all posh.'

'Bor-ing,' Liam chimes, biting a piece off and grinning before sneaking Groucho Barx a cheeky mouthful too.

Somehow, I resist imposing myself on Adam as he ruffles Liam's hair and sends him on his way. I want to hug my boy so much, but I can feel how happy Adam is watching him scamper off across the garden to where they've already carried out the kitchen table and laid it ready for a late lunch for twenty or so of their closest friends.

Adam glances across at Nelly, aged fourteen, in jeans and a crop top. She's just spotted Liam eating and now detaches herself from talking to Ngozi, Geoff and the twins to make her way towards me through the other guests. Our friends are all over by the kitchen doors, swigging back Aperol Spritzes and G&Ts.

My Nelly. Not living with Darius and Jules five thousand miles away, but here with me . . . and, Christ, I feel sick. How I could *ever* have done anything to jeopardise that? How could I have tilted my life away from something as blessed as this? For money? Out of jealousy? I swear to God, never again. Just give me this chance to put it all right.

'What did the cheese say when it looked in the mirror?' Nelly asks as she leans up against me.

'Halloumi,' Adam tells her, because of course those cheese jokes were all the rage this year. 'But why did the cheesemonger lean to the left?'

'I don't know.'

'Because he only had one Stilton.'

She groans, her beautiful blue eyes widening with derision, before she jabs a finger at the grill until Adam forks another slice of halloumi off it for her too.

'I love you, Dad,' she says casually, by way of thanks, as she saunters back up the garden to show her little brother that she's every bit as much a favourite as him.

For a second, I'm stunned. By the sheer wonder of this normal nothing moment. The kind I realise I take for granted every day. Even though I'm here to fix my future, to try and take it back, I can't quite bring myself to move. Because what if I'm about to monstrously screw things up again? What if I'm about to fuck things up even worse?

What if fucking up is all I ever do?

Because I thought I could control this last time too, didn't I? I thought I could dictate how things would be, but I got it all wrong.

As someone turns up Talking Heads' 'Once in a Lifetime' on the speaker and David Byrne starts warning, of all things, about the various versions of your life you might end up living, Adam feels a warm body pressing up close behind him and smiles.

Because this really is his beautiful wife.

Jules.

'The garlic and rosemary brioches will be done in twenty,' she tells him, softly kissing the back of his neck, 'so do you want to get going on the butterflied lamb?'

'Already on it,' Adam says. And he is. He's got two grills going, with the lamb already steaming in blistering San Miguel lager inside a tent of tinfoil on the further one.

'Oh, and keep the veggies totally separate,' she reminds me. 'Geoff will go nuts if he catches you using the same tongs.'

'On that too,' Adam says, and from his memories I can tell that he really is. That he really wants Jules to have a good time and not to have to do all the cheffing for once. Because forty-two, it's the meaning of life, right? Something he wrote on her birthday card this morning – even though he knows she doesn't know or care who Douglas Adams is.

I can't help picking up on other things too. More recent memories. Like how they just kissed for five whole minutes in bed this morning before the kids came in with her presents. This is still back in those two years when everything felt like a second honeymoon to them. With me and Darius busy working on our business plan together and starting to put together the finances, and me and Jules building up to our move to the States, and her work going so well now too, with her French cooking skills developing week by week, leaving her happier than I'd ever known her in her life.

Cold sickness sends a shiver down my spine. The knowledge of what will happen when they do get to the States. Unless I can turn things around.

'Oh, and here's a little something for you,' she says, pressing something into Adam's hand. 'To say thanks for making such an effort today.'

'Wow,' he says, clearly delighted, as he glances down at the *BBQ King 2014* CD.

He turns to thank her, but she's already moving off, dressed in hot-pink trousers and a jewel-encrusted top. Again, it's all I can do not to impose myself and run after her, kiss her and hold her and tell her how sorry I am for losing her in America – and how I'll never put anything before her again.

Especially not myself.

'Careful you don't burn them, Ads.'

Darius. Sidling up next to him. Always with the managerial advice these days, Adam thinks. But kind of admiring him for it too. Whereas me – future me – I feel nothing but darkness in my heart. Because even if I drove Jules away on that last timeline, he still dated her behind my back before he moved in with her, didn't he?

I still remember how that felt – how that felt to that other me. That betrayal in another universe. That *loss*.

Even if . . . even if it *was* my fault too.

But here that contract's not even written yet. Not for another two years. Here none of that's yet happened.

'They need another minute,' Adam says, flipping the slices again, to make sure they're all nicely browned – and, naturally, losing one through the grill slots to the fiery ember netherworld below, because that's just what halloumi does.

I impose myself on my old self. 'Listen, Darius, we need to talk.'

'Ooh, sounds serious,' he answers mockingly.

'It is.' Glancing across at him, I watch those intelligent eyes of his focusing in. He's dressed in a white Fred Perry shirt, crisp white shorts and brand-new Adidas tennis shoes, like he's about to serve a Wimbledon ace. Reaching down, he plucks a piece of halloumi off the grill, without even asking – or flinching, like his fingers are made of iron.

'So shoot,' he says.

'I'm out,' I tell him. 'Of Sirius.'

'Oh, Adam. Not again.'

Right, because Adam has already expressed his doubts several times before. 'I mean it,' I make Adam say.

Darius still thinks he's kidding. 'You cannot be Sirius,' he says. A John McEnroe tennis joke? Because of what he's wearing? I don't even let Adam crack a smile.

'I'm sorry, but that's my decision,' I get him to say flatly instead.

'What is?' asks Jules, coming over and stepping in between us, her expression clouded with worry, because even though she doesn't yet know what we're talking about, she can clearly read the determination on my face.

'Adam's bailing on Totally Sirius,' Darius tells her. 'Or at least that's what he says . . .'

'Ads?'

And I hate it. The look of concern . . . no, of sheer *fear*, on her face. That this thing she wants so much, it's about to be taken away.

'I'm sorry,' I make Adam go on. 'To both of you, for wasting your time.' But then I hit them with it. All the reasons why this won't work. Adam's real reasons. The ones that led him to not signing that damned contract on our original timeline. Him not trusting Darius's business record. Not wanting to risk getting in debt. I don't stop until they both get it. Until they both understand that what I'm saying here is irrevocable. That Totally Sirius – for me, and for him – is now done.

I ruin Jules's birthday, of course. And even though she manages to swallow back the tears and keep her cool, I can still see the fury and resentment in her eyes, before she turns her back on me.

I also know, just *know*, that this will never fully go away. Just like me not signing that deal in our original universe never did.

But I also know that the alternative is so, so much worse.

I let go of the controls then, with Darius still telling Adam what a mistake he's making. But as freaked out as I feel over what I've just done and how much I've just upset Jules by nipping this whole Totally Sirius idea in the bud, Adam holds his ground. Independent of me. Because all those arguments I just said through his mouth make sense to him too. Just like they once did to me.

In fact, he's relieved.

As everyone starts to gather around the table for the meal, he ducks into the shed, ostensibly to dig Doodles out, but also just to get away from Darius's and Jules's glares.

'Hey, man, how's it hanging?' Doodles asks from where he's sprawled out gaming on the sofa, with Bowie's 'Absolute Beginners' *bum-bum-ba-ooh*-ing on Dad's B&O.

'All good,' Adam lies, his heart still pounding over what he's just done. 'But food's ready.'

'Oh, OK . . .' Only Doodles is having trouble pulling his eyes away from whatever game it is he's playing on the screen.

Only he's not actually playing it at all, is he? Adam now notices. He's not even holding a control.

'What's that?' Adam asks, intrigued, and almost glad for the distraction after the total mind-bomb of a conversation he just had outside.

'A new thing called Twitch,' Doodles says. 'And get this, it lets you play games live online for other people to see. Livestreaming, they're calling it . . . and, like, anyone can do it. So, like, I'm now watching someone I don't know playing this right now . . . and you know what? I reckon it's going to be huge . . .'

The second I wake up back in the shed in the future, I can feel my heart thundering.

But thank God! Yes. Look . . . my bikes, gym equipment, toned reflection . . . everything's as it was before.

Leaping up, I quickly check outside, but everything's looking good here too. The tapes and CDs are still exactly where Jules left them. Meaning nothing else here on this new timeline can have changed.

I've done it. I really have put everything back.

I laugh out loud. Just from the relief that that other universe where I lost Jules isn't my reality any more. Only then – mid fist pump – it hits me. That other universe *does* still exist, and always will. Along with that other doomed me. That me without her. That me who *I* screwed up. Because he wouldn't exist if I hadn't rewound time to sign that contract. If I hadn't tried to play God.

Because God, the real God, the universe, whatever . . . comes with scales, right? How the hell else to explain that by trying to take something for just me, I ended up having something else taken in return?

Pulse pounding, I stare down at the tapes and CDs. The ones I now know I need to burn. Even though every atom in my mind is screaming at me not to. Not to destroy something as powerful, as incredible, as this.

But Jules is right. I can't be trusted. Neither of us can. Maybe the only real perfection there is in this damned universe is the kind of makeshift perfection you have to build yourself.

The only way I can think of to prove to Jules how much I love her is to do what she's asked.

With shaking hands, I continue building her pyre on the barbecue – just like Liam did ten years ago when he burned Luke Skywalker and the rest.

I open the box of matches.

I pull one out to strike.

Only then I hear Groucho Barx barking and I turn round to see Jules glaring at me from the gate.

Chapter Fifteen

Jules – 'Across the Universe'

I've spent the last two hours of my beach march with Groucho *trying* to calm the hell down, by telling myself that *at least* by now Adam will have destroyed all the tapes and CDs. Meaning that the threat of him changing my life or his – or of me doing the same to him – is over for good.

After everything that's gone on, we'll just have to commit to where and who we are now and find a way forward. All of us. With Nelly, by supporting her, and maybe even getting some family counselling. Liam needs us too. Just because he's successful, doesn't mean he's as happy as Adam's determined for him to be. I'm still worried about how he sounded on the phone, and even though he said he would, he hasn't called back.

Only then I see Adam at the end of the garden, with the tapes and CDs *still there* on the barbecue, not burned or even smoking, and like a needle scratching across a record, any ideas of us patching things up screech to a halt.

I march over.

'OK, OK, I'm doing it,' he stutters. 'You're right. We shouldn't mess with the past . . . with any of this any more.'

He won't look me in the eye. As he holds up the box of matches and the match he hasn't yet struck, I notice his hands are shaking.

Then I know. I just *know*. He's done it again, hasn't he? He's broken his promise and he's gone back in.

'What. Did. You. Do?' My voice is steely.

He closes his eyes, wincing. Then speaks fast. 'I just thought that if I took the deal and we went to San Francisco, then . . .'

Oh my God. He means the deal with Darius. 'Then *what*?' I demand.

'Then . . . then you'd be happy. Because I know you've always thought half of that money from Totally Sirius should have been mine. *Ours*,' he stumbles on his words. 'And so I went back and signed.'

From the state of him, it's glaringly obvious that didn't go well.

'And? What happened?' I ask, tensing up even more.

'It didn't work out,' he says. Then it's anger I see in his face. 'You left me. For Darius.'

I can't believe what I'm hearing. 'What the fuck?'

'So I had to go back in again. To change things round so I *didn't* take the deal. So we *didn't* go to America. So we didn't break up . . .'

I put my hands over my face, feeling dizzy.

'But it's OK now,' he says. 'Everything's fine –'

Just as I'm about to explode at him that everything certainly *isn't* fine, and *how fucking dare he*, I'm interrupted by my phone. Furiously, I pull it out of my pocket, but then I see it's Max's mobile.

'Max?'

'Hey . . . Jules.'

Right away his tone makes my heart thump. My eyes flick to Adam and, livid as I am, I put the phone on speaker.

'What's happened?' I ask.

'There's been an . . . incident,' Max says.

'*Incident*?' I grip the phone. 'What are you saying?' My voice is high, but already I'm remembering what Saori said about them playing too hard. Good God, did she mean drugs? As in something more than weed. Drugs that have now led to –

'Liam . .' Max takes a difficult breath. 'He overdosed or would have – I found him before he lost consciousness.'

I let out a feral cry, my knees buckling.

'I'm so sorry, Jules. I should have kept a closer eye on him. He's been struggling. Definitely the last few weeks. I genuinely think it was just a mistake . . .' Max chokes up and I realise he's started to cry.

'And now?' Adam's voice trembles. He's clinging to me.

'He's stable.'

Stable. What does that mean? My heart feels like it's been clawed in two.

'Where are you? I'll come,' I manage.

Adam nods. *We'll* come, he means.

Max says he'll text me the details of the hospital, then rings off.

'You still think you *fixed* him?' I rail at Adam, shoving the phone forcibly at him. I feel like I'm sinking down into the ground.

'I'm so, so sorry,' he says, the blood draining from his face.

Sorry. Like that word is enough. Could *ever* be.

He looks suddenly young, hopeless, wiping his nose across the back of his hand. Like Liam did, when Liam was a child.

'But . . . but, OK, I fucked up and should have listened to you, but we *can* still make this right,' he says, looking at the tapes and CDs, like he's an addict himself – addicted to *them*.

Only he's the one who caused this whole bloody mess in the first place.

'No. I'm done,' I tell him, my voice and body both shaking. '*Done* with them. And *done* with *you*.'

'You can't mean that –' He makes a grab for my hands, but I quickly push him off.

'*Out!* I want you out,' I scream at him. 'Pack a fucking bag and fucking leave.'

He just stares at me for a second, his eyes bright with tears. Like he's going to say something. Then he turns and heads towards the house.

Striking a match, I toss it onto the barbecue of tapes and CDs, choking on my own tears, as black smoke curls up into the sky.

Adam is packed and gone in under ten minutes. Packed with what? I don't know. Going where? I don't care. All I can think about is Liam.

My little boy.

Guilt thrums through me like a low, reverberating chord. What mother doesn't know her son's in that much trouble? Only on some level I *did* know. Which makes it even worse.

And what happens now? What if rehab is only the start? What if in six months' time Liam comes out and overdoses again? What then?

My breath catches in fearful sobs as I stare at the flames licking over the tapes and CDs. Then, checking they're truly alight, I run inside and get online as fast as I can, determined to book flights to Japan tonight. Only there aren't any available for days.

I bury my head in my hands, trying to comprehend everything that's happening on the other side of the world.

Where I should be, not here.

It's all because of Adam and the total and utter fuck-up he's made of it all.

Then I remember everything he said about San Francisco. How nothing worked out. Maybe there never *was* going to be a happy ending for us? Even with our multiverse machine, even with all those second chances, and brave new worlds, no matter what we've done, we've still ended up broken, haven't we?

Then it hits me. What *I* could do.

I feel the immediate sting of hypocrisy for even *thinking* it after the row I've just had with Adam. But in this he may have been right. What other choice is there?

Because I have to do *something*.

What if I could use the machine to create one last timeline? One where I could stop Liam leaving so soon. Where I could keep him with me and watch him more closely. Yes . . . yes . . . and save him from what's already done . . . One where I could make everything better. Where I could help Nelly to be happier and healthier. And I could be happier too.

I rush down the garden, holding my arm up against the billowing heat and peer through the swirling smoke. There's one CD left still unburned, with an image of my face on the cover. I snatch it off with my asbestos chef's fingers and squint down at the words written in Adam's writing – *Beach Party 2016*.

Like it's fate.

I run into the shed and straight to the old Sony and click the CD into it.

As 'This Is What You Came For' by Calvin Harris and Rihanna starts to play, I dive greedily into that spinning tornado again . . .

I land in 2016 in the kind of sweltering day the newspapers like to report with accompanying pictures of bare-chested Brits gurning for the camera from seaside pubs, and old people on deckchairs with melting ice creams.

It seems like the inhabitants of the entire city of Brighton & Hove, as well as half of London and most of the Home Counties, have been emptied out onto the beach, where they're basking in the heat, like a frothing colony of shit-faced seals.

Jules's shoulders are stinging, and her skin is slick with sun lotion as she guards their patch of picnic blankets. She kneels up and shades her eyes to look out to sea, where Liam and Nelly and their mates are in the inflatable kayak Liam got for his thirteenth birthday – Liam, my safe, happy little boy.

Further out, she tries to spot Adam, who's 'testing himself', swimming between the two piers.

'I think that's him,' she tells Doodles, pointing to a dim figure in the distance, an orange float bobbing behind.

'He looks like a scientifically tagged radioactive turtle,' Doodles says and Jules laughs. 'A good name for a band, that,' he considers. 'He's making good progress, though.'

Jules admires the way Doodles supports Adam in all his endeavours, while not giving a monkey's about exercising himself. But she also knows she's got an hour before Adam gets back to join them, and she already resents that they'll all then have to fan his ego and tell him how amazing he is. What's he so busy getting fit for these days anyway? He used to say it was to keep him at the top of his game for their move to America, but two years have passed since he put the mockers on that at her birthday barbecue, and other than exercise, he doesn't seem to have much ambition of any sort left.

'Why does every single social event these days have to involve some kind of sporting activity?' she says aloud.

'What? Like professional cigarette-rolling?' Doodles smirks, lighting one up. 'Any more beers?'

'Here you go,' she says, delving into the bottom of the cool box for the second-to-last of the beers and passing it over to him. She's never seen such white legs and knows Doodles hates being out in the sun.

He only made it today because it's Ngozi's birthday and Jules is sure Doodles has a crush on her, a suspicion that's now confirmed, as Ngozi walks up the beach towards us in a stunning orange bikini and Doodles quickly springs into action and hands her a towel.

'Thanks,' she says, taking it from him. She nods to the sea. 'I left Geoff to it. Got too splashy for me.'

On the scratched Discman 'Cake by the Ocean' by DNCE is playing and I nod along, listening to Doodles and Ngozi chatting. There's no need to panic yet, is there? The reason I'm back here, what I've come back here *for*, is going to happen anyway, isn't it? Just not yet.

Even though I'm feeling increasingly nervous about this coming moment, it's not enough to stop me appreciating simply being here too, under this beautiful blue sky with my friends, enjoying a mind so clear compared with my own. A mind not yet faced with the consequences of finding a portal to the multiverse.

And all the shit that will bring.

The song comes to an end and I reach for the CD player.

'Aha. That reminds me,' Doodles says, through a puff of cigarette smoke. 'Adam left this for you. To play on that piece of old crap.'

He hands over a new CD and Jules takes it. *Beach Party 2016*, she reads, grinning. She slides it out of its sleeve, glad Adam finished it in time. It's got one of Doodles' mixes of Tinie Tempah at the start, she sees, popping it on. Jess Glynne singing 'Not Letting Go' blares out.

'Choon,' Doodles nods and Ngozi high-fives him, agreeing.

Meanwhile, I'm concentrating hard. The CD handover has happened, which means I only have thirty-four minutes left. I feel my heart thump right alongside Jules's, as she spots Darius searching the crowd and she stands and shouts his name. Waving, he works his way over, dressed in shorts and a stylish black shirt.

It's always been Darius I associate with this CD, because he now picks it up and stares at the photo of me on the front cover and grins.

'Beautiful. You really look beautiful on there,' he says quietly just to me, before catching himself out and blushing, fully blushing, as he quickly turns away to greet the others.

There, that was it. Why I'm here. The first moment I knew, really knew, that he liked me like that . . .

Recovering his composure and acting like he never said anything, he kneels down and takes the last beer from the cool box.

'Hmm. Why don't I get us some cold ones?' he offers, putting the warm beer back.

Jules feels it as a criticism. She's done her best to make a perfect picnic for Ngozi, but she knows Darius has increasingly high standards these days.

It's only two weeks until he emigrates to America and Jules feels a shard of deep envy. *She* should be going too.

As Darius gets up and smiles down at Jules, I take over.

Because I'm doing this.

I *am*.

'I'll come with you,' I say, causing Jules a little inadvertent thrill of surprise. 'You guys want anything?' I ask Doodles and Ngozi.

'Cornetto,' he says. 'Double choc.'

'And for the grown-ups, some ice,' Ngozi adds, rolling her eyes at him. 'I've got prosecco going warm in my hamper.'

Jules pulls on her red-checked sundress and flip-flops and Darius picks up the cool box, holding her arm with his other hand as they gingerly step between the tourists.

They head up the steps by the bandstand and up Sillwood Road to the Waitrose at the top. It's a treat to be in the air-conditioned aisles browsing the shelves with Darius, who thinks nothing of going for the most expensive brands instead of searching the shelves for what's going cheap.

'Let's not go back just yet,' I make Jules say once they've queued, paid and everything is packed under the ice in the cool box. She likes the idea and even thinks it's her own. 'Pint in the Robin Hood?'

As they wander down through Norfolk Square, they talk about Darius's mum and how much he's going to miss her and worries about her. She's always been sharp as a pin, but recently she's been forgetting things. That must have been the start of the onset of her dementia, I realise, thinking of his poor mum now.

Once inside the pub, they wait at the bar as the landlord serves them, and They Might Be Giants' 'Birdhouse in your Soul' plays tinnily over the speakers. Jules sees there's a bench seat over in the shadows, where the daylight hasn't properly penetrated.

Heading over, they sit side by side on a prickly velvet banquette. Darius takes a sip of his lager. He's going to give up drinking when he gets to California, he says.

'You won't miss it?' Jules asks. Drinking has been so much a part of our group's culture, but of course Darius has already started his metamorphosis into Californian Tech Giant.

'No,' he says. 'I'm actually looking forward to it.'

'And . . . are you going to miss me?' I make Jules ask, because I already know that in a week, at his leaving party, he'll ask her to leave Adam and go with him. So, he must already be thinking about it. 'Because . . . because I wish I was coming with you,' I make her continue. 'I hate Adam for pulling the plug.'

Jules knows this is a dangerous, dangerous conversation to be having and she can't quite believe she's having it, but already the world – *this* world – is turning, and she's slipping, sliding, moving with it . . . to where, she doesn't yet know . . .

'What if it wasn't too late?' he asks.

'You mean . . . leave Adam?' I make her say. Even though she's already thinking it. I can sense how shocked she is by this turn in the conversation, every bit as shocked as *I* really would be a week from now on my original timeline, when he suggested the exact same thing.

'You know how I feel about you, Jules, how I've always felt about you,' Darius says, gently, reverently, tucking her hair behind her ear, as if it's the most precious thing in the world. 'You must do.'

Having another man touch her like this is so new. So shocking. Something inside her already knows that by not moving away or saying 'No', she's crossed a line from which she can't come back.

A line *I*'ve never crossed. Not on any timeline before.

But I can see what I couldn't see then. That he really wants me. That he even loves me.

Because in that other universe Adam created when Adam signed the contract – Darius and I *were* together, weren't we? We'd somehow made it work.

Imposing myself, I make Jules take his hand in hers.

'Do you mean it?' she says, but her voice is already a whisper. It's not *me* making her say it, just her.

Darius nods, his hand still touching her hair, his face close. 'Let's go, Jules. You, me . . . and the kids.'

He clasps his other hand over hers and Jules looks at the union of their fingers. She's terrified and her instinct is to snatch her hand away, but I override her.

Instead, slowly ... deliberately ... I make her lean forward and finally kiss him on the lips.

Darkness.

Where am I?

I stretch. I'm in bed. I can feel the soft mattress below me.

My fuzzy brain comes round as if from a deep, dark oily pool and, as I surface, I grope for the details of my astonishing, mind-bending dream ...

Wow. That was far out. Me, half drunk in the Robin Hood, coming on to Darius and then accepting his pass ... Jesus, even kissing him on the lips ...

My thoughts are interrupted by a long, disgusting fart.

'Close the door,' I mumble, turning on the soft pillow.

After such a weird but oddly blissful dream, the last thing I need is the sound of Adam on the loo.

'Sorry,' followed by a flushing sound. 'It's those French lentils you cooked.'

I freeze.

That's not Adam's voice.

Sitting bolt upright, I rip off the eye mask I'm wearing just in time to see Darius coming out of a giant en suite bathroom and buttoning up his shorts.

'I got you a coffee,' he says, nodding to the large mug steaming on the bedside table.

He grabs his golf putter and marches whistling out of the room.

My heart is thundering.

What the hell is happening?

I shut my eyes. Shake my head. It's got to be a dream. I'm definitely still in a dream.

Only then someone's shaking my shoulder.

'Mommy ...' A young girl's voice. An American accent.

A child is standing next to the bed. Maybe six. Maybe seven. No, six. Born 12 November 2017. And for her last birthday party, she went to see *Matilda* in New York. She has *my* face shape and eyes, but Darius's mouth, and his little gap between her teeth.

Holy mother of God.

Me and Darius.

We have a child.

New memories start hitting me like arrows.

'Hi, baby,' I hear myself say, feeling my face break into a smile and swoosh of love, as I lean in to grab her, tenderly rubbing the tips of our noses together, something she still finds funny.

Oh, she's beautiful.

'Get up. We're gonna be late,' she says.

Phoebe. This is Phoebe. I know this is Phoebe. Just as I know that she's my entire world and that my day will revolve around her, just like every day does. Starting with her riding lesson in half an hour. Which is why she's already dressed in jodhpurs and a hacking jacket, as she scampers back out of the room.

What the hell is happening?

My stomach – I mean, the real me's metaphysical stomach – is dropping through the floor, but this other me, this new Jules doesn't even notice. Even though I'm joining with her here on this new timeline.

She gets up, patting her flat real stomach, before touching her toes twenty times. She's got my fantasy middle-aged body. Nothing like any real body I've ever actually had.

Then she's hot-footing it into the bathroom. The giant bathroom that looks like it belongs in a hotel. And quickly opening the window – automatically – pinching her nostrils and counting to ten, because this is sometimes just what married life is like.

Married?

They're married. *I'm* married. I'm Mrs Angelopoulos. I look down at my ring finger. The little diamond engagement ring Adam gave me on one knee up on that roof in 1998 is gone, along with my wedding ring. Instead, I've got this massive rock of a diamond that I could probably trade in for a house.

Only not this house because that would cost a lot more. The very same house up on Tongdean Avenue where Darius threw his pool party in another life, another universe. Only now I live here too, after moving back here to the UK with him a month ago, after he exited Totally Sirius in the States for a cool fifty million.

I quickly find myself tapping into more and more of this Jules's 'new' memories, bringing myself rapidly up to speed on the last eight years of my – *our* – life since I kissed Darius in the Robin Hood pub.

And oh my . . . the sheer *devastation* of that kiss. One that Darius still sees as a triumph, but she – I? – as a detonation. The magnitude of the hurt I've caused floors me, as Jules steps into the shower.

What have I *done*? And not just to Adam, but . . . oh my God . . . the kids.

More new memories. Of how I told the kids I wanted them to come to America with me. How I'd find a way, no matter what. Or at least that's what I told little thirteen-year-old Liam and sixteen-year-old Nelly when I first left Adam for Darius.

I also really believed I could do it, didn't I? That Adam would let me, that he wouldn't fight.

But they hated me. All of them. They hated me for what I'd done. For selfishly putting my own happiness ahead of theirs. They never did come to America to join me. They flatly refused.

I left my children.
I left Adam.

I scream inside my mind.

Then, of course, I burnt my bridges with them all for good when I got pregnant.

I was convinced I was too old and too pre-menopausal for it to be possible. But when Darius found out, he hailed it as a miracle and was over the moon.

As Jules – as *I* – gets dressed, the new memories just keep coming, drowning me inside her, leaving me gasping for air. How in the US me and Darius just moved from one property to the next, each one bigger than the last, in tandem with Totally Sirius's meteoric rise. How, bit by bit, he burrowed deeper and deeper into his work, just like Adam once had with his cycling and his shed – and with me too busy mumming a small baby to be able to even think about a career of my own.

Yet all these memories I have seeping into me – of her wedding to Darius, of her pregnancy, of giving birth, of Phoebe's first baby smile and word and baby steps – they're not really mine, are they? They're hers. *She* made them. She built this new life.

I'm nothing but a cuckoo in her nest.

But . . . but I love her, my six-year-old Phoebe. Now my only child.

Nelly still barely speaks to me, even after the countless trips I've made home over the years to try and patch things up. And Liam . . . he's dropped out of uni and doesn't speak to me at all. He never did take up music again.

Oh God, oh God, oh God . . .

And it's not just me who thinks this, is it? It's her. This other me, who I'm becoming. She regrets it. Achingly. Painfully. Deep down in her gut. I can feel that too. No matter how much she loves Phoebe and – yes, in her own way – Darius too, she'll never truly get over the consequences of that kiss in the Robin Hood and how it veered her life so off course.

But she didn't do that. *I* did. This is *my* fault.

I have to change things back right now.

Adam . . . I need to see Adam. He's got to help me. He *must*.

And so I fight. I fight for *myself*, for my life. I fight to resist the terrible pull to just sink into her, to become one with this other new Jules, to end up here forever with her . . .

Until I finally feel myself slowly peeling my being away from her like a strip of Velcro, becoming two instead of one.

I walk her quickly downstairs and out to her red Porsche – even though they normally walk to the stables where Phoebe keeps her horse – and then I call Phoebe out to join her and tell her Mummy's got an errand to run.

Then I sit back again and leave the driving to Jules, who puts on her and Phoebe's Taylor Swift playlist, and the two of them sing along to 'Anti-Hero'.

Phoebe gets out at the stables and Jules blows her kisses as, grinning and laughing, she rushes off to join her friends.

Then it's me in charge again, taking control before Jules even has time to react – making her drive to our cul-de-sac back down in town.

Alongside the cool matt-black VW camper van parked outside our house is some kind of hire lorry with its side door open, our rusty old Skoda nowhere to be seen. A guy in brown overalls is carrying a heavy-looking cardboard box in through the front door, where a pretty young woman is standing wearing shades with her blonde hair tied up in a bandanna.

I make Jules get out of the Porsche and approach the house.

'Oh, wow. OK.' The woman looks shocked to see me. 'Jules, right?' she then says, trying to regather her composure.

I recognise her the second she takes off her shades – Meredith. What the hell is *she* doing here?

'Um . . . just put it through there,' she tells the overalls guy, and beyond her, I see that our hall is chocka with sealed boxes.

It's not just me who's realised who she is, Jules has too. I get another cascade of new memories, about how Adam has a girlfriend. An office romance, no less. And she's his volleyball partner too.

'It's so nice to finally meet you.' Meredith smiles, holding out her hand.

'You're moving in?' I make Jules ask, but her voice is tight. This is clearly freaking the hell out of her too.

Meredith's cheeks colour. 'Look, I know things with Adam didn't end well, but maybe this can be a new chapter? No reason why we can't all get along. I mean, I get that it must be strange for you too.' She glances back at what I now see is a removal lorry. 'But you moved on a long time ago,' she points out. 'And Adam and I . . . well, I really love him, and I know he feels the same about me.'

Jules and I both want to scream at her. But we don't have the right, do we? We caused this. *We* left Adam.

'Can I see him?' I make Jules say.

Meredith hesitates. 'He's in the studio.'

The *studio*?

'The old shed,' she explains, and before she can change her mind, I quickly march Jules past her.

The dining-room wall has been knocked down to make it open plan – which actually looks great. As does the kitchen with its new sliding French windows. Framed on the wall is a large photograph of a mud-splattered Nelly and Adam on their mountain bikes, brandishing two gold medals around their necks.

My Nelly.

And looking good. *Healthy*, thank God.

Then I see that all Adam's other clutter has gone . . .

Over by a retro turntable – but a good one, not like all that crap he kept in the shed – there's a series of award certificates framed on the walls from various international gamer sites. Photos of Adam and Doodles, going by the name the 'Dadass Dudes' – and Jules's memories come thick and fast hot off the press on this too, about how she's heard on the grapevine that Adam and Doodles teamed up to get into games streaming together. In one photo, she spots Ngozi looking sensational in a hot red satin jumpsuit. Flanked by Adam and Doodles, she's holding a large 'Media Agent of the Year' trophy and Jules remembers hearing that she'd left her law firm to become an agent.

Ngozi. Her best friend. The one who took Adam's side.

Jules gets a fresh wave of bitter pain as she remembers the row she and Ngozi had just before she'd got into the cab to go to the airport. It had been one of the only times Jules had ever seen Ngozi cry, as she'd begged Jules to reconsider, telling her over and over that she was making the biggest mistake of her life.

Hearing a familiar bark, I continue to control Jules, making her walk out into the garden. I straight away notice that the shed is twice the size it was, but the garden somehow looks bigger too, with its scrappy old borders now neatly manicured.

Groucho Barx blocks the path. Wanting to cuddle him so much, I quickly step towards him, but he growls and bares his teeth, like he doesn't recognise me. Or refuses to. Another one on Adam's side.

Gingerly, I skirt round him and open the shed door.

Inside, there's a lighting rig and cameras set up facing two scruffy leather armchairs. As Adam looks up at me, Jules's stomach flips, as does mine.

'Adam,' I say. 'It's me.'

He laughs, but without humour. 'Yeah. I know. But what are you doing here, Jules?'

Meredith appears at the door behind me.

'It's OK, babe,' he says. 'We won't be a mo.'

Smiling, secure, just using her eyes to convey this, she shuts the door, and I hate seeing this level of communication between them. Like me and Adam when he was still mine.

'Adam. Listen.' I don't know how to say this and so I'm just going to spit it out. 'We're still married. Or at least we were. Until about two hours ago,' I tell him, grabbing his arm, 'or at least that's how it feels to me . . .'

'*Ooo*-kay,' he says on an exhalation.

'The thing is we . . . well, actually, *you* . . . discovered a time machine multiverse thingy . . .'

'Have you been drinking?' He peers into Jules's eyes. But whatever he sees there only makes him frown.

'No, I'm serious, Adam,' I make her say. 'I'm not this person. I never went to San Francisco. Not on our original timeline. On our original timeline, we stayed here. We were happy. Or, OK, not *happy*. But not fucked up. Or not as fucked up as I thought we were. We were actually doing OK.'

Or rather we *were*, until we *weren't*.

Adam's still just staring at me, freaked.

'And you know, I don't know, but maybe I think we'd just forgotten how to be kind to each other, and listen,' I hurry on, trying to explain. 'We'd just forgotten . . . who we *were* . . .'

'Jules. Please. Enough. Why don't you let me call . . . well, not Darius,' he says, his expression darkening, 'but maybe a doctor? A friend?'

'You're not listening. It *is* possible,' I tell him, staring imploringly into his eyes. 'Time travel. And not only that. The multiverse. It's real.'

And there, just there, I see a tiny flicker of interest. He's probably thinking how the hell do I even know what the multiverse is? But how to convince him before he kicks me out?

'It's like, I mean,' I say, suddenly remembering what he said, 'haven't you ever wondered – and I *know* that you have – about what happens to Captain Kirk after he teleports? Whether the next him who materialises is even the same Captain Kirk at all?'

His eyes widen.

'Or whether that even matters?' I quickly add. 'So long as he's still out there kicking arse for a better intergalactic future for us all?'

And – finally – finally, I see I've got my nerdy husband hooked.

'How the hell do you know that I've –'

'For the same reason I know about cosmic strings and traversable wormholes and even the Alcubierre drive, because *you* told me about them when you were trying to explain time travel to me,' I say.

Next thing I know I'm babbling at him and telling him everything all at once, about the old tapes and CDs, and how he put one in the old Sony and went back into his seventeen-year-old self, and then I went back too.

Not pausing for breath, I explain how we changed things, at first by accident and then on purpose, and then sneakily behind each other's backs, and how I got so totally cross because of him changing Liam that I set fire to the tapes and CDs right here in this garden and then went back and stupidly kissed Darius and started a whole new life with him in San Francisco.

'Oh, but Adam, you've got to believe me, it was the biggest mistake of my life,' I tell him.

Apart from little Phoebe, I can't help thinking. Apart from little Phoebe who's not mine, and who belongs to this other, new Jules, whose love for Phoebe I can feel flooding me.

'Yeah, well, everyone knows *that*,' he half jokes in answer to what I just said about leaving him being a mistake. But his frown deepens. His *thinking* face I know so well. 'Theoretically,' he ponders, 'for time travel to be possible, you'd need an insanely complicated machine and an enormous amount of energy.'

'Ha! Adam, *my* Adam, on *my* original timeline, in my original universe, he said almost exactly the same thing.'

'Ah, yes, well, no doubt all great Adams think alike,' Adam says, shooting me a bashful little smile.

'Because *he* didn't get it either,' I explain. 'How the tapes and CDs and the stereo kept sending us back. There. That. The Sony.' I point to the familiar machine that's now in its own compartment of a sleek new shelf unit but only there to look retro and hip.

'Well, you know plenty of musicians claim it's love that makes the world go round,' he says, before staring at me curiously and, for a glorious second, I think he's seeing the real me here inside. 'And who knows? Maybe it does. Not, of course, that any of this, what we're talking about here, is real.'

'Love. Yes, Adam, love. Because it has to be, right? And if it *is* something like love that's driving all this, then what if it can undo bad things too? Everything that I . . . that *we've* done? Because I need to get out of this universe, Adam, to make another one – or somehow remake *my* own. And maybe it really *is* love that will get us back to *us*.'

He stares at me. Like I've just told him I still love him. Which in a weird, messed-up way, I suppose I have.

'Please, Adam . . . I'm begging you to help me. I need you to go upstairs and get another one of our old mixtapes or CDs. You know, the ones in that box in the loft?'

'Ah.' Adam grimaces. 'Well, I'm afraid that's going to be a problem. You see, I chucked them all out.'

'*What?* But . . . but you can't have? You *never* throw anything out.'

'I needed a fresh start. With Meredith. And so I got rid of . . . well, pretty much everything.'

I feel like the breath has just been sucked out of my body.

'But if there's no tapes or CDs, then there's no multiverse machine,' I finally manage to say. 'And if there's no multiverse machine, then . . . then I can't get back. To my Adam. To me.'

Adam shrugs in a fatalistic kind of way. Like maybe that's just how the universe is.

I feel a well of tears building up. A torrent of tears for Nelly, for Liam, for us and our family. Tears for Adam who won't ever take this new Jules back in this new universe. Adam, who new Jules could never go back to anyway, because she has her own new husband and child and life.

'I'm sorry I couldn't be more help,' Adam tells her, before steering us kindly, but firmly, towards the shed door.

Having picked up Phoebe from riding, a seriously dazed Jules – now back in control – stands at the marble island in the kitchen, absent-mindedly chopping courgettes and onions for the pasta sauce she's making. Helga, the maid, is on the other side of the room, vacuuming the giant sofa.

Outside, through the glass, Darius chases Phoebe across the green lawn in the sunshine, doing that zooming airplane thing they both love.

Jules is still pretty shaken up by her encounter with Adam, although she's blurry about most of the bits where I was fully in charge. She's not going to tell Darius how upset she is that Meredith is moving into her old home because anything to do with Adam is taboo in this house.

It'll just be another secret she keeps.

Like how at least half the time, she fakes orgasms, so the sex can be over. Or that sometimes she weeps so much, she can't stop, because she's trapped in a marriage where they have no way of talking about the past.

Seeing Adam has brought it all back.

Adam. The Adam she knows she loved in a way she can never love Darius.

Adam, who isn't hers any more and never will be.

And that's just *her*.

But what about *me*? What the hell am *I* supposed to do? Let go of my sense of self fully this time? Carry on blending into her memories until we really do become one? Until there's nothing left of me . . . of the me I once was? Because already I can feel that happening, like this me, the me who doesn't belong here, is gradually being erased.

But I can't let that happen. I want my own life back with all its imperfections. I don't want to be her – this other Jules – with her perfect house and servants to clean up her mess. I just want to be *me*. In my shabby house, on my own crummy sofa.

She jumps as Phoebe presses herself against the glass and pulls a face and Darius does the same. Jules smiles, looking at them both. She has so much, she reminds herself. A loving husband. A loving daughter.

'Daddy, please,' Phoebe says, as they fall, laughing, in through the gap in the glass doors.

'What do you reckon, Mummy?' Darius is staring at Jules.

'Ice cream,' Phoebe prompts.

'Sure, why not?' Jules says.

'I'll buy some on my way back from visiting Granny,' Darius promises.

It's already been decided that it's too nice a day for Phoebe to have to visit Darius's mother in the dementia home.

He winks at Phoebe and flips his Ferrari keys over in his hand. 'Strawberries and cream Häagen-Dazs coming right up,' he says.

As Phoebe and Jules wave him off, and the electric gate starts to close, I spot a sleek black camper van parking up on the grass verge on the road outside and my heart jolts.

Adam gets out, holding something up that almost sparkles in the sun. Something small and rectangular.

My God. It can't be. A tape?

I make Jules buzz him in through the gate, then watch him hurrying down the path towards me with one of those removal boxes under his arm, looking up at Darius's mansion for what must be the first time – in awe. Then his gaze rests on Phoebe, who stands shyly behind me. I can't read his expression. But alongside me, I feel Jules is watching closely too. Adam has never acknowledged Phoebe's existence before.

Her nerves scrunch up inside her like a fist.

But all I want to see is what he was waving.

He doesn't keep me waiting, thank God.

'Hey. So, I found this,' he says, clearly keen to get this over and done with as quickly as possible. He holds up the solitary tape box. It says *Jules Rules! 1989* on the spine in faded blue pen. 'I think it's the second one I ever gave you,' he says. 'One I forgot to throw out. I think me and Doodles used it for a livestream we did on old tech.'

'Oh, Adam.' I step towards him and take it. So relieved.

'And here's the old Sony too.' He nods down at the box. 'Because you can't time travel without it, right?' he jokes. 'Or, you know, because you kept talking about it,' he adds, seeing I'm not smiling. 'Well, whatever, we thought it might help.'

We. So him and Meredith have been discussing this. They must think I'm nuts.

'Um, thanks,' I say, taking it from him.

'Well, then. Good luck.'

He stands there awkwardly for a second. Then, quickly, I put the box down on the marble porch and hug him. Tight. For what might be the last time ever.

He looks a little embarrassed but then smiles. 'I hope you find what you're looking for, Jules.'

I'm looking for you . . .

A thought I only just manage to keep to myself.

Breaking away, he gives Phoebe a little wave – just a small one, but enough to make me think that they might not stay strangers forever on this timeline after this – before walking back up the path.

'Who was that man?' Phoebe asks as the gates close.

'He's called Adam,' I tell her, still imposing myself on Jules. 'An old friend of Mummy and Daddy's. But now I need you to do something for me, OK? Can you go and choose a movie to watch until Daddy gets back?

Even saying it brings tears springing to my eyes.

'Why?'

'Because I need to do something in the garage.'

Her big brown eyes look at me, confused. 'Can I do it too?'

'No, it's a grown-up thing. It's really boring.'

In the cinema room, we put on *Enchanted* – which is still Nelly's favourite, *my* Nelly's, even after all these years. Phoebe, just like Nelly, gets hooked by that most magical of moments, when Giselle falls through a portal from her kitsch cartoon world into the maddeningly real flesh-and-blood cacophony that is New York.

I'm left with my tummy turning from the giddy nostalgia of it all, remembering how Nelly was when she was Phoebe's age. Does she remember that, once upon a time, I used to sit with her too? How she used to put her thumb in her mouth like Phoebe's doing now? How I used to stroke her hair? How I could just gaze and gaze at her for hours?

I drink in Phoebe's beautiful face as it's lit up by the movie – her plump little cheeks and intelligent eyes – and my heart hurts, because already I miss her so much.

I can't help but love her, can I? Even though I know she's not mine.

'Don't go,' she suddenly says, grabbing on to my hand.

Like she's sensed something.

'It's OK, baby,' I make Jules say. 'I've just got this little thing to do, but then when I'm done, your mummy's going to come back in here and she'll make you the best milkshake ever with the ice cream Daddy's getting and we'll all have a happy evening together. The happiest ever, OK?'

'OK.'

'I love you,' I whisper, kissing her hair.

It hurts. Oh God, it hurts. Because this really is goodbye. I have to leave. I have to try. Even though God only knows if this is going to work.

Hopefully, just hopefully, Phoebe will be OK. That this universe *will* work out for this new Jules and new Darius and that the love they feel for this beautiful little girl will be enough to carry them all through.

It still takes all my strength to make Jules bolt the door of the garage, so that Phoebe doesn't come in – because if she does, and if she then asks me again not to go, I don't know if I'll be able to.

But for now, I hold steady, plugging in the Sony and then inserting the tape.

Because this has to work.

I need my life back.

Pressing 'Play', I hear the opening bars of one of my favourite tracks of all time kick off. 'Let's Stick Together', by Roxy Music.

Which has got to be a good sign, right?

And . . . *KKKKKRKRRRRRAAAAASSHHHH* . . .

OH. MY. GOD.

Those are my old scuffed black pixie boots on my feet – which means this can only be the eighties. It's worked! Adam's tape and the Sony have worked. I really am back before all this began. Even better, this is the corridor at the Peregrine just outside Rose's office. Meaning I'm right where I need to be.

Jules lets out a yelp of joy and is surprised by her outburst. Because it's *me* here inside her and I can't contain myself.

But I manage to hold myself back and just passenger here a moment, thinking through my plan . . . as Jules stands here with her Tupperware box full of sandwiches she's made in Rose's kitchen, waiting for Adam to turn up so they can share them outside in the sunshine in Regency Square.

Rose's office door is ajar, and I quickly grab my chance. Taking control, I walk Jules behind Rose's desk and slide a piece of paper into her old typewriter, press the caps lock and start.

The only way I can think of to save our future selves is to post them instructions, like in *Back to the Future*. To warn us and to remind us of what matters. Because the answer is right here under their – *our* – noses.

It's like what Rose said, right? That happiness is learning to love what you already have. But, boy, oh boy, haven't I just learned that lesson the hard way?

Haven't we both?

Two minutes later, as Jules hears Adam coming down the stairs, I make her rip the second hurriedly typewritten sheet out of the roller, put an envelope in the runner and type instructions. Then she folds up the sheets of paper and seals them inside. I can feel Jules feeling confused, as she licks the gum, but I know that very soon she won't remember doing this, because it's not her doing it. It's me.

I'm going to post this envelope into the solicitors' office next door. I know old Mr Hargreaves will leave his solicitors' firm to Eddy, who'll carry on drinking pints in the bar in the Peregrine for the next twenty-five years, as he slowly but surely falls in love with Rose.

He's a good man. A proper pro. He'll follow these anonymous instructions. I just know he will.

'I'm all yours,' Adam says, smiling at her from the doorway.

Oh, Adam. There you are. *My* Adam. My Adam as I first knew him. He's got a bum-fluff moustache, but his beautiful brown eyes are twinkling beneath his floppy fringe. And calling to me. The same way they always will.

We walk outside, and I continue to impose myself on Jules and make her post the letter through the Hargreaves letter box. Then I sit back inside her, enjoying the ride, as they run across the road and into Regency Square.

They head to a wooden bench, looking out towards the West Pier and the deep blue sea. And I can't help marvelling at being back here in all Brighton's seedy, tatty, dilapidated 1989 glory, as – *ahhhh* – I catch a whiff of vinegary fish and chips from the Regency chippy on the corner and the seagulls swoop and wheel and caw overhead.

I'm too enthralled by Jules and Adam to pay any more attention to what's going on around us. They're already tucking into their lunch.

'You have to put the crisps *inside*,' Adam says, opening his ham and cheese sandwich – his favourite, she already knows – and stuffing it with Walkers cheese and onion crisps.

'Heathen,' Jules laughs, taking out her brie and tomato roll.

He punches her playfully on the arm. And I remember how all the other Adams used to do this, until they stopped. Like somewhere along the way we just lost all the fun . . .

'What's that?' He turns up his nose.

'Try. Go on.'

He takes a mouthful and nods. 'Hmm. Not as bad as it smells.'

'I love French cheeses. I want to try them all when I go to Paris next year.' She's so convinced. So confident. 'What about you?'

'Dunno yet.' He shrugs. 'I'll see what comes along.'

He smiles and takes a tape out of his pocket. 'Hey. I made you another one. You want a listen?'

'Wow!' Jules says, accepting the tape case with its thick biro title. *Jules Rules! 1989*. That's so sweet, she thinks. Adam puts the tape in his Walkman and plugs in the earphones. Then he puts the Walkman on the bench between them and offers Jules one of the wires.

'This way, we can both listen and chat,' he says, pressing 'Play'.

My heart swoons as Bryan Ferry starts singing and Adam starts chatting away about the songs he's chosen. He's so funny and so earnest, somehow both at the same time, reeling off facts about the artists and who he liked seeing most on this week's *Top of the Pops*.

My beautiful music nerd.

As he speaks, I study him, and I can see so clearly the man he'll become. A man who won't be perfect, but who'll do his best when disaster strikes. A man who'll put his family first. Always. Even when he sometimes gets it wrong. And a man who will love me. Forever. Warts 'n' all.

I dawns on me now that breathing in the same air as someone for twenty-five years, sleeping together in the same bed, eating together, drinking together, parenting together, losing loved ones together . . . bonds you emotionally and spiritually in a way that no amount of universes can ever tear apart. And in the unspoken give and take, the push and pull of the minutes, hours, days, weeks, months and years, a kind of glue is formed. And the glue is the magic. The glue is love. The glue is the 'us-ness' that made me into the person I became, and the person this Adam will one day become too.

And without it, we're lost.

They're listening to a Beatles song now, 'Across the Universe', one that Adam says is his favourite. Mine too and never more poignant than right now. As John and Paul harmonise about nothing changing their world, I know what I have to do.

I have to find a way to destroy all of this so that Adam and I can't start travelling to new universe after new universe, somehow hoping each one will be better than the last. Because it doesn't always work out that way, does it? Like with Liam . . . Adam thought he'd fixed him, when he'd actually made everything so much worse. Somewhere out there in the multiverse maybe poor Liam *is* still in Kyoto going through what he's going through. And in another there's still Nelly, needing so much more than I gave. While in yet another, there's a beautiful child I had to leave behind – and am always, *always* going to miss.

Which is why Adam must never discover our machine. He must never try to be anything other than the Adam he's going to turn out to be. For love to have a chance to find its own way, we both have to be free of thinking we can change things with a click of our fingers. We have to be free to make mistakes, puzzle them out for ourselves and move on.

It's the only gift I've still got left to give.

'I prefer live music,' I make her say, forcing her to take out her earphone as the song ends. 'Actually, I'm not sure about mixtapes,' I make her continue, as kindly as she can, but she – the 1989 Jules – she's horrified that she's rejecting his lovely gesture. She already knows she wants to make Adam a mixtape in return and has a feeling, deep down, that these mixtapes will be the soundtrack of their years. That music is the thing that's starting to make their own magic glue. 'But thanks anyway,' I make her add.

'Then maybe we could go to gigs together instead?' Adam suggests after a moment's thought, hope shining in his eyes, as he tries to hide his disappointment.

I let go and put Jules back in charge. Of everything. Of her future. Her life.

'Sure,' she tells him. 'I'd like that. I'd like that a lot.' And they grin at each other, her rejection of his tape softened. 'But right now I've got to go,' she says, standing, her lunch break nearly at an end.

'Oh. OK. Well, see you,' Adam says.

She darts forward and kisses him on the cheek before walking a few steps away and, as she puts up her hand to wave him goodbye, I feel my own heart breaking, because I want this moment to last forever.

It's too late, though. I can already feel myself fading . . . Yes, every bit like that Polaroid in *Back to the Future*.

Now we're never going to have the tapes to make that multiverse time machine of ours, there'll be no time travel. Meaning I, here, simply cannot exist. I sense a deep shiver of fear at the nothing that's to come, but I also know that this is the end of just this one me. This other Jules here, she'll go on. It's her time. Her turn.

So my heart flies out to her – this young woman who'll know nothing of the adventures I've had. Nothing of the other universes I've seen.

I wish her and this Adam well. Even though they might not get to live their lives together. Something as simple as not sharing a mixtape might be enough to drive them apart . . .

But I pray that if this Jules *is* lucky enough to live out a life with this Adam, she won't change anything. She'll just do 'us', the way we did the first time round in all its imperfect glory.

Like I would. All over again. In a heartbeat.

The vortex starts to pull me, only this time as the whirlwind begins, I know it's not taking me anywhere. I'm like a candle about to be snuffed out.

And just like that . . . my time is up.

Chapter Sixteen

Adam – 'Cheek to Cheek'

After brushing my teeth to get rid of the rank taste of last night's beer and Kebab King special doner with chips, I wander downstairs in my boxer shorts and Dad's old threadbare dressing gown to our tatty kitchen with its old green eighties units that look the exact same colour as my gills.

I'm going to the shed. For what's set to be my new regular Saturday-morning workout. Even if that knackered old exercise bike didn't exactly get me pool-party ready for Darius's a couple of weeks back, the least I can do is keep using it to try and get a bit more fit.

Plus, it's not like I've got anything else to do, is it? Not now I've been fired. Or made redundant. Or however else Darius prefers to gloss over what his new management group has done.

When I rang him, admittedly bladdered, last night from the Lion & Lobster – straight after that email from HR pinged into my inbox and the inboxes of the rest of my team – I really did think he might have been able to do something to help, but he said he couldn't. His hands were tied, but that we'd talk. What does that even mean? That maybe things won't be so bad after all? Perhaps he's setting up another company entirely. One that me and my team can be brought into as well?

Only not all of us. Not Meredith. At least he's retained her. But what if that report she did for him is what led to us all getting the flick? That's what everyone was bitching about last night in the pub.

'Adam!' Jules calls out from the living room.

I don't call back right away. I'm still pissed off at her. As well as still being in the doghouse myself after getting back drunk last night and breaking the news about losing my job. Leaving her first freaking the hell out about what Darius did, before taking comfort in the fact that at least he might be up for bankrolling her pop-up, just for old times' sake. Meaning we'll be able to keep the wolf from the door.

Right.

Unless Darius *is* the damned wolf. I still can't help thinking about that too. About what I thought I saw outside the house the night before last when he dropped her home after his investor meal. Him nearly kissing Jules in his car.

Even if she swore it wasn't like that and that her chat with him was actually quite stressy because of how badly the dinner went, because he'd thought she was an expert in French cooking and spoke the language a bit as well, both things she'd exaggerated and then got caught out on.

Things kind of just blew up between us after that. She went on the offensive big time. Telling me all that stuff about our lives being in the same old holding pattern with some stupid metaphor or simile or whatever the hell it was about planes, and banging on about me never taking any risks, like not signing that bloody Totally Sirius contract way back when, which was why she was now getting Darius to back her pop-up, whether I bloody wanted her to or not.

Which isn't fair. Because I *would* help her if I had the money. Or, OK, maybe not before, but now that I can see how much it means to her. Only now I'm not just broke, I don't have any means to make money either.

I'm screwed.

'What do you want?' I glare down at Groucho Barx, who's trotted in from the garden, reeking like a compost heap, and wagging his tail with something in his mouth that he now half drops, half vomits on the floor.

No, no, please don't let this be a recently deceased mouse or baby bird, because I just can't handle that today.

Only then I see what it is, and Christ alive, it's Boba Fett. That same *Star Wars* collectors' figure of mine that Liam half melted on the barbecue – what, maybe ten years ago? My heart sinks. Because, hey, if he hadn't, I might have been able to sell it now to help fund Jules's pop-up.

But what's done is done, eh? It's not like you can go back.

Still ... my one lost chance of financial redemption being served up as such a timely reminder – it's like the universe is laughing in my face.

Kicking Boba Fett as hard in his Mandalorian nuts as I can, I send him spinning unceremoniously back out through the garden door ... watching him take off for a second, even two, as though his plastic jetpack might actually make him fly ... before he plummets into the manky water butt to drown.

'Adam!' Jules calls out again. 'Come here!'

FFS.

Scratching furiously at my beard, I reluctantly turn round with the approximate speed of a container ship reversing its course. There's no escaping her tone of voice. Whatever Jules wants to discuss, she's intent on doing it right bloody now.

'What?' I snap, finding her in the living room, hunched up on the sofa next to that *Brush Up on Your French Level 1* book she picked up in Waterstones last week. That same one that failed to help her bluff her way through Darius's investors' culinary demands the night before last.

'This just got delivered,' she says, flapping a faded envelope.

And, you know, sometimes I really hate making eye contact with her. Especially when we're fighting, because no matter how pissed off I am, I still ... I can't help liking her too. That feeling trumps everything else. Dampens down the rage.

'What is it?' I ask. 'Let me guess. Another frigging bill.' Bills I can't pay.

'No, it's addressed to us both.'

As she turns it round to face me, I see that the words 'For Adam and Jules Hole' are typed on it. No stamp. No postmark. Even weirder is what's underneath.

'From a well-wisher', along with a date.

'But that's ... today,' I say.

'You'll never guess who brought it.'

'Who?'

'Eddy, from the solicitors'. You know, who drinks in the Peregrine.

He just turned up here ten minutes ago in a suit. Said it needed to be hand-delivered.'

'What, like it was a work thing?'

She pulls a face. 'I guess. Dunno.'

'Weird.'

'So, shall we open it?'

I shrug, feeling more than a little freaked out, to be honest. Our names staring up at us like this. Sitting down beside her, I'm mindful not to scratch my belly, stretching against my threadbare *Soul Mining* T-shirt.

Jules carefully slits the envelope open with her fingernail. As she opens it, I see there are two sheets of folded paper inside. I feel this absurd intake of breath, like I'm on a game show or something, as she takes the top one out.

Across it is typed:

WHAT YOU SHOULD BE DOING FULL-TIME

Adam – the Dadass Dudes

Jules – Chez Jules at the Peregrine

That's it.

She flips the piece of paper over, but there's nothing on the back.

'What the fuck?' we both say.

'Did you do this? Is this some kind of a jo—' we both say at the exact same time.

Then stare at each other. Because, clearly, neither of us did.

'What does it even mean?' I ask.

'Well, my bit's obvious. That I should set up my restaurant.'

'And I should try and make more out of the DDs.'

'The what?'

'It's a gaming thing I've been doing with Doodles.' It's stupid, I'm about to say. But *is* it? Because, suddenly, seeing it typed out like this . . .

'Which means that whoever typed this,' Jules says, 'maybe Doodles, or Ngozi, or even Darius . . .'

'. . . they clearly know us pretty well.'

'Do you *agree*?' she says, studying the piece of paper. 'That these *are* things we should be doing?'

'Um . . .' I stare at her, thrown. 'Shouldn't we be more wondering about who the hell sent this?' Because it looks like a prime piece of mischief-making to me.

She frowns. 'Yes. But still, I'd like to know.'

'Well, I suppose maybe?' I say. 'I mean, obviously, for you, with the restaurant, that *is* what you want to do with your life.' She couldn't have made that any clearer the night before last.

She nods.

'But for me. For me and Doodles? At our age? Going pro? I mean, of course, on some fantasy level, I'd love to. But . . .' *Could* we? God, it would be fun. A hell of a lot more fun than turning up at the office every day. If I even had one left to turn up at. 'I guess it might be worth a go,' I say.

She nods again. Like this is settled. Like we've just made some kind of life choice. Like we're somehow no longer – what was that word she used? – *stuck*.

Only making monumental decisions like this, based on some bullshit someone – we don't even know who – has typed out anonymously like some serial killer on a piece of old paper . . . we must need our heads examining, right? Plus, there are wider considerations too. It's not just us we're talking about here, is it? It never is with a family.

'What about the kids?' I say.

'How will it affect them? I was thinking that too.'

Then we talk. About where they're at. About how a big shake-up like this might not have been such a good idea even just a few weeks ago. How Nelly would have gone batshit at having me and Doodles back home in her workspace. How us focusing on our new ventures might have taken our attention away from Liam too much, leaving him stewing in his room, but now he's getting out a bit more, and really does seem to have a plan for his music.

'So what's on the next page?' I ask.

She takes it out and lays it flat on the table.

This one reads:

BE HONEST. BE KIND.

Jules – tell Adam about Darius

Adam – tell Jules about Meredith

Whoa! What the hell?!

My heart races.

'OK, so whoever's doing this is just shit-stirring,' I say.

Maybe too quickly. Jules's eyes flick round to mine.

'I'm serious,' I tell her. 'There's nothing going on with Meredith.' There isn't. Hasn't been. Right?

'I believe you,' Jules says, but only after a pause.

'You do?' Again, I fail to hide it – the surprise in my voice. 'What?' I say.

'You *can* read, can't you?'

Be honest . . . that's what it says. Right here in black ink. Like whoever typed this knew we might not be.

'Honestly?' I feel my mouth drying out.

'Honestly.' Her piercing blue eyes lock on mine.

'But we don't even know who wrote this or where it came from,' I point out.

'Does it matter?'

'No, I suppose not.'

'Well, then?'

She's not blinking. I feel this hideous tension rising up inside me. Then I sigh and it's like I can feel a giant weight dropping off my shoulders. This secret I've carried too long.

'I've thought about it,' I admit.

She nods slowly. 'Go on.'

'About Meredith . . . and sometimes when you and me, when we've not been getting on . . . I've wondered what might happen, because me and her, we really do . . .'

I expect Jules to fly off the handle. I brace myself. Because I deserve it, don't I? Only the nuclear explosion I'm expecting doesn't come, and staring down at that phrase, BE KIND, I wonder if that's the only thing holding her back.

I still can't bear to look her in the face.

Then she says, 'Because we really *haven't* been getting on, have we? For too long. Too long without trying to fix things.'

'No, I guess not . . .'

'Are you and me still what you want?' she asks.

'Yes,' I answer, without hesitation. The way we're talking now . . . this letter, and what it's telling us to do . . . it's suddenly like I can see a way forward again. We've still got so much to fight for, haven't we? For us and everything we've built together. For our kids. 'And you? Is this . . . do you still want *us* too?'

I feel like I'm on the thinnest of ice. Like one wrong word and I'll be plunged into the icy, dark cold.

This time, I do look at her. She nods. Thank God. Without blinking. Like she's staring right into my soul.

'I miss you,' I tell her.

'I miss you too.'

And it's so weird, but the word 'miss', it kind of sounds like 'love'.

'And Darius?' I ask, because even though this crazy piece of paper could have been written by anyone, even *him*, I still have to know. Just asking the question is making me feel sick.

It's only then I see the tears in her eyes.

'You were right,' she says, 'he did try to kiss me the other night in the car.' She swallows, hard. 'And that wasn't the first time either. Back when we didn't go to San Francisco. He tried it then too.'

No.

I can't believe this. Don't want to.

'I should have told you back then,' Jules says, a tear rolling down her beautiful face, 'and the night before last. And I'm sorry, so sorry I didn't. But this is the truth. I'm being honest with you now, just like you've been honest with me.'

'Darius . . .' It's all I can say. I feel like I'm spinning away.

Footsteps.

Nelly walks in.

She looks from me to Jules, then back again. Clearly reading something in our expressions.

'*What* about Uncle Darius?' she asks.

'He's a prick. He just fired your dad,' Jules says, but still looking at me, that teardrop still shining.

'Are you joking?' Nelly demands.

'No,' Jules says, 'and he says it was out of his control. But that's a lie. He's a liar.' Still looking at me.

Then, perfectly timed, the unmistakable sound of Darius's Ferrari snarls into our drive.

Jules holds out her hand to me. I stare at it, but only for a second. Then take it.

'Come on,' she says, squeezing my hand tight – that tightness that always gives such strength.

I squeeze hers back, wiping her tear away with my other hand

'What's going on?' Liam asks, trotting down the stairs, scratching at his left hand the way he sometimes does when it's playing up, either alerted by Nelly's raised voice or the sound of Darius's car.

'Uncle Darius fired Dad. He's a prick,' Nelly answers him, his face registering shock.

Jules and I open the front door together and step out as Darius slowly, carefully reverses in between Dad's shonky brick wall and Mum's Skoda that Jules got towed back from the Quark Studios office yesterday.

'Guys, guys, guys,' he says, reaching out his hands. 'I had to come round because I'm genuinely sorry about what's happened. But, like I say, it really was out of my –'

'Fuck off,' Nelly tells him. She's followed us out. 'You snake.'

'Whoa,' says Liam.

'Yeah, steady on –' I find myself saying, automatically, because this is still Darius, right? Our friend. Even if –

'No,' Jules says. 'She's right. He's betrayed you.'

'It's just business,' Darius tells Jules firmly.

Jules still hasn't let go of my hand. 'Best friends *don't* do that to each other. *Any* of that. They just don't.'

'Jules . . .' says Darius – and it's impossible to miss the note of warning in his voice, because he knows what she's talking about too.

'*Leave*,' I tell him, anger bubbling up inside me. 'Now.'

He looks like he's about to say something else, but Jules speaks first. 'No,' she says. 'Not before I tell him something first.' She marches right up to him. 'What you said at your party about me and Adam and what we have and the kids, and how we really lucked out –'

'What?' He looks at her like she's gone mad.

'Well, it never was luck,' she says. 'It's been hard work, every step of the way, and will keep on being hard work. But it's also been worth it and always will be. You might act like you've got everything, but you're nothing, and you've got nothing next to him.' She points back at me. 'He's held down a job he doesn't even like for years to pay our mortgage. He's raised two kids, and he might not be a millionaire, but he's a hero.'

'Well, I wouldn't go that far,' Nelly says, but then I see it. Her mother's expression on her face. The one that warns she will not be fucked with. 'But you know what?' She glares at Darius. 'You can stick your job up your arse.'

'And your sodding music contacts,' Liam says, stepping in beside her and glaring at Darius too.

The strength I felt from Jules squeezing my hand, I feel it doubling now from the look my daughter gives me. Of total solidarity.

'Whu – what job?' I say.

'Oh, yeah.' Nelly sniffs. 'He wanted me to work for him at Quark. For him and Meredith. He said she was going to train me up.'

Jules walks back to me. Again, she takes my hand. Darius opens his mouth to speak, but then shuts it. For once, lost for words. In spite of everything he's done, I feel a swell of sympathy for him, my best friend. I can't help it. Because Jules is right. He doesn't have this, what I've got. He doesn't have any of the things that really matter.

'Just get the fuck out of here, Darius,' I say, looking my ex-best friend dead in the eyes. 'Or didn't you hear me the first time, *mate*.'

Puce-faced, he gets back into his car, and the four of us stand here together in a line, as he drives the hell out of our lives.

It takes us a good hour to calm down after that. I make us a cup of tea and a round of BLTs that we eat in the sun at the bottom of the garden by the shed.

Then Liam's off to Max's to practise and Nelly's out into town, where she's meeting Eva. Because what just happened with Darius has made up her mind that she's going to use some of that money she's been fastidiously saving for her flat to go travelling with Eva around Central and South America instead.

'I really enjoyed that, speaking my mind to someone like Darius,' she says just before she leaves. 'So much so that I've told my other boss to stick his job up his arse too.'

Not something I'd have got behind a few weeks ago. But the way she's talking, about scoping out jobs for charities abroad while she's gone, and that sparkle that's back in her eyes, like when she used to talk about saving the world as a kid, who's to deny it? Or the way she says Eva's name. With such a wide smile.

'She reminds me of us,' Jules says, after she's gone, 'when we were young.'

She's thinking about Australia and then San Francisco, of course. But it's like we still can't say it out loud.

'I wanted to go too,' I tell her. *Be honest*, right? 'What I said to you after Darius's party, I'm still so sorry. I wanted to go to Australia every bit as much as you did. I wanted to go with you everywhere. I still do.'

She nods but not like she already knew this. More like she *needed* to hear it. Her eyes glisten in the morning light, but then she takes another swig of her tea and smiles.

Then next thing I know we're talking about Liam. How I'm going to corner Rory from the Great Escape and KP from the Troubs and tell them about Liam's band and ask them if they can help out. Something I suddenly feel OK about because I'm finally starting to see that Liam's just doing the same as Nelly. Just following his heart.

Plus, what else *can* I do for him as an adult, other than be there for him and give him all the support that I can?

Finally, we talk about us, and this weird letter here on the table before us. About our futures.

'OK, so apart from the cool businesses we're going to run, what else are we going to change?' Jules says.

It's a challenge. But she's right. This is our chance to draw a line in the sand. To move on.

'OK,' I play along. 'My body. For one thing. You know, I'd like to get a bit more . . .' *buff*, I'm about to say, '. . . healthy,' I settle on instead. 'Just to keep myself more active. So, you know, you and me, we can keep on doing stuff together as we get old . . .'

Because we've stopped doing so much stuff together, haven't we? Even simple, everyday things like walking the dog.

'Good one,' she says, smiling.

'What about you?'

'Finances. I'd like to get more on top of them.'

'Yeah, well, I've messed that up, haven't I?' I say.

'No. I don't just mean your job. I mean me too. Like my credit card.'

'What credit card?'

She pulls a cartoony grin. 'The one I haven't told you about. The one I owe three grand on.' Her grin shifts to a grimace.

'Oh, Jules,' I say – I can't keep the dread from my voice, or from rising up inside me.

'I know, I'm so sorry. For lying . . . and for the debt, because I know how much that scares you,' she says. 'It's also why I think we need to listen to this letter and make these businesses work.'

She's right. We have to.

We *will*.

A few months later . . .

The Troubs save their best song for last.

Even though it's rammed up here front of stage at Concorde 2, Jules and I still manage to half elbow, half wrestle ourselves enough space to dance to 'All the Daze' right through to its thunderous end.

And, yeah, we dance crappily. Laughingly. Mum-and-dadly. *Madly*. But we don't care, because this is *our* song and it makes us feel twenty-three again, just like that night we first heard them playing live outside the Fortune of War – that first night we kissed.

I've got a rubbish memory for loads of things. So many of those early years and times we spent together are nothing but a blur. But a kiss like that. Hell, you don't forget *that*. It stays with you forever. Hopefully right up to the day that you die.

We kiss again now, as the last chords fade. But just briefly. Embarrassed. Because deep down we *do* know that maybe we ain't as young as we once were, or whatever it was the Boss sang. Even so, Doodles and Ngozi catch us out.

'Get a room,' Doodles teases, as the festival crowd starts to disperse, heading for the exits and back towards the main bar.

'Aw, leave them alone. It's their wedding anniversary. It's cute,' Ngozi chastises him, before giving him a great big kiss on the lips as well.

It's still a bit of a shocker, to be honest. Them being together. Ngozi told me the other week that this was all down to us. To the way we're still together after all these years. Since they've known each other nearly that long too. Leading to them eventually talking about how much it means having someone in your life for so much time. How much you must really have to care about them not to go your separate ways. They also both admitted they've always secretly fancied the arses off each other. So, yeah, that probably helped too.

'So, see you in the studio first thing Monday?' Doodles says.

'Right, the shortest commute in the world.' My usual gag and one that's become a bit of a catchphrase with our burgeoning army of subscribers.

Because, oh yeah. We did it. In the wake of reading that letter, Jules and I did go for its two suggestions – the Dadass Dudes and Chez Jules.

Me and Doodles clubbed our redundancy payments together and kitted out Dad's old shed into a studio – kind of like *Wayne's World*'s basement, only ours. It's now where we livestream us playing old-school games once a week, and where Kylie, and even grumpy Greg from Quark, who we've given a cut, join us on Tuesdays and Thursdays to help us push the brand.

We've got a shitload of subscribers already and our views and promotions are growing strongly too. Oh, and we're storyboarding a new game called *Earth Twin*, with a view of putting it into development and even Liam's working on it once a week. He's got ideas going way back to that long-ago staycation summer that got overshadowed by his accident.

'Hey, Dad,' he shouts, spotting me through the crowd.

He's with Max and Kai, all of them still high on the back of supporting the Troubs. ,

'So what did you think?' Liam asks.

'They were bloody brilliant. And you guys weren't too shabby either,' I tell him proudly. Truth is, I will never forget seeing him up there onstage, belting out that aching, arching bass climb that comes in about halfway through 'Ventura Highway', that America track he caught me listening to in the kitchen a few months back that his fledgling band Grass Stain then did a cover of that I then snuck to KP from the Troubs.

Or the roar of approval they got from all the younger kids who so clearly wished they'd learned more than just three songs.

And then it hits me – how I've been watching bands wrong all these years. Because it's not just about success, is it? It's about trying. It's about that moment of witnessing someone else soaring towards their potential, to where they might do anything and be anything, and willing them on.

That same moment we all have every minute of our lives, if only we could see it ourselves.

'I'm sorry,' I tell him, leaning in and whispering into his ear. 'This was never a hobby. It's your future. I just got the two things muddled up.'

He hugs me. Tight. He's taller than me now, I realise. Or maybe it's just the ridiculous cowboy boots he's got on. Then him, Max and Kai head over to help with lugging the Troubs' gear outside, and Ngozi and Doodles wend their way over to the bar.

'I still worry about him,' Jules says.

'Me too,' I say. 'But I guess that's parenting. We always will.' And I mean that. He's even kind of given us permission to, now that he's invited us back into his life.

Jules reaches into her pocket and pulls out her buzzing phone. It's Nelly, calling from Mexico.

'Yes, yes, he was brilliant,' Jules tells her, switching the phone onto video.

Our daughter waves at us from what looks like a beach bar, with Eva grinning beside her. They're thinking of staying for another couple of months, they tell us.

'Go for it,' Jules says.

'Yeah, go for it, kid,' I agree.

After we've all waved goodbye, Jules ducks over into the queue for the loo, leaving me leaning up against one of the pillars by the bar.

Then I see Meredith, coming out of the stage door. Her blonde hair is a little longer, but her grey eyes are shining as bright as ever as she looks me up and down. I've not seen her since I got fired. She did try calling a couple of times, but I never did answer the phone. I'd be lying if I said I don't feel anything now, but that *jolt*, it's so faint it's hardly there.

'Adam,' she says, coming over. 'Long time no see.'

'Hi, Meredith.'

She gives me a tentative, awkward, colleague-style hug, looking a little embarrassed too. She must know that I *know*. Who in 'Sillycon' Valley doesn't? Her and Darius are now an item.

'I was sort of hoping I'd bump into you tonight, Koala,' she says. 'You know, I really miss our old chats.'

Does she? Yeah, well, maybe I do too. But what's done is done, eh? The world's moved on. Darius walks over, slipping his arm around Meredith's waist, as he holds up his black Amex to catch the barman's eye.

'You should have seen it backstage,' he says to no one in particular. 'Those guys are so cool. And Liam, of course,' he adds. 'Although we didn't really get a chance to catch up.'

'Hey, Adam,' the Troubs' drummer, KP, butts in through the thinning crowd, with his baseball cap pulled down low. 'You want to catch a beer later? We're all heading over to the Heart and Hand.'

'I'd love to, but I can't tonight,' I say.

'No worries, next time.' He slips out through the fire escape and into the night.

Darius nods. Impressed I know him. Surprised.

'Then maybe *we* should get a drink together,' Meredith suggests, nudging Darius none-too-subtly in the ribs. 'We've both been feeling bad about what happened, haven't we, Dar? About that whole misunderstanding.'

Does she mean my job? Jules? There's no way to tell and no way I am going to ask.

'Er . . .' And for once, Darius is lost for words, as Jules walks over and stands beside me.

'Meredith here was just saying that we should all go for a drink together,' I tell her, 'Because, you know, it's been too long.'

'Right,' Meredith says, smiling. Like *I* got the memo, at least.

Then everyone's looking at me. Like this decision's somehow mine. I give my big beard an even bigger scratch.

'Sorry,' I then tell Meredith, 'it's just . . . we've got plans . . .'

'*So* many,' Jules adds, taking me by the hand and leading me off into the crowd.

*

We walk back along the seafront. It's a cold, moonlit night and we hold each other tight, with the muffled boom of the clubs up in town and the cries of the gulls ringing in our ears.

'Don't they *ever* sleep?' Jules laughs.

We walk down onto the beach and crunch across the pebbles, gazing out across the sea until we stop, without either of us mentioning it, right in front of the Fortune of War where we first kissed so long ago.

'Beautiful, isn't it?' she says.

It is. Couldn't be more so. A full moon beams down onto the glittering, flat sea. There's not a breath of wind or a wave in sight. You can even see the stars reflected in the water. A whole universe of them. Like they go on forever.

'I really do want to spend all my time with you and share everything this whole damn wide universe has to offer,' I tell her. And it's odd, because even though my memory is rubbish, I think I maybe remember saying this, or something very like it, before. Yeah, maybe up on that roof terrace of our very first home. The night we got engaged.

'Me too,' she says, and her eyes are sparkling, brighter even than the stars. 'And making the most of it. Every day. Making every single second count.'

She remembers it too.

Stepping towards her, I tuck her hair behind her ear. Her beautiful blonde hair that's now streaked with grey. This time as we kiss, it's proper. It's real. There's no one looking and it just goes on and on, as the millions and billions of stars blaze down.

'Well, A-Hole. That's what I call a proper snog,' she says, finally coming up for air.

'Yeah. Could be a record.'

She touches her fingers to my face, scratching my beard. 'I might have waited a quarter of a century for another kiss like that, but I have to say, you've still got it, you old grizzly bear, you.' She tugs at my beard, and we grin at each other, stupidly happy.

'What?' I ask.

'I was just thinking it might be fun to see you clean-shaven for once after all these years.'

'Yeah?' I think about it. Maybe a new look to go with this new phase in my life wouldn't be such a bad idea. 'Why not? Because change is good, right?'

She smiles. 'Because change is good.'

Putting my arm around her, we walk home past the Peregrine, and the 'Chez Jules' sign that's been up for two months now. She's only opening the restaurant every other Saturday to begin with, but word's already getting around and it's becoming quite the hot ticket. Especially with all the incredible new dishes she comes up with from this new French *gastronomique* course she's been doing online.

It's not the only thing we pause to look at.

There's Rose, dressed in pink dungarees, her long grey hair hanging loosely down to her waist, dancing with her solicitor 'friend' Eddy, who's twirling her round, the jukebox in the Peregrine's bar casting them both pretty in pink.

We still don't know who wrote that letter Eddy delivered. *Does it matter?* That same question Jules asked me when we first read those sheets of paper. *Does* it? If it's helped make us this happy, again? If it's helped us remember how much better we are together than alone?

'Don't they look lovely?' Jules says.

'Beautiful.'

'I hope we still dance together when we're that old.'

'Me too,' I say.

'It's funny thinking of us getting old, isn't it?'

'Well, there's nothing we can do about it.'

'Except embrace it.'

'Go down fighting.'

'Adam and Jules against the world,' she says, squeezing my hand.

We get home ten minutes later.

Mum's old Skoda glints eerily in the moonlight, though the only supernatural thing about it is that it's passed its MOT – *again*.

Even so, I've got a partner for it in mind. A little redder. A whole lot sleeker. A car that's going to make Jules smile. Of course, I've still got to save up the money first.

'Come on,' Jules says, as she takes my hand and shuts the door behind us. I give Groucho a little tickle behind his ear as I follow her into the moonlit kitchen.

BBC Radio 6 Music is playing on the speaker – I must have forgotten to turn it off earlier. Joy Division's 'Love Will Tear Us Apart', of all things.

I feel the same poignant flutter I always do as Jules takes Mum's mirrored antique box down off the shelf and opens its lid. Our time capsule of all the good times. Inside are the ticket stubs from the hundreds of music gigs we've been to over the years. As she adds this latest one – perhaps our most precious, what with it bearing Liam's band's name – the moonlight streaming in through the window is suddenly so bright, I could swear that these stubs of ours, they almost seem to glow . . .

As Joy Division fades, a piano riff breaks the spell, and the familiar tango beat of Gotan Project's 'Mi Confesión' starts crackling louchely out of the speaker. Jules and I face each other grinning, because this really is one of our favourite songs of all time.

We set off in a clumsy tango and two minutes later I'm grimacing at her laughing and wincing as I tread on her toes again.

'I'd always hoped that by this stage in our marriage I'd have mastered the intricacies of the Argentine Tango,' I say.

'What, *as well as* the Dad Dance?' she teases, stepping back and throwing a few mid-nineties ironic Pulp-style Britpop shapes into the mix.

'Hey, Mrs Hole, you were well aware of my dance moves before you married me,' I say, sweeping her up into my arms and kissing her.

Only we lurch a little to the left and nearly fall as I try to copy that cool tilting-each-other-over-in-a-swoon thing that Fred Astaire and Ginger Rogers do so well.

'I'd better take you to bed before my back goes and Liam gets home,' I tell her, laughing.

'Hmm . . . I think we might be a bit squiffy for romance,' Jules says. 'And knackered,' she admits with a sleepy smile.

'Oh.' I'm disappointed, but maybe she has a point. We have been out drinking and bopping about to bands for the last three hours.

I follow her through to the sitting room where she flops down on the moth-eaten sofa. Watching me closely, she kicks off her Doc Martens and peels off her tights.

'*Aaaaannd* now I have your attention,' she grins, 'can you tell me what I want, what I really, really want?'

'A zig-a-zig-ah?' I suggest, even though I still don't know what the hell the Spice Girls actually meant by that.

'Nope. A foot massage.'

'Really?'

'Oh, come on.' She wiggles her toes at me. 'They're bloody killing me.'

I sigh helplessly. Why is she so hard to resist? Collapsing on the sofa next to her, I take her feet in my hands.

'Mmm,' she says.

'Put something on.' I nod at the TV remote beside her.

'Why? Aren't I distracting enough?'

'It's more your feet I'm trying to distract myself *from*, actually. I'm no Tarantino, you know.'

She switches Netflix on. 'Just so long as it's not *Secrets of the Neanderthals*.'

'But –'

'But nothing. Anyway, I bet all their so-called secrets are totally rubbish. Like what tree stump Kevin the Neanderthal hid his gooseberries in. Or who Karen the Neanderthal knobbed.'

'Kevin and Karen?'

'Well, I don't know, do I?' She turns over to Prime. 'What about *When Harry Met Sally*?'

But it's more music I'm in the mood for now. Grabbing the control, I switch on Spotify.

I put on the *You & Me* playlist we made together this morning, covering all our favourite songs from the last twenty-five years.

'Lonely Planet' by The The kicks us off.

'Chuck us one of those Maltesers, will you?' I say.

'What Maltesers?'

'The ones you keep hidden under the cushion on your side.'

She pouts. Annoyed at me, but impressed too. Reluctantly, she throws one into my mouth and I let it melt, as she crunches down on two herself.

'Good this, isn't it?' she says. 'Just you and me. I mean, as much as I love the kids, it is sometimes nice being on our own.'

'Very nice indeed.'

'On our shitty sofa.'

'In our shitty house.'

'With our whole bright future still stretching ahead of us,' she says.

We cuddle up as Matt Johnson sings something about changing yourself if you can't change your world, or maybe it's the other way round, and me and Jules both sing along.

'I bloody love you, Mrs Hole,' I say.

'Just as well,' she says, 'because you're stuck with me for eternity. Or didn't you realise that yet?'

THE END

Acknowledgements

[4 pages To Come]

HARVILL

We hope you enjoyed joining Adam, Jules
and the Hole family on their multiversal adventure!
If you did, we'd love you to spread the word about
You & Me & You & Me & You & Me – whether
that's on social media, by leaving a review online
or recommending it to a friend.

We love to hear what our readers think.

You can find out more about our books here:

@harvillbooks

www.penguin.co.uk/discover/newsletters/vintage